Praise for Stephen Leather's bestselling thrillers

'Exciting stuff with plenty of heart-palpitating action gingered up by mystery and intrigue . . . Leather is an intelligent thriller writer' *Daily Mail* on *The Tunnel Rats*

'As high-tech and as world-class as the thriller genre gets' *Express on Sunday* on *The Bombmaker*

'A whirlwind of action, suspense and vivid excitement' *Irish Times* on *The Birthday Girl*

'An ingenious plot, plenty of action and solid, believable characters, wrapped up in taut, snappy prose that grabs your attention by the throat . . . A top-notch thriller which whips the reader along at breakneck speed' *Yorkshire Post* on *The Long Shot*

'A gripping story sped along by admirable uncluttered prose' *Daily Telegraph* on *The Chinaman*

About the author

Stephen Leather was a journalist for more than ten years on newspapers such as *The Times*, the *Daily Mail* and the *South China Morning Post* in Hong Kong. Before that, he was employed as a biochemist for ICI, shovelled limestone in a quarry, worked as a baker, a petrol pump attendant, a barman, and worked for the Inland Revenue. He began writing full-time in 1992 and *The Eyewitness* is his fourteenth novel. His bestsellers have been translated into more than ten languages, and *The Stretch* and *The Bombmaker* have been filmed for television. He has also written for television shows such as *London's Burning*, *The Knock* and the BBC's *Murder in Mind*.

Stephen Leather now lives in Dublin. You can visit his website at www.stephenleather.com

STEPHEN LEATHER

The Eyewitness

CORONET BOOKS

Hodder & Stoughton

First published in Great Britain in 2003 by Hodder and Stoughton
A division of Hodder Headline

A Coronet Paperback

The right of Stephen Leather to be identified as the Author of the
Work has been asserted by him in accordance with the Copyright,
Designs and Patents Act 1988.

1 3 5 7 9 10 8 6 4 2

All characters in this book are fictitious and any resemblance to real
persons, living or dead, is purely coincidental.

A CIP catalogue record for this title is available from the British
Library

ISBN 0340 73409 4

Typeset in 10/12.5pt Plantin Light by
Phoenix Typesetting, Burley-in-Wharfedale, West Yorkshire

Printed and bound in Great Britain by
Clays Ltd, St Ives plc

Hodder and Stoughton
A division of Hodder Headline
338 Euston Road
London NW1 3BH

For Ildiko

ACKNOWLEDGEMENTS

I am indebted to Gordon Bacon, OBE, Chief of Staff at the International Commission on Missing Persons, for his hospitality in Sarajevo and for opening my eyes to the work of his organisation, which identifies the war dead in the former Yugoslavia. Bob Graham was an invaluable source of information on human trafficking out of the Balkans and Luigji Ndou helped keep me on track about Muslim life in the region. Any errors of fact are mine, not theirs.

Most of the working girls that spoke to me about prostitution and trafficking wouldn't want to be identified for obvious reasons, but I want to thank Angela, Francesca, Jessica, Kim and Sophie. Not their real names, but they know who they are.

I am grateful to Denis O'Donoghue and Barbara Schmeling for casting their professional eyes over the manuscript and to Hazel Orme who helped me get it into shape for publication. Carolyn Mays at Hodder and Stoughton oversaw *The Eyewitness* from conception to production and the book is all the better for her enthusiasm, support and professionalism.

There should have been ghosts – four and a half thousand body-bags, every one containing the remains of a human being who had met a violent death – and yet as Jack Solomon walked down the length of the storage facility there were no whisperings of vengeful thoughts, no movements in the shadows, not even a prickling of the hairs on the back of his neck. There was nothing, just the hum of the air-conditioning units that kept the temperature at between two and eight degrees Celsius. Did that mean that four and a half thousand souls had moved on to whatever form of afterlife lay beyond? Solomon doubted it. Solomon didn't believe in an after-life. He didn't believe in God, either. He'd seen the aftermath of too many atrocities committed in the name of religion to believe in god. In any god.

A technician was using an electric saw to slice off a piece of a femur that had been gripped in a carpenter's vice. He was wearing a white coat, surgical gloves and a cotton mask, and nodded as Solomon walked by. Another technician in dark blue overalls was cleaning the concrete floor with an industrial vacuum-cleaner. He, too, wore a mask.

The white body-bags were stored in metal racks, seven high, each with an identification number scrawled in black ink. Above them were rows of brown-paper bags, each with a number on it. For each body-bag, there was a corresponding brown-paper bag.

Solomon had two numbers on a computer printout and he kept looking back and forth between the numbers on the printout and the numbers on the body-bags. The numbers were consecutive. The bodies had been pulled from the same communal grave.

The body-bags that matched the numbers on the printout were lying next to each other in the centre of one of the racks. One of the bags, Solomon knew, contained just a torso and a leg. The head had not been found. That was the elder of the two brothers. The skeleton of the younger man was virtually intact. Solomon had read both post-mortem reports, written in perfect English by a German doctor who had carried out the autopsies in a Portakabin close to the mass grave where they had been found. Both men had been shot in the back at close range. Not once but more than a dozen times. And a hatchet had been used to hack at their legs. The German doctor had been unable to say whether this had been done before or after death, but Solomon knew that there would have been no point in inflicting the injuries afterwards. They'd been mutilated, thrown on the ground, and raked with machine-gun fire.

Solomon pulled over a metal ladder and climbed it slowly to reach the two brown-paper bags that went with the body-bags.

He took them down a white-painted corridor to the viewing room. Two Muslim women were sitting there with the interpreter, a mother and daughter. Mothers were always the worst and Solomon was grateful for the presence of the interpreter. The interpreter was a buffer, a filter for the bad news, and it kept Solomon one step

2

removed from the horror of the situation. The interpreter was a man in his late thirties, a former soldier who had been trained to liaise with the families of the missing.

The room had been made as comfortable as possible, with two small sofas, and posters of country scenes on the wall. There was a vase of sweet-smelling white flowers on a side table. Two large books lay on a coffee table: one contained photographs of the clothes and personal effects taken from bodies that had been buried, the other images of bodies that had been left lying on the ground. Solomon had never discovered the reason for this distinction. There were so many other ways in which the dead could have been segregated – by sex, age, manner of death. Before DNA testing, the photographs had been the main key to identifying the dead.

The mother and daughter had already looked through them and had recognised the clothing that had belonged to two bodies in the holding facility. They had given blood samples, and their DNA had been checked against DNA taken from the bones. It was a perfect match.

That the woman and her daughter had been called back meant that they were already expecting the worst. But Solomon knew from past experience that they wouldn't believe it until they had heard it from him, and had viewed the possessions found with the remains. After denial would come acceptance, and then the questions.

They wore yellow and blue headscarves and padded sleeveless jackets over cheap cotton skirts. Their clothing was threadbare but clean, and Solomon knew they'd put on their best for him. The daughter's boots had no laces and neither woman wore any jewellery. Solomon put the bags on the table and sat down, forcing a smile.

Both women thanked him. '*Hvala lijepo. Hvala za sve.*'

Thank you for everything. The people in the viewing room always thanked him – even though he only ever brought bad news.

Solomon pushed one of the bags towards the daughter, but it was the mother who reached for it. If there had been any doubt about the identification, the old woman and her daughter would have worn surgical gloves to prevent contamination. But in this case there was no doubt. She opened it and took out a black jacket, edged with gold, with a picture of Elvis Presley on the back. The old woman gasped and put a hand to her mouth. The jacket was the first thing they had recognised in the book. It was distinctive, and Solomon doubted that there was another like it anywhere in the Balkans. It had been cleaned and there were creases along the sleeves where it had been ironed. Down the corridor was a laundry room where every item of clothing was washed and ironed before being placed in a bag. It was horrific enough to view clothing taken from the dead; it would be a thousand times worse for the relatives to see them in the state in which they arrived at the facility.

The old woman laid out the jacket on the table. There were five ragged holes in the back. The woman poked her finger into one, frowning. Her daughter leaned over and whispered, '*Metaci*.' Bullets. The old woman wailed and sat back, her hands on either side of her weathered face. The daughter took a pair of socks out of the bag. They had been neatly folded. She opened one out and examined the heel, then took a deep breath and blinked back tears. She spoke to the interpreter, the words tumbling out faster and faster, until she sat back, gasping.

'She darned the socks for her brother the day before the

Serbs came and took the men away,' said the interpreter. 'She says his wife couldn't sew, she was always pricking herself with the needle, so she did it for him.'

Solomon nodded and smiled. There was nothing he could say. He wondered where the wife was, but the fact that she wasn't there probably meant she was dead, too.

The daughter took the rest of the clothing from the bag and laid it out carefully. She bit down on her lower lip. There were rips in the cotton trousers, at the back of the knees. Solomon knew they were from the hatchet blows, but the bloodstains had come out in the wash.

She found a rusting wristwatch at the bottom of the bag, and the old woman took it from her and stroked it.

The second bag contained just a shoe with the upper coming away from the sole, and a torn plaid shirt. Like the Elvis jacket, it was peppered with bullet-holes. The daughter peered into the bag. Solomon knew that she was wondering where the rest of her brothers' belongings were. He did not want to explain that the bodies had been moved several times by Serbs trying to cover up the evidence of their crimes, and that in the process many had fallen apart, and the remains mixed up.

Solomon spoke in English, pausing to allow the interpreter to translate. 'I want to explain what has happened, so that there is no confusion,' he said. 'The DNA we have taken from your blood matches two of the bodies we have in this facility. The belongings we have here were taken from the remains, but it is the DNA that gives conclusive proof.' Solomon turned so that he was facing the younger woman. Siblings were always easier to deal with. The pain was bad, but not as bad as for a mother who had to accept that her child had been murdered.

'There is no doubt that they were your brothers. We can make arrangements for you to collect the remains so that they can be buried according to your religion.'

'We have no money for a funeral,' said the daughter.

The interpreter translated, and Solomon said, 'There are charities that can help. We can tell you who to contact.'

The old woman spoke quickly, almost jabbering, her hands stabbing at the air.

The interpreter translated: the old woman had said that she was certain there had been a mistake, that her sons were not dead but were being held in a concentration camp deep inside Serbia.

'I'm sorry,' said Solomon slowly. 'With DNA, there is no mistake. I know that mistakes were made in the past, that funerals were held and then those who were thought dead returned, but that was before we had DNA. There is no doubt. I am sorry. It is time to bury your sons and to mourn. It is time to accept that they have gone.'

The old woman looked at him with tear-filled eyes and nodded slowly.

Solomon stood up. The interpreter could give them any more information they needed. His own work was done.

The daughter grabbed the hem of his jacket and spoke to him in rapid Serbo-Croatian. The interpreter translated: she wanted to see the bodies.

Solomon always had to say the same thing: 'It is not possible. Not at the moment.'

It was, of course, perfectly possible. The two women could have been taken into the room and shown the two body-bags among the four and a half thousand. But then they would have asked for the body-bags to be opened,

6

and Solomon knew that the sight of what was inside would stay with them for ever. Best that they remembered their loved ones as they had known them, not as the bones and grinning skulls in the white bags. He shrugged and repeated that it wasn't possible.

He left the viewing room and walked back down the corridor to the exit. He passed the photographic room, where a man was arranging a pair of trousers on the floor and positioning a camera above it. The work went on. There were more books to be filled with photographs and sent round the world so that relatives overseas could look through them in the hope of identifying something that had come from the missing. Solomon found the books more disturbing than the facility with its thousands of dead. The body-bags were cold and impersonal, but the books were chilling catalogues, every item personal, taken from the body of a murder victim.

He had to unlock the door to get out of the facility, then relock it behind him. It was always locked so that no one could enter by mistake.

Solomon climbed into his white Nissan Patrol four-wheel-drive, with its diplomatic plates, and drove away. He was always glad to leave Tuzla, partly because the storage facility was such a depressing place, but also because the air was so polluted that his throat was red raw after a few hours. The vehicle bucked and rocked over the uneven road surfaces as he headed out of town. Tuzla was built on a huge underground salt lake that had been mined for hundreds of years. The town had started to sink as the mine works collapsed, so some bright Communist engineer who had forgotten his basic chemistry decided to pump in water. It dissolved the salt and the collapse increased: now driving around the town in a regular car meant a broken exhaust-pipe and scraped bodywork. After the war, there had been no money to repair the roads so the sinking continued.

He drove past the huge coal-fired power station on the edge of town, a massive remnant of the Communist system that had once dominated the region. Huge cooling towers belched clouds of steam into the air, but the damage was done by the coal-furnace chimney from which eye-watering smoke poured over the town twenty-four hours a day, and by the chemical plants built around the power station.

The road to Sarajevo was a single carriageway that wound its way through mountains and gorges, past small villages where every house had been reduced to rubble, and fields with red signs warning of mines. Some areas had been cordoned off with yellow tape to await the arrival of mine-clearance charities. It was only 130 kilometres to Sarajevo, but Solomon had never made the drive in under two and a half hours. There were two mountain ranges to cross and a farm vehicle, bus or a slow-moving army patrol meant a frustrating tailback; even on a clear road the hillside fell away so sharply that Solomon rarely got into top gear.

About an hour outside Sarajevo, his mobile phone rang as he was negotiating a hairpin turn in second gear behind a truck piled high with boxes of toilet paper. He held the phone between his shoulder and ear so that he could keep both hands on the steering-wheel.

It was his boss. Chuck Miller was an American who had worked for a succession of non-governmental organisations around the world, including spells in Sierra Leone, Mongolia and Bangladesh. His stint with the International War-dead Commission was just another line on his curriculum vitae. He was a manager and a grant-getter, an administrator who knew how to play the funding game, and it was as a result of his efforts that the Commission's budget had more than doubled since he'd joined four years earlier. 'Jack, where are you?' he asked.

'Just about to drive into a gorge,' said Solomon, pulling hard on the wheel and stamping on the brake.

'Take it easy,' said Miller. 'Good co-ordinators are hard to find. Can you talk?'

'Yeah, go on,' said Solomon. 'The road doesn't get any better for the next ten kilometres.'

'Remember that case you handled three years back outside Priština?'

'Sure.' It had been one of the first that Solomon had handled on his arrival in the Balkans. An entire family had disappeared from a farm on the outskirts of Priština, the capital of neighbouring Kosovo. It had happened during the spring. A farmer had seen the women tilling the fields in the morning; a Kosovar army patrol had gone past in the afternoon and a sergeant recalled seeing two men from the farm working on a broken-down tractor. The next day, at about three o'clock, a shop-keeper from Priština had driven down the half-mile track to the farm to buy eggs, which were in short supply: he could get four times the price for them that he paid the farmer so he made the trip several times a week. There had been no one in the rambling farm-house, and although he had pounded on his car horn, no one had come. No one ever came. The entire family had disappeared. There was a kettle on the stove, boiled dry. Half a dozen cows in a nearby field were gathered at the gate, waiting to be milked. There had been a broken bowl in the kitchen, and a small pool of dried blood on the stone-flagged hallway, the only signs that the family had not left by choice.

The Commission had been notified, but all Solomon had been able to do was compile information on the missing people. No one knew for sure how many had vanished from the farm, but after speaking to the neighbours Solomon had twenty-one names – men, women and children, old and young, all related, all Kosovar Albanian Muslims in an area populated by Serbs. No one had seen or heard anything. They might have been telling the truth, but Solomon knew that even if they had seen something, they wouldn't have told him. Right across the former Yugoslavia innocent civilians had been maimed and murdered, some in their own homes, others taken away at gunpoint, and no one had seen a thing. Houses had been looted and burned, cars stripped and set on fire, and those left unharmed – those who had been of the right race or religion – had turned their backs.

'They've turned up, near the border with Serbia,' said Miller.

'Alive?' asked Solomon. As soon as the question left his mouth, he realised how stupid it was.

'Get a grip, Jack,' said Miller. 'If they were alive, why would I be calling you? KFOR have found a truck in a lake about fifty kilometres from Priština, close to the border with Serbia.' KFOR was the Kosovo Force, the multinational grouping of foreign armies that were in the country to ensure that the various factions lived together in relative harmony. A similar group, Stabilisation Force or SFOR, was based in Bosnia.

'Do you want me there?'

'Tim is up to his eyes in Belgrade. They're opening up

two mass graves this week and he has to be there to co-ordinate. Can you go first thing? Take Kimete with you.'
Kimete was one of the Commission's interpreters.

'Sure. I'll swing by the office first thing and pick up the file.' Solomon screeched to a halt inches from the truck. He cursed profusely, then apologised to Miller and cut the connection.

He got caught in early-evening traffic when he reached Sarajevo, and it was almost six o'clock when he parked in front of his apartment block, one of the first to be repaired after the four-year siege had ended. It was a modern brick block on Alipasina Street, home to many of the city's top politicians and businessmen. Barely had the fighting stopped than builders had moved in to renovate and repair it. Solomon's apartment had originally been owned by a Serbian businessman who ran a string of garages on the outskirts of the city. The Serb, along with many others, had left the week before the siege started, fore-warned by relatives in the Serbian military. He had never returned and after the siege had sold the apartment to a Muslim landlord, who now owned several dozen up-market homes that he let to internationals.

Solomon walked up to the third floor and let himself in. He took a can of Heineken out of the fridge and walked on to the large balcony. There he lit a Marlboro and looked out over the huge Catholic graveyard that faced the apartment block on the other side of the road. The sun was going down and a cool breeze ruffled his hair. There were really only two seasons in Bosnia, summer and winter – the transitions between too short to be con-sidered seasons. Three days earlier it would have been too cold to stand on the balcony without a thick coat and gloves, yet already the city-centre café tables were full of students in summer clothes and sunglasses, smoking and drinking coffee as they discussed ways to study or work overseas.

With the end of winter came the start of the exhumation season. The graves had been identified and marked, but it was only with the thaw that the digging could start. A few more days and more body-bags would have been filled and the photographers would be working overtime to capture clothing and personal effects on film.

Kimete was in Solomon's office waiting for him, drinking coffee. She raised her paper cup in salute and asked if he wanted some. Solomon said no, he'd already had a Bosnian breakfast – coffee and cigarettes – at home. Kimete was tiny, barely over five feet tall, but she seemed taller because she always wore boots with high heels and thick soles. She was in her early thirties but looked a good ten years younger than that, with her shoulder-length curly black hair and boyish figure. Her English was close to fluent, and when she translated from Bosnian she could convey the inferences and subtleties of what was being said. She also spoke Serbo-Croatian, Albanian and Russian, and Solomon had seen her flirt so effectively with an Italian army captain in his own language that the man had run after her in the street begging for her phone number. Before the war she'd been a teacher, but when there had been no money to pay her salary she'd become a translator, working first for the police and then the Commission. She knew when to ask questions of her own, and when to stick rigidly to what the co-ordinator was asking.

Solomon briefed her as he took out the file on the Priština case. Then they went down to his car and drove out of the city towards Serbia. She lit a Marlboro with an SFOR Zippo and handed it to him, then lit one for herself. Most Bosnians smoked: cigarettes were cheap and plentiful, and during four years of almost constant shelling and sniper fire by the Serbian army they had been one of the few pleasures available to the population. Until she had started to work for the Commission, she'd smoked one of the foul-smelling local brands and Solomon had introduced her to the milder Marlboro Lights that he favoured. He'd realised recently, though, that she only smoked them when she was with him. Otherwise she smoked her old brand.

'So they've been in water for three years?' asked Kimete. She grimaced.

'That's what Chuck says,' said Solomon.

Six black SFOR helicopters clattered overhead in the direction of the border with Serbia. Kimete glanced up at them. 'That's the way to get around,' she said.

'Stop complaining,' said Solomon, and laughed. 'It's not as if you've got to drive.'

It took just over four hours to reach the lake, which was well away from any major roads. There were no signposts and they had to rely on a map that Kimete had open on her lap.

They knew they were on the right road when they saw two Humvee armoured cars and a group of American soldiers with automatic weapons. One held up his hand and Solomon brought the four-wheel-drive to a halt. He flashed his Commission credentials. A young American soldier in full battledress nodded, then insisted that Kimete also showed her ID. Solomon explained they were there to see the remains taken from the lake. The soldier told him to wait, then went over to one of the Humvees and used a radio. He came back to Solomon's vehicle and gave him directions to a nearby farm.

Solomon wove past the Humvees and followed the directions. The farm was at the end of a half-mile-long rutted track at the bottom of a heavily wooded hill. Stone buildings formed a U-shape around a cobbled courtyard, in which three grey US Army Humvees were lined up, along with several blue police vans and two US Army Jeeps in camouflage livery. Half a dozen US troopers stood in a circle, smoking and talking. They glanced at the Nissan Patrol's diplomatic plates and carried on their conversation.

To the right of a stone farmhouse was a large corrugated-iron barn. Two soldiers were standing at the entrance.

Solomon and Kimete walked up to them and showed their IDs. One called into the barn, and a lieutenant in a dark blue flak-jacket came out and shook their hands. He spoke with a deep south drawl and the fingers of his right hand were stained with nicotine. Solomon offered him a Marlboro, then handed the packet to Kimete. The lieutenant took them inside the barn and Solomon lit their cigarettes. They gazed at a large refrigerator truck, covered in thick brown slime, its rear doors unlocked but almost closed.

'How was it discovered?' asked Solomon.

'UN helicopter flying low over the lake last week,' said the lieutenant. 'The co-pilot called in that he'd seen something in the water but we were only able to get to it yesterday. We used a Chinook to pull it out. Hell of a job.'

Solomon nodded at the rear doors. 'You opened it, yeah?'

The lieutenant nodded and took a long draw on his

cigarette. 'Cut the padlock and opened it by the lake, then had it moved it here.' He shuddered.

'What about the driver?'

'The cab was empty.'

'Do you have body-bags?' asked Solomon.

'They're on their way from Belgrade. Should be here this afternoon.'

'How many bodies are in the truck?'

'I made it twenty-six. Some are just babies.' Kimete took a step towards the truck. The lieutenant laid a hand on her arm. 'I wouldn't, miss. It's not very pretty.'

She flashed him a tight smile. 'I was in Sarajevo right through the siege, Lieutenant. I helped bury my brother and two cousins. And I've seen hundreds of remains since the war ended.'

The lieutenant nodded. 'Okay. But these aren't remains. They're bodies.'

Solomon frowned. 'If it's the family I think it is, that truck has been in the water for three years.'

'That's right, but the rear of the truck was airtight. No water got in. And the water was cold, not much above freezing. They're preserved. It's like it happened yesterday.'

'You've examined them, right?'

The lieutenant shook his head. 'Not my prerogative,' he said. 'We notified the police and moved it here.'

'I was told it was a missing family from Priština.'

'That's what the cops think. They had a look through some of the personal effects.' The lieutenant sensed Solomon's unease. 'They were in the back for ten minutes, no more.' He said. 'Since then, no one else has been inside.'

Somebody shouted at them from the back of the barn

in guttural Serbo-Croatian. A Kosovar police captain walked over to them, his beer-drinker's paunch riding up over a thick leather belt. He carried a large automatic in a scuffed leather holster. Kimete explained in Bosnian who they were, the policeman asked to see their IDs, and Solomon and Kimete flashed their credentials again.

'I don't see why the International War-dead Commission is involved in this,' said the policeman, scratching his ear. Kimete translated.

'They appear to be victims of ethnic cleansing,' said Solomon, then paused to allow Kimete to translate. 'We have to be present at the exhumation, and if there is evidence of a war crime, we notify the War Crimes Tribunal. Until we have assessed the scene, it has to be secured by KFOR.'

The policeman brushed away Kimete's translation with an impatient wave of his hand. 'This is a crime scene. A police matter.'

'If it's the family we think it is, they are Kosovar Albanian Muslims who were abducted from their farm outside Priština.'

The police captain shook his head, his lips pressed tightly together. He jerked a thumb at the truck. 'It might have been an accident. Until we have examined the vehicle we cannot be sure.'

Kimete translated what he had said. 'I think his nose is out of joint,' she said.

'They were getting heavy,' said the lieutenant. 'My men had to draw their weapons before they'd leave the truck. We were concerned about looting.'

'You did the right thing,' said Solomon. He turned to Kimete. 'Remind him of the rules regarding exhumation,' he said, then waited while Kimete explained that KFOR had jurisdiction, and that the lieutenant had been within his rights to exclude the local police from the preliminary investigation.

The policeman listened in silence, staring at Solomon with hard eyes. He opened his mouth to speak but Solomon forestalled him. 'Tell him that we are grateful for the speed with which he identified the family,' said Solomon, 'and ask him if he'd accompany me into the back of the truck.'

Kimete translated, and the policeman nodded, his lips pressed so tightly together that they had virtually disappeared.

The American lieutenant dropped his cigarette butt on the floor and ground it with his heel. He called over to his men and they pulled open the rear doors of the truck. Solomon extinguished his cigarette, then the lieutenant helped him climb up and handed him a chunky army torch. Solomon held out a hand to haul the policeman up. Kimete pulled herself up with feline grace before the lieutenant could offer to help her.

Solomon turned on the torch and played the beam around the inside of the truck. The first thing he saw was an old man and an old woman, lying on the floor, embracing like young lovers. Their eyes were wide and staring, their mouths open.

'My God,' whispered Solomon.

'It's hard to believe this happened three years ago,' said Kimete.

The policeman switched on his torch and shone it at a middle-aged man by the door. He was lying face down, and Solomon saw that his hands were black with dried blood, the nails ripped off. The policeman spoke to Kimete.

17

'This is the man he got the identification from,' explained Kimete. 'Agim Shala.'

Solomon knelt down and examined the man's injured hands. There were two bloody fingernails on the metal floor of the truck. Solomon pulled on a pair of surgical gloves and picked one up.

The policeman spoke again in rapid Bosnian.

'He was trying to claw his way out,' Kimete explained. 'Several of the men have similar injuries.'

Solomon straightened up and walked further into the truck, passing his torch over the bodies, counting. There were several men in their twenties and thirties close to the door; the women were at the back with the children. He saw two young girls, barely into their teens, hugging each other. A small boy of seven or eight was curled into a foetal ball, his eyes closed as if he'd just fallen asleep.

At the end of the truck, pressed against the metal wall, lay a young couple, their arms around a little girl. Her eyes were closed and she was holding a small teddy bear. She couldn't have been more than eighteen months and looked as if she were fast asleep. The teddy bear had been worn smooth by years of cuddling, probably handed down from generation to generation. One glass eye was missing and a replacement had been darned in with brown thread. Solomon felt a hand touch his shoulder and he looked up at Kimete. 'Are you okay?' she asked.

Solomon felt tears prick his eyes and he turned away. In the four years that he'd been working for the International War-dead Commission, he had been present at several dozen exhumations and had been involved in the identification of hundreds of men, women and children, but the remains had been generally little more than skeletons, barely human. This little girl was real, a child who had laughed and played, and now she was dead. The mother and father had obviously been trying to comfort her. It would have been dark. And cold. The truck would have rocked and bucked as it went down the bank, and then the splash as it went into the water. What had it been like inside the truck when they'd realised that they were in the water and nobody was coming to help them? There'd have been shouts and screams. Maybe someone had tried to take charge, had told them to relax, not to use up the air so quickly, that they'd live longer if they all stayed quiet. And the men had clawed at the back until their fingers were shredded and bloody.

There'd have been panic and fear and anger, with the women huddling together for comfort, probably praying. The old couple must have just sat down and held each other, waiting to die. The young couple had probably tried to comfort the little girl, soothing her with quiet words, trying to get her to sleep, whispering to her that everything was going to be all right, even though they knew that they were all dying.

The policeman came up behind Solomon and said something in Bosnian.

'He says it might have been an accident,' Kimete told him.

Solomon stood up. 'Bullshit. The door was padlocked.'

Kimete translated. The policeman shrugged and spoke again, gesturing at the bodies with the torch. 'He says maybe they were refugees, being smuggled across country. The truck ran off the road, went into the lake.'

'They were driving towards Serbia. Tell him that Kosovar Albanians wouldn't have been seeking refuge in Serbia. And if it was an accident, why wasn't it reported?'

Kimete spoke to the policeman, then listened as he replied.

'He says they might have been cutting through Serbia to Croatia,' said Kimete, 'that if they were people smugglers and there was an accident they wouldn't have hung around. If it was ethnic cleansing, why put them in a truck? Why drive them into Serbia?'

Solomon shook his head. There was no point in arguing with the man. Divisions between the ethnic groups in the Balkans were as deep and as bitter as they had ever been. It was only the presence of KFOR and SFOR that was keeping a lid on the situation, forcing the various factions to live together in a semblance of peace. He had no doubt that if the troops pulled out, the killing would start again within days.

'Tell him that the Commission has jurisdiction, and that KFOR will be in charge of securing the truck and the bodies. We'll be handling the identification, then passing the files on to the War Crimes Tribunal. If he thinks that this was an accident, he's more than welcome to tell that to the Tribunal investigators – but as far as I'm concerned he can shove his explanation up his arse.' Kimete began to speak but Solomon put his hand on her shoulder. 'Forget the last bit.'

'I was going to,' she said.

Solomon walked back to the rear of the truck, counting bodies. He jumped down and the American lieutenant steadied him. 'I make it twenty-six, too,' said Solomon.

'Why would they do that to women and children?'

'What's your name?' asked Solomon.

'Matt,' said the lieutenant. 'Matt Richards.'

'How long have you been with KFOR, Matt?'

'Six weeks.'

Solomon gave him another cigarette and lit it, then lit one for himself. 'You're asking the one question that can't be answered, Matt,' said Solomon. 'We can find out what happened, and when, and we can identify the dead and maybe even the men who killed them, but we aren't going to get inside the heads of the people here to find out why. It's a frog-and-scorpion thing. Instinct.'

'But kids. Old people.'

'The Germans sent old people and children to the gas chambers.'

'I can't get my head around it,' Richards said.

'You'll get used to it,' said Solomon. 'You won't go far wrong if you just assume that people are basically evil.'

'I can't accept that. I let Jesus Christ into my life when I was in college.'

For a moment Solomon thought he was joking, then saw, from the intense look on his face, that he was not.

Solomon tried to blow a smoke-ring, but failed. 'Okay, this is what's going to happen now,' he said. 'Keep the truck secured until the coroner arrives. He'll carry out autopsies to determine cause of death. Then the bodies are to be bagged. We're short-staffed so if you could get your guys to do it, I'd be grateful. Make sure they wear gloves to avoid contamination. Then the bodies will be taken to our facility in Belgrade.'

'What happens there?'

'We take DNA samples and compare them with the DNA from relatives, if we can find any. And assuming the coroner says it's murder, it gets passed to the War Crimes Tribunal.'

'You do this a lot?'

'It's my job.'

'How do you deal with it?' asked the American.

'Deal with what?'

'What you see. What they've done to each other.'

'You're a soldier,' said Solomon, surprised. 'You must have seen worse.'

Richards took a long pull on his cigarette. 'These are the first bodies I've seen,' he said. He gestured at the truck. 'That's the work of the devil.'

'It's the work of human beings, Matt. We've got almost ten thousand bodies to identify, and probably as many still in the ground. And not one died peacefully. I try not to think what happened to them. I just do my job.'

Kimete jumped down from the back of the truck, leaving the policeman inside it.

'Is he okay?' asked Solomon.

'I've smoothed his feathers, he's fine.' She paused. 'It's different, isn't it, when you can see their faces?'

Solomon nodded. The remains in the body-bags at Tuzla didn't have faces. They were just bones, like museum exhibits.

'Are you feeling all right?' Kimete asked. 'You look pale.'

Solomon swallowed. There was a bad taste in his mouth, bitter and acrid. 'I'm okay.'

'Shall I get you a glass of water from the farmhouse?'

Solomon swallowed again. 'Yeah, thanks.' Suddenly he threw up. Richards and Kimete jumped back. After a moment, she put a hand on his back and patted him.

Solomon heard laughing and he looked across at the policeman, who was standing now with two of his men at the back of the truck. He took a step towards the man but Kimete grasped his wrist. 'It's not worth it,' she said. 'He's not worth it.'

Solomon glared at the three policemen who were still

laughing at him. Gradually his anger subsided. 'Yeah, you're right,' he said.

He and Kimete went over to the farmhouse. On the way, he collected the file from his car.

Two US troopers were standing at the farmhouse door and one pushed it open for them. An old couple were sitting by an open-hearth fire, warming themselves. Kimete explained who they were. The old man, his face weathered to the consistency of leather, spoke to her in Serbo-Croatian as the old woman poured them cups of strong coffee. 'He wants to know if he will be reimbursed for the use of his barn,' said Kimete.

'Tell him he will be,' said Solomon.

'Is that true?' she asked.

'Hell, I don't know and, frankly, I don't care,' said Solomon. 'By the look of it, the barn wasn't being used before they put the truck in it. Just say the Serbo-Croatian equivalent of "The cheque's in the post" and leave it at that.'

Kimete spoke briefly, the old man beamed and Solomon raised his coffee cup in salute. Twenty-six men, women and children lay dead just a hundred yards away and all the old man was concerned about was money. Solomon wondered how long Matt Richards would retain his born-again faith surrounded by people who happily saw their neighbours shipped out to murder camps and communal graves.

'And ask him if it's okay if we stay here until we've got the bodies processed,' said Solomon. 'Should all be done by this evening.'

He began to read through the slim file as Kimete translated. The reports had been handwritten in Serbo-Croatian but translated and typed in English.

Of the twenty-one names of those believed to be missing, fifteen were female. Two were infants. A missing-person's report had been compiled for each name; in most cases it consisted of a single sheet on which there was a name and an approximate age. There were no photographs, no medical details, nothing Solomon could use to match the missing with the bodies in the truck.

The reports had been prepared by the federal police in Priština, and in the absence of evidence that a crime had been committed they had clearly decided just to go through the motions. The Priština police probably took the same view as the policeman: that the family might have decided to leave voluntarily in the hope of making a new life for themselves elsewhere.

There was only one next-of-kin named, a woman who was now living in Bosnia: Teuter Berisha, aged seventy-two. She was the aunt of the owner of the farm outside Priština, Agim Shala; his wife was Drita. There was nothing in the file to suggest that Teuter Berisha had been contacted about the missing family.

A horn sounded outside and Solomon put down the file. He and Kimete went to the door of the farmhouse. A grey-haired man with piercing blue eyes was parking a white four-wheel-drive with UN on its side in big black letters. Solomon waved to him. It was Alain Audette, a Canadian doctor who had worked as a UN coroner in Belgrade for the past two years. He had a dry sense of humour and a love of single malt whisky, which meant most of Solomon's encounters with him ended in a raging hangover.

Audette climbed out of the vehicle and opened the back as Solomon and Kimete walked over to him. 'I brought the bags with me,' said Audette. 'Save time, hey?'

Solomon shook hands with him, and Kimete gave him a hug and accepted a kiss on both cheeks. Audette was a good twenty-five years older than Kimete but whenever he saw her the look in his eyes was anything but avuncular. After their first meeting Kimete had seemed quite interested, until Solomon had told her about the Canadian's three ex-wives and half-dozen children in Montréal.

'Twenty-six,' said Solomon.

'I brought thirty to be on the safe side,' said Audette. 'Where are they?'

'The barn,' said Solomon. 'Are you going to do the autopsies here?'

'*Twenty-six?* I'm a coroner, not a short-order cook, Jack. There's procedures to be followed. I'll give them the once-over *in situ* then we'll bag them and take them back to Belgrade.'

Matt Richards walked over from the barn and introduced himself to Audette. The Canadian explained that he was going to carry out a preliminary examination, and that he'd need the troopers to place the bodies in bags. Richards threw him a crisp salute and went to talk to his men. Audette nodded at Solomon. 'Let's get on with it,' he said.

Solomon and Kimete followed him into the barn. Solomon helped him into the back of the truck but didn't climb in with him.

Audette had a small dictating machine and he moved through the truck, whispering into it.

'Are you okay, Jack?' asked Kimete.

'Will you stop asking me if I'm okay?' said Solomon. 'I bought some grilled chicken at the market yesterday. Probably wasn't cooked enough.'

Kimete nodded, but it was clear from her expression that she didn't believe him.

Audette spent half an hour in the truck, then jumped down next to Solomon. 'Not often we get to see bodies in such good condition, hey?' said the Canadian.

'Other than them being dead, you mean?' asked Solomon.

Audette ignored the sarcasm. 'Cause of death in all cases appears to be suffocation,' he said. 'Two of the men had gunshot wounds, non-fatal. One in the leg, one in the arm.'

'So they were forced into the truck against their will?'

'I'd say so. I found a skull fracture on one of the men consistent with a blow. A rifle butt, maybe. I'll be able to tell you more once I've got them on the table. All Muslims, right?'

'Looks like it. All from one family farm outside Priština. Neighbours are Serbs, but nobody saw anything. Hear no evil, see no evil.'

'There were atrocities on both sides, Jack,' said Audette quietly.

'I know,' said Solomon.

Audette put a hand on Solomon's shoulder and squeezed gently. 'It's about time we had a night on the town, isn't it? Why don't you fix up a trip to my neck of the woods? I picked up a couple of fifteen-year-old malts last time I was in Zurich airport.'

Solomon nodded without enthusiasm.

'It's a shit job, Jack, but if we didn't do it, this place would be a darn sight shittier than it is.'

'Yeah, I know.'

Audette gestured towards the farmhouse. 'They got coffee in there?'

26

A few minutes later Solomon, Audette and Kimete were sitting at the table in the farmhouse kitchen drinking coffee and swapping stories while the KFOR troopers put the bodies into bags, then into a UN truck, which had arrived as the sun was going down.

Matt Richards came over to say goodbye, gave Kimete a wistful look, then climbed into one of the Humvees and led the convoy out of the farmyard, down the rutted track. Audette climbed into his four-wheel-drive and followed them.

Solomon lit a Marlboro and blew a tight plume of smoke towards the floor. He stared at the barn, frowning.

'What's wrong?' asked Kimete.

'Just give me a minute,' he said.

He walked over to the barn. The policeman was still there, talking to his men. He pointed at the man's torch, and the policeman handed it to him. He stood at the rear of the truck and played the beam around the interior.

Kimete came up behind up. 'What are you looking for?' she asked.

'The teddy bear,' he said quietly. 'I wanted to make sure they hadn't forgotten it.'

'What teddy bear?'

'The little girl was holding her teddy. I thought they might have left it behind.'

'They probably put it into the bag with her,' said Kimete softly.

Solomon switched off the torch. 'I hope so,' he said.

Two days later Audette faxed through his autopsy reports, with a handwritten reminder for Solomon to visit Belgrade for a malt-tasting session. The reports confirmed the Canadian's initial observations, that all twenty-six had died of suffocation. Several of the men had fractured bones and two had non-fatal bullet wounds.

Solomon picked up the faxed sheets and walked along the corridor to Chuck Miller's office. Miller's secretary, a middle-aged woman called Arnela, was on the phone and waved him through. The American was lying back in his leather chair, his tasselled loafers up on his expansive teak-veneer desk, the keyboard of his computer on his lap. 'Hiya, Jack,' said Miller, his eyes still on his VDU. 'What's up?' There were three framed photographs by his feet: one of his wife and two children, all with blonde hair, perfect skin and gleaming teeth, one of Miller surrounded by Mongolian tribesmen, and another of him receiving a Peace Corps commendation.

'I've got the reports on the Priština bodies,' said Solomon. 'They're doing the DNA analysis, should have the results by the end of the week.'

'What about relatives?'

'I don't think there's any doubt,' said Solomon, 'but there's one family member I'm going to see today. I'll get a sample from her for corroboration. I'm going to take Kimete.'

'Let me know what happens,' said Miller, his eyes still glued to his screen.

On the way out Arnela offered him a plate of biscuits and Solomon took one. Arnela's left hand was false, a realistic plastic model that had been made for her by an American charity. The original had been blown away by a Serbian sniper as she went to fetch water for her three young children one cold winter morning at the height of the siege of Sarajevo.

Solomon left the file in his office, put on his sheepskin

jacket and collected the keys to his Nissan Patrol from the hook by the door.

He drove to the east of the city and stopped in front of the run-down apartment block where Kimete lived. There was a shell-hole in the concrete by the front door that filled with water when it rained, a memorial to the mortar that had killed a two-year-old boy and blown off his mother's leg. Solomon never stepped over the scarred concrete without wondering if the Serb who had fired the mortar knew that he'd killed a child and maimed a twenty-five-year-old woman. Or if he knew that his victims were Serbs too.

He rang Kimete's bell and she told him she'd be right down. Solomon went back to his car and tapped his fingers on the steering-wheel as he waited. The lifts must have been out of order because Kimete took almost five minutes to get to him and she was panting. 'Sorry,' she said, getting into the front passenger seat.

Solomon filled her in on Teuter Berisha's details as he drove down the Mese Selimovica boulevard, the main route out of the city heading towards Mostar. They passed the mustard yellow Holiday Inn on their right, then a rattling electric tram.

'Why is a Kosovar Albanian woman living in Bosnia?' she asked. 'Why didn't she stay with her family?'

'Let's not look a gift horse in the mouth, Kimete,' said Solomon, braking to avoid a rusty red VW Golf that had swerved into his path without indicating. 'If she'd stayed with the family she'd be one of the bodies we're trying to identify.' The red VW swerved back to its original lane. Inside the car four young men in black-leather jackets were laughing and nodding in time to whatever was playing on the car's stereo. Solomon slowed the Nissan to give them plenty of room. Driving on Bosnian roads was dangerous at the best of times: it was as if surviving the war had given the locals a sense of invulnerability. If the Serbs couldn't kill them with tanks, mortars and sniper fire, then nothing as banal as a road-traffic accident would.

'I'm just saying, there must have been a reason.'

'She's originally from Bosnia, from a small village not far from Mostar. She married an Albanian and moved to Kosovo to be with his family. He died, but she stayed in Kosovo to raise her kids. In 'ninety-four her relatives in Bosnia were pretty much wiped out by the Serbs. There were a couple of teenagers who needed looking after, so she went back. Her kids had grown up by then and I think she just wanted to get back to her roots. I think the fact that they risked losing their land had something to do with it.'

'She's going to be distraught when she finds out what's happened,' said Kimete. 'Did she report them missing?'

Solomon wound down his window a fraction to let in some fresh air. On his left were austere tower blocks, many still bearing the scars of shrapnel hits, the hillside to his right dotted with brown houses that had new orange-tiled roofs. Virtually all the houses on the hillsides around the city had been devastated by the fighting, and after the war builders had made fortunes repairing the damage.

'No, it was a neighbour. Back then there was no procedure for contacting relatives, and because the bodies weren't found they weren't included in our database. The police didn't take a statement from her and certainly no blood sample – they didn't do that back then.'

They drove past factories empty since the war and out of the city. They curved round to the south-east and followed the Neretva river to the town of Jablanica, then along the twisting road through heavily wooded hills and rocky gorges.

It started to rain so Solomon flicked on the windscreen wipers and his side-lights. When they were ninety kilometres outside Sarajevo, Solomon passed a map to Kimete and tapped on the road they were looking for.

They turned off the main road and headed up a hill, then Kimete told Solomon to turn again and he urged the four-wheel-drive down a narrow, rutted track. They rumbled over an ancient stone bridge speckled with bullet strikes, then went through a small village with cobbled roads. More than half of the houses were roofless and every building had been pockmarked by shrapnel. They passed an orchard of fruit trees, the trunks painted white with quicklime to keep insects away, and Kimete pointed to a single-storey stone cottage. 'There it is,' she said. It was a long, low building with a pitched orange-tiled roof and a small chimney at one end. The walls had been painted white, probably with the same lime that had been used to protect the trees. Set into the wall by the door was an alcove filled with neatly chopped firewood. A lonely cow was tethered to a tree-stump, cropping a clump of tired grass. Solomon pulled up the collar of his sheepskin jacket and jogged along a rough gravel path to the front door, Kimete following close behind. There was a big brass knocker in the shape of a coil of rope and he banged it against the door. The blows echoed dully around the cottage. Solomon stood with his back pressed up against the door, trying to shelter from the rain. After a couple of minutes he knocked again, harder this time. There was still no reply. He shivered as cold water trickled down the back of his neck.

He walked along the side of the house, squelching through mud. He came to a window and peered inside. An old woman was sitting in a wooden rocking-chair, huddled over a small black stove. Solomon rapped on the window. The old woman didn't react. He knocked harder, cursing under his breath. When she didn't look away from the stove, he banged on the window with the flat of his hand, so hard that he feared the glass might break.

The woman turned to the window. Then she screwed up her eyes and craned her neck, like an inquisitive bird.

Solomon waved and nodded. 'Mrs Berisha?' he shouted. 'Teuter Berisha?'

She made a patting movement with her hand, groping for a walking-stick that was leaning against the armchair, then pushed herself slowly to her feet.

'It's okay, Mrs Berisha,' shouted Solomon, in Bosnian. 'You stay where you are.' He pointed at the front door. 'The door, it's open?'

The old woman nodded and sank back into her chair.

Solomon walked back to the door and pushed down on the rusting latch. It creaked open, scraping across worn grey slate tiles. He went in. 'My name is Jack Solomon,' he said to the woman, in Bosnian. 'I work for the International War-dead Commission.'

She frowned, not understanding.

Kimete stepped in beside him, and explained again who they were.

'Come in, come in, the heat's going,' snapped the old woman.

Solomon closed the door behind him, took off his mud-caked shoes and put them on the rack by the door. Kimete did the same.

'Put them by the stove to dry,' said the old woman. She gestured at a stack of old newspapers 'On there.'

Solomon and Kimete did as they had been told.

'Do you want coffee?' asked Mrs Berisha.

'Yes, please,' said Solomon.

She started to get to her feet again, but he waved her back. 'Let me, Mrs Berisha.'

'No, no, you are my guests,' she insisted, and stood up.

Solomon wanted to help her, but he could see that the old woman prided herself on her independence. He and Kimete watched as she reached up for an old wood and metal grinder on a shelf and a jar of coffee beans. She poured beans carefully into the grinder, then sat down and slowly turned the handle, every circuit taking almost ten seconds.

'Who takes care of you, Nana?' asked Solomon. Grandmother.

She shrugged away his concern. 'I can take care of myself,' she said. 'We lived through the war. Anyone can take care of themselves during the peace.'

Solomon indicated at the stove. 'Who chops wood for you? Who shops for your food?'

'A boy comes in every morning with wood and food, and he helps me to bed at night.' Solomon didn't understand, and Kimete translated.

'A relative?'

'The son of a cousin. A distant relative. But a good boy. He respects his elders.'

'You have other relatives here?'

'Cousins. I had a brother, but he died. He had two sons, but they died, too.' She continued to grind the beans slowly. 'It doesn't matter,' she said.

Solomon looked across at Kimete: she should explain

33

to the old woman what they needed. She was about to speak when Mrs Berisha pushed herself to her feet again, went over to the stove and spooned the ground coffee into a large *dzezva*, a conical brass pot with a long handle. She put it on the stove, jiggled the handle as the coffee toasted, then poured in hot water from a battered metal kettle. She brought it to the boil and added more hot water. Then she put the *dzezva* and three cups on a metal tray and carried it over to Solomon and Kimete. She laid it on a three-legged wooden stool and poured the thick, treacly coffee. 'I've no sugar or milk,' she said apologetically.

'This is fine,' said Solomon. He sipped: it was strong and bitter, not a brew for the faint-hearted. He smacked his lips and smiled. '*Ukusan*,' he said. Delicious.

The old woman hobbled back to her chair and lowered herself into it with a groan. Kimete took a cup to her and put it down at her side.

'Nana, we need you to do something for us,' said Kimete.

The old woman snorted. 'I am an old woman, I can barely walk and my eyes are no good.' She fixed them on Solomon. 'What did you say your name was?' she asked.

'Jack. Jack Solomon.'

'So, what do you need an old woman for, Mr Solomon?'

'You can call me Jack, for a start.'

'Are you flirting with me?' She cackled, her eyes twinkling as Kimete translated. Then looked at Kimete and said something Solomon couldn't catch. Kimete laughed, and he waited for an explanation, but clearly Kimete wasn't going to give him one.

Solomon smiled. 'No, Nana. But if I was a few years younger.'

She didn't understand his Bosnian so Kimete translated, and the old woman cackled again, then brushed a lock of wispy grey hair behind her ear.

'Have you heard of the International War-dead Commission, Mrs Berisha?' asked Kimete.

The old woman shook her head.

'Our job is to identify the victims of the war. To put names to the dead.'

'A big job, I'd have thought.'

'Jack has been doing it for more than two years, and I help him.'

The old woman's eyes narrowed to little more than slits in her parchment-like face. 'You have found them?'

'Possibly,' Kimete said cautiously. 'We have found bodies. That's why we've come to see you.' The old woman looked confused. 'We need some blood from you, Nana,' Kimete continued. 'So that we can check your DNA against the DNA of the—' She cut herself short. Solomon knew that she had been about to say *tijela* – bodies. 'The DNA will show us if it was members of your family who were killed.'

'And this DNA is in my blood?'

'It's in all your cells, but blood is easier for us.'

Kimete reached into her bag and took out a grey plastic pouch, which she handed to Solomon, and the paperwork, which she kept. 'Jack will take the sample,' she said, taking out a cheap Biro.

'He likes to inflict pain, does he?' asked the old woman.

Kimete translated and Solomon smiled as he tore open the plastic pouch. Inside was a small piece of card, used to collect four bloodstains, two surgical gloves, a sterile alcohol preparation pad, a blue and white plastic lancet and a piece of plaster.

Kimete started to ask the routine questions. Name. ID number. Her family history.

'I hate needles,' she said. 'I've always hated needles.'

'Don't worry,' said Kimete. 'It's not really a needle. You don't see it and you don't feel it.' She asked him to show Mrs Berisha the lancet. It looked like a tiny stapler. He showed her the nozzle, which was placed against the skin. When the button was pressed a small needle flicked in and out quicker than the eye could follow.

'*Ne brinite se*,' said Solomon. Don't worry. 'I've done this a thousand times.'

Mrs Berisha put her head on one side. 'A thousand times?'

Solomon nodded. 'At least.'

'But you are not a doctor?'

'No.'

'So every time you do this, it is because someone has died?'

'That's right.'

'And your job is to find out who has died? And to tell their relatives? To tell them that their loved ones have been murdered?'

Solomon couldn't follow what she was saying. He looked across at Kimete, who translated as he put on the gloves.

Then he said, 'That's what I do, Nana. We call it closure. That's my job.'

The old woman screwed up her face as if she was in pain. 'Why would any man want to do a job like that?' she whispered to Kimete. 'You never bring good news, do you? You either tell people that their loved ones are dead or you can tell them nothing.'

'Someone has to do it, Nana,' Kimete said softly.

Solomon tore off the corner sheet from the card, revealing the four printed circles where the blood drops were to be collected. He put it on the table next to him.

The old woman nodded at Solomon. 'But he is not a soldier, is he?' she asked Kimete.

Solomon understood what she had said. V*ojnik*. Soldier. 'No, I'm not a soldier,' he said.

'So you do what you do from choice?'

'Give me your hand, please, Nana.'

The old woman did as he asked. Her arm was stick-thin, the skin surprisingly smooth and white on the forearm, a stark contrast to the liver-spotted wrinkled hands. He turned the palm upward. The nails were yellow and curved, the knuckles gnarled with rheumatoid arthritis. Solomon swabbed her ring finger with the preparation pad. He nodded at a black-and-white photograph on the wall: a stunningly pretty girl with shoulder-length wavy hair on the arm of a tall, good-looking man in evening dress. 'Is that you, Nana? And your husband?'

The old woman looked across at the picture. 'Handsome, isn't he? All the girls in the village said I was lucky to have him, but they didn't know what he was like. Not really.'

As she talked, Solomon pricked her finger with the lancet. A small drop of blood blossomed at the tip. He put the lancet on the table.

'He had a temper and he was a big man.' She smiled at the photograph. 'The things you put up with when you are in love.' She looked down at her finger. 'You've started already?'

'It's done, Nana. I said it wouldn't hurt. We've almost finished.'

He took her hand and gently pressed the finger against each of the four printed circles, then stuck the plaster over the tiny wound. 'That's it,' he said, putting the card on the table to dry.

'When will you know?' she asked.

'A few days.'

'Where were they found?'

Solomon swallowed.

She saw his hesitation. 'It was bad?' She looked across at Kimete. 'It was bad?' she repeated.

'It's always bad, Nana,' said Kimete. 'They were cruel times.' She reached over and held the old woman's hand. 'But we don't think there's much doubt. We have to be sure before we say anything officially, but I think you must prepare yourself for the worst.'

'What happened to them?' she asked.

Solomon sighed 'Nana . . .'

The old woman spoke to Kimete. 'I have a right to know. I might be a silly old woman who's no use to anyone, but I have a right to know.' She leaned forward so that her wrinkled face was only inches from Kimete's. 'I know they're dead. I accepted that long ago. If any of them was alive they would have been in touch. But I have a right to know how they died. Don't I?' She looked across at Solomon, her hand still in Kimete's. 'Don't I?' she repeated.

Solomon took a deep breath. 'They were put into a truck, Nana,' he said, in Bosnian. 'A refrigerator truck used to carry meat. Some of the men fought back and they were shot. The doors were locked and the truck was driven into a lake.'

She frowned. 'They drowned?'

'The back of the truck was airtight so they suffocated.'

Kimete translated.

'*Posto*?' asked the old woman. How many?

'Twenty-six.'

'Twenty-six,' repeated the old woman. 'There were children?'

'Four boys. And three girls. One was a toddler. Two years old, maybe.'

Kimete translated.

'A baby girl?'

'Yes.'

'Shpresa,' whispered the old woman. 'My great grand-daughter.' Tears ran down her wrinkled cheeks but she made no move to brush them away.

Shpresa. Now the child had a name. The image of the little girl, clutching her teddy to her chest, cradled in the arms of her mother, flashed into Solomon's mind and he felt tears at the back of his eyes. But he was damned if he'd cry.

'It would be a help, Nana, if you could give me the names of the people at the farm,' he said.

The old woman groped for her stick and pushed herself to her feet.

'What's wrong?' he asked.

'I have photographs,' she said.

Solomon stood up. 'Let me get them for you,' he said. 'Where are they?'

The woman sighed and lowered herself back into her chair. She gestured with her walking-stick at a low wooden sideboard. 'The top drawer,' she said.

Solomon went over to it and pulled open the drawer. Inside there was a large album with thick cardboard covers. He moved his chair so that he could sit down next to Mrs Berisha, and placed the album on his knees.

'It was a wedding,' said the old woman. 'My grandson. Three years ago. I couldn't go because of my legs so my daughter sent me the album. Do you have a cigarette?'

A look of surprise flashed across Solomon's face.

'Oh come on, young man,' Mrs Berisha said tartly. 'You think that just because I'm an old woman I've said goodbye to all pleasures?'

Solomon laughed as Kimete translated. 'I suppose I'm surprised that a smoker has lived so long,' he said.

'It's not the tobacco, it's the chemicals they mix with it,' said the old woman. 'Decent tobacco never hurt anyone. My father smoked a pipe every day for seventy years. Now, do you have a cigarette or not?'

Solomon fished a packet of Marlboro out of his jacket pocket and handed her a cigarette. She had trouble moving the first finger of her right hand, the tip of which was curled into her palm, so she pushed the cigarette between her second and third fingers. He lit it for her with his Zippo. She inhaled deeply and closed her eyes as she held the smoke in her lungs. Then opened them, exhaled and smiled at him. 'That's better,' she said.

Solomon gave a cigarette to Kimete, took one himself, lit them, and put the packet on the table. 'Keep them for later,' he said.

He opened the album. The pages were separated by sheets of tissue paper and he turned them carefully. The photographs hadn't been taken by a professional. Many were out of focus and framed badly, but there was no mistaking the joy on the faces of the subjects. The groom was a stocky man in his late twenties with wide shoulders and a strong jaw. Farming stock. His wife was maybe five years younger, a frail-looking girl with long black hair and a slightly upturned nose. She had a mischievous smile

and in most of the photographs she was gazing up ador-
ingly at her new husband.

'They're a lovely couple,' said Solomon, and shuddered. They had died in the back of that truck less than a
year after the photograph was taken. 'The little girl wasn't
hers?' he asked.

Kimete translated, and the old woman shook her
head. 'No. Shpresa was born just a few days after the
wedding.' She tapped one of the photographs – a group
of six women, one of whom was heavily pregnant. 'My
nephew's wife.' She used her stick to pull a brass ashtray
in the shape of a leaf across the table towards her, then
deftly flicked ash into it.

Solomon flicked through the pages of the album. There
were pictures of two parties: the women, dancing and
drinking wine, the men, drinking beer and smoking. At
Muslim weddings, it was traditional for the two sexes to
celebrate separately. The last photograph was of a large
group of people, men and women, standing in front of a
farmhouse: all the wedding guests gathered together.
Solomon showed it to the old woman, 'Are they all
family?' he asked.

She peered down at the picture through narrowed eyes,
then tutted impatiently. She waved at a bookcase by a
narrow wooden staircase. 'Over there, a magnifying-
glass,' she said to Kimete.

Kimete retrieved it and handed it to her. The old
woman grasped it with her left hand, bent over the photograph and examined it. 'Some are family. Some are
friends.'

'Do you know them all?'

'I know the family, of course. Some of the others, no.
It's been many years since I was there.'

'Can I borrow this photograph,' asked Solomon, 'to help with identification?'

Kimete translated and the old woman nodded. 'You need all of them?'

Solomon pulled the group photograph away from the page. It had been stuck on with a small loop of sellotape and came away easily. 'Just this one will be enough.'

He placed it on the table and made a quick sketch in his notebook before numbering the figures. There were thirty-eight. Solomon asked the old woman to tell him the names of the people she knew. It took her the best part of an hour and five of his cigarettes, squinting through the magnifying-glass before she had finished. Twenty-seven of the people at the wedding were members of the immediate family. One was a cousin of the bride who had been killed by a landmine just weeks afterwards. Six were friends of the bride and groom, whom she knew by name. She didn't know who the remaining five were, but she was sure they weren't relatives. For each person she identified, Kimete filled out a missing person's information form, with as many details as possible, when and where they had last been seen. Teuter Berisha's information was sketchy at best: in many cases all she had was a name and how its owner was related to her.

When they had finished, Solomon thanked her and put away the notebook. He folded up the bloodstained card. On the back there were four identical bar codes on self-adhesive labels. He pulled one off and gave it to Kimete, who stuck it on to the top of the blood-donor's information sheet. When the sample went to the lab no one would know who had given it or where it had come from. The bar code was the only form of identification.

Solomon put the card into a foil zip-lock pouch and sealed it.

'What happens now?' the old woman asked Kimete.

'We isolate your DNA from the blood sample, and we compare it with DNA samples from the bodies,' said Kimete. 'We do that in our lab in Sarajevo. Then I'll come back. As I said, it shouldn't take more than a few days.'

Before he left, Solomon shoved two logs into the stove and wrapped the old woman's shawl around her shoulders before kissing her forehead lightly. 'Bring more cigarettes next time,' she said.

Solomon stood back and studied the photographs on the whiteboard. Alain Audette had couriered from Belgrade photographs of the twenty-six bodies in the truck. Solomon had stuck them around the edge of the board. In some cases Audette had been able to obtain names from information found on the bodies, and Solomon had written them under the respective photographs with a black marker-pen.

In the centre of the whiteboard he had stuck a copy of the photograph that Teuter Berisha had given him. He'd used his computer to blow it up to four times its original size so that he could see the faces more clearly. In many cases he could match the faces of the dead with faces in the wedding picture.

The five people in the wedding photograph that Teuter Berisha hadn't been able to identify didn't appear to be among the dead, and neither did the six friends of the bride. That left twenty-seven people in the wedding photograph, and Solomon could match all but one to the smaller photographs around the edge of the whiteboard.

Chuck Miller knocked on Solomon's open door. 'How's it going, Jack?' he asked.

'Identification's easy,' said Solomon. 'Doubt we're even going to need the DNA evidence.'

Miller waved the file he was holding. 'So this is a waste of six thousand bucks, then?' he said.

'Those are the results?'

'Hot off the presses.'

Solomon held out his hand and Miller gave him the file. It contained the DNA profiles from the bodies in the truck, and the blood taken from Teuter Berisha. A computer program had compared the samples and high-lighted similarities that pointed to a genetic link. The closer the old woman's relationship to the dead, the more genetic similarities there were. Mother–child relation-ships were the easiest to spot, followed by siblings, but the program was accurate enough to pinpoint more distant relationships. Solomon went through the twenty-six reports. In more than half of the cases there was a clear genetic link to Teuter Berisha's blood sample.

'Seems pretty conclusive,' said Miller, as he walked over to the whiteboard.

'Yeah, the pictures are, too.'

Miller studied the wedding photograph. 'Jeez . . . so everyone at that wedding was killed?'

Solomon shook his head. 'Not all of them. But the ones in the truck were all members of the same family and lived on the farm.'

'I gather there's no question that it was ethnic cleansing?'

'Muslim family, Serbian neighbours.'

'You'll pass it on to the War Crimes Tribunal, then?'

'Soon as I've informed the relative.'

'The old woman who gave the blood sample?'

'Yeah. I'm going to drive over this afternoon with Kimete.'

'Rather you than me,' Miller said. He looked at his watch. 'I've got a conference call with London,' he said. 'Catch you later.'

He left and Solomon stood for a while staring at the wedding photograph. Happy faces. The men in jackets and ties, the women in long dresses. The bride and groom.

Solomon used the marker pen to draw circles around the faces that he'd matched with the dead, then drew lines connecting them with the corresponding photographs on the edge of the whiteboard. He took a step back and scrutinised his handiwork. It looked like one of the diagrams that Miller used to flesh out the quarterly reports sent to the various funding groups that supported the Commission. But this was no organisational flow-chart. Every line represented a journey: from joyful wedding guest to victim of ethnic cleansing. A journey that had ended with lungs heaving, throats burning, the taste of blood, eyes bulging. And a little girl, clutching her teddy bear to her chest as she died.

Solomon turned away from the whiteboard.

Kimete was waiting for him in the car park. She was wearing a thick wool coat with the collar turned up against the wind and smoking a Croatian cigarette. She stubbed it out as Solomon walked up. The Walter Wolf brand she favoured was about half the price of Marlboro, and twice the strength. She had brought half a dozen black-market cassette tapes, mainly rap music, and they played them at full volume as they drove to Mostar.

It was just after midday when Solomon parked the four-wheel-drive outside Teuter Berisha's cottage and walked with Kimete to the front door. The ground under their feet was wet from recent rain, but the sky overhead was clear blue and the stone of the cottage was bone dry from the northerly wind that cut across the bleak country-side.

Solomon knocked on the door with the flat of his gloved hand, then turned the rusting metal handle. 'Nana?' he called, as he pushed open the heavy wooden door.

The old woman was sitting by her stove, sipping from a small white bowl. She grinned when she saw him, and put down the bowl on a wooden tray that lay on her lap. 'Come in, young man,' she said, 'and close the door before I freeze. Have you brought that pretty girl with you?'

Kimete popped her head around the door. The old woman grinned when she saw her. '*Slobodno!*' she said. Come in. She cupped her hands around her bowl and nodded at a metal pot on the stove. 'There's soup – help yourselves. Bowls are in the kitchen.' Then she spotted the carton of Marlboro under Solomon's arm. She beamed as he put them on the table next to her rocking-chair.

Solomon took off his shoes, then handed her the carrier-bag he'd brought with him. The old woman opened it and took out a packet of biscuits, two cans of coffee and a kilo bag of sugar lumps – he'd purloined it all from the office canteen. 'Are you married, young man?' she enquired. 'Because if you've no one to warm your bed at home you're welcome to move in with me.'

Kimete fetched two bowls from the cramped kitchen,

46

which smelt of damp. A grey cloth hung on a hook at the side of the stove and she used it to hold one of the handles of the pan as she poured out the lumpy green vegetable soup.

Solomon sat down on a wooden chair and took a mouthful. It was good, sweet onions, cabbage and a strong garlicky aftertaste. 'You made this, Nana?'

She wrinkled her nose. 'My cousin's wife. Not a patch on my cooking but my hands aren't up to much, these days. What do you think?'

Solomon took another sip. 'It could do with a little more seasoning,' he said.

The old woman's eyes brightened. 'Exactly!' she said. 'She's a miser with salt and pepper, always has been. Treats it like gold dust.' She held the bowl to her lips, then grimaced as she swallowed. She wiped her chin with her clawed right hand. 'Still, beggars can't be choosers,' she said, and laughed harshly.

Solomon put down his bowl on a three-legged wooden stool and took out his notebook and the wedding photograph. The old woman's face fell. 'It was them, wasn't it?' she said.

Solomon nodded.

She closed her eyes and muttered something under her breath. Solomon looked down at his notebook and riffled through the pages. When he looked up again, her eyes were still closed, her back ramrod straight.

'I'm sorry, Nana,' he said.

'It's not a surprise,' she said quietly. 'I knew they were dead. Of course they were dead, they had to be. But knowing and believing aren't the same thing.'

Solomon knew what she meant. Time and time again he'd broken bad news to people who already knew that the worst had happened, but until they heard it from him, the official harbinger of death, there was always some slim hope to cling to. It was his job to take it away.

The old woman opened her eyes and forced a thin smile. 'I don't know how you can do the job you do, Jack Solomon,' she said, as if she'd been reading his mind.

'Someone has to do it, Nana,' he said, but even as the words left his lips he realised how banal they sounded. And how much he was beginning to hate his work.

He placed the photograph on the table in front of her.

'All of the dead in the truck were family members,' he said, his voice flat and emotionless – as it always was when he had to rehearse the details of death. It was easier to deliver bad news if he made it sound neutral. As if he was reading a weather forecast. 'Twenty-six in all. Would you like me to go through their names?'

He waited while Kimete translated. '*Nema potrebe*,' Mrs Berisha said quietly. 'There's no need.'

'The twenty-six includes the little girl. Your great granddaughter.'

'Shpresa.'

Solomon spoke slowly, giving Kimete time to translate. 'That's right. Shpresa. Twenty-six including her. Now, in the wedding photograph, there are twenty-seven relatives, and that doesn't include Shpresa.'

'Because she hadn't been born then.'

'That's right.' Solomon tapped the man who'd been blown up by a landmine shortly after the wedding. 'And this man died, you said.'

She nodded.

Then Solomon pointed to the teenage girl. 'Which

leaves this girl,' he said. 'She is definitely not among the dead in the truck.'

'Nicoletta.'

'Yes, Nicoletta. Nicoletta Shala, you said.' He pointed at the man and woman who stood at either side of her. 'Agim Shala and Drita Shala. Her father and mother?'

'Yes. He is my brother's son. My nephew.'

The cottage door creaked open. Solomon jumped, then relaxed when he saw that the visitor was a gangly boy barely into his teens, his skin peppered with acne and his dark hair lank and greasy. The old woman waved him in impatiently. 'Close the door. The heat's getting out and firewood doesn't grow on trees.'

The boy did as he was told. 'You always say that, Nana,' he said. 'It might have been funny fifty years ago, but it's an old joke now.'

The old woman picked up her walking-stick and waggled it at the boy. 'I've already told Mr Solomon that you're a good boy who respects his elders, so don't go proving me wrong,' she said.

The boy was holding a large brown-paper bag, which he carried into the kitchen. Then he returned and sat down on a stool.

'This is Mr Solomon,' said Mrs Berisha. 'I told you about him, remember? And this is his friend, Kimete.'

The boy kept his head down, his fringe hanging like a curtain over his eyes. 'The policeman from Sarajevo,' he muttered. He spoke in English, heavily accented.

'I'm not a policeman,' said Solomon. 'I work with the police, but I'm not a policeman. You speak good English.'

The boy shrugged, but steadfastly refused to look at him.

Solomon turned to the old woman. 'I was saying, Nicoletta wasn't among the victims.'

At the mention of the name, the boy jerked as if he'd been stung.

'You know Nicoletta?' Solomon asked.

The boy shrugged again.

'They were at school together for a while, before his family moved away,' said the old woman. 'He spent holidays on their farm.' She reached over and pinched the boy's cheek with a gnarled hand. 'Mr Solomon won't bite, you can talk to him,' she said. 'You can practise your English.'

The boy looked down again, his cheeks reddening. 'She didn't like to be called Nicoletta,' he said quietly. 'She wanted everyone to call her Nicole. Like Nicole Kidman. The movie star.'

'Pretty lady,' said Solomon.

'Nicole was prettier. She could have been a movie star, too. I kept telling her. If she could just get to Hollywood, she'd be rich and famous.' The boy went quiet.

'Anyway, as I was saying, Nicoletta wasn't in the truck . . .' The boy glared at him and Solomon smiled an apology. 'Nicole wasn't in the truck, so I wanted to ask you if she had definitely been on the farm at the time of the . . . incident.'

Kimete translated for the old woman.

'I don't think she would have gone anywhere else,' said the old woman.

Solomon picked up the photograph and scanned the faces. Most of them the faces of the dead. An image flashed through his mind, of screams and shouts and fingernails clawing at the locked door, and in a corner of the truck the parents cuddling their little girl, trying to comfort her even though they knew they were all going to die. Solomon shuddered.

'The thing is, Nana, if she was away from the farm on an errand, or if she had hidden when it happened, she'd have sought help afterwards, wouldn't she?'

'*Tako pretpostavljam,*' she said. 'I suppose so.'

'And the farm has been thoroughly searched so we're sure she's not there.' He chose his words carefully: her body wasn't there, was what he meant.

'What happened to her family?' asked the boy quietly, in English. He looked up and brushed his fringe away from his eyes,

'They were killed,' said Solomon.

The boy's eyes narrowed. 'How?'

'That doesn't matter,' said Solomon. 'It's more important now that we find out who did it.'

The old woman snorted. 'We know who did it. The bastard Serbs killed them. Who else would do such a thing?'

'Nana, please . . .' Solomon said. It was important to keep emotion out of the investigation. All he wanted were the facts. 'I just need to know how I can find Nicole.'

Kimete translated.

'Why?' the boy asked Solomon. 'Why do you want to find her?'

'She might be a witness,' said Solomon. 'She might have seen what happened to her family.' Solomon looked across at the old woman. 'What do you think, Nana?'

The old woman sighed.

'Can you think of anywhere she might have gone?'

'She was sixteen. A child.'

'She didn't come here?'

'My memory might be failing, young man, but I'm

51

not yet senile. If she had come here, I would have told you so.'

'I know, Nana. I'm sorry. It's just that I can't understand why she didn't go for help,' said Solomon.

'Help from whom?' the old woman sneered. 'The neighbours were all bastard Serbs. Do you think they would have helped? Do you think the Serbian army would have helped? If it was me, I'd have run and kept on running.'

'Do you think that's what she did, Nana?'

'I don't know. I hope so, because if she didn't she's dead.'

'Why can't you leave her alone?' shouted the boy, startling them all. 'Why are you picking at their bones like vultures? They're dead and there's nothing anyone can do!' He jumped to his feet, knocking over his stool, and ran from the cottage.

He left the door open. Solomon got up and closed it. 'He was a good friend of Nicole's?' he asked.

'I think he had a crush on her, like a lovesick puppy,' Mrs Berisha told him.

Solomon took out his wallet and placed his business card on the table next to her. 'I know it's unlikely, Nana, but if Nicole gets in touch with you, can you phone me? Or get her to call me?'

Kimete translated.

'After three years? You think after all this time she'll come back?'

'It's possible.'

The old woman made a *moue*, as if she had a bad taste in her mouth. 'I'll keep your card, but don't hold your breath.'

Solomon was heading out of his office when one of the typists called after him. 'Mr Solomon! Phone!'

Solomon groaned. He was already late for an appointment with the chief forensics officer and he had to get to the other side of the city. 'Who is it?'

'He wouldn't say,' said the typist, a fortysomething battleaxe of a woman with savagely permed hair. 'A boy, I think.'

It had been more than a week since Solomon had visited Teuter Berisha's cottage, but he knew immediately who was on the line and hurried back to his desk. 'This is Jack Solomon,' he said. There was no reply, just a static buzz on the line. 'Hello?' he said. 'This is Jack Solomon.'

'Nicole isn't dead,' said a small voice.

Solomon racked his brains for the boy's name. 'I hope that's true,' he said. Had the old woman even told him what it was? Perhaps not.

'But she doesn't want anyone looking for her.'

'You've spoken to her?'

'She wants to be left alone,' said the boy, ignoring Solomon's question.

'Can I see you?' asked Solomon. 'I need to talk to you.'

'Why?'

'Because there are things we have to talk about. What happened on the farm, what happened to Nicole's family. We can't let the people who did it get away with it.'

'There's no point,' said the boy flatly.

'No point in what?' pressed Solomon. 'In catching the men or meeting me?'

'Both. Neither. I don't know, you're trying to trick me.'

'I'm not,' said Solomon. 'I just want to talk to you, face to face. Look, I can drive to where you are. I can be there in two hours.'

'No!' said the boy. 'I don't want Nana to know that I've been talking to you.'

'Well, come and see me.'

'I can't go to Sarajevo on my own. And I have to take food to Nana before it gets dark.'

'Tell me a place, then,' said Solomon, reaching for a notepad and pen. 'I only want to talk.'

There was a long pause. All Solomon could hear was the boy's ragged breathing. 'You know the bridge with all the bullet-holes just outside the village?' the boy said eventually.

'Yes.'

'Don't go over the bridge. Turn to the right and drive about a hundred metres. There's an old barn there. It was burnt down but the walls are still standing.'

'I'll find it,' said Solomon. 'I can be there in two hours. I'll see you there, yeah?'

The line went dead. Solomon replaced the receiver.

'You okay, Jack?'

Solomon flinched.

'Hell, Jack, didn't mean to startle you.' It was Chuck Miller.

'You didn't. I just had something on my mind that's all.'

Miller was holding a steaming mug. He gestured at the phone. 'Important?'

'Could be. It's that Priština case. The truck.'

Miller frowned. 'I thought we were done with that. All identified, right?'

'Yeah, they were all members of the same family.'

54

Solomon jerked a thumb at the telephone. 'That was a boy who's been in touch with one of the survivors.'

'Which involves you how?'

'She might have seen something.'

'So what's that to do with you? The remains are identified, we inform the relatives and the Tribunal, and we move on.' Remains. Miller always said 'remains'. Solomon had never once heard him refer to 'victims', or 'bodies'. And he never used names. Ever. It was either their reference number, or 'remains'. 'Remains': that which was left behind after the soul had departed. 'If the survivor is an eyewitness, the Tribunal's investigators will follow it up,' Miller continued. 'We have to stay within our brief. Pass on the name and get on with the next case.' He nodded at the whiteboard and its collection of photographs. 'You can get rid of them, too,' he said. 'I've got visitors coming tomorrow and a wall full of corpses is going to put them off their lunch.' Miller sipped his coffee. 'Aren't you supposed to be with Lisa Tourell over at Forensics?'

'Just on my way,' said Solomon.

Solomon headed downstairs and out to the car park. As he climbed into his four-wheel-drive he saw Miller watching him from the window.

As he drove out of Sarajevo, Solomon called Lisa Tourell on his mobile to reschedule their appointment. She was a forensic anthropologist, one of several working for the Commission in identifying the war dead. DNA testing was an expensive business and the forensic anthropologists were helpful in the early stages, ruling out matches based on age, sex, height and previous injuries. Her voicemail kicked in and Solomon left a message.

It took him an hour and a half to reach the ruined

barn. There was no sign of the boy. He sounded the horn and a group of crows rose up from the field to his right, cawing angrily at the disturbance. A murder of crows. Solomon smiled thinly. A murder. The collective noun for a group of crows. He sounded his horn again, three long blasts.

He waited for several minutes, listening to the metallic clicks of the engine as it cooled. Then he climbed out and walked towards the barn. The roof had been destroyed by fire leaving two blackened beams at one end, sticking up like a church spire. Sheets of rusting corrugated iron had been hammered over the space where the main door had been, but one sheet was pulled back and flapped in the wind.

Solomon shivered and raised the collar of his sheep-skin jacket. 'Hello?' he called. 'It's Jack Solomon.' His voice echoed around the ruin. He stooped and eased himself through the gap into the barn. The boy was crouching in the far corner, his knees against his chest, his head resting on his arms. Solomon walked towards him, stepping over broken roof tiles and blackened embers. 'Are you okay?' he asked softly. The boy didn't look up. Solomon bent and put a hand on his shoulder. 'Are you all right?'

The boy looked up. His eyes were red from crying. 'Do you have a cigarette?' he asked.

'How old are you?'

He glared up at Solomon. 'Do you know how many dead people I've seen? Do you know how many times I've had a gun pointed at me? How many times I've been told I'm a filthy piece of Albanian shit and that death is too good for me? Do you think I'm scared of a few cigarettes?'

Solomon took his hand off the boy's shoulder and crouched next to him, his shoulders pressing against the rough stone. He took out his packet of Marlboro, tapped one out and offered it. The boy took it without a word. Solomon lit it with his Zippo, then lit one for himself. They blew smoke up at the sky.

'Look, I'm sorry, but I don't know your name. Nana didn't tell me.'

'Emir,' said the boy.

'Pleased to meet you, Emir.'

'No, you're not,' said the boy bitterly. 'You don't care about me. You're a foreigner, and foreigners don't care what happens here.'

'That's not true,' said Solomon. 'There *are* people who care. People who are working to make Yugoslavia a better place.'

'Because you're paid,' said Emir. 'You do it for the money, not because you want to help.' He took another long drag on his cigarette. 'No one wants to help, not really. Other Europeans are scared that the fighting will spill over into their countries so they send their soldiers to keep order. They send charities so that we won't starve, and they put the generals on trial so that it looks like they're doing something – but they don't really care. If they could build a wall around us and let us get on with killing ourselves, they'd do it.'

Solomon looked across at the teenager. In any other situation he'd be wondering why someone so young could be so bitter, but not in Yugoslavia. The whole world knew the havoc that the warring factions had wreaked on each other. Genocide. Mutilation. Rape. Emir was right. Solomon had no idea how many dead people he'd seen, but however many it was, the boy had earned the right to be cynical. He flicked ash on the floor. 'When did you see Nicole?'

'What do you mean?'

'On the phone you said you had spoken to her. After her family were killed.'

Emir shook his head. 'I didn't talk to her. She wrote me a letter. I haven't seen her since the football match.'

'Football match?'

'My school was playing against a team that had come over from Ireland. I was in goal. Nicole came to watch.'

'All the way from Priština? She must like you a lot.'

'Not as much as I like her,' said Emir, flatly. 'I love her.' He wiped his eyes with the back of his hand.

'How old are you, Emir?'

'What's that got to do with anything?' said the boy, fiercely. 'You're just like her – she said I was too young. She was only three years older than me but she made it sound like she was ancient. She's nineteen now. I'm sixteen. Big deal. I told her that when I'm ninety-seven she'll be a hundred. So what?'

His hands began to shake and he put the cigarette to his mouth, his left hand supporting his right wrist as he inhaled.

'She must have thought a lot of you, to send you the letter,' Solomon said quietly. 'She didn't tell Nana where she'd gone. She didn't tell anyone. Only you.'

'She said I had to forget her. She said that the old Nicole was dead and that she was starting again. A new life.'

'Did she say where she was going?'

Emir shook his head.

'Did you keep the letter?'

Emir nodded.

'Can I see it?'

Overhead a helicopter clattered. Solomon looked up but the sky was obscured with a thick layer of grey cloud. When he looked back at Emir, the boy was holding a crumpled envelope. Solomon pulled it slowly from between his fingers. It was a pale blue airmail envelope but the postmark was Sarajevo. Dated just a month after the family had been herded into the truck.

Solomon lifted the flap and slid out the letter. It was handwritten on a sheet of lined white paper that had been torn from an exercise book. The edges were grubby from countless readings, and tear stained.

The handwriting was a childish scrawl and he had trouble deciphering some of the words, but he didn't want to ask Emir for help. His spoken Bosnian was just about good enough to hold a simple conversation, but his reading and writing skills were basic. However, Nicole's message was simple: she had seen her family taken away at gunpoint, and had no doubt that they had been killed. She was running away from the farm, away from Priština, away from Kosovo. She had considered killing herself, but said she didn't have the courage so she was going to forget everything – the life she once had, the people she knew. She was starting a new life, with a new name, and she was never coming back. She told Emir to forget her. Then she spoilt it by signing it 'always in my heart'. With a pay-off like that, Solomon knew that Emir would never forget her. And maybe she had known it, too.

'She's hurt,' said Solomon quietly. 'She wrote this because she was hurt. She's trying to blot out what happened.'

'I know that,' said Emir. 'I'm not stupid.'

Nowhere in the letter did it say where she was going or

what she was planning to do. 'Did she have friends in the city? Someone who might have given her somewhere to stay?'

Emir shook his head again, vehemently this time. 'I was her friend. If she was going to stay with anyone she would have stayed with my family.'

'But you're not in the city, are you? You live quite a way outside. Maybe she wanted to stay in the city.'

'No. She didn't know anyone. She had friends in Priština, but not in Sarajevo.'

'Can I borrow this?' Solomon asked, holding up the letter. 'Just for a while?'

'No!' Emir snatched it out of Solomon's hand. A small piece tore off in Solomon's fingers. 'Now look what you've done!' Emir hissed.

'I'm sorry,' said Solomon quickly. He gave the scrap to the boy. 'It's okay, there's no writing on it, and you can stick it together again.'

Emir ignored him. He put the torn piece in the middle of the letter, folded it and slid it back into the envelope.

'The letter might help me find Nicole,' said Solomon.

'She doesn't want to be found,' said Emir.

'That's what she says, but that's not what she means. Sometimes people try to push away those they love when they really want to be helped.'

'I can't help her.'

'No, but maybe I can,' said Solomon, holding out his hand.

Emir stuffed the envelope into his jacket.

'It's important that we find out who killed Nicole's family,' said Solomon.

'Important to whom?'

'Don't *you* want to know?'

'It won't bring them back, will it? Besides, we know who did it. Like Nana said, the bastard Serbs.'

'But which Serbs? We need to catch the men responsible and put them on trial.'

'You don't get it, do you?' Emir sneered. 'It's all Serbs. They want us dead. For every one you catch and put in prison, there's a thousand who would do just the same. It's just like it was after the Second World War. You put a few hundred Nazis on trial, but all of Germany knew what was going on in the camps. They knew that the Jews were being rounded up and taken away and they were glad. It was the same in Bosnia and Kosovo. Putting Milosevic on trial was great publicity, but if the people hadn't backed him, he wouldn't have been able to do what he did. If you think that putting a few Serbs on trial is going to make a difference, you're a fool.' He stood up. 'I shouldn't have come.'

'Then why did you?' asked Solomon. He stayed where he was, crouched against the wall, and looked up at the boy.

Emir didn't answer. He tossed away the butt of his cigarette.

'Because you want me to find her,' said Solomon.

Emir snorted softly. 'You think so?'

'You want me to find her so that you know she's all right,' said Solomon. 'Because that letter isn't enough, is it? No matter how many times you take it out and read it, it's not the same as knowing where she is and what she's doing. I'll find her, Emir, I promise.'

The boy opened his mouth to speak, then changed his mind and ran out, rattling the corrugated iron sheet aside and bolting through the gap like a frightened rat.

Solomon finished his cigarette, then returned to his car,

thinking about what Emir had said. Maybe he had been right. Maybe putting a few Serbs in the dock wouldn't make a difference, not to the grand scheme of things. But as Solomon climbed behind the wheel, he swore to himself that he would find Nicole, and the men who'd killed her family. He'd find them and make sure they paid for their crime. If nothing else, he'd get justice for the men and women who'd died in the back of the truck . . . and for the little girl with the teddy bear.

When Solomon got back to his office he found Chuck Miller sitting in his chair, his feet up on Solomon's desk. 'So how was the lovely Ms Tourell?' Miller asked, raising his eyebrows expectantly.

Solomon cursed under his breath. 'She called, yeah?' he said.

'Damn right she called,' said Miller, swinging his feet off the desk. 'Half an hour after you hightailed it out of here. Said she could reschedule for Friday but it'd mean turning her diary upside down. What the hell are you doing? Playing fast and loose with one of the interpreters? Quick bang in a cheap hotel room?'

'Don't be ridiculous!' snapped Solomon.

'Ridiculous?' said Miller. 'I'm not the one flaunting office procedures. We have diaries, Jack,' Miller pushed Solomon's across the desk, 'so that we know where our people are. Then, if anything goes pear-shaped, we know where to look.'

'I didn't have time to change the diary,' said Solomon.

'Bull-fucking-shit, Jack. I was here when you left remember? You lied to me.'

'I was planning to see Lisa,' said Solomon, 'just not today.'

'That's not the point, I'm your boss. There has to be trust for the relationship to work.'

Solomon sighed. 'Look, Chuck, I knew you'd be pissed off if I cancelled Lisa so I didn't tell you. And it wasn't a quick screw.'

'Whatever it was, it better have been damn important for you to lie to me.'

'It was the Priština case. The truck.'

Miller jabbed a finger at Solomon's chest. 'I knew it.'

'Well, if you knew that's what I was doing, why the accusations?' asked Solomon.

'I wanted to hear it from your lips. I told you, that case is over. We've identified the remains, you wrap up the file and pass it on. We don't have the resources for you to play detective.'

'I'm not playing anything,' retorted Solomon. 'I'm trying to track down an eyewitness.'

'The Tribunal will do that,' said Miller.

Solomon tutted. 'They're as stretched as we are,' he said. 'They're only after the big fish these days, or the easy cases. This isn't an easy case. There's only one witness and she's vanished. If I send over the file now, it'll get lost.'

'Twenty-six deaths, you said?'

'That's right. Women. Children. Grandparents.'

'And clearly racial?'

'All ethnic Albanians.'

Miller threw up his hands. 'So it's a perfect case for the Tribunal. It's a war crime, clear-cut. Twenty-six deaths, they'll follow it up.'

'I don't think they will,' said Solomon. 'No one other than the missing witness saw what happened. All we know is that twenty-six people were herded into a truck,

63

and the truck ended up at the bottom of a lake. Without the eyewitness, there'll be no case.'

Miller jabbed his finger at Solomon's chest again. 'That's not your problem! Our budget is stretched as far as it can go. I've a list of cases pending as long as my arm and I can't afford to have you playing the maverick. End of story.'

'Fine,' said Solomon, flatly.

'Fine isn't good enough, Jack. I want your word that you'll drop this case.'

'How about I work it on my own time?'

'Haven't you heard a word I've said? The file goes to the Tribunal. Today.'

'Okay.'

Miller gestured at the whiteboard. 'And they come down off your wall. Today.'

'Okay,' said Solomon.

'I mean it.'

'I said okay.'

Miller stared at him. 'Okay. No hard feelings, yeah?'

'You're the boss.'

'That's right.' Miller gripped Solomon's shoulder. 'We should have a drink some time, after work.' He left the room.

'Sure,' said Solomon to himself.

He removed the photographs from the whiteboard and put them into a desk drawer, then wiped off the black felt-tip marks he'd used to link the pictures of the dead with the faces in the wedding photograph.

He sat down at his desk and tapped at his computer keyboard, then got up and walked over to the framed Sarajevo street map that hung by the door. He ran his finger along Obala Kulina Bana Road and found the main post-office building. Virtually destroyed during the siege of Sarajevo, it had been painstakingly rebuilt and was now one of the most impressive buildings facing the Miljacka river. Inside it was all gleaming brass and polished mahogany with marble floors, but so much money had been spent restoring it to its former glory that there was little left to pay staff. Whenever Solomon had been there the queues had been horrendous. Even if Nicole had posted her letter there Solomon doubted that anyone would remember her.

When Solomon arrived at work the next morning, a type-written memo from Chuck Miller was tucked under his keyboard. He groaned as he sat down and read it. Evidently Miller hadn't felt that the verbal warning was enough, or that an email would be a permanent enough record of his instructions. Solomon had no doubt that a copy had been placed in his personnel file.

Miller was a seasoned memo writer and never used one word where half a dozen would do, but the meaning was clear: drop all interest in the Priština truck case – referred to in the memo only by its reference number – and pass it to the Tribunal investigators. And keep the appointments diary up to date. Solomon screwed it up and tossed it into his wastepaper basket.

He opened the top drawer of his desk and took out the Priština truck file. He signed it off, scribbled a note that it was to be forwarded to the War Crimes Tribunal and dropped it into his out-tray.

A stack of manila files was waiting for his attention and he picked one up and opened it: six Albanian factory workers had been taken off a works bus at gunpoint, marched into a wood and clubbed to death with rifle butts then doused with petrol and set on fire. The problem wasn't identifying the dead – their names were all on a roster at the factory – it was finding out who was who from a pile of charred bones. A Serbian army unit had been responsible: the police had taken statements from the rest of the workers on the bus, almost all of whom were Serbs. To a man they had refused to say anything other than that soldiers had boarded the bus and ordered off the Albanians. Hear no evil, see no evil, speak no evil. Solomon wondered what sort of men would allow their workmates to be murdered, then refuse to identify the perpetrators. It wasn't that they were scared of the repercussions, Solomon knew: it was that they almost certainly supported what the soldiers had done.

All Solomon had to do was to cross-check the DNA samples from the charred remains with DNA taken from relatives and ensure that the individual remains were given to the right families. Wherever possible they would be returned by a worker from the Family Outreach Programme, men and women trained to deal with grieving families.

Solomon flicked through the file. There were no photographs, just closely typed pages and computer printouts. It was the sort of case that would make Miller's statistics look good: six bodies identified; six sets of relatives informed. End of story. Case closed.

Solomon swore. At Miller. At the Commission. At the bloody futility of it all. Then he picked up the truck file from his out-tray and went over to the photocopier. It took him twenty minutes to photocopy every document. He also made several copies of Nicole's picture, a blow-up of the smiling face in the wedding photograph. The Tribunal could do what they wanted with the case, but as far as Solomon was concerned, he was still working on it. No matter what Miller said.

It was a great name for a policeman, Solomon thought, as he started on his second bottle of Heineken. Dragan Jovanovic. The name 'Dragan' inspired trepidation, if not fear, before you even met the man. A shovel-like hand fell on his shoulder and thick sausage-sized fingers squeezed. He winced. 'Started without me, did you? And why are you drinking that foreign muck? Sarajevsko Pivo not good enough for you, huh?'

'You're late, Dragan,' said Solomon, without turning.

'Yeah, well, I've got more to do than shuffle papers,' said Dragan, sliding on to the stool next to him.

Solomon ordered him a bottle of Sarajevsko beer, and they clinked bottles. '*Zivjeli*!' said Solomon. Cheers.

Dragan worked for the Sektor Kriminalisticke Policije, the equivalent of the British CID, and was based at the Sarajevo Canton Headquarters in La Benevolencije Street, off Mis Irbina Street. He was one of the first police-men Solomon had met in Sarajevo and, like detectives the world over, he enjoyed a drink and the opportunity to swap stories. 'So, how is life Jack?' he asked. He was a big man, well over six and a half feet tall with a barrel chest that strained to burst out of his cheap dark blue suit, and weight-lifter's thighs that threatened to do similar damage to his trousers. His hair was close-cropped and greying at the temples, although he was only in his early thirties.

Solomon pulled a face. 'Like you say, I shuffle papers. I cross-reference DNA samples, and then I break bad news, like I was the fifth horseman.'

Dragan's huge craggy face creased into pained frown. 'Horseman?'

'Death, war, pestilence and famine. The Four Horsemen of the Apocalypse. I feel like I'm riding behind them on some clapped-out old nag, the fifth – the bringer of bad news.'

The frown slackened, but Solomon could see his friend was still confused. 'Forget it, Dragan, I'm having a bad day, that's all.'

'Can't be any worse than mine, old friend,' he said, wiping the top of his bottle with the flat of his hand. 'Butcher killed his wife and . . .'

'Butchered her?'

Dragan flashed a lop-sided grin, showing a row of greying slab-like teeth. 'Sausages.'

'For God's sake.'

Jovanovic raised his eyebrows. 'She was half gone by the time one of the customers complained.'

'The taste?'

'Found a fingernail.'

Solomon groaned. 'Oh, God, Dragan, that's fucking disgusting.' He took a long swig of beer, then wiped his mouth with the back of his hand. 'What about the skull? The hips? The big stuff?'

'All went through the grinder.' Dragan drained his bottle and slammed it down on the bar. The barman looked over at him, and he motioned for two more beers. 'Both Sarajevsko this time,' Dragan said. 'No more of that foreign muck for my friend. He drinks with Bosnians, he drinks Bosnian beer. Okay, Jack?'

'You buy it, I'll drink it,' said Solomon.

Dragan nodded, satisfied. 'So, other than papers and bad news, what's bothering you?'

'A case. Down in Priština. A family were taken from their farm and put in the back of a truck. That was three years ago. The truck's just turned up in a lake in Serbia. Twenty-six dead.'

The two beers arrived, the men clinked bottles again and drank.

Solomon continued, 'I think there's an eyewitness. A girl. She was sixteen when it happened, nineteen now. Her name's Nicole Shala. Her parents were both in the truck. Agim Shala and Drita Shala.'

'She saw who did it?'

'I'm guessing so, and that's why she's running.'

Jovanovic nodded slowly. 'Victims were Albanians?'

'You ought to be a detective.' Solomon smiled. It was no great leap of intuition for the policeman. The surname alone was enough to identify the family background.

'Priština three years ago? A lot of Serb special forces were killing back then. If she saw anything, it was probably just uniforms and camouflage makeup.'

'Do you start all your investigations with this negative attitude?'

'Just the difficult ones. Is the Tribunal on the case?'

'Miller says I'm to pass on the file, and I'm doing that. But you know as well as I do how stretched they are. They'll take one look at it and say exactly what you said.'

Dragan drank some beer. 'The victims, they were shot?'

'Three were, to get them into the truck. But they all died of suffocation when the truck went into the lake.'

Dragan exhaled through pursed lips. 'So she didn't see them killed?'

'Probably not. Why?'

'Because if no one saw the truck go into the river, who's to say it wasn't an accident?'

'Come on, Dragan, you know it was murder. Had to be.'

'I'm just playing devil's avocado.'

'Advocate. Devil's advocate.'

'What's avocado?' asked Dragan, frowning.

'That green fruit thing. Soft inside, with a stone.' Solomon slid an envelope out of his pocket and placed it on the bar in front of the policeman. 'She came to Sarajevo about three years ago. I want to find her. That's her details, and her family's. And most of the Commission paperwork on the case. The last contact she had with her family was about four weeks after the abduction. She wrote to a friend outside Sarajevo. Said she was starting a new life.'

'Got the letter?'

Solomon shook his head. 'The guy she wrote to has a hard-on for her. It was all I could do to persuade him to let me read it. But it had a Sarajevo postmark.'

'That's not much help,' said Dragan. 'All mail posted in the canton has a Sarajevo postmark. Anyway, if she was smart, she wouldn't have posted it close to where she lived.'

'I don't think she's that smart,' said Solomon. 'And I don't think she expects anyone to be after her. I think she just wanted to tell this boy that she was all right and that he was to forget about her. She's a teenager, Dragan.'

'Back then kids grew up early in Yugoslavia. That's if they got to grow up at all. This girl, she had friends here? Someone who might take care of her?'

'I don't think so. The impression I got was that she came to Sarajevo precisely because she didn't know anyone here.'

'And why didn't she go to the police?'

'Hell, Dragan. I don't know. She'd seen her family forced into a truck at gunpoint. She'd seen three of them shot. That's got to be enough to make anyone act irrationally.'

'And no one's heard from her since?'

'Just the letter.'

Dragan sucked air through his teeth. 'It does not look good.'

Solomon jerked his thumb at the envelope. 'You can look for her, yeah?'

Dragan picked up the envelope and took out the sheaf of papers. He licked his thumb and forefinger, then flicked through them. He stopped when he got to the photocopied photograph of Nicole. 'Pretty girl,' he said. 'And it's not easy for a young girl to survive here on her own.'

'What are you getting at, Dragan?'

'You were in Vice in the UK, weren't you? You know what I'm getting at.' He waved the picture in front of Solomon. 'A young girl looking like this arrives in Sarajevo, the pimps are around her like dogs to a wounded rabbit. Hadn't you thought that?'

Solomon hadn't. He hadn't even noticed how pretty Nicole was. To him she was just a scared teenager on the run. He took the picture from Dragan and stared at it. Shoulder-length blonde hair with a slight curl, a cute upturned nose, high cheek-bones and full lips. She was pretty, all right. She was tall, almost as tall as her father, and the dress she was wearing was cut just low enough to suggest that even at sixteen she had a good figure. Dragan was right. A pretty, vulnerable girl would be easy prey for the Sarajevo pimps.

Dragan took back the picture. 'What was she? A farm girl?'

'Still at school, I think.'

71

'They'll have had her in a brothel within an hour of her setting foot in the city.'

'When did you get so cynical?' asked Solomon, but the question was rhetorical. Solomon had been a policeman for ten years in London, five in plain clothes, three in Vice, and cynicism went with the job. He motioned to the barman for two more beers. 'Assuming you're right, where could she be?'

Dragan laughed harshly. 'Pretty blonde girl, still in her teens? They'd break her in here, sell her to the highest bidder. By now she could be anywhere in Europe.'

Sarajevsko beer generally came in squat brown bottles, but one of the beers that the barman put in front of them was in a green one. Dragan reached for it and took several deep gulps. Most Bosnians insisted that the beer tasted better out of the green bottles, although the labels were identical. Solomon picked up the brown one. It all tasted the same to him.

Dragan burped nosily. 'It's the way it goes,' he said. 'We're a trading post for prostitutes all over Central Europe, you know that. They can't get into the EC from their own countries anywhere near as easily as they can through the Balkans. And the real money's made in Italy, Germany or the UK. They can earn ten times as much in a Rome brothel as they can here.'

'So you're saying she's not in Sarajevo?' Solomon tapped out a Marlboro and offered it to the policeman who took it and used his thumbnail to ignite a match. Solomon stuck a cigarette in his mouth and leaned forward to take a light from Dragan.

'I'd say there's a good chance. That or she's dead.'

'Oh, come on, Dragan. Now you're overplaying the hard-boiled detective.'

Dragan shrugged carelessly. 'Do you want to know how many dead hookers I have to deal with in a month? Overdoses, suicides, pimps slitting their throats, customers strangling them? Prostitution isn't a long-term career. Not here.'

'Let's try looking on the bright side, shall we? Let's suppose for a moment that she's not dead, and that she's still in Sarajevo. Where might she be?'

'Nightclub, if she's lucky. A brothel if she isn't.'

'Could you find her?'

'Needle in a haystack.'

'Haystack,' said Solomon.

'Thank you for the English lesson,' said Dragan. 'But you understand what I am saying?'

'I didn't ask if it was easy, Dragan. I asked if you could do it.'

Dragan narrowed his eyes. 'Make it a challenge and I'll do your work for you, is that what you think?'

'Hell, Dragan, would you rather I tried to bribe you?'

Dragan chuckled throatily. 'Okay, I'll try. But first I'll check that she's not turned up dead. That's easy enough. Then I can check arrest records through our information section, but without fingerprints I only have a name and a three-year-old photograph to go on.'

'What about running it past the federal police? If she was trafficked, they might have come across her.' Dragan had spent six years with the federal police, the country's equivalent of the FBI, dealing with countrywide and international crime, before joining the Sarajevo canton police. He'd been an inspector with the Odjeljenje Za Organizovani Kriminalitec I Droge, the department investigating organised crime and drugs.

He shrugged. 'Sure I'll try. A lot of my contacts have

moved on, but I'll see if I can get someone to access their records.'

'What about trawling through the bars?'

The policeman chortled. 'Do you know how many cases my boss has given me this week?'

'That's a no, then, is it?'

Dragan laughed and slapped Solomon on the back, hard. 'I love the English and their sense of humour,' he said.

'It's irony,' said Solomon. 'Verging on sarcasm.'

Dragan waved for another two bottles of beer.

'These bars where the hookers work, how dangerous are they?' Solomon asked.

'You've never been?'

'Never felt the urge,' said Solomon.

Dragan looked at him in disbelief. 'Bullshit,' he said.

'I worked in Vice for three years, which pretty much got it out of my system,' said Solomon. 'Plus, it's illegal here and I wouldn't want to go breaking any Bosnian law.'

'It is illegal in England too, no?'

'It's complicated,' said Solomon. He drained his bottle as the barman placed a fresh one in front of him. 'Prostitution as such isn't illegal. You can pay for sex without any problems. What's illegal is to offer to pay for sex. That's importuning. And it's illegal to offer sex in exchange for money. That's soliciting. It's the proposal that's illegal, not the act itself.'

'That's crazy.'

'You're probably right. But because it's such a grey area, Vice cops don't bother busting the girls, unless they're too blatant and the neighbours start to complain.'

Dragan was frowning, deep furrows cutting across his brow. 'So let me get this right. If the girl doesn't say how much she's charging, she can't be done for prostitution.'

'She wouldn't be done for prostitution anyway, it would be soliciting.'

'Isn't that what a lawyer does? You call them solicitors, right?'

'That's different.'

Dragan jabbed a finger at Solomon. 'Got you!' He laughed. 'English humour.'

Solomon leaned back on his stool. 'Screw you, Dragan. If you're going to take the piss, forget it.'

Dragan gripped his shoulder and shook him, like a grizzly bear showing affection to its cub. 'Don't get upset, Jack. You know I love you.'

'I don't know why I put up with you. You butcher the English language and you never buy your round.'

'Because we're the same, you and I. We know that nothing we do really makes a difference. But if we didn't do what we do, the world would be an even worse place than it is.'

'That's one hell of a philosophy,' said Solomon. 'Once you unscramble it.'

Dragan threw back his head and guffawed, slapping Solomon's back so hard that his head jerked backwards. He drained his beer and winked at the barman, who was already reaching for two fresh bottles. 'So the prostitutes in London, they are not breaking the law?' he asked.

'So long as they're not on the streets, approaching men, then what they do is legal. But they have to work on their own. One girl in a flat seeing men is legal, but if it's two girls or more it's a brothel and that's illegal.'

'More nonsense,' said Dragan.

'It's even crazier than that,' said Solomon. 'They're allowed another girl in the flat, but she can only work as

75

a maid – answering phones, letting people in and out, changing the bed linen.'

'And the cops check that?'

'Nah. They used to, but these days they're way too stretched. They're more interested in putting the pimps away.'

'So pimping is illegal? At least you are doing something right. Pimps are the scum of the earth.'

'Oh, sure. Pimping always has been a crime. Carries a maximum sentence of seven years. Living off immoral earnings, they call it – if it's a man. If it's a woman it's controlling prostitution for gain. But the girls themselves aren't breaking the law. Do you fancy a drink somewhere else?'

Dragan looked at him suspiciously. 'Like where?'

Solomon slid off his stool. 'Oh, I don't know,' he said innocently. 'I thought maybe you could show me one of those nightclubs you were talking about.' He ducked as Dragan tried to slap him again.

'You are a bad man for leading me astray like this,' he said. The policeman got off his stool, drained his bottle and slammed it down on the bar. 'What will I say to my wife?'

'She's a policeman's wife, she's used to you coming home late at night.'

'Coming home late from work is one thing. Coming home late smelling of cheap perfume after a night out with Jack Solomon is a different kettle of fish,' said Dragan.

'I'll explain,' said Solomon. 'She likes me.'

'She tolerates you,' said Dragan. 'The same as I do.' He pushed Solomon towards the door. 'Go on. If you're going to lead me astray, get on with it.'

Dragan drove north out of the city in his almost-new black VW Golf, his pride and joy. 'They make great cars, the Germàns,' he said, winding down his window and blowing out smoke. 'VW, Mercedes, Audi, BMW, Rolls-Royce.'

'Don't start, Dragan,' said Solomon. 'You know I'm not going to rise to it.'

'But it must be galling, no? To have Germans running your most famous car company?'

'Dragan, the chances of me ever owning a Rolls-Royce are so remote that I couldn't give a monkey's who owns the company, be it Germans, French or Lithuanians.'

'A monkey's?' asked Dragan.

'It means I don't give a shit. Where are we going?'

'The Purple Pussycat. Wine, women and song.'

'But why's it all the way out here?'

'Because such places are illegal. If they were in the city, they would draw attention to themselves. Here they are out of sight, out of mind.'

Solomon took a long drag on his Marlboro as Dragan negotiated a series of stomach-churning hairpin bends with the engine at full revs. The policeman took it as a personal insult whenever he had to change down a gear, and while Solomon knew that his friend had never been involved in an accident, he still found sitting in the passenger seat stressful and had to stop himself stamping on a non-existent brake pedal. Whenever Dragan saw the involuntary movement, he drove all the faster.

'How do people know where to go?' asked Solomon.

'They know,' said Dragan, overtaking a truck belching black smoke from an exhaust held in place with knotted wire from the tailgate. 'Word gets round. The SFOR

Americans have a list of approved places their people can visit.'

'They what?'

'Approved places. Places where they won't be busted.'

'But they're still illegal?' said Solomon.

'Sure. But I guess the Americans have different degrees of illegality.'

'That's like different degrees of pregnancy,' said Solomon. 'It doesn't work that way. Either you're pregnant or you're not. No half-way stage.'

Dragan swerved to avoid a tractor, then accelerated over a hump in the road. Solomon's stomach lurched and the policeman flashed him a grin. 'Not going too fast for you, am I?'

'I was wondering why you were so slow tonight,' replied Solomon.

Dragan roared with laughter. A car coming towards them swerved into their lane to overtake but the policeman made no move to avoid it. He just flashed his lights and accelerated. The car braked hard, pulled over and sounded its horn as the VW swept by. 'Bosnian drivers are the worst in the world,' said Dragan.

'I couldn't agree with you more.'

'Did you know that Bosnia is one of the only countries that has more cars than people?'

Solomon sighed. 'Yes, Dragan, you told me.' There were two reasons for this. The population of Bosnia had been almost halved during the war, and the country was used as a dumping ground for unwanted vehicles from all over Europe. Some academic had calculated that there were now two vehicles for every man, woman and child.

Dragan pointed to the left. 'There it is,' he said.

Solomon saw a two-storey house with an orange-tiled

roof, no different from the rest that dotted the hillsides around Sarajevo. There was no sign, no neon lights, nothing to indicate that it was anything other than an ordinary house. As they turned off the main road and drove down a single-lane track, he saw a dozen or so vehicles parked, including two white UN four-wheel-drives.

Dragan parked in the road behind four saloons, all with SFOR plates. 'If it wasn't for the internationals, these places wouldn't survive,' he said.

'What's the difference between an approved place and one that isn't?' asked Solomon, as they walked towards the front door. He could hear the thudding bass of a rock track through the shuttered windows.

'Drugs. Underage girls. Violence.'

'Those would be negatives, right?'

'I love your English humour,' said the policeman. 'Some of the guys running these places are heavy-duty gangsters. They deal in drugs as well as girls. The SFOR people are warned about them, and if they get caught they're sent home. The approved places don't get busted – at least, not until they're put off limits.'

'That's perilously close to corruption, isn't it?'

Dragan shrugged his massive shoulders. 'Most of the internationals are single men, or men away from their families for long periods,' he said. 'They've got needs, and they've got money. Prostitution is going to happen no matter what the law says. By confining it to safe places, there's less trouble all round.'

'And what about the places that aren't approved?'

Dragan pulled a face. 'That's where the real corruption is,' he said. 'They pay off whoever needs paying off. Big money. When there's a crackdown the gangsters are tipped off and they move most of the girls out before they're busted. They just set up somewhere else.'

They reached the front door and Dragan knocked. A small hatch snapped open at eye level. They were scrutinised by a thick-set man with a single eyebrow, then the hatch snapped back into place and bolts were drawn back.

The door opened and the man waved them inside. A Rolling Stones song was playing: 'Paint it Black'.

In the centre of the room a blonde girl in a black bikini was dancing around a silver pole on a podium. Half a dozen others were sitting on an L-shaped sofa in one corner of the room, wrapped in identical plum silk dressing-gowns and drinking beer. 'Salubrious,' said Solomon.

'What does that mean?' asked Dragan, pointing at an empty sofa and gesturing to a waiter at the far end of the bar.

'Salubrious? It means respectable. I was being sarcastic.'

'Ah,' said Dragan. 'This constant double-talking cost you an empire, didn't it?'

'Now you're trying to be sarcastic, right?' said Solomon.

Dragan winked and they sat down. The waiter came over and he ordered two local beers, then motioned at Solomon for a cigarette.

'So why is it called the Purple Pussycat?' asked Solomon.

'They change the name every time they're busted. It used to be the Red Rover. There's never a sign outside, so the name doesn't really matter. I don't think the décor has changed in the past five years.'

'So you've been here before?'

The policeman pointed a warning finger at Solomon. 'I was on a few raids,' he said. 'I don't want you telling anyone that I came here for pleasure.'

'Perish the thought, Dragan.'

The track ended and the blonde skipped off the podium. She went to sit with her co-workers, and her place at the pole was taken by a buxom redhead. The waiter brought their beers and Dragan settled back to leer at the dancer.

'The girls are all available, are they?' asked Solomon.

'For sex? Sure.'

'How does it work?'

'You ask the barman or a waiter. He gets the girl you want to come over. You can buy her a drink and chat to her, and if you want to go upstairs you tell the waiter.'

'How much does it cost?'

'Fifty konvertible marks for half an hour. A hundred for an hour.' Dragan grinned. 'Last time I checked.' When western forces had moved in to the fractured Yugoslavia, they had established a new currency, the konvertible mark, linked to the German Deutschmark. Even though the Euro had replaced the Deutschmark, the konvertible mark remained the local currency.

Dragan waved at the waiter, then pointed at two of the girls. He went over to them, and they jumped to their feet, then tottered on high heels to where Dragan and Solomon were sitting. Dragan told them to sit down. The taller of the two, a brunette with a wide smile and surprised eyes, sat down next to Solomon and put a hand on his thigh. She spoke to him in a language that sounded like Bosnian but he didn't recognise any of the words.

The other girl, a lanky blonde with breasts so large they

could only have been implants, sat down next to Dragan and put an arm round his shoulders. He spoke to her for a few minutes, then leaned towards Solomon. 'Belarussians,' he said. 'All the girls who work here are from Belarus.'

'How many girls are there?'

'Twenty, she says. Another dozen arrive next week. From Belarus, too.'

'Is that normal?' asked Solomon. 'I'd have thought there'd be more than enough local girls who needed the money.'

'The foreigners are cheaper,' said Dragan. 'The Ukraine, Latvia, Belarus – the daily wage there is a fraction of what it is here. Give these girls a couple of dollars a day and they think they're rich.'

The girl next to Solomon began to rub his groin suggestively. 'Can you tell her I'll buy her a drink but that I don't want to go with her?' said Solomon.

'Tell her that and she'll walk away,' said Dragan. 'They're not interested in customers who are here just to drink. We'll buy them drinks and say we're deciding which girl to take. Okay?'

'Fine,' said Solomon.

Dragan ordered for the girls. He spoke to the blonde for a few minutes, then tapped Solomon's leg. He disentangled himself from the brunette and leaned across the sofa so that the policeman could whisper in his ear. 'She says the guy here has a deal with Mafia guys in Belarus. He brings them in direct. I don't think it's worth even showing them your girl's picture. They won't have seen her, and we sure as hell don't want her asking her pimp.'

'All I'm trying to do is find her,' said Solomon. 'We can explain that I'm not a cop.'

'No, but I am. And, besides, these people are breaking the law. If this place gets busted, and the girls are sent back where they came from, they lose everything. And if the pimp gets busted he goes to jail, or he spends a hell of a lot of money buying his way out. They're not going to risk that by spilling their guts to a stranger.'

Two bright green drinks in small glasses arrived but the girls didn't touch them. The brunette's groin-rubbing became more insistent. Solomon smiled at her, took her hand and held it. Immediately the other found its way between his legs. She nuzzled his neck and he felt her lick his chin. She whispered in his ear.

'I'm sorry,' said Solomon. 'I only speak English.'

'I want you fuck me,' she whispered.

'You speak English?'

'I want you fuck me,' she repeated.

'That's all the English you know, right?'

'I want you fuck me.'

Despite himself, Solomon smiled. She nodded encouragingly. Solomon shook his head. Her expression hardened. She stood up, spoke to the other girl, then flounced off, tossing her long, dark brown hair like a race-horse ready for the off.

The remaining girl whispered in Dragan's ear and when he shook his head she went off to join the other girl.

'See?' he said. 'They're only interested in screwing.'

'Are all the places like this?'

'Some are, some aren't. Some are more relaxed and the girls will chat to you. Depends on the management. Here they just want them dancing or screwing.'

Two large men in overalls spoke to a waiter, who crossed to speak to the two girls who'd been at Solomon and Dragan's table. They went to join the men and five minutes later the four were heading through a door at the back of the room.

'Do customers ever take the girls out?' asked Solomon. 'Back to their homes or hotels?'

'I doubt it,' said Dragan. 'By keeping them here the pimps have control. The girls never get the money, it's paid to the pimp and he pays the girl. Also, if their papers are not in order, the girls will be taking a risk in leaving the bar.' The policeman drained his bottle. 'What do you want to do?'

'There are other bars we can try?'

'If that's what you want.'

Solomon waved for the bill. 'Maybe a couple more.'

'Your wish is my command,' said Dragan, getting to his feet. 'Just so long as you keep buying the drinks.'

The fax machine kicked into life and a sheet of paper curled out. Solomon went to stand by it.

'That's not from New York, is it?' shouted Miller, from the corridor.

Solomon cursed under his breath. The last thing he wanted was for his boss to see the list of nightclubs that his SFOR contact was sending over. 'No, it's for me,' he said. 'I'll give you a shout if yours arrives.'

Miller headed back to his office as the first sheet of paper was ejected into the wire tray at the bottom of the machine. Solomon pulled it out. Across the top, JC had scrawled, 'You didn't get this from me.' Beneath was a typewritten list of two dozen bars and clubs and their addresses. A second sheet dropped into the basket and the fax machine clicked off. At the top of the second sheet JC had written in capital letters, 'AND YOU DEFINITELY

DIDN'T GET THIS FROM ME!' On the sheet were four handwritten names and addresses.

JC was an American sergeant who worked at the airport as an air-traffic controller, responsible for all US flights into and out of Sarajevo. Solomon had met him in an Irish bar in the city centre shortly after he'd arrived in Bosnia and they'd spent a highly enjoyable evening contrasting the merits of Irish whiskey and Scotch. They both enjoyed soccer: JC supported Manchester United and had been amazed to discover that the city had a second football team, and even more amazed that Solomon supported it. Like many natives of Manchester, Solomon regarded Manchester City as the true local team and Manchester United as a group of highly paid poster boys more interested in sponsorship and advertising than in the Beautiful Game. They'd become good friends and whenever there was a big match on they met in the Irish bar to get drunk and watch the game on the bar's big-screen TV.

Solomon had phoned JC and had asked him if it was true that the Americans in SFOR had been given a list of approved nightclubs. JC had laughed and said that it depended on Solomon's definition of 'approved'. There was a list in circulation but it didn't mean that the SFOR top brass condoned their staff visiting them.

Solomon had asked him to send over the approved list, and also the names of any other bars he knew where girls were available.

Solomon took the fax back to his office. The Purple Pussycat was on the approved list, as were the two other bars that Dragan had taken him to the previous night. All three had been pretty much the same in layout and function, but the second two had offered a mixture of girls, from the Ukraine, Latvia, Slovakia, Moldavia, Romania and Lithuania, as well as a few locals. Solomon had shown them the photograph of Nicole, but no one recalled seeing her. 'A needle in a hâystack,' Jovanovic kept repeating.

'You busy?' asked Miller.

Solomon hadn't heard the American walk down the corridor. He opened his top drawer and put away the two pieces of paper. 'No more than usual,' he said.

'They could do with you in Tuzla,' said Miller. 'We've just got a dozen matches come through. Are you up for it?'

A dozen matches. That meant a dozen remains identified. Twelve sets of grieving relatives. It was time for the fifth horseman to saddle up again. Solomon nodded. 'I'll drive up this afternoon.'

'Good man, they're expecting you. Did you pass the truck case on to the War Crimes Tribunal?'

'Absolutely,' said Solomon.

Miller flashed him a smile and went back to his office.

Solomon spent the night in Tuzla, staying with one of the Commission's forensic anthropologists, and got back to Sarajevo late the following evening. As always, his throat was sore from the city's polluted air and he showered for twenty minutes to get the dirt out of his skin and hair.

He towelled himself dry and changed into a clean pair of jeans and a denim shirt, then telephoned Dragan. The policeman's mobile was switched off and Solomon didn't leave a message. He made a cup of coffee, then took out the two sheets that JC had faxed, sat down on one of his sofas and read through the typed list.

All but one, the Moulin Rouge, had an English name,

perhaps because the clientele was mainly international, Solomon thought. Concessions were rarely made to English speakers in Bosnia: signs in English were few and far between and the city's news-vendors almost never stocked English or American papers.

Solomon turned to the handwritten list. The four bars weren't approved by SFOR but JC had said they were regularly visited by friends of his who claimed that the music was better and the girls were prettier. The only downside was the risk of a raid, but JC said that happened only rarely and that as SFOR troops often conducted them, unofficial advance warning was usually given.

Dragan had said that drug-use was one reason that a bar might not be on the approved list, but in the approved bars to which the policeman had taken him Solomon had seen evidence of drug-taking among girls – dilated pupils, hyperactivity, sniffing, nose-rubbing.

One of the bars on the list, the Butterfly, was in a small village to the south of Sarajevo. Solomon had been there several times to organise the collection of blood samples from Kosovan refugees. He'd been planning on an early night but instead he decided to drive out to the Butterfly. As it wasn't approved he doubted that Dragan would take him.

He put a photograph of Nicole into his jacket pocket and went down to where he'd parked his four-wheel-drive, then had second thoughts. It wouldn't be a good move to leave the vehicle with its diplomatic plates and International War-dead Commission logo parked outside a brothel.

He walked to the main road and flagged down a taxi. He told the driver where he wanted to go and they headed out of the city and up into the mountains.

The Butterfly was at the edge of the village, in a new building, by the look of it, or one that had been substantially rebuilt after the war. There was parking for two dozen vehicles, but only five cars were there, all Volkswagens.

Solomon asked the driver if he'd wait for him, but the man shook his head and held out his hand for the fare. Solomon paid him, got out, and stood looking at the house as the taxi drove away. He was already regretting not using his own car. He'd just have to hope he could phone for a taxi from the bar when he was ready to go home.

He walked up to the front door and raised his hand to knock, but the door opened before he could do so and two men staggered out, smelling of whisky and Turkish cigarettes. They grinned amiably at Solomon and staggered towards one of the Volkswagens. Solomon walked into the bar.

The management hadn't chosen its name at random: it had a butterfly theme with framed photographs of different species on the wall and paper butterflies hanging from the ceiling, their wings wafting in the cigarette smoke. The whole ground floor of the house was open plan, with small wicker sofas facing each other across wicker and glass coffee tables. On each table there were large ashtrays in the shape of butterflies.

A teenage waiter with a pencil-thin moustache and a ponytail came over carrying a metal tray and showed Solomon to an empty sofa. He ordered a Heineken.

'Do you want a girl?' asked the waiter in Bosnian, and jerked his head at half a dozen dancers who were sitting on stools at a bar that ran the length of the room. They were wearing wraparound silk dressing-gowns of various colours with butterfly motifs on the back. They all swivelled to face him, smiling brightly. One allowed her dressing-gown to fall open, revealing a white bikini. Two more girls were dancing around a silver pole on an oval podium in the centre of the bar. They also beamed at Solomon and one jiggled her breasts in his direction.

'Maybe in a while,' he said.

He settled back and looked around the room. The girls at the bar swivelled so that their backs were to him. Four big men, in leather jackets with bottles of Sarajevsko in front of them, were sitting by the door. They had all turned to look at him. He nodded a greeting and one raised his beer bottle, smiling with cold eyes. Security, no doubt.

There were two dozen customers, most of them sitting next to girls, and almost everyone was smoking.

Solomon lit a Marlboro. The waiter returned with his beer and a glass bowl of salted peanuts. Solomon indicated the girls at the bar. 'Do any of them speak Bosnian?' he asked.

'Sure,' said the waiter, scratching at his moustache. 'But you don't have to talk to them to have sex with them. See the one with the long blonde hair?'

'She speaks Bosnian?'

The waiter grinned. 'No, but she does anything you want.' He leaned close to Solomon. 'I mean anything. You can hurt her if she wants. She loves it. Begs for more.'

'I want a girl who speaks Bosnian,' said Solomon, fighting an urge to punch him.

'There aren't any Bosnian girls working here,' he said. 'We have girls from Latvia and the Ukraine.'

'I don't care where she's from,' said Solomon, 'but I want a girl who can speak Bosnian. Or, better still, English.'

The waiter pointed at a girl on the right of the group at the bar. 'She is from the Ukraine, but she speaks English. Many of the internationals like her.' The girl was a brunette, her hair cropped short. She was resting her head on the shoulder of the girl next to her.

'Okay,' said Solomon. 'Send her over.'

'You can go upstairs now,' said the waiter. 'There's a room free. Fifty marks for half an hour, everything included. We have condoms in the room.'

'Let me buy her a drink first,' said Solomon.

The waiter shrugged and went over to the bar. He spoke to the brunette, who looked over her shoulder at Solomon, then nodded. Seconds later she had sat down opposite him. Close up, Solomon could see that she was very young. Probably still in her teens.

'The waiter said you want girl who can speak English,' she said. She had a thick accent.

'Yeah. I'm Jack,' he said, and held out his hand.

She smiled, showing teeth that gleamed so brightly he thought they'd been cosmetically whitened. The fingers of her right hand were stained with nicotine. 'Lyudmilla,' she said.

'Pretty name,' said Solomon. 'You're from the Ukraine?'

'How do you know?' she said, nervous. 'You see me before?'

Solomon smiled, trying to put her at ease. 'The waiter said you were Ukrainian,' he said. 'He said you spoke very good English.'

'Not so good,' she said. 'I go school in Ukraine but not much.'

'You're a long way from home,' he said.

'Not really,' she said. 'What about you? You are American?'

'English.'

'But you like American cigarettes?' She reached across and pulled one from his packet, then gently scraped his skin with a bright red fingernail as he lit it for her with his Zippo.

'How did you end up in Sarajevo?' Solomon asked.

'I came to work.'

'The money's better here?' he said.

'Of course,' she said, and snorted contemptuously. 'There is nothing in the Ukraine. Here there are UN workers, charity workers, soldiers. All with money to spend.' She smiled coquettishly. 'What about you, Jack? Do you have money to spend?'

'How old are you, Lyudmilla?' Solomon asked.

'You think I'm too old?' she asked.

'I think I'm old enough to be your father,' he said.

'I like older men,' she said, reaching under the table and giving his leg a squeeze.

The waiter reappeared and Solomon asked him to bring over whatever Lyudmilla was drinking. She grinned. 'So, you like me?'

'Of course I like you,' he said.

'Do you want to go upstairs with me?'

'Lyudmilla, I just want a drink.'

'You don't want me?'

Solomon looked her up and down. Dark green eyes, soft, full lips, pale white skin that looked as if it had never seen the sun, firm breasts that seemed to be trying to push themselves out of her bikini top, and long silky legs. If she wasn't a prostitute who'd slept with God knew how many men to get from the Ukraine to Sarajevo, and if she wasn't young enough to be his daughter, yes, he'd have wanted her.

She misunderstood his look and stroked his leg again, closer to the groin this time. She raised her eyebrows expectantly. 'There's a room upstairs we can use,' she said. 'Only fifty marks for half an hour. The sheets are clean.'

Solomon put his hand on hers and moved it away from his groin. 'I'm married,' he lied.

'Most of the men who go with me are married,' she said. She batted her long eyelashes and Solomon laughed. She pouted and crossed her legs away from him. 'You are making fun of me,' she said crossly.

'I'm not. Really, I'm not.' The waiter brought over a glass of what looked like cola and placed it in front of her. She sipped it, then licked her upper lip. Solomon took out the photograph of Nicole – the head and shoulders shot taken from the wedding photograph.

'Who's that? Your wife?' asked Lyudmilla, still pretending to be annoyed.

'Someone I'm looking for,' said Solomon, handing the picture to her. 'Have you seen her?'

She looked at the photograph. He saw the flash of recognition, then her attempt to hide it. 'Why do you want to find her?' she asked.

'Have you seen her?' Solomon repeated.

'I'm not sure,' she said. 'I could ask the other girls.'

'Her name is Nicole. That's an old photograph. Three years ago.'

'No one uses their real name here,' she said. 'First thing you change, your name. Are you police?'

'Of course not,' said Solomon. 'I'm English. I work

for an aid agency.' He didn't want to tell her that he worked for the International War-dead Commission – it sounded too close to police work. 'A friend met her in Priština before he went back to London. She said she was moving to Sarajevo but he lost her address. That's all.'

'You could give me your friend's name and address. If I see her, I'll pass on the message.'

'So, you do know her?'

'A lot of girls pass through here. I'll pin up the photograph in the changing room.'

'She's not in any trouble, Lyudmilla, I promise.' He held out his hand for the photograph. 'She worked here, didn't she?'

Lyudmilla bit her lower lip. 'She said her name was Amy. And she had black hair, not blonde like in the picture.'

'Where is she now?'

Lyudmilla looked nervously at the four men sitting by the door.

'Is she still in Sarajevo?'

'London. She went to London four months ago.' Lyudmilla looked down at the photograph in her hands and smiled.

'What's she doing in London?' asked Solomon.

She snorted again. 'What do you think she's doing? She's working.'

'Who sent her?'

'Why do you want to know?'

'Just curious.'

'You said a friend wanted to write to her.'

Solomon tried to smile reassuringly. 'He'll want to know where she is and what she's doing, that's all.'

'You ask questions like a policeman.' She put the photograph on the table and stood up.

'You haven't finished your drink,' said Solomon.

She didn't answer, just walked away. She went into the ladies', giving him one last look over her shoulder before the door closed behind her.

Solomon sipped his Heineken, then stubbed out his cigarette in the butterfly ashtray. He headed for the gents', but at the last moment pushed his way through the door of the ladies'. Lyudmilla was standing in front of a mirror, applying mascara to her long lashes. She turned and took a step away from him. 'You shouldn't be in here,' she said.

'Are you worried about the guys by the door? We could go somewhere else – you could say I'm taking you to a hotel.'

'I cannot go hotel,' she said, glancing nervously across at the door. 'We go upstairs with customers. Cannot go outside. Please, go away. Someone might have seen you come in here.'

'I'll pay you,' he said.

'You want to sleep with me?'

'I want to talk to you.'

She opened her mouth, but before she could speak the door was thrown open. 'Who the hell are you?' snarled a short, stocky man in a brown leather safari jacket. He was holding the photograph of Nicole, which Solomon had left on the table. He had receding hair cropped short, thin lips and a square chin with a large dimple in the centre. He was one of the four who had been sitting by the door.

'I just wanted to talk to Lyudmilla,' said Solomon.

The man waved the photograph under his nose. 'Where did you get this?'

Solomon swatted away his arm. 'I don't want any trouble,' he said.

'I don't care what you want,' said the man. 'I want to know what you're doing asking questions in my bar.'

Lyudmilla was trembling. 'He was just looking for Amy—' The man cut her off with a menacing look.

'I'm not talking to you, whore,' he said. 'Get out there and earn some money or I'll get the boys to take you upstairs.'

Tears welled in Lyudmilla's eyes and she hurried out.

'You get a kick out of terrorising women, do you?' asked Solomon.

'Give me your wallet,' the man said to Solomon,

'Like hell,' said Solomon.

The man reached into his jacket and took out a gun, which he levelled at Solomon's chest. 'Your wallet.'

'There's no need for this,' said Solomon, backing away.

'I want to know who you are. Give me your wallet.' The man's finger tightened on the trigger.

'There's no need for this. I'm just looking for the girl in the photograph, that's all.'

The man screwed up the photograph with his left hand and threw it in Solomon's face. 'You think you can come into my bar, asking questions, bothering my girls? If that's what you think, you're wrong.' He jabbed the barrel of the gun into Solomon's stomach. 'Your wallet.'

Solomon took it out slowly and opened it to show his Commission identification.

The man sneered at Solomon. 'So you're a cop.'

'No. I'm a co-ordinator. I make sure everything is handled properly.'

'I know what you people do. You accuse people of war crimes.'

'No, we're forensic investigators. We identify the dead.'

The man snarled and whipped the barrel of the pistol across the side of Solomon's face. He felt a flash of pain and blood spurted down his cheek. The man raised the gun again and Solomon lashed out with his fist. He hit the man on the chin and his head snapped back.

Solomon caught sight of his reflection in the mirror: his left cheek was smeared with blood and there was a near-manic look in his eyes. He hadn't been in a fist fight for more than ten years and on the last occasion he'd had two detectives and six uniforms backing him up.

The man roared and pointed the gun at Solomon's face. Solomon grabbed for the weapon with his right hand and clawed at the man's face with his left. He managed to get his thumb on the hammer and forced the barrel away to the side. The man brought up his knee and Solomon twisted to the side to protect his groin. He screwed his fingernails into the man's cheek, then rammed his head back against the mirror so hard that the glass shattered.

Now the man brought his knee up again and this time he caught Solomon sharply in the belly. Solomon gasped, and let go of the gun. He punched the man on the side of the head, then slammed his elbow against his chin. The man's eyes glazed over briefly, then focused again. He brought the butt of the gun crashing down on Solomon's head. Solomon staggered back and the man pointed his weapon at his groin, then tightened his finger on the trigger.

Solomon kicked out and the gun jerked upwards as it fired. The bullet whizzed by his head and buried itself in the ceiling. His ears buzzed and he kicked out again, connecting with flesh. The man doubled over and

Solomon stepped forward, grabbed him by the shoulders and slammed him into the wall, head-first. He slumped to the floor and rolled on to his back. The gun was still on his hand and Solomon lashed out with his foot and knocked it to the side. He kicked again and connected with the man's elbow. The gun fell from the man's nerveless fingers and clattered on the toilet floor.

The man cursed and groped for it with his left hand. Solomon kicked him hard in the ribs, but the man was strong and reached again for the weapon. Solomon kicked him until he eventually lay still.

Solomon stood looking down at him, breathing heavily. He knelt down, felt for a pulse in the man's thick neck and found one, regular and strong. As he got to his feet the door burst open and two more heavies rushed in, their guns held high.

One grabbed Solomon by the collar and swung him against a cubicle door, knocking the breath out of him. The other hurried over to check the injured man.

'He was going to kill me,' gasped Solomon, in Bosnian. The man who'd grabbed him shoved him towards the door and into the bar.

Solomon tried to twist round, but his legs were kicked out from underneath him and he crashed to the floor, face down. He felt a gun barrel press against the back of his neck. 'You're dead,' hissed the man.

Solomon tried to roll over but a booted foot hacked into the small of his back. He heard the click of the hammer being drawn back and cursed himself for going into the bar alone.

Then he heard a loud bang: the sound of a door crashing open. He twisted his head in the direction of the noise. Four uniformed policemen stood at the entrance to the bar in dark blue uniforms. They were all holding handguns and shouted at Solomon's captor to drop his weapon.

'Fuck you,' snarled the man.

Solomon rolled towards the wall as the man who'd been holding him down swung his handgun to point it at the police.

'Down!' shouted the sergeant. 'Put the gun down now!'

The girls sitting at the bar screamed and scattered. The men behind it dropped down out of sight. At the far end, customers hunched into corners or fell to the floor and tried to hide behind the wicker sofas.

The thug who'd stayed in the ladies' room charged out and two of the policemen swung their guns to cover him.

'Put your weapons on the floor or we'll fire!' yelled the sergeant, taking a step towards the man who'd kicked Solomon. 'This is your last chance.' He was a heavy-set man with a thick moustache and day-old stubble over this chin.

The man ignored him. He shouted over at the security man who was still sitting at the table by the door. 'Get your gun out!

He pushed back his chair and pulled out his handgun. The police officers bunched together, suddenly less sure of their authority.

The sergeant ignored the man by the door and walked up to the one who had pushed Solomon to the ground, keeping his gun pointing at the man's face.

Solomon sat against the wall, unable to take his eyes off the sergeant's face. He was glaring at his opponent, his jaw clenched. They were both big men and neither looked as if they were used to backing down. They kept their guns levelled at each other's faces.

'I will shoot you,' said the sergeant.

'Fuck you,' said the man.

'Put down your gun.'

'Put down yours.'

The sergeant's lips tightened until they almost disappeared. Even from where he was sitting, Solomon could see his trigger finger whitening.

'This is our territory,' the man said to the sergeant. 'We are the law here.'

The sergeant said nothing.

One of the girls started to sob. They had all gathered together and were hugging each other in terror. Lyudmilla was somewhere in the middle of the group, a handkerchief clutched to her lips.

The other policemen tried to reassert their authority, holding their guns with both hands and shouting staccato commands. 'Drop your guns! We'll fire! Do it!'

Solomon heard them but he couldn't tear his eyes away from the sergeant. The sergeant must have known that at the moment he pulled the trigger all hell would break loose. Even if he fired first and killed the man in front of him, the other security men would start shooting and so would the police. God alone knew how many would die. But the sergeant was past being concerned about anyone else in the bar: he was focused on the man in front of him.

'Do you know who we are? Who we work for?' the man asked the sergeant. 'This is Petrovic's bar. Do you know what Petrovic can do to you? To your family? You think that if we back down now that's the end of it? Think again, my friend. It will only be the beginning.'

For the first time Solomon saw a flicker of doubt on the sergeant's face.

'Go now, and this will be forgotten,' said the man, his gun still pointing at the sergeant's face.

The sergeant looked across at Solomon. 'He's going to kill me,' said Solomon. 'If you leave, they'll shoot me.'

The sergeant took a step back and lowered his weapon. Solomon knew that it was over. The man with the gun grinned in triumph, but before he could say anything, the door to the bar was kicked open and half a dozen American soldiers piled in, armed with semi-automatic weapons. They were wearing camouflage uniforms, helmets and flak-jackets. They rushed through the bar, shouting and waving their guns, their boots pounding on the tiled floor. The three heavies dropped their weapons and the police forced them to the ground, spreadeagled like stranded starfish.

Two of the troopers ran over to stand on either side of the sergeant and they pointed their guns at the man facing them. He stood glaring at them, his breath loud and rasping, then he lowered his gun and let it fall to the ground. The troopers stepped forward and grabbed his arms, forcing them behind his back. A policeman produced a pair of steel handcuffs and clicked them on to the man's wrists.

One of the soldiers was an officer, a lieutenant, and he nodded at the police sergeant. 'What is happening here?' he asked, in heavily accented Bosnian.

'They were going to kill me,' said Solomon, before the policeman could speak.

The officer looked quizzically at Solomon. 'You a Brit?' he asked.

'I'm with the International War-dead Commission,' said Solomon, getting to his feet. His head was aching and blood had trickled down his neck.

'Who are you?' asked the lieutenant.

'Jack Solomon,' said Solomon, offering the officer his ID.

'Who did that to you?' said the officer, nodding at the cut on Solomon's face.

One of the policemen pushed open the door to the ladies' room.

'It's nothing,' said Solomon.

The officer jerked a thumb at the man they'd handcuffed. 'It was him?'

'It's okay,' said Solomon. He just wanted to get out of the bar.

'It's not okay,' said the officer. 'We heard a shot.' He repeated what he'd said in Bosnian, looking at the sergeant.

'We had the situation under control,' said the police sergeant, in Bosnian.

'That's true,' said Solomon, speaking in the policeman's language. Backing up the sergeant seemed to be the quickest way out of the bar.

'I don't speak Bosnian,' said the officer.

The police sergeant repeated what he'd said, in English this time.

'It looked like a stand-off when we burst in,' said the officer.

'They were just about to give up their guns,' said the sergeant.

'How did it start?' the American officer asked Solomon.

'It was a misunderstanding,' said Solomon.

The policeman who'd gone into the ladies' appeared at the door. 'There's something you should see here, Sergeant,' he said.

Solomon headed for the exit, but the American lieutenant pointed a finger at him. 'You stay here,' he said. He told one of his men to stand by Solomon while he followed the sergeant. They both returned a few minutes later. 'What happened to him?' the sergeant asked Solomon. Solomon heard a policeman radioing for an ambulance.

Solomon looked at the American but the lieutenant stared impassively at him, waiting for him to answer the policeman's question.

Before Solomon could answer, the thug who'd been handcuffed kicked out at Solomon's groin. A soldier pulled him away. 'He beat him up,' the man shouted.

'He pulled a gun on me,' said Solomon. He gestured at his bleeding cheek. 'Pistol-whipped me.'

'There was no gun in there,' said the sergeant.

'His men took it.'

'What were the two of you doing in the toilet?' asked the sergeant.

'This is stupid,' said Solomon. 'I'm the one who was attacked.'

'But you're not the one lying unconscious on the floor, are you?' said the sergeant. 'You'd better come with us.'

'Am I under arrest?'

'If you refuse to come with us, I will arrest you, yes.'

'They're the ones who were going to shoot you.'

'Which will be dealt with back at the station. As will your case.'

Solomon looked across at the lieutenant. 'Are you going to let them take me?' he asked.

'Looks like a police matter,' said the American officer casually.

'Before you arrived, they were just about to cut a deal,'

said Solomon. He gestured at the police sergeant. 'They were going to back off. They were going to let them kill me.'

'That's not going to happen,' said the lieutenant. 'We'll escort you back to town. We have your details. Nothing's going to happen to you.'

Solomon realised it was futile to argue. He was taken outside by two policemen, who put him into the back of a blue van. One policeman climbed in with him.

The nightclub heavies were being loaded into another van. They had all been handcuffed.

'Have you made a will?' asked the policeman next to Solomon.

'What?'

'You know who he is, the man you hit?' He sucked his teeth. 'Big mistake,' he said. 'Big, big mistake.'

An ambulance arrived, siren wailing. Two men in green overalls rushed into the bar with a metal stretcher and reappeared less than a minute later with the injured man. They put him into the ambulance and it roared off.

The American soldiers climbed into their vehicles, a green Humvee and two Jeeps. A uniformed policeman got into the front of the van that Solomon was in and started the engine. The sergeant climbed into the front passenger seat.

They drove all the way to Sarajevo in silence. Solomon's heart sank as they parked outside the main Sarajevo canton police station on Mis Irbina Street. The American vehicles drove away as he was taken through a metal security door into a busy reception area where his watch, wallet, belt and shoes were taken from him by a female officer whose breath reeked of garlic. She gave him a form to sign. It was in Bosnian. Solomon tried to read it but she tapped it with a pudgy finger and told him to hurry up. He signed it and asked if he could make a phone call. 'Later,' she said.

Solomon turned to the sergeant, who was standing behind him. 'Do you know Dragan Jovanovic?' Solomon asked.

The sergeant pursed his lips. 'I know of him.'

'Will you find him and tell him what's happened?' Dragan was based at the Mis Irbina Street headquarters but Solomon doubted that he would be in the office so late. Someone would have to call him at home.

'Come with me,' said the female officer. She put a hand on Solomon's shoulder.

Solomon shook her off. 'Okay?' he asked the sergeant.

Before the sergeant could answer, the female officer's fingers dug into Solomon's shoulder and she pulled him away, then marched him along a stone-flagged corridor, jangling a set of keys. She pushed him into a cell with green-painted brick walls and a small barred window set close to the ceiling. There was a metal bed with a thin sheet of foam rubber over the springs and a plastic bucket that stank of stale urine. The door clanged shut. It was made of vertical metal bars less than six inches apart.

'Dragan Jovanovic,' Solomon called after her. 'Will someone call him and tell him I'm here?'

Footsteps crunched on the flagstone floor, a slow, measured tread. Solomon sat with his head in his hands and didn't look up. A pair of tasselled brown loafers topped by fawn slacks moved into view and he cursed. He knew only one person in Sarajevo who wore tasselled loafers.

'Have you any idea how much damage your escapade has done to the Commission?' asked Miller.

Solomon still didn't look up. He thought that the question was rhetorical so he didn't answer it. He had been in the cell all night and for most of the morning. The police had taken his watch from him so he didn't know for sure how long he'd been there, but it must have been more than twelve hours and he'd snatched barely a couple of hours' sleep.

'We have a certain position in this town,' continued Miller, in a dull monotone, as if he was reading from a script, 'an authority. We're doing a job that the locals can't be trusted to do, and we have to maintain an appearance of respectability. We're supposed to be better than them.'

Solomon looked up. 'Why are you here, Chuck?'

'Why do you think I'm here?'

'I don't know. To gloat?'

'This isn't about gloating,' snapped Miller. 'This is about getting your nuts out of the fire.'

'I don't need your help.'

'Oh, really?' said Miller. 'Do you know how precarious your position is?'

Solomon shrugged.

'What were you playing at?'

'I wasn't playing,' said Solomon.

'You were brawling. In a bar.'

'It wasn't like that.'

'You've put a guy in hospital.'

'He deserved it.'

'You're not in the playground, Jack. You nearly killed him. What the hell were you doing in that club? You owe me an explanation,' said Miller.

Solomon sighed. 'You won't like it,' he said.

'That's a given.'

Solomon badly wanted a cigarette but the police had taken his Marlboros and the Zippo off him when they arrested him. 'I was looking for the eyewitness. The Priština case.'

Miller slapped his hand against the bars of the cell. 'I thought I told you to pass that on to the Tribunal?'

'I did.'

'So why are you still working on it?'

'I want to find the girl. I want to know what she saw.'

'I told you to drop it. You promised you would.'

'I'm sorry.'

' "Sorry" doesn't cut it. You can't keep lying to me like this. I'm your boss, and I deserve your loyalty if not your respect.'

'What more can I say? I said I'm sorry.'

'What is so important about that case? There are forty thousand missing people in the Balkans and most of them were probably murdered. Why are you taking this one so personally?'

'Because if I don't it's going to get lost. Because someone has to care. Twenty-six men, women and children died of suffocation in the back of that truck. They died slowly and they knew they were dying, and someone has to get the men responsible.'

'And that man has to be you, does it?'

'If no one else will, yeah.' Solomon stared at Miller. 'That's the way it has to be, Chuck.'

Miller stared back at him for several seconds. 'The guy you beat up, Ivan Petrovic, he knew the girl?'

'She worked at his club until a few months ago. She was a hostess.'

'A prostitute?'

Solomon assented.

'You know how much trouble you're in, don't you?' asked Miller.

'He won't press charges,' Solomon said flatly.

'That's the least of your problems. You know who he is?'

'He's a pimp and a trafficker. He won't go running to the police.'

'He won't have to,' said Miller. 'He's going to have you killed as soon as he gets out of intensive care.'

'Bullshit,' said Solomon. He sat back on his bed and leaned against the cold stone wall.

'I'm serious. Petrovic isn't just a pimp or a bar-owner. He's one of the biggest villains in the country, as dangerous as they get. He kills people. He pays to have people killed and on occasions he does it himself. With relish.'

Solomon closed his eyes. 'How did you know I was here, Chuck?' said Solomon quietly.

'I got a call. A local. He told me what had happened and said I should get you out of Sarajevo – out of the country.'

Solomon nodded. It could only have been Dragan. The policeman had probably been reluctant to get involved once he'd discovered the identity of the man Solomon had put in hospital. With good reason: corruption was a way of life in the Bosnian force and many of Dragan's colleagues could well be on Petrovic's payroll. It was hardly surprising that so many officers were corrupt: a new recruit to the Uprava Policije, the canton police, earned just eight hundred marks a month. An inspector like Dragan would be lucky to get much more than a thousand. That was less than a tenth of the equivalent salaries in the UK.

'I spoke to the police, who said that if I guarantee you'll be on the next plane out of Sarajevo they'll look the other way.'

Solomon opened his eyes. 'You're sacking me?'

'No. Your job will still be here, but you're going to have to take the two months' leave you're owed. Plus a month's unpaid. After three months, if the heat's off, you can come back.'

'This is ridiculous,' said Solomon,

'You either do that, or I'll have to let you go,' said Miller. 'I can't afford to have a hoodlum like Petrovic coming after you with guns blazing.'

'I can take care of myself, Chuck.'

'In London, maybe. But this is Sarajevo. Life is—'

'Cheap,' Solomon finished. 'I know the cliché.'

'Clichés usually become clichés because they're true,' said Miller. 'You can't do your job here if you're looking over your shoulder all the time. Look, you're owed leave. You've barely had a day off since you started with the Commission. And you're owed a return flight home. Take the vacation. Recharge your batteries. In three months Petrovic himself might be dead, the way the gangs here are ripping into each other.'

'There's nothing for me in London.'

'You've got family.'

'I've got an ex-wife who wishes *I* was dead.'

'So go anywhere. Go lie on a beach. You get a paid-for ticket to the UK. Where you go from there is your own business.'

'Thanks a bunch, Chuck.'

Miller sighed. 'You think I'm a callous bastard, don't you?'

Solomon didn't answer.

'Just because I don't wear my heart on my sleeve doesn't mean I don't have feelings,' Miller continued. 'I did your job for two years, and we had half the staff then that we have now. We all have our way of dealing with it, and my way is to treat it like an academic exercise. They're not people. They're cases to be closed or passed on. Once you start thinking of them as people, you're lost.'

'I hear what you're saying,' said Solomon.

Miller carried on as if he hadn't heard Solomon: 'You seem to think I've stopped caring. I haven't. I just don't want to start empathising again, like I used to. I don't want to start imagining what it's like to be lined up in a field and shot in the back of the head. To be locked inside a church that's set on fire. To see my wife raped and my children killed. To be locked in a truck with twenty-five other people and watch them suffocate. I've got a pretty good imagination and I'm fucked if I'm going to use it to make my own life a living hell.'

Solomon felt a sudden rush of sympathy for the man. In the two years they'd worked together, Miller had never come close to opening up.

'I'm sorry, Chuck,' he said.

'Fuck you,' snapped Miller. 'I don't need your pity.'

'I mean I'm sorry for screwing you around like this. Sorry for the hassle.'

Miller turned his back on Solomon. 'Just go, will you?' he said. 'The cops are doing the paperwork, you'll be out in an hour or two. Go home, get some sleep, and I'll have the tickets sent round to you. Call me when you get to

London.' He walked away before Solomon could say any more.

A cloud of sweet-smelling smoke greeted Solomon when he opened the door to his flat. Dragan Jovanovic was sitting on the sofa with his feet on the coffee table.

'Don't you people need a warrant before you go breaking into people's homes?' Solomon asked, as he closed the door.

'I didn't break in. I slipped the lock.'

'And I've told you about smoking these Turkish things in here. The stink lingers for days.'

'I couldn't find your Marlboros,' said Dragan. He waved a half-empty bottle of Heineken. 'I found the beer, though. You should get some Bosnian beer in – Heinrich if you can't get Sarajevsko. I'd even rather have a Serbian beer than this shit.'

Solomon gestured at the five empty Heineken bottles lined up next to his friend's feet but didn't say anything. He went into the kitchen, took a bottle out of the ageing refrigerator, then sat down in a worn leather armchair and put his feet on the edge of the coffee table. He raised the bottle in salute. '*Zivjeli*,' he said.

Dragan did likewise. '*Zivjeli*,' he echoed. 'How were our facilities?'

'Checking out was a hell of a lot more pleasant than checking in,' said Solomon. 'A visit would have been nice.'

Dragan's face broke into his trademark lopsided grin. 'The man you put in hospital plays pool with my commander every Sunday.'

'Yeah, well, I guess this weekend's game is off,' said Solomon.

'You were lucky.'

'Lucky? I'm being run out of town, Dragan.'

'If the American patrol hadn't been passing on the way to their barracks, Petrovic's thugs would have killed you.'

'Bullshit.' As the word left Solomon's mouth he remembered the foot in the small of his back and the sound of the hammer being clicked back.

'It's not bullshit. You attacked him on his home grass. No one was expecting it. It's like you went into Buckingham Palace and headbutted the Queen.'

'Turf,' said Solomon. 'The expression is "home turf".'

'Grass, turf, it doesn't matter. If the patrol hadn't turned up, you would have been dead.' He drained his bottle, picked up a fresh one from the side of the sofa, and used his teeth to prise off the metal cap. He stubbed out his cigarette and held out his hand. Solomon took his packet of Marlboro from his jacket pocket and tossed it over. Dragan lit one.

'How bad is he?' asked Solomon.

'A mean motherfucker.'

'I meant how badly hurt is he?'

Jovanovic grimaced. 'You burst his spleen.'

'Shit.'

'Yeah. Deep shit. It's going to be a cold day in hell before he forgets what you did.'

'Miller says I can come back in three months. What do you think?'

'I think if you stay around Petrovic will kill you,' he said. 'If you leave, I doubt he'll come after you. If you come back in three months, I don't know. Three months isn't long.'

'He pulled a gun on me, Dragan. He pistol-whipped me and he was going to put a bullet in my face.' Solomon took a long drink of his beer. Foam fizzed up and dripped over his legs. He rubbed it into his trousers. 'So, I'm finished here,' he said.

'Not necessarily,' said Dragan. 'My commander's not going to want the Commission co-ordinator killed on his watch.'

'That's reassuring.'

'I'll talk to him when he's in a good mood, explain about the gun. He'll wait until Petrovic has calmed down, then have a word with him. Maybe Petrovic will agree to let bygones be bygones. Maybe he won't. We'll have to wait and see.'

'Your boss is on Petrovic's payroll?'

Dragan winced. 'Jack . . .'

'You said . . .'

'Forget what I said. If you're going to start remembering everything I say, I'm going to keep my mouth shut.'

Solomon grinned. 'That'll be a first. You said they played pool together.'

'Yeah, and that's all you're going to get out of me after six beers. Ask me again when I'm drunk.'

'So I've got to go?'

'The sooner the better. You've got my number, call me in a few weeks and I'll have a better idea of how things stand.'

'Terrific.'

'Off the record, on behalf of the members of Sarajevo police department – the ones who don't play pool – I'd like to thank you for kicking the shit out of the scumbag.' He clinked his bottle against Solomon's. 'Now, come on, let's get drunk.'

★

Solomon woke with a thumping headache and a queasy stomach. It was several seconds before he realised that someone was banging on his front door. He rolled out of bed, wrapped a towel round his waist and stumbled into the living room. More than a dozen empty Heineken bottles littered the floor and there was an empty slivovitz bottle on the coffee table. It had been two o'clock in the morning when Jovanovic had left, promising eternal love and protection.

Solomon screwed up his eyes and tried to focus on his wristwatch. It was just after eight o'clock. He groaned. He pressed his eye to the spyhole in the door but couldn't make out who it was. 'What do you want?' he croaked.

The visitor didn't respond. He slipped on the security chain and opened the door. It was one of the clerks from the Commission office.

Solomon cleared his throat. 'What do you want?' he asked, in Bosnian.

The man thrust an envelope through the gap. 'Mr Miller said you were to get this first thing,' said the man. He bent down and picked up a bulging black plastic garbage bag. 'And this.'

Solomon took the envelope and slid off the security chain. As he opened the door the man swung the garbage bag over the threshold. Solomon grabbed it and closed the door. The bag contained personal effects from his desk, the envelope a return economy ticket to London with Austrian Airlines via Vienna. The flight left at half past two. Miller was wasting no time in getting Solomon out of the country.

There was a note with the tickets. 'Jack – it's for your own good. Trust me.' Miller's scrawl of a signature was at the bottom.

'Yeah, right,' said Solomon, under his breath. He went into his bathroom and swallowed two painkillers. He shaved and showered, then drank half a carton of milk from the fridge and made himself a mug of instant coffee.

He sat down on his sofa and lit a Marlboro. There was another envelope under his ashtray. Solomon frowned and opened it. Inside were the photocopies of the Priština truck case he'd given to Dragan. The policeman must have left it. Solomon flicked through the papers and found the photograph of Nicole. He stared at it as he sipped his coffee. Miller might be running him out of town, but Solomon was damned if he was going to turn his back on the case.

The Austrian Airlines flight left Sarajevo on time and ascended into thick cloud. Solomon didn't see land again until the jet dropped down over the patchwork quilt of perfectly ordered green rectangles that was the farmland outside Vienna.

His fellow passengers were virtually all SFOR or NGO officials, and the conversations on the plane were about what grants were becoming available, which jobs were falling vacant, who was moving out and what new trouble spot needed their presence. Bosnia was rapidly becoming old news and most of the big aid agencies were cutting back or pulling out. The old hands had already seen the writing on the wall and were frantically networking to get either fresh funding or alternative employment.

The majority of passengers had connections to make in Vienna. Barely had the wheels of the plane touched the ground than people were standing up and grabbing their hand luggage. It reminded Solomon of the annual sale at

Harrods, where respectable middle-class, middle-aged men and women turned into elbow-jabbing animals. He had no option but to join the scrum: he had just twenty minutes to make his connecting flight to London.

He arrived at Heathrow as the sun was disappearing over the horizon, smearing the skyline a murky red. He caught the Heathrow Express to Paddington then picked up a black cab to Bayswater. He switched on his mobile phone: there were no messages, but he hadn't been expecting any. He flicked through the phone's address book and called Danny McLaren.

McLaren answered almost immediately. 'Danny, I'm on my way,' said Solomon.

'Hey, welcome back,' said McLaren. 'I'm going to be in the office for about another hour. I've left a set of keys with the guy who runs the noodle shop opposite Queensway tube station. His name's Mr Wong. He's expecting you. There's beer in the fridge and clean sheets on the bed.'

'Cheers, Danny. You're a lifesaver.'

'See you later,' said McLaren. 'Got to go – the news editor's breathing down my neck.' He cut the connection.

Solomon asked the driver to take him to Queensway station. He and Danny McLaren had been friends for almost ten years. McLaren was a crime reporter on the *Daily Express*. They had met when Solomon had been a detective working out of Paddington Green and McLaren had been a junior reporter on the *Evening Standard*. They had a mutual love of cricket, football, beer and Indian food. McLaren was one of the few people who'd supported Solomon's decision to leave the Met, and when he'd moved to Yugoslavia had been quick to offer his spare bedroom whenever he needed it. McLaren was the first person Solomon had called when Miller told him he had to leave Sarajevo.

Mr Wong turned out to be a squat Oriental with a clump of black hairs almost six inches long protruding from a large mole on his cheek. He squinted at Solomon suspiciously and demanded to see his passport. Solomon handed it over and Mr Wong scrutinised the picture, then smiled and handed over two keys attached to a miniature cricket ball.

He walked round the corner to Inverness Terrace. One of the keys opened the front door to a terraced house, and the other the front door of McLaren's top-floor flat. It was light and airy with two large skylights, one in the sitting room and the other in the kitchen. The spare bedroom was at the back of the flat and Solomon dropped his suitcase next to a mirrored wardrobe. He opened the sash window to allow in some fresh air, then went through to the kitchen and took out a can of Caffrey's beer.

He switched on the big-screen television, flopped down on one of two sofas and flicked through the channels until he found a cricket match. Pakistan versus South Africa. Sarajevo felt like a million miles away. The four and a half thousand body-bags in Tuzla even further.

He woke to the sound of a key being turned in the front door. Danny McLaren walked into the sitting room. 'Sorry, mate,' said McLaren. 'Got pulled on to a rewrite just as I was walking out of the office.' He flung his overcoat over the back of an armchair. 'Any beer left in the fridge?'

'Yeah, I only had one can before I fell asleep,' said Solomon.

McLaren went through to the kitchen and came back

with two. He tossed one to Solomon. 'How was the cricket?' He gestured at the television, then ran a hand through his unruly hair. That and the sprinkling of freckles across his nose and his square jaw gave him the look of an Irish farm-boy, but his piercing blue eyes burned with a fierce intelligence. He had won a scholarship to Oxford, got a first in economics, then dismayed his tutors and parents by announcing that he wanted to be a journalist. Not a heavyweight feature writer on the *Financial Times*, either, but a tabloid reporter. His parents had eventually forgiven him, but McLaren had never been back to his Oxford college.

'I hardly saw it,' said Solomon. He looked at his watch. It was just before eleven: he'd been asleep for almost four hours. He popped the tab on his can of beer and took a long drink.

'So, what's the story?' asked McLaren. 'Three months, you said.'

'Yeah, I won't impose on you for long, I promise. Just until I get myself sorted.'

'Forget it,' said McLaren, sitting down opposite him and swinging his feet up on to the coffee table. 'I'm glad of the company, mate. I'm just wondering what you did to get laid off for three months.'

Solomon told him what had happened in Sarajevo, and Miller's reaction. McLaren listened intently, leaning forward.

'Bloody hell, mate. Enemies in high places, huh?'

'Lowlife scum, more like,' said Solomon. 'Even the cops are scared of him.'

'You don't think he'll come after you?'

'Cops say no,' said Solomon, 'and I believe them. The question is, when can I go back?'

'Or if,' said McLaren.

'Exactly.'

'Shit.'

'Deep shit,' echoed Solomon, remembering what Dragan had said. It would be a cold day in hell before Petrovic forgave him.

'So, what's your game-plan?'

Solomon shrugged. 'Job-wise, I'm going to wait a couple of months. I'm getting paid, I've a few grand in the bank, so there's no need to rush into anything. By then I'll have a better idea of how the land lies. If Petrovic is still on the warpath, I either kill him or look for another job.'

McLaren's jaw dropped. 'What?'

Solomon laughed. 'I'm joking,' he said. 'I doubt I could get near him.'

'Sounds like you did okay last time,' said McLaren. He drained his can and tossed it into a bin. 'Another?'

'Sure. I caught him by surprise,' he called after McLaren. 'Doubt I'd get a second chance.'

McLaren came back with two more cans of Caffrey's. 'What about just cutting your losses and finding another job?'

'I'm thirty-five, Danny. I'm running out of options.'

'Come on, you're hardly over the hill,' McLaren remonstrated. 'You're an experienced cop. Ten years with the Met, three years with charities out in the Balkans, two years with the Commission. You'd be snapped up by any of the NGOs out there. Or in any other trouble-spot, for that matter.'

'Maybe,' said Solomon.

'If all else fails, you could always get a job in security back in the UK.'

'Sitting on a building site with a Thermos of soup? Screw that.'

'I was thinking FT-100, head of security for a big company, that sort of thing. But if you want to wallow in misery, I'm going to bed.' He stood up.

'I like the job I have, Danny.'

'Last time we spoke you said it bored you rigid.'

'Yeah, well, that was before they were trying to force me out.' Solomon finished his beer. 'Sorry, you're right. I'm wallowing. Let's have a curry tomorrow night and I'll be on better form. Do you still snore?'

'Like a bloody steam train.' McLaren headed off to his bedroom. Solomon sat up and watched an Italian football match on TV with the sound muted so as not to disturb McLaren, but he ended up falling asleep on the sofa. He woke up in the early hours, drank from the kitchen sink tap and fell into bed.

When Solomon woke, McLaren had already left for the office. He had left a note propped up against an empty Caffrey's can on the kitchen table. 'Make yourself useful – buy some more beer!' Solomon grinned and made himself some coffee.

He sat down on the sofa and considered his options. Three months was a long time to spend doing nothing. One of the reasons why he had two months' vacation owing from the Commission was that he was happier working. Two weeks' lying on a beach would drive him crazy. He had worked for a relief agency in Kosovo before joining the Commission, and he knew that several similar agencies had offices in London. If nothing else, he could offer his services as a volunteer.

He finished his coffee, then went through to his

bedroom and unpacked his suitcase. An envelope fell to the floor. Solomon picked it up. It was the report on the Priština truck case. Solomon sat down on the bed and read through the photocopied sheets. Lyudmilla had said that Nicole had gone to London. If that was true, maybe he could track her down. His pulse beat faster at the prospect. If he could find Nicole and get her to tell him what had happened on the farm outside Priština, then maybe his time in the UK wouldn't be wasted after all.

He went back into the sitting room and dialled McLaren's mobile. 'You running up my phone bill already?' McLaren asked.

'Yeah, my mobile costs an arm and a leg if I use it here,' said Solomon. 'I'll get a pay-as-you-go today. Can you do me a favour?'

'Sure,' said McLaren.

'Can you pull any info you have on prostitution in London?'

'No sweat. I've done a couple of stories myself recently. I'll get some cuts before I leave. Are you still up for a curry tonight?'

'Sure.'

'Hang on,' said McLaren. 'You're looking for that eyewitness, aren't you?'

'Maybe.'

'Be careful, Jack.'

'I'm a big boy, don't worry.'

'It's more complicated that that. I'll tell you tonight over a chicken korma.'

Dragan Jovanovic flashed his police credentials at the nurse in Reception and asked for Ivan Petrovic's room.

The nurse frowned as she tapped away on her computer keyboard. Then she said no one of that name was in the hospital. Dragan told her who Petrovic was and why he was probably in the hospital under a different name. And that he would probably have guards with him. The nurse immediately gave him a room number, on the fifth floor, but told him that no visitors were allowed. Dragan flashed her a smile and headed for the lift.

Two big men were standing outside Petrovic's room in matching dark brown leather jackets, black jeans and designer sunglasses. They put their hands inside their jackets as Dragan stepped out of the lift. He raised his arms to show that he was no threat and told them he was a police officer.

'Mr Petrovic is not seeing anyone,' said the man on the left.

'He'll see me,' said Dragan.

'He's not pressing charges,' said the man on the right. 'It's not a police matter.'

Dragan walked up to the man and stared into the dark lenses. 'I will decide what is and isn't a police matter,' he growled. 'Now, go in there and tell your boss that Dragan Jovanovic of the Sektor Kriminalisticke Policije wants to talk to him.'

The man stared at him for several seconds, then turned, opened the door and slipped inside. Dragan glared at the other guard, daring him to argue. The man stared straight ahead, refusing to look at him.

The door opened. 'Okay,' said the guard.

Dragan bared his teeth in a rictus grin and walked past the man into the room. Two more guards sat on straight-backed chairs by the window. One had a shotgun by his side, the other a chrome revolver in his lap. The guard closed the door and stood with his back to it, his hands crossed over his groin.

Petrovic was lying in bed, propped up by three pillows, and connected to a drip. He had a livid bruise across his right cheek and his right hand was bandaged.

'You don't look so bad,' said Dragan.

'I might lose my spleen,' said Petrovic.

'You can live without it.'

'How about I get my men to come round to your house and take out your spleen, Dragan? See how you like it,' said Petrovic.

'Yeah, you know where I live, I know where you live. You know where my mother lives, I know where your mother lives. You've got men with guns, I've got a whole police force standing behind me. We're not going to get anywhere threatening each other.'

'I don't see anyone standing behind you, Dragan.'

'Not everyone's on your payroll,' said the policeman.

Petrovic forced a smile. 'You think not?'

Dragan walked over to the foot of the bed. 'You know why he went to your bar?'

'He was looking for a girl. Like most men who go to my clubs.'

'He wanted a particular girl. Did he tell you about her before he beat the crap out of you?'

'He attacked me,' said Petrovic.

Dragan grinned and looked across at the two men sitting by the window. 'How many men do you have around you?' he said. 'It's obviously not enough.'

'We were in the toilet,' said Petrovic.

'This just gets better and better, doesn't it?' sneered Dragan.

'He'd gone in after a girl.'

'Why?'

'Because he thought she knew the girl he's looking for.'

'And does she?'

Petrovic narrowed his eyes. 'This isn't official, is it?'

'If it was official, we'd be taking you into the station,' said Dragan. 'This girl he's looking for, where is she?'

Petrovic stared at the policeman. Dragan stared back, poker-faced.

'London,' said Petrovic eventually.

'I know that, Petrovic. I'm not stupid. Where in London?'

Petrovic shook his head. 'She left my bar, maybe she worked somewhere else. I don't know. She told some of my girls that she was going to London.'

Dragan nodded thoughtfully. 'You know that Solomon will be searching for her?'

Petrovic looked at him suspiciously. 'Why is this girl so important to him?'

'She was an eyewitness to an atrocity in Kosovo. The only witness. He didn't tell you?'

'We didn't talk much. He said he worked for the International War-dead Commission, that's all. You're saying he's gone to London to find her?'

'To find the girl, and to keep away from you.'

Petrovic snorted. 'That's the first sensible thing he's done. What do you want, Dragan? Why are you here?'

'I want you to leave the Englishman alone.'

Petrovic laughed harshly. 'Look what he's done to me. I'm the one in the hospital bed.'

'You pulled a gun on him, he protected himself. I want that to be the end of it.'

'He burst my fucking spleen!' yelled Petrovic.

Dragan didn't react to the man's outburst, but the three bodyguards tensed. The one with the shotgun picked it up and swung it casually in his direction.

Petrovic continued to glare at the policeman, his chest heaving. A doctor in a stained white coat opened the door, but it was slammed in his face.

'Get out, Jovanovic,' said the Serbian gang boss, 'and tell the Englishman that if he shows his face in Sarajevo again he's a dead man.'

'If anything happens to him in London, you'll have me to answer to,' said Dragan.

Petrovic raised his bandaged hand and pointed at the policeman. 'You wouldn't be the first cop I've killed,' he hissed.

'I'm not looking for a fight,' said Dragan quietly. 'I just want you to know that I stand with the Englishman. If anything happens to him, I'll know where to look.'

The man with the shotgun stood up and took a step towards him. The policeman raised his hands slowly and walked towards the door, keeping his eyes on Petrovic until he left the room.

McLaren was in the office until just after ten o'clock. He phoned Solomon as he was leaving and arranged to meet him in an Indian restaurant off Queensway, a short walk from the flat.

Solomon was on his second bottle of Kingfisher when McLaren arrived, apologising profusely. He'd been grabbed by an assistant editor on the way out and drafted in to do a rewrite of a young reporter's news story. He mimed drinking beer to an elderly Indian waiter, who scurried to the bar.

'You work too hard,' said Solomon.

'The amount of money they pay me, they own me body and soul, mate,' said McLaren.

Solomon couldn't argue with McLaren's logic. His friend was one of the highest-paid journalists in the country, with an expense account to match. During a drinking bout back when he was a detective, Solomon had made the mistake of comparing wage slips. That had been six years ago, and even then McLaren had been earning three times Solomon's salary.

The waiter hurried over with a beer. 'Thanks, Rudy.' McLaren was a regular in the restaurant and knew all of the staff by name.

He clinked his glass against Solomon's. 'Cheers, mate. And welcome back.'

A young waiter was brandishing a small notebook beside them. McLaren ordered for the two of them without consulting the menu. Then when the waiter had left he took an envelope from his jacket pocket and handed it to Solomon. 'The stuff you asked for,' he said. 'My piece is in there, I was on a Vice Squad sweep through Soho. Your old mob.'

'Not my old mob,' said Solomon. 'Everyone from chief inspector down was transferred after I left.'

McLaren grinned. 'Still touchy, huh? Thought you'd have been over that by now. Anyway, you know what I mean.'

'Yeah. So why the sweep? In my day they left the Soho walk-ups alone unless punters were getting ripped off.'

'Immigration, mate. Three-quarters of the girls they pulled in were from eastern Europe, and virtually all had come through the Balkans.'

'That's new.'

'Damn right it's new. Used to be the girls were a cross-section, right? English, French, Italian, Maltese.'

'That's how it was in my day, but it was the Maltese who controlled the flats.'

'Still is, just about. But the girls are all out of the Balkans. Belarussians, Latvians, Slovakians, all the former Soviet bloc, they go through the Balkans, then here or to the rest of Europe. Albanian Mafia are the traffickers. Vicious bastards. They came here a couple of years ago and did a deal with the Maltese. Offered to supply girls who'd work cheaper. The Maltese jumped at the chance, but the Vice boys reckon there's going to be a gang war soon. The Albanians are going to want the flats and the girls.'

'The Maltese are no pushover.'

'Agreed, but they've gone soft over the years. The Albanians are hungry. That's what I meant when I said be careful if you're going to go looking for that girl. If the Albanians are running her, they'll not be best pleased to see you. This guy you beat up in Sarajevo, was he Albanian?'

Solomon shook his head. 'A Serb. The girls who were picked up were sent back, yeah?'

'That's the way the game's played. Immigration and Vice go through the flats and check their immigration status. The illegals are rounded up and questioned. Immigration want to find out how they got into the country, but of course the girls clam up. Most of them don't even have their passports – their pimps keep them as security. After a couple of days they're put on a flight home if they haven't claimed political asylum. By the time they get there a new batch of girls is working in the flats.'

'So there's a chance that Nicole is already back in Sarajevo?'

'It's possible,' said McLaren, 'but the odds are against it. In the last sweep they went into thirty flats. That's maybe a tenth of the flats in Soho. And the girls work in two or three shifts. That's between six hundred and nine hundred girls, but they deported twenty-four. It was touted as a major victory in the battle against traffickers, but we all know they're pissing in the wind. And most of the girls who were sent home were probably back here – or in Rome or Paris – a week later.'

Their food arrived and they spent the next twenty minutes wolfing down chicken korma, chicken tikka masala and lamb dansak, washing it down with Kingfisher.

They walked back to the flat and McLaren pulled a six-pack of lager from the fridge before flopping down on the sofa. Solomon switched on the television. McLaren tossed him a can and they watched an Italian soccer match.

'So, what's your plan, mate?' asked McLaren.

'What do you mean?'

'This girl. The missing witness. Are you going to look for her?'

Solomon shrugged. 'I've little else to do.'

'What's so special about her? You must come across dozens of cases like hers. It's the Commission's job, right, clearing up atrocities?'

'That's not how my boss tells it,' said Solomon bitterly. 'He says we're shuffling cases in and out.'

'But this one's different.'

Solomon lit a cigarette. He didn't offer the packet to McLaren, who had given up years ago but didn't mind others smoking in his presence. 'Most of the cases are shootings, Danny. They're horrible enough, women and children, old people, the sick, the ones who can't run away. But at least you know that it was over relatively quickly, usually. They were rounded up, they were shot, end of story. And there is almost a logic to it. One army shooting the supporters of another army. It's a war crime, of course it is, but it's almost understandable. If not forgivable.' He cleared his throat. 'I'm not explaining this right. It's not one of those things you can put into words. You had to have been there. It was just the way it was so bloody premeditated, you know? They herded them into the truck and drove it into a lake, then left them there to die. I keep imagining how it must have felt to sit there in the cold and the darkness as the air ran out. Surrounded by the people you love.' He shuddered. 'I tell you, Danny, my stomach churns just thinking about it.'

'Empathy does that, mate. My job's not quite the same as yours, but to do it properly you've got to distance yourself, take the clinical view.'

'I was a copper for ten years, Danny. Give me a break.'

'Yeah, well, being a copper's different. You're part of a team, a fraternity.' He grinned. 'You've got a support system around you, same as we journalists have. You don't have that any more. Most of your cases you handle alone, right?'

Solomon nodded. 'You reckon cabin fever?'

'I think maybe a shit job is getting on top of you. If I were you I'd go and lie on a beach for a week or two. Watch the sun go down with a beer in your hand and a bird on your arm.'

'Maybe you're right.'

'I'd feel happier if you at least tried to fake sincerity.'

McLaren knew him too well, Solomon realised. 'I'm just going to rattle a few cages. If I get lucky, fine. If I draw a blank, I'll take a holiday. Now, stop nagging.'

Petrovic tossed his fork on to the plate and told one of his men to take it away. His food was brought in from one of the best Italian restaurants in Sarajevo, but he had no appetite. No energy, either. It was all he could do to walk the few steps to his bathroom but he insisted on doing that unaided. There was no way he was going to let his men see him piss in a pot in his bed.

He cursed Jack Solomon. And the visit from the policeman had annoyed him. There was nothing Dragan could do to hurt Petrovic: he had too many friends in the canton and the federal police for them ever to act against him. From time to time they would close down one of his clubs or put away one of his foot-soldiers, but never without warning him in advance. And despite the man's threats, there was no way Jovanovic could ever hurt him. Petrovic had doubled his personal security and would never again allow himself to be caught unawares.

'Give me a phone,' he growled, and one of his guards rushed over with a mobile.

Petrovic tapped out a London number. It was answered by a gruff Russian voice. 'Sergei, it's Ivan. How is life?' He spoke in English: his Russian was non-existent and Goncharov's Bosnian and Serbo-Croatian were limited.

Sergei Goncharov was a Moscow-born former GRU officer, who had spent much of his working life based in East Berlin. He had been there when the Wall had fallen and had taken the opportunity then to move to the West to start anew with a different identity and a trunkful of counterfeit currencies, all courtesy of the GRU. He had had more than enough to pay for extensive plastic surgery in Switzerland and a new life. That was the story

Goncharov had told Petrovic one night when they had got drunk together in one of Petrovic's brothels. Petrovic wasn't sure whether it was idle boasting or based on fact, but there was no doubting the man's present position as one of the biggest human traffickers in Europe. The Russian's web of contacts stretched across the European Community, through eastern Europe and beyond into Central Asia and even China. He smuggled refugees into EC countries and helped them apply for asylum in the EC – for a fee; he worked with Hong Kong-based triads to move Chinese workers around the world; and he was a major player in the world of prostitution, arranging for girls from Third World countries to work in the West. He made several visits a year to Bosnia and Serbia, and Petrovic had supplied him with hundreds of girls.

'Life is a struggle,' said the Russian sourly. 'We are born, we struggle, we die.'

Petrovic smiled to himself. Goncharov seemed in a permanent state of depression, despite being a millionaire many times over. 'There is a matter I need help with, Sergei,' he said. He knew that the Russian had little time for social chit-chat: he lived for work, and saw anything else as a distraction to his main purpose in life – the acquisition of wealth. Even when he relaxed with Petrovic it was always in the company of girls he was sampling before deciding whether to move them to London, Berlin or Milan. 'Do you remember a girl you bought from me four months ago? Nicole, her name was. She worked as Amy.'

'From Estonia, right?' asked Goncharov.

'A local, from Kosovo,' said Petrovic. 'Nineteen. Blonde hair dyed black.'

'I think so,' said Goncharov, hesitantly. 'Let me check.'

Petrovic heard phones ringing in the background, and girls talking. Goncharov grunted and Petrovic heard fingers tapping at a keyboard. 'Nicole?'

'Nicoletta was her real name but she answered to Nicole. She worked as Amy.'

'Four months ago?'

'That's right. You took her and four Albanians.'

More tapping. 'I've got her,' said the Russian. 'She's working for one of my agencies here.' More tapping. 'I have her outcall at the moment. We're looking to fix her up with an apartment this week. Is there a problem?'

'Not with her, but there's a guy looking for her. He might be in London.'

'Might be?'

'I am fairly sure he is. He works for a group out here who identify the war-dead. This girl saw something and he wants to talk to her. The thing is, if he starts rocking the boat, we could all end up in the water.' Petrovic was choosing his words carefully. He didn't want to tell the Russian that because of Solomon he was lying in hospital with a ruptured spleen: Goncharov was more likely to help take care of Solomon if he thought it was in his own interest, rather than because Petrovic wanted revenge.

'So, what do you want me to do? Move the girl out of London? I wouldn't be happy doing that – I am nowhere near recouping my investment.'

'I've a better idea,' said Petrovic. 'A more permanent way of solving the problem. And don't worry, I'll cover any costs.'

'I would expect you to,' said the Russian. 'This is an inconvenience I can do without.'

Petrovic explained what he wanted Goncharov to do,

then agreed a fee. If it took care of Jack Solomon, Petrovic would regard it as money well spent.

Solomon walked out of Oxford Circus station. Two women in anoraks and baggy jeans were handing out leaflets advertising a local language school and he brushed past them. A young man with a shaved head had set up a display of perfume bottles on a cardboard box and was touting his wares in a loud Liverpudlian whine.

Solomon headed east down Oxford Street, weaving through the crowds. Even at two o'clock in the afternoon the pavements were packed: sales reps rushing between appointments, tourists poring over street maps, families shopping, schoolchildren playing truant. A bus pulled up with a squeal of brakes and a crowd surged to the rear of the vehicle, jostling and pushing to get on board. It seemed as though queuing had ceased to be the norm in the capital: now it was every man or woman for themselves. Solomon's visits to the UK were few and far between and each time he returned the city seemed increasingly hostile. It had been bad enough when he had been a police officer, but now it seemed that street robberies, car-jackings and shoot-outs were regular occurrences.

He turned right on to Berwick Street and walked through Soho. Once the city's most infamous red-light area, it had evolved into a thriving business and entertainment district with advertising agencies and film-production companies jostling with glossy bars and chic restaurants. But the cancerous underbelly of the sex trade was still there: it just had to be sought out.

Between a chemist and a film-processing shop a door had been propped open showing a flight of bare wooden stairs. There were two sheets of paper pinned to the wall. On one was written 'ITALIAN MODEL – FIRST FLOOR'. The other said, 'BUSTY BLONDE – SECOND FLOOR'.

Solomon walked slowly up the stairs. He knocked on the first-floor door and heard heavy footsteps. There was a pause as someone checked him out through the spyhole. The door opened. 'Come on in, darling,' said a husky voice.

Solomon stepped inside. A rotund woman wearing a fisherman's sweater and black leggings looked at him through thick black-rimmed spectacles. The maid, he deduced. 'Through there, darling,' she said, pointing down the corridor. Solomon walked past a closed door, behind which he could hear the insistent squeak of bed-springs in motion. The woman followed him, breathing heavily.

There was a single bed in the room and a straight-backed chair on which lay a well-thumbed copy of the *Sun*. Solomon picked it up and sat down. The maid asked him if he wanted a cup of tea. Solomon shook his head, and she closed the door.

Five minutes later he heard the other bedroom door open and close, a muffled man's voice, and then the front door. The maid returned. 'All right, darling, come on through,' she said, and waddled back down the corridor. She showed him into the room. 'She won't be a minute, darling,' she said, and closed the door.

Solomon could hear a shower running somewhere in the flat. The room smelt of lavender. There was a can of air-freshener on the mantelpiece above a boarded up fire-place, next to a piece of paper on which had been written a list of sexual services and how much each cost. Solomon picked it up. The prices were about double what they'd been when he'd worked in Vice. At the bottom of the list, written in capital letters, was 'I DO NOT DO ANAL SO PLEASE DO NOT ASK.'

The only items of furniture in the room were a double bed, a small wardrobe and a wooden chair, the mate of the one in the second bedroom. By the door was a plastic wastepaper bin, which had been lined with a carrier-bag. It was full of crumpled tissues. There was a padlocked chain across the handles of the wardrobe, and on top of it a suitcase, the airline tag still on the handle. Solomon stood on tiptoe and squinted at the label. BEG. Belgrade.

The shower was switched off and Solomon went to sit on the wooden chair. He looked across at the bed. There were no pillowcases on the pillows, and no blanket or quilt, just a worn orange sheet on top of which was a grubby pale blue towel that had been shaped into a bow. The walls were bare, except for a torn poster of a naked woman holding a violin.

Solomon heard rapid footsteps and the door opened. A tall brunette walked in wearing a leopard-patterned baby-doll nightgown and black high heels. She was in her early twenties with wide crimson lips and high rouged cheekbones. When she smiled Solomon saw a smear of red lipstick across one of her canines.

'So, what can I do for you?' she asked. Her pupils were dilated, and she stared fixedly at Solomon as she ran her hands over her large breasts and across her stomach. She was on cocaine, Solomon thought. Or crack.

Solomon took out his wallet and gave her forty pounds. 'I just want to talk,' he said.

The girl frowned. 'You want oral?' she said. 'Oral is fifty.' She pointed at the list on the mantelpiece. 'You can see there. It says oral is fifty.'

'Not oral,' said Solomon. 'I just want to talk.'

The girl held out her hand and took the money. The nails had been filed into talons and were painted as bright a red as her lipstick. They looked as if they'd been dipped in blood. She turned and left the room, closing the door behind her.

A few seconds later the door burst open. The maid stood there with a baseball bat in her hands. 'What the fuck do you want?' she said. She was a big woman and Solomon could tell that the bat wasn't for show.

He stood up. 'I just wanted to talk to her, that's all.'

The maid swung the bat menacingly. 'This isn't the fucking Samaritans, it's a knocking shop.'

'I'm not Vice, I'm—'

'I don't give a monkey's fuck who you are,' she said, punctuating her words with jabs from the baseball bat. 'If you want to talk, you can call a sex line. Now, get out.'

Solomon took out his wallet, 'Look, I've got more money,' he began, but the maid banged the bat against the door jamb.

'Out,' she said.

Solomon could see that there was no point in arguing. He walked down the stairs to the street. On the way he passed a middle-aged man in a dark blue suit, who grinned knowingly. 'How is she? he asked.

'An experience,' said Solomon dourly.

He walked to Wardour Street and bought a cappuccino in Starbucks. He sat on a stool and looked out of the window, deep in thought. He guessed that the maid had been jumpy because of the Vice crackdown McLaren had talked about. Punters who wanted to do no more than talk were dangerous because they might turn out to be undercover cops or immigration officers. Or journalists looking for a story. At least the maid hadn't taken a swing at him. He sipped his coffee. He had hoped that the offer of money would be enough to get the girls to talk to him, but now he knew better. The only way to get any information would be to prove that he wasn't a cop, and that meant crossing the line. At the very least he'd have to take off his clothes and accept a massage.

He finished his coffee and went out into Wardour Street. He lit a Marlboro and moved slowly through Soho looking for another walk-up. He saw a sign at the entrance to an alley: MODEL. He walked down it. There were no open doors but in the window of the second floor of a terraced house was a red sign illuminated by a light – the girl was available then. If it had been switched off, she would have been otherwise engaged. He dropped the cigarette on the ground and ground it out with his shoe. There was a small intercom at the side of the door, set into the bricks, and three call buttons. A piece of paper with 'MODEL' written on it had been taped across the middle one. Solomon pressed it with his thumb. A second or two later the lock buzzed and he pushed open the door.

He stepped over a pool of manila envelopes and junk mail and walked slowly up a narrow staircase that smelt of stale cabbage. The second-floor door was already open and a woman in her sixties peered through the gap. She showed him into a small sitting room with two sofas on either side of a teak-effect coffee table littered with cards advertising massage services and four mobile phones.

She was tiny, slightly stooped, and her face was as wrinkled as a chamois leather that had been left out in the sun. And she peered at Solomon through thick-lensed glasses. She pointed at an open door.

When he walked into the room a girl was sitting on the

bed. She was tall with an eager-to-please smile and shoulder-length dyed red hair. She waved him to an armchair that had been covered with a white sheet. Thick curtains had been drawn across the single window and the only illumination came from a small lamp on a bedside table over which hung a peach-coloured silk scarf.

'Please, sit down,' she said. Her accent was Central European. Solomon did as she asked. She was wearing a black dressing-gown over a red bra, and when she crossed her long legs he saw red stockings and caught a glimpse of red suspenders with little black bows on them.

'My name is Inga,' she said. She had high cheekbones and almond-shaped brown eyes.

'David,' lied Solomon.

'What can I do for you today?' she asked.

Solomon tried to look embarrassed. 'I'm not sure, I haven't done this before,' he said.

'It's sixty for oral, eighty for sex,' she said.

'Could I have a massage?'

'A massage and hand relief is forty,' she said. Her smile was a little less eager-to-please.

'Forty's fine,' said Solomon. He took out his wallet and gave her two twenty-pound notes. She stood up and took the money.

'Make yourself comfortable,' she said, and left him alone.

The room was as dismal as the last, and the furniture was as bleakly functional. Other than the armchair and the double bed there was only a wardrobe and a dressing-table on which were several bottles of Johnson's baby oil, a tin of talcum powder, a can of air-freshener, a box of baby wipes and a Tupperware carton filled with condoms. By the door was a rubbish bin with a swing top.

There was nothing personal in the room, no clue as to who the girl was or where she'd come from.

Solomon took off his jacket and hung it over the back of the chair. As he was unbuttoning his shirt the girl came back. 'Okay?' she asked.

'Sure,' said Solomon. 'Bit nervous, that's all.'

The girl closed the door. 'Oil or powder?'

'What?'

She gestured at the bottles on the dressing-table. 'Talcum powder or oil. For the massage.'

'Powder's fine,' said Solomon. He took off his shirt, trousers and socks and lay face down on the bed. The sheet was threadbare and smelt of stale sweat. Solomon tried not to think of the number of men who'd been on it before him.

The girl took off her dressing-gown and climbed on to the bed, still wearing her high heels. She sprinkled talcum powder on his back and smoothed it into his skin with small circular movements.

'So where are you from?' asked Solomon.

'Italy,' she said.

Solomon was sure that was a lie. Her accent certainly wasn't Italian – Bulgarian or Romanian was more likely. 'How long have you been in London?' he asked.

Her hands moved down his back. 'Two months.'

'Yeah? Do you like it here?'

'It's okay.' She sounded bored, as if her mind was elsewhere.

'Did you do this in Italy?'

'No.' She pulled down his boxer shorts and sprinkled talc over his legs.

'Good money, though?'

She grunted and began rubbing his legs. Solomon

closed his eyes. He wasn't getting anywhere, and he realised it had been naïve to expect her to say anything to a complete stranger.

'Turn over, please,' she said.

Solomon did as she asked. She sprinkled talc on his chest, then lay down next to him and ran her hand back and forth across his stomach. She kept her head down so that she didn't have to look at him.

As a Vice Officer, Solomon had worked undercover many times, but his aim then had been solely to prove that sex was being sold. All he had had to do was get the girl to say what sexual services were being offered and how much they cost. Once they'd been arrested and taken to the station, he questioned them from a position of authority. Now he was just a punter lying naked on a dirty sheet. She had no reason to answer any of his questions and more likely than not she'd lie anyway.

Inga's hand moved between his legs. She grabbed him but Solomon reached down and held her wrist. 'Just a massage is okay,' he said.

For the first time since she'd climbed on to the bed she looked him in the face. He saw suspicion in her eyes.

'I'm married,' he lied. 'I thought I could, but now . . .' He let his voice trail off, and tried to look shamefaced.

'You've been with a working girl before?' she asked.

Solomon shook his head. 'My wife and I don't . . . you know . . .'

She started massaging his chest with her right hand, and propped up her head with the left. 'You are a good-looking man,' she said.

'Thank you.'

'How old are you?'

'Thirty-five.'

'You look good for thirty-five.'

'Thanks. How old are you?'

'Twenty-two.'

Solomon thought that was another lie. She looked to be in her mid-to-late twenties. 'Your English is very good,' he said. 'Do you study here?'

She nodded. 'I go to a school in Oxford Street. Two hours every day.'

It was a standard way for prostitutes to get into the country, Solomon knew. Language schools didn't run any checks on their pupils so long as they paid their fees, and they were usually able to fast-track student visa applications. The girls would be granted a six-month visa, but once they were in the country, nobody checked whether or not they attended classes.

Inga moved down the bed and began to massage his feet. 'Do you want me to take off my bra?' she asked.

'No, it's okay,' said Solomon, opening his eyes and smiling at her.

'I like your smile,' she said.

Solomon felt a momentary twinge of guilt at the way he was lying to her but suppressed it. 'You don't live here, do you? he asked.

'No, this is a working flat,' she said. 'I work until midnight. Then another girl comes to work until midday.'

'That's a long time, twelve hours.'

'It goes quickly.'

'But you don't enjoy the work?'

'I need the money.'

She leaned over his legs and let her hair brush over his thighs. Solomon reached down and stroked it. 'Do you know a lot of the girls who work in Soho?'

She kissed the inside of his thighs, and Solomon felt

himself hardening. He pushed her shoulders and wriggled from underneath her.

'Your wife won't know,' she said.

'No, but I will.' Solomon laughed. 'Just lie with me for a while, okay?'

She looked at her cheap plastic watch. 'You only have ten minutes left.'

'That's fine,' he said. He held out his arm and she dropped down on the bed and snuggled up to him. He planted a kiss on her forehead. 'So, do you have friends here in London?'

'Not many,' she said.

'Must be lonely.'

'I'm working, or I'm at school, or I'm asleep,' she said.

'But you have friends here, yeah?'

She didn't answer.

'What about other working girls? Do you meet them?' He felt her stiffen. 'You ask a lot of questions.'

'Just curious,' he said. 'Sorry. I don't mean to pry.'

'We have to be careful,' she said. 'Police. Immigration.'

Solomon forced a laugh. 'If I was a cop, I'd hardly be lying here naked with you, would I?'

'You don't know the police,' she said bitterly. 'Sometimes they sleep with a girl, then lie afterwards. You cannot trust the police here – you cannot trust them anywhere.'

Solomon knew the girl was right. He'd never crossed the line when he'd worked for Vice, but several of the officers he'd worked with had made it no secret that they'd had sex with girls they'd been targeting. There was nothing the girls could do. If they were to stand up in court and accuse the officer, it was their word against his, and who'd believe a prostitute?

'How did you find the flat?' he asked.

'A friend told me.'

'From Italy?'

She nodded. Another lie. Solomon was sure. If he was going to get any useful information, he would have to push her. 'Someone told me that a lot of girls in Soho come from Kosovo. Or Bosnia.'

'Albanians,' she sneered.

'Not you, though?'

She propped herself up and looked at him. 'You think I am Albanian?' she said, clearly offended.

'No,' said Solomon. 'I'm just telling you what I heard. That a lot of girls come here from there.'

She pulled a face. 'I don't know,' she said.

'It's true, though, is it?'

'I don't know.'

'They said it was Albanian gangs bringing girls in.'

'You think I work for Albanians?' she said.

'No, I'm just—'

She sat up. 'You ask too many questions.' There was a quick double-knock on the door. 'That means your time is up,' she said. 'You have to go.' She slid off the bed, grabbed her dressing-gown and rushed out.

Solomon dressed. The elderly maid opened the door and showed him out. As he walked by the bathroom he heard the shower spark into life.

Solomon walked down the stairs, mentally kicking himself. He wasn't going to get anywhere walking in off the streets and expecting the girls to talk to him. Their defences were up all the time: they had to be. A prostitute never knew if her next customer would be an undercover policeman, a thief, or a pervert who wanted to slap her around. It didn't matter what story Solomon told, he was just another punter to be treated with suspicion.

Chief Inspector Colin Duggan walked out of the Lost Property Office, scratched his fleshy neck, and headed towards the pub. Solomon fell into step next to him, and grinned at the look of surprise on the man's face. 'Long time no see, Colin,' he said.

'Fuck off, Solomon,' hissed Duggan.

'I'm the one who should be bearing grudges.'

'You're the one who brought the whole house of cards tumbling down. Now, piss off, I don't want to be seen with you.'

'Your choice, Colin. We can have a chat in the pub or I can keep calling your office.'

'So, I've got my own stalker, have I? You know there are laws against that now?'

'A chat, Colin. That's all. You owe me that at least.'

'I owe you nothing, Solomon.'

'My round.'

They had almost reached the pub. 'One drink, then you piss off.'

'Scout's honour,' said Solomon.

Duggan pushed open the pub door and walked in, letting it swing behind him. Solomon caught it and followed him. 'Still on Bell's?' he asked. Duggan grunted and Solomon ordered a double whisky with ice, and a pint of lager.

'How did you know where I was?' asked Duggan.

'Couple of calls. How is it?'

'How do you think it is?' said Duggan bitterly. 'It's a lost-property office. I deal with morons who've left their mobiles in cabs, and I've another four years to go.'

Their drinks arrived. Solomon paid the barman. 'At least you're still in plain clothes.'

Duggan drained his glass and slammed it down on the bar. 'Are you stupid, Solomon? I changed in the office. I'll be in uniform until I retire. In an office with two old women who don't have a brain cell between them. And it's your fault. I'm amazed you've got the balls to show yourself in this city. There's a dozen cops, good cops, who'd like to see you in intensive care.'

Solomon waved for the barman to bring another whisky. 'I did the best I could, Colin. I walked away. Didn't say a thing.'

'Which was as good as putting your hands up for it.'

A fruit machine began to pay out and the old man playing it did a celebratory jig.

'I had two choices. I could have talked to CIB or quit. I quit. I didn't do a damn think wrong, yet I was the one who had to leave the job. How do you think I felt? I'd worked bloody hard for ten years and I had to walk away because you lot were rotten to the core.'

'We were good cops, Solomon.'

The old man began feeding coins back into the fruit machine. The second double whisky arrived and Duggan swirled it around in the glass, staring at the melting ice cubes. 'You had a third choice and you knew it. All you had to do was to stand shoulder to shoulder with us. They didn't have any proof.'

'You took bribes, Colin. You were in Montanaro's pocket – you all were.'

'Fuck you,' said Duggan. 'CIB had nothing on us, not until you resigned.'

144

'I wasn't going to lie to them. And I wasn't going to be the one responsible for sending you down.'

'So you walked away and left us to deal with the shit,' said Duggan bitterly. 'What did you think would happen, Solomon? No smoke without fire, is what they said. They wanted us to resign, like you did. I tried to get out on medical grounds but they wouldn't have it. Instead they sent me to this shit-hole. There were fourteen good guys on the team, Solomon. Now six are in Traffic, two are in recruiting offices and one spends his days telling primary-school children not to talk to strangers. The rest quit. Are you proud of yourself?'

Solomon drank some lager.

'Why did you come back?' asked Duggan eventually.

'I'm looking for a girl.'

'Try a dating agency.'

'A particular girl. From Kosovo.'

'I heard you were in forensics now. Identifying bodies.' Duggan finished his whisky and nodded at the barman for another. He didn't order one for Solomon.

'I am.' Solomon took out a photocopy of the photograph of Nicole and handed it to Duggan. 'Her name's Nicole Shala. She's from a village near Priština.' Solomon could see from the look on Duggan's face that he had no idea where Priština was. 'It's the capital of Kosovo.'

'Yugoslavia?'

'Part of former Yugoslavia.'

Duggan studied the photograph. 'Pretty girl. Fifteen?'

'Sixteen in the picture. Nineteen now.'

'And what's your interest?'

'She was a witness to a mass killing.'

Duggan raised his eyebrows. 'You don't do things by

half, do you?' He held out the picture, but Solomon didn't take it.

'I think she's working as a hooker in London.'

Duggan frowned. 'Haven't you been listening to a word I've said? I'm nothing to do with Vice. I'm in limbo until my thirty years are up and then I'm out.'

'You've got access to the police computer. Just run her name and date of birth.'

'Why the hell do you think I'd help *you*, Solomon?'

'This is important, Colin.'

'And my career isn't? You screwed me over. You screwed us all over.'

Duggan walked away and sat down at a table close to the gents'. He left the photograph on the bar.

Solomon picked it up and went to sit next to him. 'My life hasn't been a bed of roses. The easy way out would have been to spill my guts to CIB.'

'Yeah? There isn't a cop in the Met who'd have worked with you if you had.'

Solomon shook his head. 'You're wrong. Not the way the Met is now. It's not seat-of-the-pants policing any more. Everything has to be done by the book.'

'That's what you think, is it?' sneered Duggan. 'It's the same as it ever was – it's just gone deeper underground. If it wasn't for you, everything would still be right as rain.'

'For you, maybe. But I couldn't live like that. I didn't join the police to take backhanders from the bad guys.'

'You think I did?'

Solomon stayed silent. He didn't want to argue with Duggan.

'I was a bloody good detective,' said Duggan bitterly. 'When I worked Vice there wasn't a single death on our patch that was Vice-related. Not one. Any girl got assaulted, we had it sorted, be it a pimp or punter. Robberies were at a minimum. We had the patch under control.'

'You were taking bribes.'

'You call it a bribe, I'd call it commission for helping things move smoothly.'

'Montanaro controlled half the girls in Soho.'

'Still does, just about,' said Duggan. 'But if he didn't run things, someone else would.'

'Better the devil you know, is that it?'

'The system worked. There was stability. Everyone knew where they stood. Now, no one knows what the hell's going on. That girl you're looking for, came in through Kosovo, right?'

'Bosnia. Yeah.'

'That's where most of the Soho girls are from now. Most of the brasses are Central European, and they're brought in by the Albanian Mafia. Do you think the Albanians are going to stay cosy with the Maltese? Of course they're not. There's going to be a bloodbath. A turf war. Wouldn't have happened in my day. And you know why?'

Solomon sipped his lager.

'Because we had it under control,' said Duggan. 'If newcomers like the Albanians had moved in we'd have stamped on them, hard.'

'To protect Montanaro.'

'To protect the status quo,' hissed Duggan.

The fruit machine began to pay out again. The old man did another jig.

'Will you help me find this girl?' asked Solomon, holding out the photograph again.

'Why should I?' asked Duggan. He drained his glass.

Solomon got up and walked back to the bar, leaving the photograph on the table in front of Duggan. When he got back with fresh drinks, the policeman was studying the picture. 'What did she see?' Duggan asked.

'Her family were killed. By Serbs, probably.'

'Probably?'

'All I've got is twenty-six corpses. Men, women and children.' He filled in the rest of the story.

'Jesus,' whispered Duggan softly. 'Why would they do that?'

'Racial hatred. You think we have problems in Brixton and Bradford, it's nothing to what went on out there. Forty thousand missing people across Bosnia, Croatia and Kosovo. We've got over ten thousand bodies to identify.'

'And they were all murdered?'

'The ones we've found so far? Most of them, yeah. There were some military casualties, but they were usually identified straight away. Civilians were butchered and dumped in mass graves. I'll give you an example. Serb soldiers took over a hospital in Vukovar in Croatia. Anyone who wasn't a Serb was marched out at gunpoint. Didn't matter how sick they were. They were taken to a farm on the outskirts of the city where they tortured them. They cut them with knives, stubbed out cigarettes on them, beat them up. Then they took them into a field in groups of ten and shot them. Two hundred and sixty people were killed. That was on the twentieth of November 1991. I remember the date because it was the first time I saw Parkes slipping you one of Montanaro's envelopes.'

Duggan flashed him a sarcastic smile.

'I'm just saying that you and I were going about our business and hundreds of men, women and children were being shot and thrown into mass graves,' said Solomon 'And it's not on the other side of the world. It's less than a three-hour flight away. If it could happen there, it could happen anywhere. And it was still going on three years ago.' He gestured at the photograph of Nicole. 'Her family were killed in 1999. I was in the Balkans then, and we knew the Serbs were on the rampage. They were like animals. Shelling, looting, raping, murdering civilians. The whole world knew, and they just stood by and let it happen.'

'I don't think we really knew what was happening.'

'Bollocks. That's like the Germans saying they didn't know about the concentration camps where the Jews were being killed. The German people knew. And the world knew what was happening in the Balkans and didn't lift a finger to help.'

'We sent troops, didn't we?'

'Too little, too late. This is a chance to do something.'

'So, you're on a crusade.'

'I want whoever killed her family to get what they deserve. And the only way to do that is find her.'

'You think she was an eyewitness?'

'The only witness. And now she's on the run. Here in London.'

'What makes you think she's hooking?'

'She worked in a nightclub in Sarajevo.'

'Needle in a haystack,' Duggan said.

'I keep hearing that,' said Solomon. He slid a piece of paper across the table. 'That's her name and the details on her birth certificate.'

'You think she'd come here under her own name?'

'It's a possibility. Though she might be calling herself Amy.'

'So you want me to run her through the computer?'

'It'd be a start.'

'Waste of time,' said Duggan.

'Like I said, it's a start. Can you check with Immigration?'

Duggan glared at Solomon. 'I'm not your bloody manservant. I'll run a check through criminal records, but that's all. How do I reach you?'

Solomon gave him the number of the mobile he'd bought earlier in the day.

'What about dabs?' asked Duggan.

'She was never fingerprinted, as far as I know.'

'So, a name and a date of birth is all I've got.'

'And her photograph.'

Duggan sneered at Solomon. 'If you think I'm going to go looking through pictures of arrested hookers on the off-chance I come across her, you've another think coming. Besides, do you know what a small percentage of hookers are ever charged these days? The force has other priorities. So long as they stay off the streets and don't rip off their punters, they're pretty much left alone.'

'Just like the good old days, then?'

Duggan folded up the photocopy and shoved it inside his coat with the slip of paper Solomon had given him. 'I'll check to see if she's been arrested, and that's it. If I find anything, I'll call you.'

Solomon stood up and held out his hand, but Duggan stared at it as if it was a dead thing. 'Okay, have it your way,' Solomon said softly. 'I'm sorry for the way things worked out.'

'Yeah,' said Duggan, bitterly. 'Me too.'

Solomon went back to McLaren's flat, made himself beans on toast, then telephoned an old contact who worked as an immigration officer at Heathrow airport. Immigration officers had had no power to arrest when Solomon worked as a Vice officer, so police officers had had to accompany them whenever they went on raids. Solomon had met Diane Milne during his first year on Vice when immigration officers had wanted to arrest two dozen Chinese girls who were working in an illegal night-club in Chinatown. He had ended up sitting next to her at a celebratory curry afterwards. He had spared no time in introducing her to Danny McLaren and the three had spent many drunken evenings together watching football on TV at McLaren's flat, downing cans of beer and moaning about their employers. Like McLaren, Diane had remained a firm friend after he'd left the force. One of the few.

Diane was tall, striking rather than pretty, with a lingerie model's figure that turned heads wherever she went, but she was happily married to a male nurse. When they'd met Solomon had also been married, so there had never been anything sexual about their relationship. She was overjoyed to hear from him and offered to cook him dinner that evening. Solomon told her he needed a favour and she agreed to run Nicole's details through the Immigration database, so long as he promised he wasn't pursuing her for personal reasons.

'Oh, come on, Diane,' he protested. 'As if.'

'I know what divorced men are like. One sniff of a language student and they're a-quiver.'

'It's work-related,' he said.

'Which is why it's coming through official channels, yeah?'

'I'll tell all when I see you,' he promised.

★

Diane and her husband lived in Clapham so Solomon caught the tube south of the river and walked to their terraced house. Sean Milne opened the front door and pumped Solomon's hand enthusiastically. He was a big man, a good two inches taller than Solomon's six feet.

Diane was in the kitchen, prodding pasta with a fork. She hugged him, and it was only when their stomachs touched that he realised she was pregnant. 'Oh, my God, why didn't you say anything?' asked Solomon.

'It's not yours!' she laughed.

'But aren't I going to be a godfather or something?'

'You're never here. Godfathers are responsible for moral upbringing and stuff.'

'It's an honorary title.'

'Not in this family it's not,' said Sean, opening a bottle of Frascati. He poured wine into three glasses and they toasted each other.

Later, as they tucked into spaghetti carbonara, Diane told Solomon that there had been no trace of a Nicole Shala entering the country. There had been several dozen girls with the first name of Amy but none from anywhere in the Balkans.

Solomon sighed. If she had used another name the chances of finding her were next to impossible, and Duggan was certain to draw a blank when he looked on the police computer.

'Who is she?' asked Diane.

'An eyewitness to an atrocity in Kosovo. Her family were all killed.'

'So she'd have been looking for asylum, right?'

'I don't think so,' said Solomon. 'I'm pretty sure she's working as a prostitute, so she could have come under another name. I was hoping for the easy option.'

'There's a whole industry devoted to putting together false identities for prostitutes,' she said. 'She could have paid for a passport and visa, or come over under contract. Either way, the paperwork would be faultless.'

'Can't you spot them when they're coming through?' asked Sean, refilling their glasses with wine.

'You mean you can spot a hooker just by looking at her?' said Diane. 'They don't come in wearing miniskirts and fishnet stockings, love.'

'No, but if you've got a pretty young girl arriving at Heathrow with no visible means of support, you must wonder?' said Solomon.

'She might be a language student – they're allowed to work twenty hours a week to fund their studies. She might have rich parents. She might be a tourist. Our people have a few seconds to make a judgement. There might be just half a dozen officers to deal with two 747s. Seven hundred people. We don't have time to cross-examine every good-looking girl. If the passport and visa are right, they're in.'

'So nothing can be done to stop it?'

'It's the asylum-seekers who are the bigger problem. They cost the country money. Prostitutes don't go on the dole – they work and then they go home. They're not really seen as a problem, not when our resources are as stretched as thinly as they are.'

Solomon sat back in his chair. 'It's a funny old world, isn't it?' he said. 'Immigration aren't over-worried about girls coming here to work as prostitutes. The police don't care, so long as no one gets hurt. But the guys doing the trafficking are making a fortune. No one seems to be doing anything to stop it. Why don't we just legalise it and have done with it?'

'It's not a bad idea,' said Diane. 'We could issue hooking visas. Six months, renewable, subject to health checks and income-tax payments.'

'Specialist workers,' said Sean, with a grin.

'I was joking,' said Solomon.

'Well, I'm not,' said Diane. 'The going rate for a fake passport and visa out of Central Europe is about ten thousand dollars. Most of the girls have to pay off the debt when they get here, and that means working for one of the trafficking gangs. That's where the problems start. If the Government was to issue visas to working girls, it could be monitored and the girls looked after.'

'So the Government would be living off immoral earnings?'

'They sort of are already,' said Diane. 'A lot of English prostitutes pay income tax. They face more hassle from the Inland Revenue than they do from the police.'

'Yeah, maybe you're right,' said Solomon. 'Legalise it and have done with it.'

'Legalise it and regulate it,' said Diane. 'So long as the girls aren't being forced into doing it, they'd be better off. And it'd free up more resources for the real problem areas.'

'So it's the men who are running the prostitution rings who are the problem, not the girls.'

'They're just trying to earn a living,' said Diane. 'You can't blame them. There but for the grace of God . . .'

'What do you mean?' asked her husband. 'Are you saying you'd prostitute yourself?'

'If I had no other choice? What do you think?'

'You always have a choice,' said Sean.

'That's easy to say when you're living in the UK,' she said, 'but what if I'd been born in Kosovo? What if I was thrown out of my home, my country? What if half my family had been massacred? I'm bloody lucky to have been born in England, Sean. I've had choices thrown at me throughout my whole life. Good schools, good health-care, and an economic system that works.'

'But you could sleep with a stranger for money?' asked Solomon.

Diane jerked a thumb at her husband. 'I've slept with him after he's had six pints of lager and a vindaloo, and I didn't get a penny.'

Solomon laughed and Sean faked a glare at his wife.

'Come on, Jack,' said Diane. 'You must have paid for sex, right? After your divorce?'

'Thanks,' said Solomon, 'but I don't have to pay for sex.'

'Everyone pays,' said Sean, raising his glass to Diane. 'One way or another.'

'And you'll pay for that remark later,' she said. She turned back to Solomon. 'Seriously, are you saying you've never paid for it?'

'Diane . . .' he protested.

'I'll take that as a yes. And you know as well as I do that paid-for sex is a massive industry here in the UK. More money is spent on prostitution in Britain than on cinema tickets.'

'Oh, come on.'

'It's a fact. I read it in the *Sun*.'

'Oh, it must be true then.' He laughed.

'It's an industry, and with the sort of money on offer I'm not surprised that girls are queuing up to do it.'

'You're right,' said Solomon. 'I've seen where these girls come from and their choices *are* limited. Kosovo is a pretty shitty place to be just now.'

'And the collapse of Yugoslavia's made our life bloody difficult,' said Diane. 'Turks, Iraqis, Iranians, even Chinese, are all flooding into the UK through the Balkans.'

'How so?' asked Solomon.

'Tens of thousand of Iranians and Turks go to Sarajevo as tourists. They don't need a visa, payback for supporting the Muslims during the war. The Chinese can get tourist visas to Serbia pretty much on demand because of the special relationship there used to be between Beijing and Belgrade, and the Serbs were in bed with Saddam Hussein for years so they get visas without any problems, too. Hardly any go home. They slip across the border into Croatia and there they buy a package to the UK.'

'Package?' queried Sean.

'A passport and transport,' said Diane. 'Sometimes legal on a scheduled flight, sometimes overland to France and then the Eurostar, sometimes hidden in the back of a truck. As soon as they get to the UK they claim asylum. We keep asking Bosnia and Serbia to tighten up their visa requirements, but why should they listen to us?'

'But the atrocities – all those people who died. That was the Serbs, right?' said Sean.

The problem with explaining the situation in the Balkans was that it was so damned complicated, Solomon thought. There were no blacks and whites, just many shades of grey. 'There were atrocities on both sides,' he said. 'Muslims killed Serbs, Serbs killed Muslims. Serbs killed Croats. Croats killed Muslims. Everyone had it in for the Albanians. When Yugoslavia fell apart, there were a lot of old scores to settle.'

'So this girl, what is she?' asked Sean.

'Albanian Muslim,' answered Solomon.

'So Serbs killed her family?'

'Until I find her, I won't know for sure. But there were lots of Serbian troops on the rampage in Kosovo at that time.'

Diane motioned at her husband to open another bottle of wine. 'So, how are you going to find her?' she asked. 'Once someone is in the country, there's no real way of tracing them. Not if they're working for cash.'

'Yeah. No National Insurance number, they're not on the electoral roll, no State benefits. All the normal avenues are dead ends.'

'You're trying the police?' asked Diane.

'I've got a contact who'll run her through their computer, but if she's not here under her own name . . .'

Diane nodded sympathetically. 'You could try the clap clinics.'

'Sexual-health clinics, please,' said Sean.

'Thank you, darling,' said Diane, blowing him a kiss.

'Presumably she'll have health checks while she's here. There aren't that many clinics in London – you could take her photo round, see if any of the doctors recognise her.'

'Might work,' said Solomon. 'Snag is, I'm not here officially.' He explained what had happened in Bosnia and why he'd left the country.

'Bloody hell, Jack,' she said, when he'd finished. 'You still know how to win friends and influence people, don't you?'

The next day, Solomon sat in a coffee bar in Wardour Street nursing a succession of cappuccinos until he saw

Inga walking towards the alley where her flat was. She'd tied back her hair and was wearing a long leather coat, knee-length boots and a pair of sunglasses with impenetrable lenses.

Solomon hurried out of the coffee bar and caught up with her as she reached the entrance to the alley.

'Inga?' he said, touching her shoulder.

She recoiled. 'What do you want? Who are you?'

'It's David,' he said. 'I came to see you the day before yesterday.' He flashed her an open smile.

'What do you want?'

'Hey, it's okay. You remember me, don't you?'

She looked at him for several seconds, then smiled tightly. 'Okay. I remember.' She looked at her wristwatch. 'I have to go.'

'I need to talk to you.'

She pushed her sunglasses higher up her nose. 'Come and see me later. I shower and make up, then I work after midday. I am happy to see you then, okay?'

'Can I take you for a coffee? Please?'

She shook her head emphatically. Then her lips tightened – she had seen something over his shoulder. He turned. Two policemen in bright yellow fluorescent jackets were walking slowly down from Oxford Street.

'You're here illegally, aren't you?' he said.

'I have passport and visa,' she said.

'But not in your real name, right?'

'Who are you?'

'I'm someone who needs your help, Inga. That's all. Just let me talk to you for a few minutes.'

He looked over his shoulder. The policemen were less than fifty feet away.

'I'm not with the police, I'm not with Immigration. I'm

158

not here to hurt you. Five minutes, okay? And I'll pay you for your time.'

For a moment he thought she was going to turn and run down the alley, but then she nodded.

She walked with him to the coffee bar. She wanted an espresso and Solomon ordered a lemonade for himself – he'd had all the caffeine he could take.

Inga was waiting for him at a table by the window, tapping her foot impatiently. She nodded curtly when he put the coffee in front of her, but made no move to drink it. He sat down next to her. 'Look, I'm sorry about this,' he said.

'You could get me into big trouble,' she murmured. 'I'm not supposed to see customers outside work.'

'Who says?'

'My boss.'

Solomon took out the photograph of Nicole and slid it across the table towards her. 'I'm looking for this girl,' he said.

She picked up the picture and studied it. 'Why? Did she steal from you?'

'No,' said Solomon.

'You said you would pay me for talking to you,' she said, putting the photograph back on the table.

Solomon gave her forty pounds. 'The man you work for, your boss. Who is he?'

She eyed him suspiciously. 'You said you were looking for a girl. Why do you want to talk about my boss?'

'Because someone brought her over from Bosnia. I thought maybe the man who brought you over might have brought her, too.'

'She is from Bosnia?' asked Inga. Picking up the photograph again.

'Kosovo,' said Solomon.

Inga's eyebrows shot up, suddenly interested. 'She is a Serb?' she asked.

'Albanian,' said Solomon. 'What about you, Inga? Where are you from?'

'Bulgaria,' said Inga.

'Did you come here from Bulgaria?'

Inga took off her sunglasses and gave him a long, hard look. 'Why do you want this girl?' she asked.

'She witnessed a crime in Kosovo.'

'So you *are* a policeman.'

'No, I'm not,' he said firmly. 'I work in Bosnia for a charity. I'm not interested in what's happening here in London. I just want to find this girl.'

'And she is a prostitute, the same as me?'

'I think so. Yes.'

She nodded slowly. 'I, too, was in Kosovo for a while,' she said. 'It was not a nice place.'

Solomon sipped his lemonade and waited.

'My parents died when I was small,' she said. 'I lived with an aunt but she didn't want me in her house. She was a cleaner at a hotel and had no money and two children of her own. I didn't want to live with her but I didn't have anywhere else to go.' She shrugged. 'I wanted to run away but there was nowhere I could go. Then, when I was sixteen, I met Goran. He was twenty but he said he loved me. He was the first man I went with. He said we'd always be together. That we were soul-mates.' She paused. 'He told me we could work in Macedonia, in a restaurant that a friend of his owned. He said I could help in the kitchen and work as a waitress. He said we could get a flat and live together and be happy.'

She rubbed the bridge of her nose, close to tears.

'There was no restaurant?' said Solomon.

She shook her head fiercely. 'We stayed with a friend of his. Then, after a week, he said I had to sleep with his friend because we had no money. Then there was another friend. Then another. Then he brought men to the apartment and they gave him money to sleep with me. If I said no he beat me. Then he took me to a house where there were a lot of girls and left me there. I never saw him again.'

Solomon lit a Marlboro. He offered the packet to Inga but she waved it away.

'I was there for six months. Then some men came from Kosovo. I think they were the Kosovo Liberation Army. You know them?'

Solomon said he did. They were the former anti-Serbian rebel force, and were every bit as violent as the Serbs they hated.

'We were paraded naked in front of the men, I thought it was for sex, but the man who owned the house was selling us. I was sold for two thousand dollars. Six of us were put in a van and they took us to Kosovo.'

She looked out of the window, watched the traffic crawl by.

'We were held in an army camp for a year, I think. There were so many men. Sometimes twenty a day. No condoms. They gave us antibiotics every month. Beat us if we didn't take them. Then there was a problem in the camp and we were put in a motel.' She forced a smile. 'That was better. Not so many men and they gave us condoms.'

Solomon sat in silence. Outside, black cabs ferried businessmen to meetings, couriers zipped by on bicycles, all Lycra and leggings, and wannabe movie producers dressed in Armani shouted into mobile phones. Only feet away from them Inga was talking about sex slavery, girls traded like a commodity, bought, sold and repeatedly raped.

'I was in the motel for six months,' she said. 'Then we were moved again. They took us to Belgrade. There was a big auction there. Hundreds of girls. I was sold for three thousand dollars.' She smiled ruefully. 'My price had gone up. I don't know why.'

'Who bought you?'

'My boss. Sasha. He's from Albania. He bought six girls at the auction. He brought us to London and we work for him here.'

'He's your pimp?'

'He's my boss.'

'How much do you give him?'

She frowned. 'What do you mean?'

'The money you earn. How much do you give him?'

'You don't understand how it works, do you?' she said sadly.

'Tell me.'

'All the money is for him. He gives me somewhere to live and some money for my food, and I get some money to spend, but he keeps all the money the customers give.'

'That's outrageous!' said Solomon.

'He bought me,' said Inga, 'and he paid to get me into London. He paid for the passport, the visa and my ticket. He paid for the clothes I'm wearing. I have to work for him until I have paid him what I owe him.'

'How long will that be?'

'I don't know. Maybe never.'

'You don't mean that, surely.'

'He says it cost him twenty thousand dollars to get me here. I have to repay that with interest.'

'But you must earn a lot, doing what you do?'

'Not so much. Maybe ten customers a day. Sometimes more. Some pay forty pounds, some sixty, some eighty. More if they want special services.'

Solomon didn't want to know what the 'special services' were. 'So, you must make about six hundred pounds a day.'

She nodded. 'More sometimes. But that's for the flat. Not for me. There's rent for the flat, the maid's wages, the phone, the card-boy. If I earn six hundred, Sasha says my share is one hundred, and that goes to pay off my debt.'

Solomon did a quick calculation in his head. Twenty thousand dollars was about fourteen thousand pounds, give or take. At a hundred pounds a day that would take a hundred and forty days to pay off. 'Okay, so you'd have to work for him for three or four months, right?' he said. 'Then you'd be free?'

She smiled despondently. 'You are forgetting the interest. And the money for my school. I study English three times a week. And my rent. He charges me for everything and it all gets added to what I owe.'

'Have you asked him when it'll be paid back?'

'That's not something you ask Sasha. When I don't owe him anything, he'll tell me.'

'And how many girls work for him?'

Inga picked up her cup and sipped the espresso, her eyes on his face. She put the cup down slowly. 'Why do you want to know about Sasha?' she asked.

'I don't,' he said quickly. 'It just seems that what he's doing isn't fair, that's all. It's as if you're a slave.'

'I am not a slave,' she snapped.

'But you're forced to work for nothing.'

'I'm not working for nothing. I am paying off a debt.'

Solomon leaned towards her. 'But it's *his* debt, not yours. He paid money for you, at an auction, you said. Why should you have to pay that money back? He's the one who brought you to London. It's his debt not yours.'

She sighed. 'You don't understand.'

'I understand that he's ripping you off.'

'He's not ripping me off.'

'You're earning five hundred pounds a day for him. He's making a fortune from you. And the little money he says is yours goes to pay off money he says you owe him. That's crazy. Look, suppose you said you didn't want to work for him any more. Suppose you said you wanted to go back to Bulgaria?'

'I cannot go. He has my passport.'

'So you're a prisoner?'

'How am I a prisoner?' she said. 'I am here talking to you. I go to school to learn English. Every month I have a day off.'

'But don't you want to go back to your own country?'

'What do I have back there? I have no family, no job, no money. If I go back to Bulgaria I will be on my own. At least here I have . . .'

Solomon knew what she was going to say. At least she had Sasha. He sat back in his chair. He couldn't understand why she was so sanguine about her situation. She'd been taken from her country, sold into virtual slavery and forced to sleep with hundreds of men, yet there was no trace of anger or bitterness.

'I must go,' she said, standing up. 'If I am late I am fined.'

'You're what?'

'For every minute I am late, I am fined ten pounds,' she said.

Solomon scribbled his mobile-phone number on the coffee-shop receipt and gave it to her. 'If you see her, call me. Please.'

She nodded and took the piece of paper from him. She put on her sunglasses and walked away without saying goodbye.

Solomon awoke to the sound of a loud buzzing. He rolled over, groped for the alarm clock on the bedside table, then realised it was his mobile. He fumbled for it. 'Yeah?' he grunted. He squinted at the clock. It was just after one a.m. He'd only been asleep for an hour.

'David?' It was a girl. 'You are David?'

David? Who the hell was David? He was about to tell her she had a wrong number when he remembered. 'Hi,' he said. 'Who's that?'

'It's Inga. How are you?'

Solomon sat up. 'I'm fine. Are you okay?'

'I think I know where you can find the girl you're looking for.'

Suddenly Solomon was wide awake. 'Where?'

'I don't mean I know where she is, but I've spoken to a girl who's met her.'

'Here in London?'

'I think so,' she said, 'but she needs to see the photograph to be sure.'

'Who is she, this girl?'

'She does the same as me. She's from the Ukraine.'

'And she's met her? You're sure?'

'She thinks so. But she needs to see the photograph.'

Solomon heard someone whispering to her. Then the sound was cut off as if she'd put her hand across the mouthpiece. 'Inga, is the girl there now?'

There was a pause. 'She's here but she doesn't want to talk to you.' said Inga eventually. 'She wants to see the photograph. Is that okay?'

'Now?' said Solomon. 'It's one o'clock in the morning.'

'She works all day,' said Inga. 'There are many girls at the house where she stays and they're not allowed out unless one of the boss's men goes with them. Now is the only time you can see her on her own.'

'She doesn't work for Sasha?'

'No, her boss is a Russian. He beats the girls if they talk to anyone outside work. We must do this now.'

'Where are you?'

'Soho.'

'If I get a minicab I can be there in half an hour.'

Inga's hand went over the mouthpiece again. Solomon took a quick look at the screen of his mobile. The caller ID had been blocked.

'Okay, you come here,' said Inga. 'You know where you saw me?'

'Wardour Street?'

'Near there. You know Soho Square?'

'Sure.'

'There's a public toilet there. At the end near Oxford Street. We will see you there, okay?'

The phone went dead. Solomon pulled on his clothes, called a minicab firm on his mobile, then went outside to wait on the pavement. Ten minutes later, a battered Honda Civic pulled up.

As they drove to Soho, Solomon looked at Nicole's photograph. He wondered if she felt it was better to be a prostitute in the West than homeless and unwanted in her own country. Maybe Diane had a point: maybe choice was a luxury, a privilege rather than a right, and girls like

Inga and Nicole were doing the only thing they could do to survive.

He wondered, too, what he could offer Nicole to persuade her to go back with him to Sarajevo. If she'd wanted to see the men who'd murdered her family caught, then surely she'd have stayed in Kosovo and gone to the authorities. She'd made the decision to run and, like Inga, she had nothing to go back to. If she was in the UK illegally, her fingerprints and photograph would go on file and she'd find it difficult to return, legally or otherwise. She had no family left in Kosovo, and Solomon doubted that she'd be able to stay with Teuter Berisha, or even that she'd want to.

He put the photograph back into his pocket and closed his eyes.

'I drop you Charing Cross Road, okay?' asked the driver. He was watching Solomon in the rear-view mirror. He had dark eyes, almost black, and a thick stubble over his chin.

'Sure, whatever,' said Solomon.

The driver swerved to avoid a bus and pounded on the horn.

'Where are you from?' asked Solomon, suddenly curious.

'Afghanistan,' said the man.

'Have you been here long?'

'Five years,' said the man. 'Taliban kill my family. My father general, work with Russians. Taliban kill all soldiers work with Russians. Kill my father, my mother and my sister.'

'How did you get to England?'

'We pay agent in Kabul. He take us to India. Pay another agent there for passport and visa.'

'What about going back to Afghanistan? The Taliban have gone now, does that mean it's safe for you to return?'

The driver snorted derisively. 'Why go back? I get British passport soon. Soon I British, same you.' He pulled up sharply. 'Charing Cross Road,' he said.

Solomon paid him and walked past bookshops and fast-food restaurants towards Soho Square. A young man was bedding down in a bookshop doorway with a black and white collie and a bottle of Strongbow cider.

Soho Square was almost deserted. Most of the buildings that fronted it were offices or studios; the bars, nightclubs and strip-joints were further west. In the centre of the square there was a garden where, during lunchtimes on fine days, office workers flocked to eat their sandwiches. Someone was standing at the entrance – it was Inga, still wearing her sunglasses. 'Where's the girl?' Solomon asked as he reached her.

Inga seemed tense. 'She didn't want to wait here,' she said. 'She was scared somebody might see her.'

Solomon groaned. 'You mean I've wasted my time?'

'No, no,' said Inga. 'She's with a friend not far from here. We can walk.'

'Are you okay, Inga?' asked Solomon. 'You look nervous.'

'I'm okay,' she said. She slipped her arm through his and smiled. 'I'm glad to see you again.'

Solomon smiled back, but his mind was racing. Something didn't feel right. He could feel her tension – she was practically shaking. And the smile she'd given him had been more the grimace of a frightened dog.

She guided him away from the garden towards Carlisle Street. She was biting her lower lip and there were deep frown lines across her forehead. Solomon stopped and swung her round to face him. 'Inga, what's the matter?'

'Nothing.' She tugged at his arm. 'Come.'

He looked at her suspiciously. 'I'm not going anywhere until you tell me what's happening.' A blue van turned into the square. Inga glanced at it. 'It's okay, it's not the police,' said Solomon.

'Please, David . . .' said Inga.

'What?' asked Solomon. 'What's wrong?'

'Nothing's wrong. This way.' She pulled his arm and they crossed the road. The blue van stopped and its lights went off.

'Inga, where are we going?' asked Solomon.

'This way,' she said.

A car door opened behind Solomon. Then another. Two big men in long coats climbed out of a BMW. One was smoking a cigar. They slammed the doors and started to walk purposefully towards where Solomon and Inga were standing. Solomon knew it was him they were after. He tried to pull away from Inga but she held on to his arm. The men broke into a run.

Two more got out of the blue van and rushed towards Solomon. He pushed Inga away. 'What is this?' he shouted.

'I'm sorry,' she said. She was hugging herself. 'I'm sorry,' she repeated.

The men from the BMW were only yards away. Solomon put up his hands to defend himself. Both men were bigger, younger and stronger than he was. And the one who wasn't smoking had something in his right hand. A cosh or a truncheon, about eight inches long, made of black, shiny material. He stared at Solomon, his mouth set.

'What do you want?' Solomon asked.

The man with the cigar nodded at the one with the cosh and they moved apart to block Solomon's way. There were rapid steps behind him, but he couldn't turn because he knew that if he did the man with the cosh would hit him. He stepped off the pavement into the road and tried to run past the men from the BMW but, despite their bulk, they moved quickly. The man with the cigar kicked out and Solomon jumped to the side, losing his balance and slipping on the Tarmac. He fell on one knee, cursing. The cosh delivered a stinging blow to his left elbow. Solomon yelped with pain and his left arm hung uselessly at his side. As he tried to get back to his feet, he saw Inga standing on the pavement, her hands covering her face.

Then the man with the cigar kicked him in the chest and he fell back, his head slamming against the road. He lay there, head spinning. The man who'd kicked him grinned and took a deep pull on his cigar.

Then the two men from the van grabbed his arms and hauled him to his feet. He kicked at the man with the cigar but missed. The man with the cosh stepped forward, raised his arm and Solomon felt a sickening blow to the back of his head before everything went black.

A wave of nausea washed over him as he opened his eyes and he vomited. He wiped his mouth with the back of his hand and coughed, trying to clear his throat. He was lying on bare concrete, facing a brick wall. He tried to roll over but pain lanced through his left arm. He lay where he was, flexing his fingers one by one. Once he was satisfied that he could move them he checked his forearm and elbow. Nothing seemed to be broken.

He heard voices muttering somewhere behind him and

used his right arm to force himself into a sitting position. His head was throbbing and he felt close to passing out again.

Someone shone a light into his face and he turned his head away.

'Who are you?' snarled a voice.

The accent was familiar, but Solomon couldn't place it. His driving licence and credit cards were in his wallet, along with his International War-dead Commission credentials, so he knew there was no point in lying. 'Solomon,' he said. 'Jack Solomon.'

'You told the girl your name was David.'

'I don't think anyone uses their right names when they visit hookers, do they?'

He was kicked in the side, hard. 'Don't try to be clever,' said the man. 'Who do you work for?'

'A charity.'

'You look like a cop.'

Solomon spat bloody phlegm on to the floor. 'You know I'm not a cop,' he said. 'You wouldn't be doing this if you thought I was a cop.'

'You gave your phone number to my girl. Why did you do that? What did she tell you?' He was kicked again, harder this time.

'Okay, okay!' shouted Solomon. 'I'm looking for a girl from Kosovo. I asked Inga if she saw her to give me a call.'

'What's your interest in Kosovo?'

'I work out there.' He shaded his eyes with his right hand. A broad-shouldered man was sitting on a chair. Next to him was an Anglepoise lamp that had been twisted to point at Solomon. 'For who?'

'For a charity. We identify bodies.'

'You have proof of this?'

'My ID. It's in my wallet.'

'Show me.'

Solomon took out his wallet and held it towards the man, who got up and took it from him. He studied Solomon's identification, then tossed back the wallet.

'Why are you in London?' asked the man.

'I'm looking for a witness to an atrocity in Kosovo.'

'Where in Kosovo?'

'Near Priština.' He put away his wallet and rubbed his arm. 'You could have broken my elbow.'

'I could have done a lot worse.'

The man walked back to his chair, sat down and spoke in Albanian to the man who'd delivered the kick.

Solomon heard footsteps to his left, then a scraping sound. His arms were seized and he was pulled to his feet, then forced roughly on to a chair.

Fluorescent lights flickered into life. Solomon looked around him: he was in a windowless cellar with low ceilings, bare brick walls and a single wooden door. The big man from the BMW was standing with his hand on the light switch. There was a damp, musty smell, and in one corner of the room he could see a cardboard tray filled with what he assumed was rat poison. Two men were standing behind him.

The man on the chair was the man who'd been smoking the cigar. He was in his mid to late thirties with a square face, dark brown hair cut short and pale grey eyes. 'You're Sasha?' asked Solomon.

The man's eyes narrowed. 'She told you my name, did she?'

'That's all she told me,' said Solomon.

'It's more than enough,' he said.

'Look, I don't want to get anyone into trouble,' said

Solomon. 'I just want to find the girl I'm looking for.'

'What is her name, this girl?'

'Nicole. Nicole Shala. She might be calling herself Amy.'

'You have her photograph?'

Solomon took it out. The man who'd kicked him took it from him and handed it to Sasha, who grimaced as he looked at it, then shook his head. 'Kosovar Albanian?'

Solomon nodded. Sasha would have known that from her name. Names in the Balkans were as identifiable as bar codes.

'Muslim?'

Solomon nodded again.

'What happened?'

Solomon explained how Nicole's family had been killed. Sasha listened without saying anything. When he finished, the other man grunted and put the photograph into the pocket of his leather jacket. Solomon didn't object. It was the original that he'd brought from Sarajevo, but he had photocopies in McLaren's flat. 'Why do you think she is in London?' Sasha asked.

'She worked in a bar in Priština,' said Solomon. 'A lot of the girls there moved to EC countries.' That was a lie, but he couldn't take the risk that Sasha knew Ivan Petrovic. Petrovic was a Serb and Sasha was an Albanian so in theory they would be sworn enemies – but crime produced strange bedfellows.

'So London is a guess?'

Solomon shrugged. 'I had to start somewhere.'

'And you were approaching girls at random, asking if they'd seen this girl?' He patted his pocket.

'Yeah.'

'That's not much of a plan.'

'Needle in a haystack, I know. But I had to do something.'

'It is dangerous to question working girls,' said Sasha.

Solomon touched his injured arm. 'So I've discovered.'

'We have to protect our investments,' said Sasha. 'The police and Immigration want to send them back. Other gangs want to steal them. We have customers who want to rescue them.'

'Is that what you thought? That I wanted to rescue Inga?'

'I found the phone number you gave her. She told me what you had said to her, but I wanted to check for myself.' Sasha stood up. 'Do you drink whisky?'

Solomon was confused. 'What?'

'Whisky. Do you drink whisky?'

'Sure.'

Sasha turned and walked towards the door. The man by the light switch opened it for him. 'Come with me,' said Sasha.

Solomon stood up and followed him out of the cellar. The door led to a stairway. They went up it, and into a huge kitchen with gleaming stainless-steel cupboards and huge industrial-sized appliances. The fridge was the size of two telephone boxes and there were ten gas burners on the hob. Nothing appeared to have been used; every surface was pristine. The floor was polished granite.

Sasha walked through it to a living room the size of a hotel lobby. At the far end was a massive marble fireplace topped by a mirror the size of a shop window. All the furniture was ornate, with gilt frames, curves and claws and overstuffed upholstery.

Sasha waved Solomon to an uncomfortable-looking chair, then walked over to one of the sideboards, which was laden with bottles of spirits. He sloshed generous measures of Johnnie Walker Black Label into two crystal tumblers. He handed one to Solomon, then sprawled on a sofa. 'How long have you been in Bosnia?' he asked.

'Two years in Sarajevo, and I was in Kosovo for a year before that, working for the International War-dead Commission. Before that I worked for a charity delivering food and medicines throughout the Balkans.'

Sasha nodded and sipped his whisky. 'I have heard of the Commission. You identify dead Muslims, right?'

Solomon shook his head emphatically. 'We identify remains. Usually all we have to work on is a few bones, so it's down to DNA analysis. And there's no way of telling from DNA whether the person is Muslim or Christian, Albanian or Serb.'

'I lost my brother. And five cousins. Murdered by the Serbs.'

'What happened?'

'What happened?' Sasha snarled. 'The Serbs took them out and shot them, that's what happened. Then they took everything they owned out of their houses, stole what they wanted and burned the rest.'

'This was in Albania?'

'Kosovo. My family is from Albania originally, but my grandparents moved to Kosovo just before the Second World War. They were Christians. Many of my brother's neighbours were Serbs. The ones who didn't do the killing just stood by and watched. Serb families moved into their houses.'

'A lot of appalling things happened over there.'

Sasha's eyes hardened. 'You don't know what it's like until it has happened to you. To someone you know.'

There was nothing Solomon could say. He knew what it was like to watch a loved one die, to hold a dying child in his arms. But he was damned if he was going to discuss his personal life with a pimp and trafficker who'd thought nothing of abducting him and beating him up. He might have taken Solomon into his sitting room and poured him a whisky but that didn't make him any less of a thug. And Solomon wasn't taken in by the man's sudden affability. Sasha was a nasty piece of work – the sharp pain in his elbow and the ache in his ribs where he'd been kicked were testimony to that.

'We bring closure,' said Solomon. 'Thousands of people have no idea what happened to their loved ones and until they have a body to grieve over they're in limbo.'

'Shit job,' said Sasha.

Solomon said nothing. It *was* a shit job, but at least it was an honest one. Sasha made his living out of young girls prostituting themselves, and he clearly had no compunction about using threats and violence. He was a violent pimp. But Solomon didn't want to go back into the basement for another kicking so he smiled and nodded.

'Why is a Jew doing a shit job in Kosovo?'

'I'm not Jewish,' said Solomon.

'Solomon is a Jewish name,' said Sasha.

'My grandfather was Jewish, but he married a Catholic.'

'So what are you?'

It was difficult for Solomon to say exactly what he was. The easy answer was Church of England, because he'd gone to a Church of England school when he was a child, but he hadn't worshipped in a church for more than thirty years. Even his marriage had taken place in a register office. 'Agnostic, I guess,' he said.

'Agnostic means what?' asked Sasha.

'Agnostic means that I just don't know.'

'I thought that was an atheist.'

'Atheists know that there's no God. Agnostics aren't sure.'

'And that's how you feel? That maybe there's no God.'

Solomon groaned. 'Sasha, I don't know, and frankly I don't care. If there is a God, and if he's allowed the sort of things to happen that have happened in the Balkans, then I'm not sure I'd want anything to do with him.'

Sasha threw back his head and roared with laughter. 'That means that if you turn up at the gates of heaven, and he's there waiting for you, you're just going to say thanks, but no thanks?'

'There's no heaven, Sasha. There might be a hell, but it's here on earth.'

'You're a bitter, twisted man.'

Solomon raised his glass. 'Thanks for the character assessment.'

'It's probably because you're a mongrel,' said Sasha.

'What?'

'Jewish grandfather, Christian grandmother, who knows what else? Mixing blood leads to disaster. That was always the problem with Yugoslavia. Too many races forced to live together.'

Solomon sat tight-lipped. There was no way he was going to be drawn into an argument about racial integration with a man like Sasha. He just wanted to get out of the house in one piece.

Sasha drained his whisky glass in several gulps. 'Are you going to continue looking for this girl?' asked Sasha.

'Yes,' said Solomon.

'I would advise against approaching any more of my girls,' said Sasha.

'I understand. But how will I know if they work for you or not?'

Sasha flashed Solomon a tight smile. 'You can assume that if they are in Soho they work for me,' he said.

'All of them?' Solomon was surprised.

'I defend my territory, Jack,' said Sasha, 'and Soho is my territory.'

'Okay,' he agreed.

'I'm glad we understand each other,' said Sasha. He stood up and held out his arm, indicating that Solomon should leave, then showed him to the front door. 'This man will drive you to wherever you want to go,' he said.

'It's okay, I'll get a black cab.'

'My man will drive you,' repeated Sasha, his voice harder. 'Where are you staying in London?'

'Bayswater,' said Solomon.

A thug was standing next to a large Mercedes, its engine running. He stared stonily at Solomon, who felt the urge to run, but there was a high wall surrounding the garden topped with metal spikes and the wrought-iron gate at the end of the drive was shut. Sasha shouted something to the man in Albanian. It wasn't a language Solomon understood, let alone spoke, but he didn't hear the word 'Bayswater'. He climbed into the back of the car and the door slammed.

The driver turned and grinned at him and gave him an exaggerated thumbs-up. Solomon smiled uneasily. The other passenger door opened and the thug climbed in next to him. Solomon flinched as the locks clicked. The Mercedes headed down the drive and the gates swung open. Solomon twisted in his seat and caught a last glimpse of Sasha standing in his doorway, his hands on his hips, staring after the car.

Sasha walked slowly up the marble staircase, carrying the half-full bottle of Black Label. He walked down the landing, past a line of identical doors. There were two dozen bedrooms in the mansion but Sasha hadn't been inside most of them. He had paid an interior designer a small fortune to decorate and furnish them and they were kept scrupulously clean by the Albanian housekeeper and her assistant, but most of the beds had not been slept in.

He opened the door at the far end of the corridor. The girl was sitting on the edge of the king-sized bed and stood up quickly. Her face was tear-stained and her mascara had run. She wiped her face and sniffed.

Sasha kicked the door closed and took a swig of whisky. He looked slowly around the room. The designer had used a leopard theme. There was a fake leopardskin cover on the bed, and a real leopardskin on the floor. On the walls were framed paintings of the big cat, and there was a life-size porcelain model of one under the window.

Sasha wiped the back of his mouth with his hand. 'You told him my name.'

The girl sniffed again and looked down at the floor. 'I'm sorry.'

'You told him about my business.'

'I didn't,' she said.

'No more lies,' said Sasha. He took another swig from the bottle. 'Take off your dress,' he said.

She complied immediately, unzipping it at the back and stepping out of it. She placed it carefully on the bed. She was wearing her working underwear. Black bra, pants and suspenders with white stockings. There was a small gold cross at her throat.

'Everything off,' said Sasha.

The girl began to sob.

It had been a long time since Sasha had seen Inga naked. It had been in Belgrade. She hadn't been that special, and he'd probably overpaid, but he'd needed girls quickly and she had a good figure, and the friend who'd road-tested her had confirmed that she'd been well trained. She'd put on a bit of weight since the auction: now her figure was fuller and her breasts were bigger than Sasha liked. Sasha liked his girls young with boyish figures, but what he was about to do to Inga had nothing to do with sex and everything to do with control. She had to be taught a lesson.

Inga stood naked at the end of the bed, her right arm covering her breasts, her left hand over her crotch.

'Look at me,' hissed Sasha.

Inga slowly raised her tear-filled eyes. 'I'm sorry,' she whispered.

'I didn't tell you to speak, whore,' said Sasha. 'Turn and face the mirror.'

Inga did as she was told. The mirror was on top of the dressing table. She closed her eyes.

Sasha walked up behind her. He grabbed her neck and pushed her down so that she had to lean on the dressing-table. Then he undid his belt and took her from behind, roughly, cursing all the time. He didn't bother with a condom – he never did with his girls. They were checked by a doctor every two weeks, and if they were discovered to have an infection they were fined and beaten. A day off sick was a day's money lost, and that had to be made good by the girl. And a beating was necessary to make sure that they didn't make the same mistake again.

Sasha pounded into her until he came, then zipped up his trousers. Inga stayed where she was, sobbing quietly.

'Stand up,' said Sasha. She began to shake, but Sasha grabbed her by the hair and hauled her upright. He slapped her across the face, hard but not hard enough to break anything. She clamped her mouth shut, knowing that if she screamed the beating would be all the harder.

'You don't take a phone number from a punter,' he said. 'Ever.' He slapped her again. 'You don't meet a punter outside work,' he said. 'Ever.' He slapped her a third time. 'And you don't ever tell anybody my name.' Slap. 'Or my business.' Slap.

'Do you understand?'

Inga nodded and sniffed. 'Yes.'

'Lie down, on the bed.' Inga lay on her back. 'On your face, whore.'

Inga rolled over. Sasha slid off his belt and folded it double. He stood over Inga, swinging it gently. Then he laid into her.

Sasha's mansion was in West Hampstead and it was only when they drove past Maida Vale station that Solomon realised the two men really were driving him home. They hadn't said a word from the moment they'd climbed into the Mercedes and he had been gearing himself up for a last-ditch effort at either fight or escape. The two men were both bigger and stronger than he was and Solomon doubted that he could overpower one, let alone the two of them.

As the Mercedes drove down the Great Western Road, passing under the A40 Westway, Solomon asked the driver to pull up on the left. He didn't want them to know where he was staying.

The driver did as Solomon asked and pressed a button to unlock the rear passenger doors. Solomon got out and waited for them to drive away before he walked to Danny McLaren's flat. He let himself in and tiptoed to his bedroom. He wanted to soak in a bath of hot water but that might wake McLaren. He lay on the bed fully clothed, staring up at the ceiling and wondering what he should do next.

Sasha walked through Soho, his head up, his jaw thrust forward, his fists clenched. Two of his men, Karic and Rikki, followed behind. They had worked for him for more than ten years and he trusted them both with his life. During the war Karic had taken a bullet meant for Sasha. He had been running black-market food and medicine into the beleaguered city of Sarajevo when a Serbian gang had decided that they had a God-given right to a piece of the action. They hadn't put it to Sasha as directly as that, of course. They had arranged a meeting at a warehouse, ostensibly to discuss a shipment of antibiotics, when half a dozen men had opened fire with automatic weapons. If it hadn't been for the bullet-proof vest he wore under his parka and Karic pushing him out of the way, Sasha would have died that night. As it was, the Serbian gang-leader died, with four of his men.

Two young men walked by, hand in hand, simpering at each other like giggling schoolgirls. Sasha sneered at them. He hated homosexuals, hated them for their mincing ways and girlish outfits. There were no homosexuals in the Balkans. Not out in the open, anyway, but in Soho they seemed to be everywhere. It made no sense to Sasha that the city's predominant red-light area should also be home to so many gay bars.

He told Karic and Rikki to wait at the entrance to the alley while he walked down to the entrance to three of his flats. The door was open. Sasha looked up. In each window was a sign saying MODEL and all were illuminated with red lights. When Sasha had taken over the flats, the signs had been used to show whether the girls were available or not. If the signs were illuminated by a red light, the girl was free; if the light was off, she was servicing a client. One of the first things Sasha had done was to change the system – now the lights were on all the time. If necessary, the waiting clients could sit in the kitchen or the bathroom, or even a broom cupboard, and it was up to the maid to make sure that the girl kept working as efficiently as possible. If the kitchen, bathroom and broom cupboard were occupied, the maid could send the customer to another of Sasha's flats. It was all about keeping the girls on their backs with their legs open for as much of the time as possible. If they weren't screwing, they weren't earning. And if they weren't earning, they were no good to Sasha.

The girl on the first floor was a Latvian who worked under the name of Elsa. Sasha had bought her in Sarajevo for two thousand dollars and it had been money well spent. She had earned him a hundred times that over the past two years. He had introduced her to heroin – smoking not injecting because needlemarks put off the punters – soon after bringing her to London on a tourist visa, courtesy of a corrupt official at the British embassy in Sarajevo. Now Sasha charged her ten times the street price for heroin, but she was so doped up that she was none the wiser. The heroin made her more compliant, too, and there was no service she wouldn't offer, provided that the punter had enough money. She no longer asked Sasha when she would have worked off her contract. She belonged to him now, body and soul, and Sasha reckoned he could get another three years out of her before her looks faded and he sold her on.

He went up the stairs and knocked on the door to the first-floor flat. The maid opened it, a fifty-year-old woman who had worked there for more than a decade. She smiled when she saw it was Sasha and ushered him into the flat's tiny kitchen. There was a stool and a pile of well-thumbed *Penthouse* magazines. Sasha sat on the stool. The maid opened a drawer, took out a notebook and handed it to him. It had Elsa's name on the front and was a record of every customer she had seen, the time they arrived and left, the service provided and the amount of money paid. Every girl who worked for Sasha had a similar book. He flicked through to that day's entries. From the time that she'd opened for business at eleven o'clock in the morning, there were barely any gaps between clients, four minutes at most. 'Well done, Liz,' he said.

Liz groaned. 'She's a good worker, the punters like her. Lots of regulars.' Liz and the rest of the maids who worked in Sasha's flats were the eyes and ears of his business, and he treated them with respect. Girls he could buy by the dozen, but experienced maids were hard to find. They could spot if a girl was ripping him off, if she was getting too attached to a particular punter, or if she was getting lazy or giving clients poor service. A good maid would always talk to the punter on the way out, to check that everything had been satisfactory, and that he hadn't been asked to pay for any extras mid-session. And Liz, like all Sasha's maids, would search the bedroom periodically for hidden money when the girls were in the bathroom.

'No problems?' Sasha asked.

'Everything's hunky-dory,' she said. She opened another drawer and took out that day's earnings, the banknotes folded into one-hundred-pound bundles. Seven in all. Seven hundred pounds, and Elsa was barely half-way through her shift. Sasha pocketed it.

'Do you want a coffee?' asked Liz. She looked a good decade older than her true age, the result of too many cigarettes, a liking for neat gin and twenty years on the game. Her main claim to fame was three years as mistress to a well-known TV game-show host who had put her up in an apartment in Knightsbridge, leased her a convertible Mercedes, and spent every Wednesday afternoon making love to her while he was dressed in a black cocktail dress and a long blonde wig.

'No, thank you,' said Sasha, pocketing the money. 'I just want a word with Elsa and then I'll be off.'

The bedroom door opened and they heard Elsa pad to the bathroom. Liz left the kitchen and showed the punter out. She came back grinning and waving a five-pound note. 'Another satisfied customer, and a tip too,' she said. She slipped the money into her purse.

Sasha went out into the hallway and banged on the door. 'Bedroom, Elsa,' he said.

'Sasha?'

'You're expecting someone else? And don't waste hot water. Do you have any idea what my bills are for this place?'

He walked into the bedroom and sat down on the bed. The room was illuminated with a red bulb. Girls always looked better under red light. Sexier. There was a vase of flowers on a table by the bed, and a teddy bear holding a red heart with 'I love you' written on it.

Elsa appeared in the doorway, wearing matching black

bra, suspenders and pants. She slipped on her high heels and smiled at Sasha, then her lip trembled as she saw that he was holding the bear. 'It's not mine,' she said. 'It was here when I came. It must be Abi's.'

Abi was the girl who worked the night shift. A Latvian. Her English was good and she loved to talk. She had the knack of making her more susceptible clients fall for her. It usually started with flowers and soft toys, then perfume, and before long they'd be offering to marry her or set her up as a mistress if they already had a wife. Sasha had already got heavy with two who'd lost their hearts to her, and he'd thrashed her twice in an attempt to teach her the error of her ways. She was there to screw, not to flirt. Encouraging repeat business was all well and good, but lovesick punters were at best an inconvenience, and at worst a danger. Many of Sasha's girls had overstayed their visas and a call to Immigration might mean deportation.

Sasha smiled at Elsa and put the bear back on the bedside table. He patted the bed next to him and told her to sit down. She did as she was told, her hands in her lap. She was a bit thin even for Sasha's taste, a result of her heroin addiction, but she looked about sixteen in the school uniform that a lot of her clients asked her to wear. And the uniform meant an extra ten pounds. Sasha had drummed that into all his girls. Whatever the customer wanted, he got. For a price. If they wanted to spank her, that was an extra twenty pounds. Oral without a condom another twenty. It was the McDonald's principle. A customer drops in for a burger, but McDonald's won't let him get away that lightly. You want fries with that? How about a Coke? If a punter walked in off the street for a hand-job or a blow-job, he was looking to pay thirty or forty pounds. If the girl could talk him into a few extras, he would pay sixty or seventy. And if she could talk him into the works she would get a hundred and sixty for an hour, which more often than not she could turn into a forty-five-minute session. Providing the guy had come and come well, there was no reason for him to hang around.

Sasha took the photograph of the Kosovar girl from his jacket pocket. 'Have you seen this girl?' he asked.

Elsa brushed her long black hair behind her ear. 'I don't think so,' she said.

'Her name's Nicole. Or Amy.'

'Sasha, you know I don't go out with the other girls.'

Sasha put a hand on her leg and squeezed gently. 'Elsa, I'm not accusing you of anything.' Sasha made it clear to the girls that they weren't to socialise with girls who worked for other employers, but he was enough of a realist to know that they would bump into other prostitutes from time to time. 'I just want to know if you've seen her. You go to discos in Leicester Square, I know that. I'm just asking if you remember seeing her. Or if anyone has mentioned a girl from Kosovo called Amy or Nicole.'

Elsa shook her head. 'No. I am sure.'

Sasha took the picture from her and held it close to her face. 'I want you to remember this face, Elsa, and if you see her I want you to phone me.'

Elsa nodded.

'Good girl. I'll send Karic up with your present,' said Sasha. He never carried drugs himself. It wasn't worth the risk.

'Thank you,' said Elsa.

'How about showing me how grateful you are?' said Sasha.

Elsa slid off the bed and on to her knees. Sasha opened

his legs and lay back on the bed as she eased down his zip. He looked at his watch as Elsa went down on him. It was important to have the girls service him because it reminded them that he owned them, that he was the only man who could have them for free. But he was only going to give her ten minutes. Every minute she had him in her mouth was a minute when she could be opening her legs for a paying punter.

Solomon took off his clothes and handed them to the big man. 'Okay?' he asked. The big man scowled at Solomon and made a small circling gesture with his index finger. Solomon turned slowly. The big man grunted, handed Solomon a fleecy white towel and opened the door to the sauna. Hot, cloying steam billowed out and condensed on his face.

Solomon stepped inside. It was lined with pine benches racked up to head height with space for fifty people to sit, but only one man was inside, ladling water on to a pile of hot stones. There was a hiss and clouds of steam swirled up towards the ceilings. 'Hot enough for you, Solomon?' asked the man, grinning. Rolls of fat cascaded over the towel around his waist and his several chins dripped sweat. His hair, so black that it must have been dyed, was swept back and he had a thick moustache.

'Do you take all your meetings in here, Marco?' asked Solomon. The door closed shut behind him.

Marco Montanaro tossed the ladle into a wooden pail of water. 'Just cops,' he said, and sat back. 'First, there's nowhere to hide a recording device. Second, no transmitting signal can get through the metal walls behind the wood. Third, I like to see cops sweat.'

'Haven't you heard I'm not with the Met any more?'

Montanaro waved at the bank of benches to Solomon's right. Solomon sat down and opened his mouth wide to draw more air into his lungs. Montanaro grinned at his discomfort. 'Your phone call came out of the blue. You wanted nothing to do with me when you were in Vice.'

'I just wanted a chat,' said Solomon.

'I hope you're not asking for money.'

'I didn't want your money then and I don't want it now. But I need some information.'

Montanaro laughed harshly. 'You want me to give you information? Why, in God's name, would I tell you anything?'

Because you owe me,' said Solomon. 'If I'd told CIB what I knew way back when, you'd have gone down.'

'You're not going to tell me you acted out of altruistic reasons, are you? You didn't grass on your colleagues because you were scared of what they'd do to you.'

'It was more complicated than that,' said Solomon.

'I think you've confused me with someone who gives a shit,' said Montanaro. He ladled more water on to the hot stones. 'You ruined a lot of lives – but not mine.'

'I know,' said Solomon.

'Duggan was a good cop. Things ran smoothly while he was top dog. Do you know what he's doing now?'

Solomon nodded.

'And what about your own life, Solomon? Is it better now? Did you profit from your altruism?'

'It's . . . different,' said Solomon. 'But I don't regret what I did.'

'How very fucking noble of you,' said Montanaro. He spread his legs wide and leaned back against the wooden bench.

Solomon wiped his hands across his face. They came away soaking wet. The heat was stifling and he had to fight to stop himself panting. 'What's the story with these Albanians?' he asked.

Montanaro shifted a little. 'That's what you wanted to talk about? The Albanians?'

'I'm told that you and the Albanians are in bed together, pretty much. That they're moving their girls into London – and into your flats.'

'That's old news. What's your interest?'

'I'm trying to find a girl – a working girl. I think she's here in London, but I've had a run-in with an Albanian guy who says he controls Soho. Now, the way I remember it it was the Maltese who ran Soho.'

'We still do,' said Montanaro tersely.

'Do you know a guy called Sasha?'

'Ah,' said Montanaro. 'He's been filling your head with nonsense, has he?'

'So you know him?'

Montanaro smiled thinly. 'We have a business arrangement.'

'He supplies the girls, they work out of your flats?'

Montanaro nodded.

'He didn't strike me as the sort of man who'd be satisfied with an equal partnership,' said Solomon.

Montanaro shrugged.

'When I worked Vice, you had the flats and you had the girls. Plus the clubs and the massage parlours. No one else got a look in. Why are you so keen to work with the Albanians now?'

'They've got good-quality girls. They work cheap, they do anything – they know what'll happen if they don't.'

'I seem to remember that you weren't a soft touch with your girls,' said Solomon.

'The Albanians are something else,' said Montanaro.

'This doesn't add up,' Solomon said. 'You're letting them walk all over you.'

'Fuck off!' Montanaro jabbed his finger at Solomon. 'No one walks over me! No one!'

Solomon held up his hands in surrender. There was nothing to be gained from upsetting Montanaro. Solomon needed his help. 'No offence,' he said.

Montanaro glared at Solomon for a few seconds, then smiled slowly. 'You've got balls, Solomon. Big, clanging balls. You've no back-up now, no team behind you, and you know that I could crush you like an ant and no one in the world would give a shit. True?'

'Pretty much.'

'Yet still you give me a hard time.'

'Frankly, Marco, I've nothing left to lose.'

Montanaro picked up a bottle of Evian and drank from it, then wiped his mouth with a small towel, which he draped round his neck. He poured some of the Evian water over his hair and let it cascade down his back. 'So is your interest the girl, or this Albanian?'

'The girl. But I thought if I could understand what's going on with the Albanians, I might have more chance of finding her. He says he doesn't know her, but he also says he controls all the girls in Soho.'

'Yeah, well, that's bollocks,' said Montanaro. 'He has a big chunk of them, but there are others. And we still have some. Then there's the blacks, and the triads in Chinatown.'

'But you're pulling out.'

'We own the flats. The Albanians are supplying us with girls.'

'But the money from the girls goes to their pimps, right? The Albanians?'

'We get well paid for the flats they use.'

'So your girls are working elsewhere?'

'Now you're getting the picture.'

'But where? Soho and Chinatown have always been the centre of the sex trade. How's that changed?'

Montanaro's grin widened. 'The Internet,' he said. 'The sex trade is right across London now, Soho's days are numbered, but the Albanians haven't realised it yet.'

Solomon frowned. 'The Internet? You mean virtual sex?'

Montanaro laughed out loud. 'There's nothing virtual about it, Solomon. It's real sex, but instead of postcards in phone-boxes, we advertise on the Internet. Escort-agency websites. Our girls can be based anywhere in London. The West End. The City. South of the river. We can put the girls where the punters are.'

'How do the punters find the girls?'

'They go on line, they visit a website, then they call a number. They say which girl they want, we give them the address. The website's got photographs, descriptions, general location, the price. The punter can choose exactly what he wants at a price he can afford.' Montanaro poured more water over his head and shook his wet hair. Drops of water splashed over Solomon's face. 'It's big business, Solomon. Huge. The first agencies went on line in the late nineties, now there are hundreds. And we've got some of the biggest. The money's way more than we got from the Soho walk-ups. We've got one up-market agency where the girls charge five hundred quid an hour.'

Solomon's jaw dropped. 'People pay that?'

'Thousands of people pay that. And more. The girls charge three grand for an overnight and men are queuing up to pay. Some of our girls are booked weeks in advance.'

'More money than sense,' said Solomon. He tried to work out what a girl charging five hundred pounds an hour could earn in a year. It was lottery money.

'High-rollers,' said Montanaro. 'Guy works for a bank in New York. His bosses send him to London for a few days. He can go to the Internet, find the girl he wants, pre-book her with an email, then pay with his credit card. The credit-card slip will show he paid for a meal at a restaurant. He gets the best sex of his life and his company pays for it.'

Solomon stared longingly at Montanaro's bottle of Evian water, but the Maltese clearly had no intention of sharing it.

'We've got other agencies where the girls charge a couple of hundred quid an hour, we've got a domination site for the City types who want to pay for a trashing, and we've started bringing over Thai girls to work for an Oriental site. Bargain basement, a hundred and twenty quid an hour. Something for everyone.'

'And Vice leave you alone?'

'Vice couldn't give a shit, and it doesn't cost us a penny in backhanders,' said Montanaro. 'We're taking it off the streets. No phone-box advertising, no signs in doorways, no hookers harassing civilians. Just nice apartments in nice areas, all discreet, all above board.'

'But still illegal, right?'

Montanaro laughed. 'You know the legalities as well as I do, Solomon. But with all the info on the Internet, solicitation isn't an issue. The punter knows what he's going to get before he calls us.'

'You list the services on the site?'

'Nah, that'd be a red rag to Vice. But we don't have to. The prostitute-review sites take care of that.'

'What are they?' asked Solomon.

Montanaro ladled more water on the hot stones and breathed in the steam. 'Why the hell am I helping you, Solomon? What have you ever done for me?'

Solomon didn't reply. Now that he was no longer working for the Met, he wasn't a threat, and Montanaro probably didn't get too many opportunities to boast.

'Okay,' said Montanaro eventually. 'This is how it works. Prostitute-review sites are like restaurant-review columns. Punters write about the girls they've seen, how much they paid, what the girls did. There's one called Punternet.com that we use – our people file reviews saying what the girls do. That way the girls never have to solicit. If a punter started trying to get them to list their services, they'd smell a rat. There's no need any more – it's all there on the Internet. It's as close to legal as it's possible to be.'

'Except for you living off immoral earnings?'

'Almost impossible to prove. As I said, my girls are right across London. We've got them in serviced apart-ments in Chelsea, riverside apartments on the Isle of Dogs, mews houses in Chelsea. Vice don't have the resources to mount an investigation into our operation. We're just too big. And if they did, do you think the girls would give evidence? Of course they wouldn't. Do you think they'd be able to follow the money trail? Of course they couldn't. My money's well hidden. Millions, all salted away.' He leaned forward conspiratorially. 'Do you have any idea how much we made from the agencies last year?' he asked.

Solomon shook his head.

'Eight million pounds,' said Montanaro. 'And that's profit, not turnover.'

Montanaro grinned at Solomon's look of disbelief.

'That's right. It's big business, Solomon. Now you understand why we're happy to let the Albanians into Soho. We get the rents from the flats, but we're going to sell them soon. If the Albanians want to buy, fine. If not, we'll sell to any one of a hundred property-development firms who are dying to get into Soho. Have you any idea what our portfolio's worth? Tens of millions. We've had some of those flats since the fifties, when no one wanted to buy there. How much did you make last year, Solomon?'

'Enough for me,' said Solomon. 'I've got simple tastes.'

Montanaro laughed. 'How long did you work Vice?'

'Five years.'

'And what did you achieve, huh?'

It wasn't an argument Solomon wanted to be drawn into, because he knew what Montanaro was getting at. When it came to prostitution, the legal system was pretty much a revolving door. Prostitutes charged with soliciting would be fined and back on the streets to earn the money to pay the fine within an hour of walking out of the court. If the police went after the pimps, the maximum sentence for living off immoral earnings was seven years and most ended up serving a year or so. But the girls simply found another pimp and carried on working. When the police went in with immigration officers, they'd deport girls who were working illegally after photographing and finger-printing them – but new girls would be moved into the flats before the old ones were on the plane home. And more often than not the girls they deported would be back in the United Kingdom within weeks on a different passport. When neighbours complained about streetwalking prostitutes, Vice could move the girls on – but they didn't stop working, they just moved to another location. If they closed down a brothel, another would open up elsewhere.

'Now ask me what I achieved over those five years, Solomon.'

Solomon didn't have to. He'd seen Montanaro's file five years earlier. Seen the surveillance photographs of his house in Belgravia. The imported cars. The yacht. The private jet. He could only imagine how much the man had moved on since then. 'You don't have to rub my nose in it, Marco.'

'I know I don't have to, but it makes me feel good,' said Montanaro gleefully. 'You wasted those years, Solomon. You think the public cares about prostitutes plying their trade? Most people would sooner have it legalised. At least then the hookers would be paying tax. And charging VAT.'

'I've heard the same argument a million times about drugs,' said Solomon.

'Drugs are different,' said Montanaro. 'No one ever died from an overdose of sex.'

'There's Aids.'

'Hookers don't get Aids, and if they do it's from drugs. Hookers know all about safe sex, Solomon. You won't find any of our girls doing anything without a condom. If they get Aids it's because they're screwing a dodgy boyfriend or sharing needles. And any punter who screws a working girl without protection deserves everything he gets. Prostitution is a victimless crime and in a few years the Government is going to recognise that and legalise it. Trust me.' He took a swig of Evian. 'Anything else I can help you with?' he asked sarcastically.

'If I showed you a photograph of the girl I'm looking for, would you tell me if she works for you?'

'Where's she from?'

'Kosovo. Near Priština. She came through Sarajevo.'

Montanaro grimaced. 'Most of the girls we use in our agencies are from the EU,' he said. 'No immigration hassles that way. We use Thais and Chinese, but only if they've got valid student visas.' He chuckled. 'We've got Tony Blair to thank for that. Language students can legally work twenty hours a week, and Immigration aren't concerned about the type of work they do. Escorting is a valid job, so providing they don't get caught soliciting, they're not breaking the law.'

'You don't use girls from the Balkans, then?'

'A few, maybe. They have to speak good English because in our business they work alone. In the walk-ups it's different because there's a maid who can do the talking. And we need the cream of the girls because their photographs are on the website. With the walk-ups it's less important because by the time a punter's through the door he's usually too wound up to change his mind.'

'This girl's pretty,' said Solomon. 'And young.'

Montanaro nodded. 'Give the picture to the man outside, and a phone number. Someone'll be in touch.'

Solomon stood up and stretched out his hand. 'Thanks.'

Montanaro stared at the outstretched hand with a frown. Then he offered his own. The two men shook. 'I really don't understand you, Solomon,' said Montanaro.

'I'm not sure I understand myself,' said Solomon.

The big man was waiting outside with his clothes. Solomon took out a copy of the photograph of Nicole and scribbled his mobile phone number at the bottom. 'Mr Montanaro is expecting this,' he said. The big man took it but said nothing. He watched silently as Solomon dressed, then showed him out.

Solomon caught a black cab to Bayswater and found an Internet café in a road off Queensway. He bought a double espresso and a bottle of water and sat down opposite a terminal in the corner. He drank half the bottle of water, then clicked on to Internet Explorer.

There were two dozen screens in the room, and all but a handful were occupied, mainly by foreign students tapping away at emails. Solomon turned his to the side so that no one could see what he was looking at.

He tapped in 'www.punternet.com', sipped his espresso and waited. The home page welcomed him to Punternet and offered him a list of services including Field Reports, Message Board, Service Provider Database and Amateur Photos.

Solomon clicked on the Service Provider Database link, smiling at the euphemism. It took him to a list of escort agencies and independent working girls, almost all of whom had their own websites. He clicked through to the website of a girl called Alison. It was professionally done, with pages devoted to the services she provided – pretty much everything, so far as Solomon could tell – her prices, and two galleries of photographs. She was a pretty girl, Latvian, with long blonde hair, long legs and surgically enhanced breasts. There was an email address.

Solomon clicked back to the Service Provider Database. There were screens full of entries. The agencies had names like Fine Date, Photogirls, AAA-Gal, Agency Provocateur, Legal Escorts, and Oriental Angels. Solomon clicked through some of the links at random. Most had a dozen girls or so on their books, but some had more than fifty. The websites differed in layout, but the content was pretty much the same. Pictures of girls, sometimes with faces obscured or blurred, but more often than not there was no attempt to hide their features. Descriptions of the girl, including the all-important measurements, the rates, the cost per hour. They didn't mention sex, just the cost for an hour of the girl's time. Montanaro was right: with no mention of sex on the site it would be difficult for the police ever to prove that agency owners were involved in prostitution.

There must have been thousands of girls on the Punternet database, and Solomon smiled as Dragan Jovanovic's voice echoed in his mind: 'A needle in a haystick.'

He clicked back to Punternet and ran down the list of names in the database. There was no Nicole. Two girls called Amy were working as independents and he clicked through to them. One was an overweight brunette with a penchant for anal sex – educated to A-level standard, as she coyly described it – while the other was a black girl based in Bristol.

Solomon clicked on the link to the Message Board, where prostitutes and punters could leave messages for each other. Like scribbling notes on a lavatory wall, thought Solomon. He flicked through the message threads. Juvenile chat, mostly. Punters looking for hookers, prostitutes complaining about clients, inane poetry and juvenile rantings. Solomon clicked on to a message from a man using the handle 'Wonderboy', who wanted advice on a rash that had appeared on his genitals. The general feeling among the Punternet community was that he should see his GP.

He clicked through to Field Reports, and called up all the ones that had been posted over the past seven days. There were just under three hundred.

He sat back, sipping his espresso. The search engine showed the name of the girl being reviewed and her location. He chose one at random. Helen of North London.

The report followed a standard template: the name of the girl, the name of the reviewer, the location, time of day, how much the experience had cost, how long it had lasted, and details of how to contact the girl, including a phone number. The reviewer who'd written about Helen used the handle BigTodger. The report was the sort of thing a schoolboy might have written, full of spelling mistakes. Big Todger described the flat where Helen worked, the state of the bedroom, what she looked like without her clothes, what she had done to him and he to her. It was more information than Solomon needed or wanted. But he could see what Montanaro meant: once a punter had read the review, there was no need for solicitation or importuning. Both parties would know exactly what was on offer.

He read a dozen reports, then used the search engine to see if there were any reports of a Nicole. There were none. He looked for reports on anyone called Amy and came up with several dozen from girls across the country. He read them all. None sounded like Nicole.

Solomon sighed. If he didn't know the name she was using, it would take for ever to find her.

His mobile phone warbled and he answered it.

'Jack Solomon?' grunted a man.

'Yeah.'

'Mr Montanaro said I should call you.'

'Yeah.'

'This girl. The picture you gave Mr Montanaro. She's not one of ours.'

'Right. Thanks,' said Solomon. The line went dead. Solomon slipped the phone back into his pocket. He waved at a waitress and ordered a second espresso. He might be looking for a needle in a haystack, but he could do it faster on the Internet than visiting Soho walk-ups. He clicked back to the Punternet database and started at the top, clicking through to the website of AAA-Gals. There were half a dozen pretty Oriental girls. Solomon sighed. One down, several hundred to go.

Colin Duggan buttoned his coat and walked out into the street, his shoulders hunched against the wind. He hated his job, but he was stuck with it until his retirement date, and that was three years away. If he left before then, his pension would be cut to ribbons. He was little more than a clerk, taking in lost items and keeping the office's computerised inventory up to date. The high spot of his day had been the young secretary who'd turned up to claim the mobile phone she'd left in the back of a black cab. She'd been wearing a low-cut top and, so far as Duggan could tell, no bra.

'Penny for them,' said a voice to Duggan's left.

'Fuck off, Solomon,' snarled Duggan, without looking round.

'Free country, last I heard,' said Solomon, lighting a Marlboro.

He shoved the packet under Duggan's nose. Duggan shook his head. 'What do you want?'

'The girl. Nicole Shala. Any joy?'

'If there'd been any joy I'd have called, wouldn't I?'

'Not in the mood you're in.'

Duggan glared at him. 'The way we left it was that I'd phone you if I found anything. I didn't phone you. You used to be a fucking detective, draw your own conclusions.'

'So there was nothing on the computer?'

Duggan stopped and stared at Solomon. 'I ran her name through CRO. Nothing. I got a mate to run her picture through the Home Office computer and she hasn't been deported. That's all I can do.'

Solomon blew smoke up into the air. 'Fancy a drink?'

'I'm going home.'

'One for the road?'

Duggan swore and started walking again. Solomon followed him. Duggan headed for the pub. He had nothing to rush home for: his wife had died ten years earlier, and even Solomon was better company than the television set and a microwaved dinner. Duggan pushed open the pub door, walked to a table and sat down while Solomon bought the drinks.

Solomon put a tumbler of Bell's and ice in front of him and sat down. 'I went to see Montanaro,' he said.

Duggan spluttered into his whisky, 'You did what?' He looked at Solomon as if he'd lost his mind. 'What game are you playing? You go to see him and then you come and see me. What is this? A fucking set-up?'

'Don't be ridiculous.'

Duggan leaned over and patted Solomon's chest, then ran his hand down his shirt to his stomach.

'I'm not wearing a wire,' said Solomon.

Duggan didn't say anything as he ran his hand around Solomon's back and up between his shoulders.

'Colin, for God's sake . . .'

Duggan removed his hand. 'Why don't you just sod off back to Bosnia?' he asked.

'Not until I've found the girl.'

'Well, keep the hell away from me. Haven't you screwed me over enough as it is? How's it going to look if you're seen with Montanaro, then spotted talking to me?'

'No one's following me. No one even knows I'm in town.' Solomon sipped his lager. He gestured at Duggan's now-empty glass. 'You want another?'

Duggan sat fuming until Solomon returned with another whisky. 'Why did you go to see him?' he asked.

'He controls a big chunk of the Soho girls. I wanted to know if he'd seen Nicole.'

'And had he?'

'Says not.'

'Believe him?'

Solomon looked pained. 'No need for him to lie, not now.'

'Maybe he just wanted you to piss off.'

'He'd be in good company, then,' said Solomon.

Despite himself Duggan grinned.

'He seemed pretty sanguine about getting into bed with the Albanians,' asked Solomon. 'The way Montanaro tells it, he's moving into the Internet escort-agency business and the Albanians are putting their girls into the Soho walk-ups.'

'Sounds right.'

'The Albanians are a mean bunch,' said Solomon.

'Who isn't, these days?' said Duggan. 'Yardies, Russians. Colombians – London's full of tough bastards. The home-grown villains don't stand a chance.'

'Thing is, the Albanians aren't going to be happy with a profit-sharing arrangement. They went head to head with the Mafia in Italy and won.'

'Let me think if I give a shit,' said Duggan. He sat in silence for a few seconds. 'No, I don't,' he said.

'You don't want to see a gang war, do you? You're still a cop,' said Solomon.

Duggan smiled thinly. 'No, I'm not. I'm just marking time until retirement.'

'Bullshit,' said Solomon. 'Once a cop, always a cop.'

Duggan drained his glass. 'What are you going to do now?' he asked.

'I'm working through the Internet sites. At least they've got photographs.'

'They're not all genuine. Same as the postcards in phone-boxes. What you see isn't necessarily what you get.'

'Is that the voice of experience?'

'I never went with a brass. Never have done and never will. Some of the guys didn't mind dipping their wick, but that's one line I never crossed.'

'I was joking.'

'Yeah, well, that sense of humour is going to put you in hospital one day.'

Solomon finished his lager. 'Another?'

Duggan shook his head, and Solomon stood up. Duggan watched him leave. Despite everything that had happened, Duggan liked Solomon. Not that he'd ever tell him – not after the damage he'd done. He went to the bar and ordered another double Bell's and ice. He hadn't planned on drinking but, these days, once he'd started, he found it difficult to stop.

★

Solomon sipped his double espresso and clicked back to the Punternet database. He was about half-way through the list of escort agencies and independent girls and so far he had three possibilities. He was working his way alphabetically down the list and checking every photograph on the sites. The independent girls were easy to rule out, but the agencies took more time. They tended to have a page of pictures of all the girls on their books, and clicking on one of the individual photographs led to another page devoted to that particular girl with more photographs and a potted biography. Solomon could dismiss Oriental and black girls immediately, but he checked every page of Caucasian girls, blonde, brunette or redhead. Nicole was a natural blonde but she'd dyed her hair black when she went to Sarajevo and might have changed it again.

The girls who caused Solomon the most problems were those whose faces were obscured by computer-generated blurring or black strips across the eyes. Then he had to go by body shape and that was difficult because Nicole had been wearing a long dress in the wedding photograph: on the websites most of the girls wore the minimum of clothing and in many cases were naked.

He could rule out a lot of the girls by age. Nicole was nineteen and he dismissed anyone who described herself as twenty-five or older.

Of the three on his short-list, the faces of two had been obscured electronically. Both were blondes and worked for agencies. One was using the name Savana, the other Bianca. The third girl was an independent, based in Earl's Court, and was calling herself Nikita. Her face wasn't blurred or blacked out, but in all the photographs it was turned away from the camera.

He'd obtained colour printouts of the three girls from the young Arab man who ran the Internet café. The first time the guy had grinned knowingly and winked, but Solomon had given him a withering look and the second and third had been handed over without comment.

Solomon clicked on to a website run by an agency called Legal Escorts. The home page showed a pretty brunette smiling slyly at the camera. Beneath the photograph was a warning that the site contained information of a sexual nature and anyone under eighteen should click on a red 'exit' button. Solomon clicked on 'enter'.

The next page was a group of thumbnail photographs of girls, more than twenty in all. No names, no details. Four were Oriental and two were black. One by one Solomon clicked on the Caucasian girls and went through to their individual pages. The sixth girl he clicked on was called Amy, and when her page filled the screen Solomon knew he'd found Nicole. There were eight photographs on the page. In most her face was turned away, but in one she was facing the camera. She was wearing a school uniform with white knee socks and her hair was tied in two pigtails. She was sitting on a bed with an ornate wooden headboard, her legs apart.

Below the photographs was a list of prices and 'outcall only'. That meant Solomon couldn't visit her at her flat: she had to come to him. The agency charged £200 for an hour, and up to £1500 for an all-night stay. There were two phone numbers, both mobiles.

Solomon clicked on 'print', then went over to the cash desk to collect the sheet of paper and pay for his session. He stared at the picture. Nicole's hair was dark brown, several inches longer than it had been in the wedding photograph, and her breasts looked a little fuller, but her smile was an exact match. A little sly, mischievous, nervous.

He read through her details. The biography said that she was from Italy, but he decided the agency owners preferred to advertise their girls as being from the European Union rather than the Balkans. He folded the sheet of paper and slid it into his inside pocket. It had been a needle in a haystack, but he had found her.

Solomon sipped his Kingfisher as McLaren rattled off the order without consulting the menu. The Indian waiter was equally casual, not using a notebook. 'And two more Kingfishers,' said McLaren. 'Large ones.' It was just before nine and the restaurant was almost empty. The real trade started as the pubs closed but McLaren hadn't had any lunch so he'd been eager for an early dinner. Early for McLaren, anyway – he didn't usually eat until midnight. His eating habits went against all medical advice but in the years Solomon had known him he'd never had a day off work and there wasn't an ounce of fat on him.

'I need a favour,' said Solomon.

'Sure,' said McLaren.

'I need to borrow the flat,' said Solomon.

'You know you can stay as long as you want.'

'It's a bit more specific than that.' Solomon slid the printout of Nicole's web page across the table.

McLaren scanned it, then grinned. 'Outcall only,' he said.

'Yeah, so it's either your place or a hotel.'

'So my flat's going to be a knocking shop, is that it?'

'I'm not planning to have sex with her. Cross my heart.'

'Wouldn't blame you if you did, mate. She's a little cutie. School uniforms always do it for me.'

'Stupid thing to ask, right?' said Solomon.

McLaren raised his glass of beer in salute. 'You go for it,' he said. 'You sure she'll come to a private address?'

'It says she visits hotels and homes in Central London. You know you're going to have to be out?'

McLaren grinned. 'Threesome's out of the question, then?'

'I'm serious, Danny. If there's two guys in the flat, it'll spook her.'

The waiter brought over a plate of poppadums and pickle tray. Danny pressed his fingers into the centre of the stack, then dipped a shard into the mango chutney. 'What time were you thinking of?'

'Dunno,' said Solomon.

'They charge by the hour, right, so she's not going to be there overnight.'

'You know how much it costs for her to stay overnight?' McLaren raised an eyebrow. 'One and a half grand, said Solomon. McLaren gasped. 'Back in Sarajevo it would set you back a hundred quid.'

'The girl did good.'

'Not necessarily,' said Solomon. 'If she's got a pimp, she might not be seeing any of the money.'

'But how long's she going to be in the flat?'

'I'm going to pay for an hour, but I'm hoping she'll talk to me for longer. I'm going to ask her to go back with me to Sarajevo.'

'At one and a half grand a day, that's going to cost you,' said McLaren.

'Her family were murdered, and she must want that avenged.'

'So why's she in London?' asked McLaren.

Solomon didn't reply. It was the one question he

couldn't answer. But maybe Nicole could. The curries arrived, with two fresh beers. McLaren reached over and clinked his bottle against Solomon's. 'Just be careful, yeah? You've already had one run-in with a pimp.'

'Two, actually.'

'What?'

'It's a long story.'

Solomon sat down on McLaren's sofa and studied the notebook on the coffee table. He had written down the number of the pay-as-you-go mobile that he was using, the name he was planning to use to book Nicole, McLaren's address and 'AMY'. He rehearsed in his mind exactly what he was going to say, then tapped out the number on the mobile.

A woman answered, middle-aged with an East European accent. She didn't give the name of the agency, just asked if she could help.

'Is that Legal Escorts?' asked Solomon.

'It is. How can I help you?'

'I'd like to book Amy for an hour today. Is that okay?'

'Have you used the agency before?'

'No, I haven't.'

'What time would you like to see Amy?'

'Six o'clock,' said Solomon. It was just after four.

'And your name is?'

'Richard Williams.'

'And what is the name of your hotel, Richard?'

'Er, I was wondering if Amy could come and see me at my home. In Bayswater.'

'Of course. I'll have to confirm the appointment with her and call you back. What is your number?'

Solomon gave her the number of his mobile. Then he

paced up and down until the woman called him back. She confirmed the appointment for six and wrote down his address. 'The fee for an hour of Amy's time will be two hundred pounds,' she said. 'She might ask you to contribute towards her taxi fare, but that is your choice, Richard. Thank you for calling.'

She cut the connection. There had been no mention of sex, no discussion of the services Amy would offer. No solicitation, no importuning. A totally legal transaction so far.

The intercom buzzed and Solomon jumped. He picked up the receiver. 'Yeah, hello?' he said.

'This is Amy,' said a voice.

'Amy, come on up,' said Solomon, and pressed the button to unlock the street door. When the flat bell rang, he took a couple of deep breaths, then opened the door. His face fell when he saw the girl standing there. It wasn't Nicole.

She smiled brightly at him, showing crooked teeth. 'Hi, I'm Amy,' she said. She was tall, an inch or two below six feet, with long brown hair, parted in the middle, her eyes a blue so deep that he was sure she was wearing tinted contact lenses. She was wearing a grey fake fur coat with the collar turned up, tight black trousers and high-heeled black-leather boots.

Solomon said nothing. He stood where he was, his hand on the door, staring at her. He'd asked for Amy and there had been only one girl called Amy on the Legal Escorts website. The girl in front of him was taller, older, with a squarish jaw and a more prominent nose. She was pretty, striking even, but she wasn't Amy. The girl's smile tightened a fraction. 'Aren't you going to ask me in?' she said.

Solomon forced a smile and opened the door. 'Sorry,' he said.

She walked past him, took off her coat and tossed it on to one of the sofas. 'You have my money?' she asked.

He took a wad of ten twenty-pound notes from his back pocket and gave it to her. She counted it, then pulled a Nokia mobile from her bag. 'I'm just going to call the agency to let them know that everything is okay,' she said.

She turned her back on him as she made the call, talking to the woman at the agency in what sounded like Russian, then turned back to him. 'Can I use your bathroom, please?' she asked.

Solomon nodded and showed her where it was. She smiled, blew him a kiss, and closed the door. He heard a tap running.

His mind was in a whirl. The last thing he'd expected was the wrong girl to turn up. If he told the agency he wanted the girl on the website instead, they'd wonder why. He'd already told the woman on the phone that he'd never met Amy. He'd paid this girl two hundred pounds for her time, so if he didn't have sex with her she'd suspect something was wrong. He grabbed his mobile and called McLaren, saying a silent prayer that he wasn't out of the office or on another call. His luck was in – his friend answered on the second ring. Solomon spoke quickly, keeping his voice low. 'Danny, call me back in ten minutes. Pretend you're my boss and I'm needed in the office.'

'Pig ugly is she, mate?'

'Just do it, please,' said Solomon. 'I'll explain later.'

The tap stopped running. Solomon put his mobile on the coffee table. 'Can I get you a drink?' he shouted.

'No, thank you,' the girl shouted back.

Solomon got a can of lager from the fridge and sat down on one of the sofas. He popped the tab and sipped it.

A minute or so later the bathroom door opened. The girl had taken off her clothes and wrapped a towel around herself. It reached to just below her bottom, showing off her long, coltish legs. She dropped her clothes on the arm of the sofa and put her boots on the floor. 'Shall we go to the bedroom?' she asked.

Solomon grinned and waved at the sofa. 'Slow down,' he said. 'I like to take it slowly.'

Her smile widened. 'Ah, you like to be seduced, do you?' she asked. She walked slowly towards him, licking her upper lip. 'That's good, because I like to seduce men.'

Solomon took another drink from his can of lager as she slid on to the sofa next to him and ran her fingertips along his inner thigh, staring into his eyes and pouting. Solomon had to force himself not to laugh – she was a terrible actress. 'You're very pretty,' he said. That much at least was true. Her skin was soft, white and flawless, and he could see an impressive cleavage above the towel. She had small, perfect toes with nails painted a bright red, and she ran one foot up and down the back of his calf.

'Thank you,' she said. 'And you are a very handsome man.' She blew in his ear and stroked the back of his neck with her right hand while her left continued to wander up and down his thigh.

'But you're not Amy, are you?'

Her hands stopped moving. 'You do not like me?' she asked.

'I like you fine, but I asked for Amy.'

'You don't want me?' There was a hard edge to her voice, and the hand on his neck was no longer stroking him but gripping tightly.

'No, I'm more than happy with you,' said Solomon. He leaned forward and kissed her. Her lips parted, and she slipped her tongue inside his mouth, moaning softly. Her hand caressed his neck again and she slid her leg over his so that she was sitting astride him.

Solomon broke away, gasping for breath. 'Hey, slowly,' he said.

She started to unbutton his shirt and tried to kiss him again. Solomon felt himself grow hard and pushed her away, laughing. 'You're terrible!' he said.

Her face fell. 'What you mean, I'm terrible?'

'I don't mean you're bad, I mean you're . . . it's hard to explain. It's like you're trying to rape me.'

Her face brightened. 'Ah, is that what you like? I can tie you to the bed. You want that? I tie you to the bed and rape you?'

If the truth were told, Solomon found the idea a hell of an attractive proposition, but this wasn't the time or the place. He put a finger to the girl's lips. 'Slowly, is what I like,' he said. 'Talk to me, get comfortable with me, then we'll make love. Like boyfriend and girlfriend, okay?'

She nodded enthusiastically. 'Okay,' she said. 'We go to the bedroom now?'

'In a bit,' said Solomon. He eased her off his lap and put an arm around her as she snuggled against his chest. 'So what's your name, really?'

'Tanya,' she said.

'Where are you from?'

'The Ukraine,' she said quietly. 'Have you ever been there?'

'No.'

'It is a beautiful country.'

'I'm sure.'

She twisted round to look up at him. 'Why do you say that?'

'It must be a pretty place to produce such a pretty girl.'

She smiled and tried to kiss him again but Solomon laughed and moved his head away. 'I am being terrible again?' she asked.

'Yes,' he murmured. 'You are.' He drank some lager and she sat back, pushing her hair behind her ears. 'What happened to Amy?'

'Today she has her period,' said Tanya. 'She cannot work.'

'Why didn't the agency say something?'

She shrugged. 'Maybe they were scared you'd go to another.'

'How long have you worked for them?'

'Two months.'

'And they're a good company to work for?'

'They're okay.'

Then she tickled his ribs, grabbed his ears and kissed him hard on the mouth. He tried to push her away but she held him tight, grinding her hips against him and pushing her tongue deep into his mouth. Solomon felt himself grow hard again, and she felt it, too, because she started to ride him more rhythmically and moaned softly as she kissed him. Her towel slipped down and her full breasts pressed against his chest. Solomon tried to protest but she kept her lips pressed against his. He could barely breathe.

The mobile phone rang. Solomon pushed her away. 'I'm sorry, Tanya, I have to get that.'

She was gasping, as out of breath as he was. 'Are you sure?' she asked.

For a moment he wasn't. She was young, pretty and paid for, and it would have been the easiest thing in the world to pick her up and carry her into the bedroom. She smiled, sensing his indecision, but he answered the mobile. It was McLaren. 'How's it going, mate?' asked the journalist.

'I'm at home,' said Solomon. 'What's wrong?'

'You're needed in the office. Why the hell am I bothering? She can't hear what I'm saying, can she?'

'What? Now? Can't someone else do it?'

'Blah, blah, blah,' said McLaren, in a sing-song voice. 'Blah, blah, blah.'

'Okay, but I'm not happy about this,' said Solomon, flashing Tanya a smile. She picked up the towel and wrapped it around herself again.

'Well, you could stay and give the dog a bone if you'd prefer,' said McLaren.

'No, I understand,' said Solomon, looking at his wristwatch. 'I'll be there in half an hour. Tell them I'm on my way.' He cut the connection. 'Tanya, I'm sorry, I have to go to the office. They've a problem and I have to sort it out. Keep the money.'

'We can make love first,' she said eagerly. 'We can do it quickly.'

Solomon picked up her clothes and handed them to her, apologising profusely. She took them into the bathroom and returned a few minutes later, dressed. She sat down on the sofa to put on her boots.

'I'm sorry about this,' said Solomon.

'It's okay,' she said. 'Call for me again, yeah?'

'Of course,' lied Solomon.

He showed her out, then leaned on the door, cursing his bad luck.

Sasha walked out of the airport terminal and shivered despite his full-length Armani leather coat. Karic and Rikki followed just behind him. Karic had a metal brief-case attached to his wrist by a thin chrome chain.

There were three black Mercedes with tinted windows parked in the No Waiting zone. Two men stood by each vehicle their eyes sweeping the crowds, looking for trouble even though they were on their home turf. Belgrade was a dangerous place, even for a man as well protected and connected as Sasha.

One of the men stepped forward and gave Sasha a bruising bear-hug. 'Good to have you back, little brother,' he said.

Sasha hugged him in return, trying to squeeze the air from his lungs. It was a childish game they played when-ever they met, a trial of strength that neither man wanted to win. 'Have you stopped working out, Markovic? You don't seem as toned as last time I was here.'

Markovic guffawed and tightened his grip. 'How's that feel, little brother?'

Sasha laughed. Markovic always referred to him as his little brother, though they weren't related. At forty-one, he was Sasha's senior by five years but he looked older, mainly because he shaved his head and his face was lined and weathered from a childhood spent working on the family farm in the south of Serbia. Sasha gave Markovic a final squeeze. 'Come on, we've work to do,' he said.

One of the Serbs opened the rear door of the middle Mercedes and Sasha climbed in, followed by Karic.

Richmond £375,000

A delightful two bedroom refurbished end of terrace home situated in
the cul-de-sac within 1/2 mile of Kew Gardens and Station. Tiered
landscaped southerly aspect garden and off street parking for two.
Contact Richm

...ful Victorian cottage presented in very good order throughout, two double bedrooms, reception room with bay window, formal dining room, galley kitchen and utility room. Lovely enclosed rear garden, very attractive property with character and charm.

For details contact 0208 941 7900

TWICKENHAM
£187,500

Recently the subject of refurbishment by owners and presented in immaculate order. This one bedroom modern semi detached house is the ideal first purchase. Located close to Fulwell main line station with regular bus links into nearby Twickenham, Hampton or Teddington. The property benefits from its quiet cul-de-sac location, conservatory, south facing garden and off street parking.

For details contact Wayne Englishby 07949 169431

Markovic got into the front seat. The driver already had the engine running.

The first Mercedes pulled away from the kerb. Four of Markovic's men were inside it, and Sasha knew they would all be heavily armed. The second and third Mercedes followed in convoy. The cars were all armoured with bullet-proof windows and could withstand a direct hit from a grenade or a landmine.

Markovic opened the glove compartment and took out two Glocks. He handed one to Sasha and one to Karic. Sasha checked the weapon, satisfied himself that the safety was on, and slid it into his pocket. It felt good to be carrying again. It wasn't something he could risk in the UK, where possession of a handgun could result in a seven-year prison sentence.

'So, how is business, little brother?' asked Markovic, unscrewing the top of a silver hip flask. He offered it to Sasha.

Sasha took a swig of Cognac and handed it back. 'Business is great,' he said. 'I want to pick up another eight girls this trip, and I reckon on ten next month. How about you?'

'Getting better by the day,' said Markovic. 'We're shifting a hundred kilos a week into Germany and fifty into Italy.'

Like Sasha, Markovic had made his money out of the four-year siege of Sarajevo, but while Sasha had been smuggling food and medicine into the city, Markovic had been smuggling things out. People. People with enough money to pay to escape the near-constant sniping and shelling. Ten thousand people died during the siege, and Markovic made more than a million dollars. Once the war was over and the multinational peacekeepers had arrived in the former Yugoslavia, Markovic had moved into prostitution and drugs, initially supplying the local population and the internationals, but quickly moving abroad, bringing in heroin from Afghanistan and transporting it across Europe. Recently he had been pressing Sasha to set up a heroin-distribution network in London, but Sasha was reluctant to expand into drugs. Prostitution in the UK was more profitable than drugs, and came with much less risk.

The convoy drove to a hotel some three miles from the airport. It was a concrete cube eight storeys high, built in austere Communist style during the Tito era. It was now owned by Jon Nikolic, a Serbian Mafia boss who only kept it functioning as a hotel to launder drugs and trafficking profits. The four lower floors were occupied by paying guests; the top four were used by Nikolic's gang. The hotel was given a wide berth by the local and federal police; those who weren't on Nikolic's payroll knew that to cross the Mafia boss would bring a premature end to their careers or their lives. For the last two years it had been the venue for the country's biggest prostitute auctions.

The convoy drove up to the front of the hotel. Four men in long black coats stood guard at the entrance. They wore earpieces and dark glasses, and their hands were never far from their concealed weapons.

The men from the first Mercedes rushed over to the second and third and opened the rear doors. Markovic walked into the reception area with Sasha. There were several plastic sofas, cheap wooden coffee tables and artificial plants that hadn't been dusted for years. There was a shabby feel to the place, which was exactly what

Nikolic intended. All the money had been spent on the upper floors.

Markovic and three of his crew went over to two of the sofas. Other groups of heavies had congregated in different parts of the ground floor of the building. Only the buyer, his money man and an assistant were allowed on to the fifth floor during an auction. Two more men in black coats stood guard at the lifts. One had the doors open for Sasha, who walked in, followed by Karic and Rikki.

The lift doors rattled shut and they went up to the fifth floor in silence. Here, two more guards were waiting when the doors opened, but this time their weaponry was on display. They each had a Kalashnikov AK-47 slung over their shoulders. Only Nikolic's men were allowed to carry weapons. It was all down to trusting him. That was how the system worked.

A table stood beside the lift, and next to it a metal detector, the sort used to screen passengers at airports. Without being asked, Sasha, Karic and Rikki handed over their Glocks. An unsmiling man in wraparound sunglasses made a note of the guns in a ledger and placed them on a rack behind him. A couple of dozen handguns were already hanging there, along with several machine pistols and two hand grenades.

Karic opened the metal suitcase and displayed the contents. Bundles of fifty-pound notes. The man moved the top layer to check that there were only notes underneath, then replaced them. He nodded at Sasha and told him which room they were to go to.

Karic clicked the locks shut, unchained the briefcase from his wrist, and walked through the metal detector. He held out his hand and the man passed him the case. Sasha and Rikki passed through the metal detector, and the three men walked together down the corridor to the meeting room.

In the early days of the auctions, the potential buyers had gathered together in one room and bid against each other for the girls on offer. That had stopped after a Russian mobster had pulled out a gun and shot an Italian in the head at point-blank range during a dispute over who should be allowed to buy pretty twins from Montenegro. The body had been taken away and the Russian had been billed for the cost of replacing the carpet and repainting the walls. From then on guns had been checked in on arrival and the buyers were kept separate. Nikolic moved between the rooms, showing which girls were on offer and taking bids. It was a safer system, but it depended on all the buyers trusting him: he was in a perfect position to manipulate prices.

Sasha walked into the room and sat down at the head of a large, oval, mahogany table. Karic put the briefcase on the table in front of him, then went to stand by the door. Rikki stood at the window, arms folded across his chest, face impassive.

Nikolic arrived, with two bodyguards in tow. They had large handguns in shoulder holsters.

Sasha stood up and accepted a crushing bear-hug from the Serb. Nikolic was Sasha's height but about twice his girth. He had several chins and his gold-ringed fingers were puffed up like sausages. 'Sasha, you are one of the last,' wheezed Nikolic. 'Now we can start.'

'The plane was delayed,' said Sasha. 'My apologies.'

Nikolic waved him to a seat. 'I'm glad you made it. We have some excellent girls on offer, first-class specimens. How many are you looking for this trip?'

'Eight would fulfil my needs, but you know what an impulse buyer I am.'

Nikolic laughed, his hands on his massive stomach as if he feared it would burst.

'Before we start, I've a question for you,' said Sasha, taking the picture of Nicole from his jacket pocket. 'Is this one of yours?'

Nikolic frowned. 'I thought you didn't like the young ones,' he said. 'What is she? Sixteen?'

'Nineteen now,' said Sasha. 'Her hair might be darker.'

'So many girls pass through here, Sasha. I can't be expected to remember them all.'

'Nicole, her name is. Or Amy.'

'Names mean nothing, you know that. What is your interest?'

'Five thousand US, if you can tell me where she is.'

Nikolic rubbed his face. 'Sasha, there's nothing I'd like better than to take your money, but she is just one face among many.'

'She might have gone to London.'

'So, she is a face among thousands.' He handed back the picture. 'I'm sorry. Now, give me five minutes to talk to the Russians, then I will be back.'

'Is there anyone else here from London?' Sasha asked. He knew that at least two of his competitors were in the hotel – he had recognised their men at Reception.

Nikolic pointed a warning finger at him. 'You know that's not allowed, Sasha,' he admonished him good-naturedly. 'You can meet the other bidders after the auction, if you wish. Can we get you anything?'

There were bottles of water, glasses and an ice bucket on the table. Sasha said that water would be fine: the time for drinking would be after the auction.

He sat patiently for ten minutes until Nikolic returned. This time he was carrying a Gucci attaché case, which he placed on the table before lowering himself on to one of the high-backed leather chairs.

'So, what are you looking for, Sasha?' he asked, as he opened the case.

'What do you have?' asked Sasha.

Nikolic reached into his briefcase and handed over twenty Polaroid photographs. 'Moldavians,' he said. 'I have a bid on the table already for five thousand pounds apiece but I am willing to sell them individually.'

Sasha sorted through the Polaroids. Several he dismissed as too old, too fat or too ugly. In some parts of Europe it didn't matter what a girl looked like – men were just grateful to be with a woman – but the UK was a richer market and men who wanted to pay for sex could afford to be choosy.

He put two of the Polaroids down in front of Nikolic. They were both brunettes, one with short hair, the other with long hair in plaits. 'How old are they?'

Nikolic wrinkled his nose. 'I have passports for both showing that they are twenty,' he said.

Sasha smiled tightly. Nikolic hadn't answered his question.

Nikolic threw up his hands. 'Okay, okay,' he said. He tapped the picture of the girl with short hair. 'Fifteen,' he said. 'The one with long hair is her sister. Seventeen.'

Sasha tossed the picture of the fifteen-year-old on to the discard pile. He never touched underage girls. It wasn't just because of the potential problems if the police or Immigration discovered her true age; the real downside was that they weren't experienced enough to handle the customers. Sasha didn't want virgins or girls who had

222

only had sex a few times. He wanted them seasoned. Broken in. Girls who could screw two dozen times a day without complaining.

That left him with fourteen. He spread out the pictures. 'I need girls who can speak some English,' he said. 'Just the basics.'

Nikolic nodded and, one by one, pushed five Polaroids towards him. The seventeen-year-old was among them.

'They are all upstairs,' said Nikolic. 'Feel free to test the merchandise.'

Sasha waved Karic and Rikki over. He kept the Polaroid of the seventeen-year-old for himself but gave the other four to his men. Nikolic handed over four hotel keys. Karic and Rikki left the room. They knew what to do.

Nikolic gave Sasha the key to the seventeen-year-old's room and winked. 'You'll like her, Sasha. I should be charging you extra for her.'

Sasha pocketed the key. 'What else do you have?'

'I have Belarussians. But, frankly, they are not up to your standards. Farm-girls. I don't think I would fuck them with your dick, Sasha.' Nikolic roared with laughter at his own joke and banged on the table with the flat of his hand. 'I also have girls from Latvia, the Ukraine, and Bulgaria.'

'What about Kosovans? Or Bosnians?'

Nikolic scratched his chin. 'I have two, but they speak no English.'

'I want to see them.'

Nikolic sorted through the photographs in his briefcase and passed across two. 'Seriously, Sasha, I wouldn't bother with them. Not your type at all. Second-rate. I was planning to send them to Hong Kong. The Chinese will screw any white woman and think she's Julia Roberts.'

'They are in the hotel?'

Nikolic shrugged. 'Of course.'

Sasha held out his hand and the Serb gave him two room keys. 'The one in six thirty-six is from Sarajevo, the other from Priština. I must warn you, Sasha, they have medical certificates but I wouldn't trust them.'

Sasha stood up. 'Let me see for myself.' He left the room and walked to the lifts. One of Nikolic's men stood aside to let him enter. He pressed the button for the sixth floor.

He unlocked the door to 636 without knocking. The girl was a brunette in her late twenties with large, pendulous breasts and wide hips. She was wearing a black négligé, black lacy briefs and high heels that were several sizes too big for her. She smiled at him nervously and undid the front of the négligé. Her stomach was scarred and wrinkled. She'd had two or three children, at least. Her mouth was a vivid slash of scarlet and she'd applied too much blue mascara to her lashes. She took a step towards him, cupping her breasts, but Sasha waved her away.

'I don't want to screw you,' he said, in Serbo-Croatian. He took out the picture of Nicole from his jacket pocket and showed it to her. 'This girl, have you ever seen her? She's older now, with dark hair.'

The woman shook her head.

'You're sure? Look at the picture.'

The woman frowned, then shook her head again.

Sasha took the picture from her and turned to go.

'Where are you from?' asked the woman.

'Albania, but my business is in London.'

'I want to work in London,' said the woman.

Sasha opened his mouth to speak. He wanted to tell her that she was too old, too ugly, too scarred to make a living as a hooker in London, that there were younger, prettier girls queuing up for the opportunity to sell themselves, but he could see from her eyes that she already knew the truth. She had already given up hope, had slept with God knew how many men just to get to the hotel room in Belgrade where she would be sold like an animal.

'London is difficult at the moment,' said Sasha. 'There's a lot of competition. Where are your children?'

'My husband is taking care of them,' she said. 'Our farm is mined, we can make no money from the land.'

'He knows what you are doing?'

The woman looked down. 'We have nothing,' she said. 'They said it would be six years, maybe more, before they come to take away the mines. They have other priorities – land belonging to more important people than us.'

'Why don't you work in Sarajevo? You would be closer to your family.'

The woman pulled her négligé around herself, still looking down at the floor. 'The man who gave me my job in Sarajevo has sold my contract. I wanted to stay but he said I had to come here.'

Sasha nodded.

'You can take me to London?' she asked hopefully.

'I'm sorry, no,' he said.

She nodded and sat down on the bed, her hands in her lap. Her nails were painted a dark red, but they were bitten to the quick.

The girl from Priština was in the room next door. When Sasha opened the door she was reading a magazine but she stood up quickly, pushed out her breasts, sucked in her stomach, and smiled seductively. Sasha nodded.

She had been well trained. Her makeup was good, just enough to put some colour in her cheeks and lips, and she was wearing a translucent dressing-gown, pull-up stockings and a bra that was slightly too small. No briefs – another sign that she had been well trained. By showing the punter what was on offer, he was more likely to plunge straight into sex; the less time spent on foreplay the quicker the turnover.

She had a pretty face framed by dark brown hair with red tints, a professional cut. She also had a series of old razor cuts down the inside of her left arm. Not serious attempts at suicide, just attention-seeking self-mutilation. That was reason enough for Sasha to reject her.

'Can you speak English?' Sasha asked, in English. The girl looked at him blankly. Sasha took out the picture of Nicole and showed it to her. 'You know her?' he asked, in Bosnian.

The girl nodded. 'Yes. We worked in the same bar in Priština.'

Sasha was stunned. 'You're sure?'

The girl looked at him as if he was stupid. Under other circumstances that would have earned her a slap, but Sasha was too surprised at what she'd said to take offence.

'She was a waitress for about a week. Then she started dancing. After a month the boss sold her on to a bar in Sarajevo.'

'Definitely the same girl?'

'Sure. She was blonde like this when she turned up at the bar asking for work, but she dyed it black after a couple of days.'

'The bar in Sarajevo, what was it called?'

'I don't know.'

'Think.'

'No one told me. I turned up for work one day and she'd gone. I asked what had happened to her and they said the boss had sold her to a bar-owner in Sarajevo. That's all I know.'

'The bar-owner, what was his name?'

Another shake of the head. 'I don't know.'

Sasha took the picture from her and went out of the room.

He took the stairs up to the next floor and let himself into the Moldavian sisters' room. Both girls were in there, sitting on the bed. He closed the door behind him. The younger of the two looked even younger than she had in the photograph. If he hadn't known her real age he'd have taken her for thirteen or fourteen.

'What is your name?' he asked the older girl, in English.

She stood up, smiling. 'Katrina,' she said. Her hair was in two plaits, and she was wearing a long red satin robe, tied loosely at the waist.

'How old are you?'

'Seventeen,' she said. 'This is my sister. She is sixteen.'

Sasha ignored the lie. If the younger sister had looked older, perhaps he might have taken her to the UK on the fake passport, but she was never going to look like anything other than an underage girl. She was tiny, a little over five feet, and had barely any curves. 'You know what anal is?' asked Sasha.

Katrina nodded.

'And you are okay with that?'

'If it doesn't hurt,' she said.

Sasha's face hardened. 'I don't care if it hurts or not,' he said. 'I want to know if you are happy to do it. Customers pay more for it in London.'

At the mention of London the girl's smile widened.

'I'm happy to do it,' she said. She put a hand on her sister's shoulder. 'My sister, too.'

'You know what oral is?'

Katrina nodded and mimed putting something towards her mouth. Her sister giggled.

'What about oral without?' said Sasha. 'What does that mean?'

'No condom,' said Katrina.

'Take off your robe,' he said.

Katrina did as she was told, and he looked her up and down. Her skin was pale and flawless, her breasts firm, her stomach flat and unmarked. She turned round without being asked. High, tight buttocks, long legs, emphasised by her high heels. He liked what he saw.

There were condoms and a box of tissues on the bedside table. There was no point in paying thousands of pounds only to discover when a girl got to London that she was lousy at her job. Sasha told the younger sister to give him a condom as he unbuckled his belt. Katrina walked towards him. 'Let me do that,' she said.

Sasha smiled. It showed she'd been well trained. Katrina knelt down, unzipped his trousers and took him in her mouth. She kept looking up at his face as she moved back and forth. A nice touch. Eye-contact made it seem personal.

Sasha felt hands stroking his back. The younger girl was standing behind him. She handed him a condom, the packet already torn open. Sasha took it and gave it to the girl on her knees. She slipped it on while the other's hands moved round his waist and started pulling out his shirt.

Sasha told the older sister to stand up, then lifted her and drove into her as she gripped him with her knees, urging him on. He shuffled over to the dressing-table and sat her on it as he pounded into her. 'Yes, darling, yes, darling, I love it, I love it,' she gasped. The girl was good, thought Sasha. She made it seem as if she was enjoying it, as if he was special, and that was important because the more special a punter felt, the more likely he was to return.

Sasha came with a grunt, and the girl kissed his cheek and hugged him. He pulled away. The younger sister had slipped off her robe and tried to drag him towards the bed, but Sasha pulled up his trousers, went to the bathroom and flushed away the condom. He wiped the girl's lipstick off his cheek with a tissue. When he walked back into the bedroom, the two girls were wearing their robes and sitting together on the bed, whispering in their own language.

Sasha pointed at Katrina. 'I will take you to London,' he said.

Katrina beamed, then put her arm around her sister's shoulders. 'And my sister?' she asked.

'When she is older,' said Sasha. 'I cannot use underage girls in London. In two years, when she is ready, I will bring her. But not now.'

Katrina opened her mouth to protest, but Sasha silenced her with a warning finger. 'You will do as you are told,' he said. 'I am the boss, you obey me, do you understand?'

Katrina took her arm from around her sister and nodded.

'Good. If you remember that we will get on fine.' Sasha didn't bother explaining that Katrina would have to work to pay off her debt once she got to London. If there were any problems, he'd explain it to her when it was too late.

The younger sister would give him leverage, too. Katrina wouldn't know where she was, but Sasha would.

He went back to the meeting room and sat down. Karic and Rikki were already there. They gave him the four Polaroids and said that the girls were fine. They were well versed in checking, and Sasha trusted their judgement. He poured himself a glass of water and was about to add ice cubes when Nikolic came back into the room. 'How is everything?' he asked, dropping into the chair opposite Sasha and opening his attaché case.

Sasha pushed the Polaroid of Katrina across the table towards him.

'Ah, by far the prettier of the two,' said Sasha. 'An excellent choice. I already have an offer of fifteen thousand euros for her.'

'You said five thousand pounds before.'

'The bids have started, Sasha, and the sisters are pretty and talented. I have an offer of fifteen thousand euros for her. And fifteen for the sister.'

'I'm not interested in the sister,' said Sasha. 'I'll give twelve thousand pounds for her.'

Nikolic scribbled in a small leather notebook.

Sasha passed over the photograph of the four other Moldavians. 'And I'll pay six thousand pounds apiece for these.'

'I already have an offer of ten thousand US dollars for this girl,' said Nikolic, tapping one of the pictures.

'Okay, eight thousand pounds for her. Six for the rest.'

Nikolic made another note, then took a handful of photographs out of his attaché case. 'I have these for your consideration,' he said. 'All English speakers.'

Sasha settled back in his chair and flicked through the Polaroids. The bidding had now started in earnest and would go on for much of the day. He was certain of one thing: he was going to buy Katrina, no matter how much she cost him. Not that the money mattered – she would repay it: he knew he would have fun with her himself.

Solomon was sipping his espresso and looking at the Legal Escorts website when his mobile rang. It was Danny McLaren.

'Looks like you've got the flat to yourself for a few days, mate,' said the journalist. 'Things are starting to move Iraq-wise so they're sending me out to Saudi this afternoon. Probably all turn to shit but I won't be back before the weekend, whatever happens. I've got to handhold one of our star feature writers, get her the quotes so she can win another award. And I say that without a trace of bitterness.'

Solomon said he could look after himself. McLaren asked him what he was doing. 'Going over the agency's website,' he said.

'Have you found out who it's registered to?' asked McLaren. 'Probably hidden but you should give it a go.'

'How?'

'Go to a domain-checker. There's one at www.registryweb.com. They'll tell you who it's registered to, who the technical people are, how long they've had the domain, stuff like that. Does this mean you'll be inviting young Miss Whatsername back to my humble abode?'

'No need,' said Solomon. 'According to the site she's available for incall now. Maybe that's what the fiasco was about last time. She was probably too busy moving into the new place.'

'Don't think they have to move much, mate. They don't usually live in the flats.'

'Escort agencies are different,' said Solomon. 'No maids, and the girls often sleep where they work.'

McLaren laughed. 'Sounds like you're becoming an expert,' he said.

'Got it from the horse's mouth, a Maltese. He says he's got girls right across London. I'll try to fix up a date with her tonight.'

McLaren laughed again. 'A date? Is that what you call it? You old romantic, you.'

'Less of the old,' said Solomon. He wished his friend a safe trip and cut the connection.

Then he clicked through to RegistryWeb and typed in the URL for Legal-escorts.com. After a few seconds the details of the website owner popped up, but it appeared to be an Internet company in Surrey. They had probably registered it on behalf of the true owner. They had bought the domain in March 2000.

He went back to McLaren's flat before phoning the agency. A girl answered, younger the first, and her accent was less pronounced. He asked if he could book Amy for an hour's incall at four o'clock, but was told she was busy until later that evening. 'Would you be interested in another girl?' asked the receptionist.

'What time would Amy be available?' asked Solomon.

'Not until nine, I'm afraid,' said the receptionist.

'Can I book her for an hour then?' asked Solomon.

'No problem,' said the girl. 'Have you seen Amy before?'

'No, I haven't,' said Solomon.

'And your name is?'

Solomon froze. He couldn't remember the name he'd booked under last time. He was using his mobile and if they were anywhere close to efficient they'd have taken a note of his name and number. He looked frantically for his notebook. 'I'm sorry, you're breaking up,' he said, playing for time. 'I didn't catch what you said.'

Then he remembered. The bedroom. He rushed down the hallway as the receptionist repeated what she'd said.

The notebook was on the floor and Solomon grabbed it. 'Richard,' he said, fighting to keep his breathing steady. 'Richard Williams.'

'I'll call you back to confirm, Richard. What's your number?'

Solomon gave it to her. Five minutes later she called back and gave him an address in St John's Wood.

Solomon fetched a beer from McLaren's fridge, sat down in the kitchen and worked out what he was going to say to Nicole Shala.

The sky had darkened outside the hotel when the auction finished and Nikolic presented Sasha with his bill. Eighty-five thousand pounds, plus a commission charge of twenty per cent: Nikolic took a cut from both buyer and seller.

Sasha opened his metal briefcase and took out bundles of banknotes.

'I wish these Brits would adopt the Euro,' said Nikolic. 'It would make life so much easier.'

Sasha stacked the money beside the case. One hundred and two thousand pounds. He had agreed on twenty thousand pounds for Katrina; the most he had ever paid for a girl. He had bought two Latvian girls for five thousand apiece and two pretty Ukrainians for seven and a half each. The four Moldavians had cost him a total of thirty-five thousand. Nikolic had also talked him into taking a Bulgarian girl who specialised in domination work. While Sasha wasn't interested in that side of the sex industry he knew of a woman who ran a dungeon in the City who would give him three times what he'd paid to take over her contract.

'The woman in six thirty-six, is anyone bidding for her?' asked Sasha.

Nikolic shrugged carelessly. 'The Bosnian? There has been some interest, but no bids.'

'How much do you want for her?'

'You are joking?'

'Does it look like I am joking?'

Nikolic stopped laughing. 'The triads would pay me eight thousand,' he said.

'That would be Hong Kong dollars?'

'US,' said Nikolic, smiling thinly.

'Do I look like I was born yesterday? I'll give you two thousand pounds.'

'Four.'

'Three.'

'Three thousand five hundred.'

Sasha sighed. 'I'm too tired to argue,' he said, and counted out bundles of banknotes. He gave the money to Nikolic, then told Karic to lock the briefcase. He said he would return in a couple of months.

Markovic was waiting for him in Reception. 'How did it go?' he asked.

'I took ten,' said Sasha. 'Good merchandise. And one other. A girl from Sarajevo. Get someone to collect her. Nikolic will have her ready for you. You've still got that bar outside Sarajevo, the one where the federal cops drink?'

Markovic nodded.

'Give her a job as a waitress, or in the kitchen. Pay her

well, yeah? Not stupidly well, but I want her taken care of.'

Markovic slapped him on the back. 'Not getting soft, are we?'

Sasha reached down and grabbed Markovic's balls. 'You want to see how soft I am just carry on talking like that,' he said.

Both men laughed and they walked towards the waiting cars with their arms around each other.

Anna knocked on the door to his office and Sergei Goncharov looked up from the spreadsheet on his computer screen.

Anna smiled brightly, not put off by the frown on the Russian's face. She had worked with him for almost four years and was used to his black moods. She was from Estonia, a tall, striking blonde with a supermodel's figure, who had been one of Goncharov's highest-earning girls during the three years she had worked as an escort. She'd approached him directly after making her own way to London on a fiancé visa that an Englishman she'd met in Moscow had obtained for her. She'd dumped him within days of arriving in the city and had started working for Goncharov a week later. Because she wasn't on a contract she could work for him on the same terms as the English girls at the agency and kept two-thirds of the money she earned. After three years she had amassed more than a quarter of a million pounds in the bank, a two-bedroomed mews house in Knightsbridge and half a dozen marriage proposals from City lawyers, stockbrokers, TV executives and a schoolteacher who lived with his aged mother. For some reason that Goncharov could never fathom, she'd agreed to marry the schoolteacher and stop working as an escort. Goncharov had been more than happy to keep her on as one of his receptionists: she was professional with a good phone voice and acted as a substitute mother to the younger girls, even though she was only in her mid-twenties.

'Sergei, you remember you asked us keep an eye on Amy?' She always spoke to him in Russian, partly because she knew he preferred his own language but also because it gave her an edge over the rest of the office staff who couldn't speak it.

Sergei nodded but didn't say anything.

'We've just had a booking from a new client. Richard Williams. He booked Amy two days ago but she wasn't available so we sent Tanya instead. Today he has called for Amy and I've arranged one hour incall.'

'So? Amy is a popular girl.'

'I phoned Tanya to see how he'd been with her, and she says he was a bit strange. He seemed uneasy, didn't want to have sex, and kept asking about Amy, even though he'd never met her. Then there was a phone call saying he had to work. The appointment was cut short but he didn't query the money.'

Goncharov leaned forward, his interest piqued. 'What was he like, this Williams?'

'Tanya said he was in his mid-thirties, quite good-looking. Brown hair. Brown eyes. About six foot.'

'He didn't mention Bosnia?'

'No.'

'And he's seeing her at nine?'

'That's right. What do you want me to do?'

For the first time in several days, a smile spread across the Russian's face. 'Nothing, Anna. I'll take care of it. And thank you, you've done well.'

236

The smile vanished and Goncharov went back to his spreadsheet. Business was good, and growing fast. Income from Legal Escorts amounted to more than a hundred and forty thousand pounds in the previous month, and it was only one of several agencies he owned. With the saunas, walk-ups and drinking clubs he was earning close to a million pounds a month in London alone.

The money didn't remain in the UK for long. Goncharov moved it through a daisy chain of bank accounts, then into a commodities company based in Budapest. The company made bulk purchases of easily resaleable items, anything from children's shoes to second-hand cars, which were then shipped around the world. Its subsidiaries received payment for the goods, and the money was moved through more offshore bank accounts until it was virtually untraceable. Goncharov had made sure that in the unlikely event that the British police or Europol targeted him for trafficking or living off immoral earnings, the money would be unreachable. Everything he used in the UK was leased or rented: his mansion in Kensington, his fleet of cars, his cruiser moored at Chelsea Harbour. None of it belonged to him and he could walk away from it without a moment's hesitation.

Nicole's flat was in an apartment block close to St John's Wood tube station, a ten-storey, featureless building with more than fifty bells at the main entrance. A small brass plate detailed instructions for contacting the various apartments. Solomon pressed the 'clear' button, then the flat number, then the star button. The intercom made a harsh repetitive buzzing noise, then there was static hiss, then he heard a girl's voice. 'Yes?'

'Amy?' said Solomon. 'It's Richard.'

'Come on up, Richard.' The lock clicked and Solomon pushed open the heavy wood and glass door. He took the lift to the second floor. The corridor was expensively carpeted and there were pretty brass light fittings every half-dozen steps. He went along to Nicole's flat and knocked at the door. It opened almost immediately and Nicole Shala smiled at him.

She was taller than Solomon had thought, although she was wearing three-inch heels, and she looked older than he knew she was in a sheer leopard-patterned robe. 'Come in,' she said.

Solomon smelt jasmine as he walked past her into a large sitting room with a fireplace above which hung an ornate gilt mirror. He watched her reflection as she closed the door and walked up behind him. She put her hands on his shoulders and massaged them gently. 'Would you like a drink?' she asked.

'Yes, please,' said Solomon. He turned to face her. She was wearing a lot of makeup – heavy foundation, thick mascara and bright red lipstick.

'Whisky, beer, Coke?'

'Water would be fine.'

She put a hand up to his cheek. 'Make yourself comfortable,' she said, then headed for the kitchen.

There were two Louis XIV-style sofas at either side of the fireplace and Solomon sat down on one. Gilt-framed paintings were on all the walls, scenes of various European capitals. A crystal chandelier hung from the centre of an ornate carving that was almost certainly plastic. Solomon realised that the whole room was a fake – the reproduction antique furniture, the old-master prints. And Nicole? A cheap copy of a mistress: a sexual experience bought and paid for without any emotional involvement . . .

'You look worried,' said Nicole, coming back from the kitchen.

'Just thinking,' he said.

'Better not to think,' she said, and handed him a glass.

'Is that how you feel?' asked Solomon, and put it on a marble coffee table.

'Thinking doesn't help.' She sat down on the sofa next to him and put her hand on his leg. 'So, what do you like to do?' she asked.

'What do you mean?'

'In bed?'

'Ah, I don't know. I really just wanted to talk'

She raised her eyebrows. 'Talking is good,' she said. 'Do you want me to tell you what I want you to do to me?' Her hand slid up his thigh.

'Nicole . . .' said Solomon, and she froze.

'What did you say?'

'Your name's Nicole, right?'

She stood up. 'Who are you?'

'My name's Jack. I just want to talk to you.'

'You must go,' she said, nervously. 'Go now.'

'Please, Nicole, sit down. Just give me a few minutes.' He took out his wallet and held up two hundred pounds. 'Look, here's the money. Phone the agency and tell them I'm here, then listen to what I have to say. Please.'

'How do you know my name? How did you find me?'

Solomon held out the money but she ignored it. 'I was looking for you in Sarajevo,' he said. 'I spoke to Emir.'

'Emir?' She sat down, her hands clasped together. 'How is he? What's he doing?'

'He's fine, he misses you – he's read and reread that letter you sent him a million times.'

'He loves me,' she said, flatly.

'There's no doubting that,' said Solomon. 'You should get in touch, let him know you're okay.'

'Nicole isn't okay, Nicole Shala is dead.'

'That's not true, Nicole,' said Solomon softly.

'Nicole died three years ago. My name is Amy.'

'Nicole—'

'Don't call me that!' she hissed.

'Okay, okay,' said Solomon. 'If you want me to call you Amy, I'll call you Amy.'

'I want you to go,' said Nicole. She stood up. 'I want you to go now.'

'We've found your family,' said Solomon.

For a moment her eyes brightened, but the look of hope vanished just as quickly. 'They're dead,' she said.

Solomon nodded slowly.

'All of them?'

'The truck was at the bottom of a lake.'

Nicole wrapped her arms around herself. 'It was my fault,' she said, and tears trickled down her cheeks.

Solomon stood up and went over to her. 'It wasn't your fault,' he said, putting his hands on her shoulders. 'You mustn't say that.'

She began to sob and Solomon put his arms round her. As he held her, she crumpled against him. He could smell her jasmine perfume, and stroked the back of her neck, not sure what to say.

A mobile phone beeped into life. *The William Tell Overture*. She pushed him away and rushed over to it. She wiped her eyes with the back of her hand and sniffed loudly, then answered the call. 'Hello, yes, yes, he's here.'

She turned her back on Solomon. 'I was just going to call. Yes, everything's fine.' She cut the connection and tossed the phone on to one of the sofas. Then she turned to Solomon. Her face was streaked with tears. 'Please, just go. You don't have to pay me, just go.'

'We need to talk,' said Solomon.

'No!' she hissed, then rushed across the room, disappeared through an open door and slammed it behind her.

Solomon could hear her crying softly. 'Nicole,' he called, 'come out and talk to me.' There was no answer. He knocked. 'Nicole, please.' Still no reply. He tried the door but it was locked.

Solomon sat down with his back to the door and lit a Marlboro. 'I'm going to wait here until you come out, Nicole,' he said, 'you have to talk to me. You have to tell me what happened three years ago. You're the only witness to what happened, Nicole. You're the only person who can get justice for your family. I understand why you wanted to run away. I understand why you wanted to forget that it ever happened, but you have to face up to it now. If you don't speak up, if you don't tell the world what happened, the men who did it will get away with it.'

He heard a click. He scrambled to his feet and stubbed out his cigarette in an ashtray then went to the door. It led into a bedroom, small but prettily furnished with a brass-framed bed, a white dressing-table and built-in mirrored wardrobes. There were feminine touches throughout the room – a crystal vase of long-stemmed roses, a gilt-framed photograph of Nicole, a twelve by ten of one of the pictures on the website, and four toy rabbits with different-coloured bow-ties. On the dressing-table were a dozen different perfumes, all expensive brands. Probably gifts from admirers, thought Solomon.

Nicole was sitting on a small stool, staring into the dressing-table mirror.

'It's safe to go back now,' said Solomon. 'Kosovo's a different place from what it was three years ago. The Americans are there, European soldiers are there, the UN is watching. They're there to make sure that justice is done. There are people there who'll help you, in Kosovo or Bosnia. There's a whole organisation geared up to tracking down war criminals and bringing them to justice.'

Nicole stood up and turned to face him. In her right hand she held a small metal nail file. She held it to her left wrist, the point pricking her skin. 'If you don't go, I will kill myself,' she said. There was a faraway look in her eyes.

'Nicole, this is stupid,' said Solomon.

Nicole pressed the file harder. 'I mean it.'

'Stop this,' said Solomon urgently. 'I'm not going to hurt you, I just want to talk.'

'I've nothing to say to you. Now go, or I will cut my wrists.'

Solomon was four paces away from her and saw that he could probably reach her before she did herself any serious damage – but then what could he do? If she was serious about killing herself there would be nothing to stop her doing it after he'd left.

Solomon held up his hands. 'Okay, I'll go,' he said. 'But can I leave you my phone number, and if you change your mind will you call me?'

'I won't change my mind,' she said. She held out her hands towards him, the point of the file still pressed against her wrist.

He backed out of the bedroom. Nicole went with him but stopped at the doorway.

He went to the front door and reached for the handle. 'Nicole, can I just say one thing?'

She flinched, and he saw a drop of blood blossom at the end of the nail file and dribble down her wrist.

'Please, stop that, will you? said Solomon.

Her right hand was shaking and she was biting down on her lower lip as if preparing to cut deeper.

He took out his wallet. Inside was a card that had come with the pay-as-you-go phone he'd bought. He knelt down and placed it on the floor. 'That's my mobile number,' he said. 'Think about it, really think about it. I can help you. Together we can track down the men responsible for murdering your family. They deserve justice, Nicole. And you are the only one who can get it for them.'

'Go,' she said, scraping the point of the file down her wrist. More blood flowed.

Solomon pulled open the door and went out. He shut it behind him. He stood on the landing for almost a minute, wondering whether or not to ring the bell again, but he knew there was no point. There was nothing he could say to her that he hadn't already said. All he could do was hope she'd have a change of heart.

Sergei Goncharov scratched his groin as he watched the girl flop on to a sofa and curl up into a ball as she sobbed. He felt no sympathy for her. She was a commodity, a revenue generator, nothing more. She had another client due at ten thirty and if she wasn't over her crying fit by then he'd send round one of his men to straighten her out.

Goncharov picked up his phone and tapped out a number. Aleksei Leskov answered on the second ring.

'Have you got him?' asked Goncharov.

'He's in a black cab, heading south,' said Leskov.

'Don't lose him,' said Goncharov, but the instruction was unnecessary. Leskov had spent two decades working for the KGB in Kiev and had few equals when it came to surveillance or counter-surveillance. Leskov would have no problem in following the man called Richard Williams back to his home. Or in doing whatever else was necessary.

Goncharov cut the connection and studied the CCTV monitor on his desk. There were two hidden cameras in the girl's apartment; one in the light fitting in the sitting room, one in a smoke detector in the bedroom, and microphones in four of the flat's electrical sockets. He had watched all visitors to the apartment, even if they hadn't fitted the description Petrovic had given him

The conversation had intrigued the Russian and he wondered what the girl had seen in Kosovo. His years as a GRU investigator had provided him with all the techniques he'd need to get the information out of her. The threat of a little blood from her wrist wouldn't have deterred Goncharov. He'd have let her cut herself, then patched her up and asked her the question again. He smiled to himself. The man was a fool, and a weakling.

Goncharov had known Petrovic for more than a decade. The Bosnian was a nasty piece of work but a useful contact, and Goncharov had been paid enough for him to ignore the questions that were buzzing in his mind. Petrovic had wanted the man found and killed, and Goncharov was happy to oblige. What the girl had seen would remain a mystery.

Solomon closed his eyes and rubbed the back of his neck. He had the beginnings of a headache. He couldn't believe how badly he'd handled the situation. He'd gone in too hard, confronting her immediately, when he should have brought up the real reason for his visit only after he'd won her confidence. She was little more than a child, a child whose family had been massacred, and he'd treated her with all the subtlety of a sledgehammer.

He stared out of the window of the taxi. At least he'd found her. If nothing else, he could tell the War Crimes Tribunal where she was and they could pick her up. The Tribunal's investigators were professionals and they would probably do a better job of questioning her. And they'd be able to reassure her that she'd be protected, that she wouldn't suffer the same fate as her family. Maybe then she'd tell what she knew.

He shuddered as he remembered how she'd punctured her wrist with the nail file. It hadn't seemed like a bluff. What had she seen that she would rather kill herself than speak about it?

As a uniformed beat policeman, Solomon had done his fair share of breaking bad news. He'd turned up on doorsteps in the middle of the night to tell mothers and fathers that their children had been killed in road accidents. He'd explained to a wife how a mugging had turned violent and her husband had been shot in the chest. Told a man that his wife had been raped, then murdered, while he was at work. Explained about drug overdoses and drunken falls and suicides on railway lines. And later, working for the International War-dead Commission, he'd broken the bad news to hundreds of grieving relatives. Almost without exception the reaction had been the same: they'd wanted to talk about what had happened, how their loved ones had died, the memories they had, the way they felt. Talking was part of the grieving process that had to be gone through before they could move on with their lives. Nicole had never talked about what she'd seen.

Whatever had happened had been so traumatic that she'd blocked it out. But as far as he was aware, she had only seen her family herded into a truck. The true horror had happened hours later, far from the farm. There'd been violence at the farm, of course – men had been shot and slashed with hatchets – but Solomon had spoken to survivors of worse massacres and they had always been willing to talk. They'd been driven to tell him every detail, and to implore him for justice.

Nicole's silence made no sense to him.

'Inverness Terrace, yeah?' asked the cab driver.

'Yeah, but drop me in Queensway. Thanks.'

Solomon had finished the last can of beer in McLaren's fridge and there was hardly any milk left, so he spent half an hour in a supermarket stocking up with provisions. He walked back to Inverness Terrace with four carrier-bags, deep in thought. He wanted another crack at Nicole Shala. It was like questioning a suspect: even the most hardened criminal, backed up by his solicitor, could be made to talk, providing you could find the key. Sometimes it was ego, or a desire to be understood, or an urge to contradict, but handled the right way anyone could be made to open up. They might not confess, they might do nothing but lie, but at least they would start a dialogue.

He unlocked the front door and walked slowly up to McLaren's top-floor flat. He made himself a cheese omelette and toast, drank four cans of McEwan's lager as he watched football on Sky Sport, and went to bed, promising himself that he would go round and see Nicole the next day.

Aleksei Leskov put his hands deep into his overcoat pockets and coughed. He had smoked sixty cigarettes a day during the twenty-two years he had spent as a KGB officer in Kiev, and had cut down to twenty since leaving to set up his own security company. The cough was getting worse but he steadfastly refused to visit a doctor. He didn't trust doctors. His mother had died in a Kiev hospital, from liver cancer. His father had died, under medical care, from heart disease. Leskov ignored the cough and the occasional flecks of blood on his handkerchief.

There were three men with him, men who worked for him and whom he trusted. Two were Russians and the third was from the Ukraine. They had followed the man called Richard Williams from the flat in St John's Wood to Queensway in two cars. As soon as Williams had climbed out of the black cab two of Leskov's men had followed on foot. It had been easy. The man went to a supermarket, then walked to Inverness Terrace and inside a building that contained several flats. He didn't look round. Even if he had, he would not have spotted Leskov's men. Shortly after he had entered the building, lights went on in the top-floor flat.

Leskov had sent the Ukrainian to check the lock. It was a simple Yale. Any of his men could pick it in under a minute.

They took it in turns to watch the flat, retiring to a pub in Queensway, drinking vodka and smoking unfiltered cigarettes. Leskov was on watch when the lights went out. He waited five minutes to reassure himself that the man wasn't leaving the building, then went back to the pub, bought a round of drinks, then sat and smoked and talked until the barman shouted that it was closing time. Then Leskov left with two of his men.

They'd parked the cars in a multistorey close to

Whiteley's shopping centre; they threaded their way along the still-crowded pavements and up the concrete stairs to the third level. The Ukrainian opened the boot of one of the cars and pulled the rubber cover away from the spare wheel to reveal four handguns, each wrapped in a piece of cloth.

Leskov gave his men their weapons, then checked his own, a Russian-made semi-automatic, already loaded. There was a silencer for each. The men put the guns and silencers in their coat pockets and the Ukrainian slammed the boot.

Leskov briefed the men quickly. The Ukrainian and one of the Russians were to go into the flat. The second Russian was to wait on the pavement opposite the front entrance to the building. Leskov would wait at the rear. He sent the Ukrainian to deal with the lock while he and the two Russians walked up and down Queensway, looking into the windows of the packed restaurants and gift shops. Once the Ukrainian was inside he phoned Leskov, who sent one of the Russians to join him.

Leskov left the second Russian in Inverness Terrace while he walked down an alley that led to the rear of the terrace. Each block had its own neatly-tended garden. Leskov stood in the shadows and slowly screwed the silencer into the barrel of the gun.

Solomon rolled over, half asleep. His throat was dry and he groped around for the mug of water he'd left on his bedside table. His hand knocked the alarm clock on to the floor. He cursed and sat up. As he bent to pick it up he heard a metallic click from the hallway.

His first thought was that McLaren had got home, but the clicking wasn't the sound of a key being slotted into a lock. It was more persistent. Click, click, click. Solomon rolled off the bed and put his ear to the bedroom door. Click, click, click.

He pulled on a pair of jeans, opened the door and tiptoed down the hallway. The clicking was coming from the front door. As he got half-way down the hall the sound stopped. He froze, and heard muffled voices talking in what sounded like Russian.

Solomon pressed himself against the wall, his heart racing. The front door creaked open. He looked around for something to use as a weapon but the only thing within reach was the telephone.

There were more muffled voices, then footsteps. They were inside. The hallway was T-shaped: one of the small arms of the T led to the front door and the long leg to the bedroom behind him. Two steps and the men at the door would see him.

He tiptoed across the hallway to the kitchen, holding his breath. The floorboards creaked and he froze. The front door clicked shut. He stepped into the kitchen. The floor was tiled so his bare feet made no noise as he padded across to the sink. He picked up a plastic-handled bread-knife and went back to the kitchen door.

He peered carefully around the door jamb. He saw something dark, moving at waist height, and his breath caught in his throat. A gun, with a long, thin silencer.

Solomon's legs began to shake. Why was a man with a gun in McLaren's flat? Burglars in London didn't often carry guns. No one knew that Solomon was staying with McLaren. And surely anyone who was planning to attack McLaren would know that he was out of town. They'd have waited outside until they were sure he was at home.

A floorboard creaked. Solomon gripped the knife so tightly that his knuckles cracked. He forced himself to relax. They weren't burglars and they weren't there for McLaren. That meant they could only be after him, but who knew where he was staying? Only Diane. And Chuck Miller in Sarajevo. A few of McLaren's friends. Certainly no one who would want to do him any harm.

Solomon knew that a knife would be no match for a gun. Or guns. There were at least two men in the flat and Solomon doubted that only one would be armed. Two men, two guns. His best chance was to phone the police but there was no way he could use the phone in the hall, and his mobile was in the back bedroom.

He heard footsteps moving slowly down the hallway. Solomon stepped back into the kitchen. He had only seconds in which to decide what to do. He could stay hidden in the kitchen and gamble that they would go straight to either the main bedroom or the back bedroom. If they went past the kitchen, he stood a chance of running for the door and reaching it before they started shooting. But if they checked the kitchen, they'd have him cold.

His only other option was to confront them in the hallway. He'd have the advantage of surprise, but that was all.

Another creaking floorboard. And a sniff. Sweat was pouring down Solomon's back but his mouth was so dry he could barely swallow.

Russians. It had to be the agency. They must have followed him from Nicole's flat. He dropped to a crouch and moved to the kitchen door, his ears straining for any clue as to how far the men had moved down the hall. He glanced at the knife. It was more than a foot long with a serrated edge, designed for slicing, not stabbing. His eyes sought something else he could use as a weapon. There was a wine rack under the kitchen table and he pulled out a bottle of champagne. Then stood up at the side of the door.

Another creak of a floorboard. The silencer appeared in the doorway, pointing towards the bedroom.

Solomon stepped out of the kitchen and brought the bottle down hard on the man's wrist. The man screamed and the gun clattered to the floor. Solomon brought the bottle up again. The two men in the hallway stood still. They were both big men in long, dark coats. The one Solomon had hit was the bigger, with wide shoulders and a close-cropped haircut that emphasised the bullet shape of his head. The second man had a more angular face. He raised his gun and pushed the first man to the side to give himself a clearer shot.

Solomon threw the champagne bottle at him. It spun through the air and smacked into his face. The man staggered back with blood streaming from his nose. The first was bending down to retrieve his gun. Solomon brought his knee up hard and felt the man's nose break as his head jerked back, but the man had the gun in his hand again. Solomon slashed at him with the knife but it glanced off his sleeve. He slashed again, going for the throat, but the man fell backwards and the blow missed.

The men were blocking the hallway so he couldn't get to the front door. He turned and ran back to his bedroom. As he reached the door, he turned and threw the bread-knife at them, then slammed the door and pushed the bed against it. He knew that it wouldn't stop the two men – and the door panels were thin so a bullet would pass straight through. He picked up his mobile phone and tapped out nine-nine-nine, but he'd barely pressed the third nine before a bullet slammed through the door in a shower of splinters and embedded itself in the wall next to the window. There was surprisingly little noise.

Solomon pressed himself into the corner and put the phone to his ear. It was ringing, unanswered. Another bullet thwacked through the door. Solomon heard muffled voices. 'I'm phoning the police!' he shouted. 'Can you hear me? I'm calling the police!'

Another shot. A bullet smacked into the wall by his head. The phone continued to ring out.

Something banged into the door hard enough to jolt the bed. Solomon didn't know if it was a foot or a shoulder, but it was a heavy enough blow to push the bed several inches across the carpet. He pushed it back, tucked the phone into his jeans, bent down and rushed over to the window. He ripped open the curtains and tried to pull up the lower sash. It wouldn't move.

Again the door smacked into the bed, which scraped across the carpet. He kicked it back, then tried the window again. The muscles in his arms screamed with pain. Then he realised that there was a lock at the top of the window. He didn't have the key.

There was another heavy blow to the door, the top panel bowed in and the bed moved several inches.

'The police are on the way!' shouted Solomon. He pushed the bed back against the door.

There was a short silence, followed by a whispered conversation. Then nothing. For a moment Solomon thought they'd gone, but then there were four rapid gunshots, the sound of splintering wood and the window exploded in a shower of glass.

Solomon grabbed for his mobile. A woman was on the line, asking which service he wanted. He shouted his address down the phone then shoved it back into his pocket and headed for the window. He used a pillow to push out the remaining shards of glass. Behind him, shoulders pounded against the door. Solomon put the pillow on the bottom of the window frame and looked out. There was a cast-iron drainpipe some three feet to the left of the window. If he leaned out he'd be able to grab it and climb down the three storeys to the ground.

He swung his legs through the window and reached for the drainpipe. The door pounded again and the bed moved a good six inches across the floor. A gun appeared in the gap. A bullet slammed into the wall by the window.

Solomon grabbed for the drainpipe, his bare feet scrabbling against the wall. The bricks were damp, his feet slipped, and he took all of his weight on his arms. He pushed his knees against the bricks, then managed to get his feet up. He began to move down the drainpipe, hand over hand, trying to keep his arms outstretched so that his weight forced his feet against the wall.

He heard the door being hammered and he moved faster, scraping his knuckles against the bricks. He was breathing heavily and his heart was pounding. He passed a window on his left. The second floor. He looked down. Twenty-five feet. Maybe more. Below was a concrete patio and beyond it a small lawn that ran up to a brick wall.

In the distance he heard a siren. He couldn't tell if it was a police car, a fire engine or an ambulance, but part of him knew it was too soon for the police to have reacted to his call.

Above him he heard the door crash open. Solomon continued to scramble downwards, his breath coming in ragged gasps. Then he realised that the texture of the

253

pipe had changed: it was plastic rather than cast iron. A second later, it ripped away from the wall and he fell backwards.

He hit the concrete hard and heard, as much as felt, his left leg snap just below the knee. He pitched sideways and his head slammed into the ground. As he struggled to sit up he saw a shard of cracked bone sticking through the flesh.

Then he looked up. One of his attackers was leaning out of the third-floor window. Solomon crawled away from the rear of the building towards the lawn. The man pointed his gun and fired. A bullet kicked up a puff of dust in the concrete by his head. Solomon crawled faster, dragging his injured leg. Every movement sent spasms of red-hot pain through the limb, and he could feel blood pulsing from the wound under his knee. He heard a second loud pop from the upstairs window and his right arm jerked as a bullet smacked into his shoulder. The pain hit a second later, and Solomon screamed. He rolled over and started crawling again. That was when he saw the big man in the dark coat standing by the wall. He was aiming a gun at Solomon's face.

Leskov shouted up at the Ukrainian to get out of the flat and the man disappeared from the window. His finger tightened on the trigger. 'What are you doing?' asked a stern voice. A woman. Leskov looked round to see who it was. 'I've called the police,' shouted the woman. Leskov still couldn't see where she was.

The man on the patio groaned and tried to crawl towards a garden shed. He was only twenty feet from Leskov. The siren was getting louder. Heading his way. It was joined by a second, fainter but moving closer.

Leskov had to know how far away the woman was and if she was in a position to identify him. Further down the terrace there was a light on in a window, a figure silhouetted against it. He pointed the gun at it and the figure ducked.

Then Leskov heard the squeal of brakes followed, a second or two later, by car-doors opening and shouts. It had to be the police.

He turned to look at the man on the ground. He took a step forward, aiming his gun. The man had rolled up against the garden shed. Leskov fired. The man jerked and was still.

The footsteps were louder and Leskov knew that he had no time for a second shot. He turned and ran down the alley that led away from the terrace, unscrewing the silencer then shoving it and the gun into his pocket.

Oval shapes were spinning around a bright white light and shadowy figures were mumbling. Something was howling, a dog or a wolf, and the world was in the grip of an earthquake, shaking Solomon from side to side. He wasn't sure what had happened, but he knew it was bad. Now, though, he felt warm and comfortable, and let himself drift towards the white light.

'Stay with me!' A woman's voice, urgent and demanding. The voice of a woman who expected to be obeyed. Like a teacher or a soldier. Solomon tried to tell her to leave him alone, that he wanted to sleep, but he couldn't talk. There was something hard in his throat, but it didn't stop him breathing.

'Come on, stay with me!' The voice sounded more urgent this time but Solomon ignored it. He felt as if he was floating in a warm, wet cloud.

'Daddy?'

Solomon tried to smile but the hard object in his throat wouldn't let him.

'Daddy?'

He saw her then, four years old with long blonde hair.

'Daddy, what are you doing?' She reached out and stroked his forehead. 'Shall I kiss it better, Daddy?' she asked.

Solomon tried to nod but he couldn't move his head. He wanted to tell her that he missed her, that he loved her, and that he was sorry for what had happened, but his throat was hurting.

She slapped his face, hard. Solomon was confused. Why was she hitting him? Another slap, harder this time, then fingers gripped his face. Big fingers, not the fingers of a four-year-old child.

'Stay with me, damn it!' The woman was back. So was the howling wolf. Something pulled back his left eyelid and a masked face looked down at him, a face wearing thick, protective glasses. She was in her early thirties with black hair pulled back from her face. 'Can you hear me?' she shouted.

Solomon nodded. She let go of his face. The metal stretcher he was lying on lurched to the left. 'For God's sake,' said the woman, 'take it easy! Blood's pouring out of him.'

There was a man behind her. He was also wearing a mask and glasses, and a yellow and green jacket.

Solomon was sliding back into unconsciousness, but the woman pulled up his eyelid again and shone a beam of light into his eye. 'Can you hear me?' she asked.

Solomon nodded again. The howling wolf was louder now. It was a siren wailing. He was in an ambulance.

Images flashed through his mind. Throwing the champagne bottle at the man in McLaren's flat. The drainpipe coming away. The crack as his leg broke. The bullet slamming into his shoulder.

'We're on the way to hospital. I've given you something for the pain, but I need you to stay conscious. Do you understand?'

Solomon couldn't talk because of the plastic pipe in his airway and had to nod again. He wanted to ask the paramedic if he was going to die, but instead he concentrated on breathing. There was a bag of clear liquid hanging from a hook, which swung from side to side as the ambulance rushed, siren blaring, through the city streets. The siren started to fade and he closed his eyes again. The girl was back, stroking his forehead. 'Daddy?' she whispered, and Solomon smiled.

Goncharov tapped out Ivan Petrovic's number and glared at Leskov as he waited for the Bosnian to answer.

'It wasn't our fault – he should have been asleep,' said Leskov. Goncharov cut him off with an impatient wave of his hand.

Petrovic answered and Goncharov explained what had happened.

'So, is he dead or not?' asked the Bosnian.

'He was shot twice and he fell from a third-floor window,' said Goncharov.

'You are not answering my question,' said Petrovic.

'The police intervened before we could be sure,' said Goncharov. 'An ambulance was called and the siren was on when it drove away.'

'I suppose there is no doubt that he was shot?' asked Petrovic, his voice loaded with sarcasm.

'Twice,' said Goncharov. 'One of my men shot him in the arm, another shot him in the side.'

Petrovic chuckled. 'Two men with guns, and they couldn't finish him off?'

'They're good men, generally,' said Goncharov. 'They were interrupted by the police. What do you want me do? We can finish him off at the hospital, or wait until he returns home.'

For a few seconds Petrovic said nothing. Then he chuckled again. 'Let it go. He won't come back to Sarajevo, not after this. The scars will be a permanent reminder of what's waiting for him.'

'You're sure?' asked Goncharov.

'Don't worry, Sergei. You'll get your money.'

Goncharov flushed. He hadn't been worried about payment for the shooting; he was more concerned that Petrovic thought he'd been less than professional.

'What about the girl?' asked Petrovic. 'The man went to see her, did he?'

'We used her as bait,' said Goncharov. 'That's how we got him. We followed him home.' He wanted the Bosnian to know that the hit had been well planned, even if it had been clumsily executed.

'If he's not dead, he'll tell the police about her.'

'I've already moved her,' said Goncharov.

'It would be better if she were out of the country,' said the Bosnian.

'I would lose money on her if she leaves now,' said Goncharov.

'I'll buy back her contract,' said Petrovic, 'providing you don't try to screw me.'

'I paid you ten thousand.'

'I remember.'

'But there have been extra expenses.'

'I said I didn't want you to screw me, you thieving bastard. I'd already arranged the paperwork, and you just paid for her flight.'

'There have been expenses in London,' said Goncharov.

'Send her back to me – I can use her somewhere,' said Petrovic. 'Put her on the next plane and I'll give you a credit of twelve thousand dollars against the next batch.'

'Agreed,' said Goncharov.

'The girl, she talked to this man?'

'Briefly,' said Goncharov.

'Do you know what was said?'

He had asked the question casually, but Goncharov knew instinctively that he should choose his words carefully. 'He wasn't with her long,' he said. 'When it became clear that he didn't want sex she asked him to leave.'

'He was questioning her?'

'He said he wanted to talk. She asked him to leave. That's all I know.' There was a long silence, and for a moment Goncharov wondered if the connection had been lost. 'Hello?' he said.

'Send her back to Sarajevo. I'll see you next month.'

Goncharov put down his mobile phone on the desk. There were dozens of questions he had wanted to ask Petrovic. He wanted to know who the man was, and what the girl had seen in Kosovo. He wanted to know why she was running, and who from. But Goncharov knew that some questions were best left unanswered, especially when it came to a man like Ivan Petrovic.

Jack Solomon opened his eyes to a regular electronic beeping. There was something comforting about the monotonous sound, and as he struggled to focus he realised that it coincided with his heartbeat.

He turned his head to the left. There was a bank of monitors on a metal trolley next to his bed and a large card with a teddy bear on it holding a bunch of flowers and a balloon with 'Get Well Soon' on it.

'Mr Solomon?'

It was a woman's voice. Solomon turned back. A black nurse was smiling down at him, a stethoscope slung around her neck. He tried to speak but his mouth was so dry that his tongue was stuck to the floor of his mouth. He grunted.

'That's okay, Mr Solomon, don't try to talk. I can't give you any water but you've got a drip there so don't worry.'

Solomon grunted again. He wanted to know if he was going to die.

'You're in intensive care but you're going to be all right,' she said, as if reading his mind. 'You just have to relax and let us take care of you. Do you understand?'

Solomon nodded.

'That's good,' she said. 'Get some rest.'

He closed his eyes.

The immigration officer barely glanced at Nicole's passport. It was Croatian. The name wasn't hers, neither was the date of birth, but it was her photograph. Nicole was more nervous at the airport in Sarajevo than she had been at Heathrow. At the London airport she'd had a minder, whom Petrovic had laughingly called her jockey. He was a student from south London who had been paid a thousand dollars to fly with her, posing as her boyfriend. On the way back to Sarajevo she was alone. Two of Goncharov's men had taken her to the airport. She'd kept asking them what was wrong and why she was being thrown out of the country, but they had steadfastly refused to answer her questions.

'Why?' she'd asked tearfully, after they'd checked her in and walked her to the departure area. 'Why are you doing this to me? What did I do wrong?'

There had been another man waiting for her at Vienna airport, and he, too, had refused to speak to her. He'd just stayed close by her until her connecting flight was due to depart then watched until she'd walked to the plane.

Nicole had cried all the way from Vienna to Sarajevo. The stewardesses had asked if she was sick, but she'd covered her face with a handkerchief. She had no idea what had gone wrong. She knew what the rules were: Anna had explained them the day she'd started working for the agency. No talking to clients about the agency, no leaving the flat without telephoning the agency first, no socialising with anyone who wasn't with the agency, no contact with clients outside work, never to give out her phone number, never to answer the door unless she was expecting a client. There were rules about handling the money, rules about hygiene and cleanliness, rules about what she should do in bed. There were rules for everything and, so far as Nicole was aware, she hadn't broken any of them.

It had to have been the man from Bosnia, she'd realised at some point during the flight to Sarajevo. The man called Jack. Maybe he'd complained to the agency. Or maybe they'd discovered he wanted to talk to her about what had happened in Kosovo. If she was being sent home because of him, it wasn't fair because she hadn't answered any questions. She'd refused to speak to him, point-blank.

She'd only stopped crying when the wheels of the plane had screeched on the runway and the plane had taxied to the terminal building. She knew that someone would be waiting for her. She just didn't know who it would be.

The immigration officer gave her back the passport. She slipped it into her bag and walked through to the baggage-reclaim area. She had no suitcase to collect. The two men in London hadn't allowed her to take anything with her. Everything she owned was still in the St John's Wood flat.

She walked through the Nothing To Declare channel and into the arrivals area. She kept her head down and her bag clutched to her chest as she walked quickly to the exit.

'Not so fast, little sister,' said a guttural voice to her left.

Nicole stumbled and the man reached out to steady her.

Another appeared at her right shoulder. 'We're here to drive you,' he said.

Both men were tall and thin, wearing leather bomber jackets and blue jeans. She could tell from their accents that they were Bosnian Serbs. She kept her head down so that they wouldn't see how scared she was.

'Don't be frightened, little sister,' said the first man, patting her on the shoulder.

'I didn't do anything wrong,' she said.

'You've nothing to worry about,' said the man.

'Where are you taking me?' she asked.

The man grinned cruelly. 'Arizona,' he said.

Nicole's heart sank. She knew what awaited her in Arizona. The tears started again, but the two men ignored her anguish and guided her towards the exit.

Solomon knew before they opened their mouths that they were police. Two men, one in his late twenties in a dark blue pinstripe suit with a crisp white shirt and a red tie, the other in his mid-thirties in a blue blazer and black trousers. Both wore shoes chosen for comfort rather than style.

They were laughing as they walked down the ward to his bed. Solomon guessed that the older detective would be an inspector, his sidekick a DC. By the look of the suit he was a university graduate on the fast-track promotion scheme.

'Jack Solomon?' asked the older policeman.

'That's what it says on the chart,' said Solomon.

'Detective Inspector Bob Hitchcock, and this is Detective Constable Paul Owen. How are you feeling?'

Solomon smiled tightly. It was a difficult question to answer. His leg had metal pins sticking out of it and even the most optimistic prognosis had been that he'd always limp. The two bullet wounds were healing but he'd be scarred for life. He was still in intensive care hooked up to machines measuring his bodily functions, and he was doped up to the eyeballs with painkillers. But he was alive and he was grateful for that. 'Fine,' he said.

Owen pulled up two plastic chairs and they sat down. The younger man carefully straightened his trousers, then took a small black notebook and a silver pen from his jacket pocket.

'Do you know who attacked you?' asked Hitchcock. He was a stocky man with receding hair and intense blue eyes.

'Two men. I think they were Russian.'

'Why do you think that?'

'They spoke to each other in Russian. You know I was in the job?'

'We're aware of your background.'

Solomon had no doubt that Hitchcock had pulled his file. He'd know why he'd left the Met.

'Can you identify them?' asked Hitchcock.

Solomon said he could and gave them a full description of the two men, speaking slowly so that Owen could take it all down.

'Why would anyone want to kill you, Mr Solomon?' asked Hitchcock, once Owen had finished writing.

Solomon had given a lot of thought to that question, and to what he should tell the police. He'd reached the conclusion that there was no reason not to tell them everything. He told them about the massacre in Kosovo, about Nicole coming to London, about finding her picture on the Internet, and about visiting her flat in St John's Wood.

Hitchcock listened patiently. 'Did you give her your address?'

Solomon shook his head. 'I gave her my mobile number, that's all. And it's a pay-as-you-go – I couldn't be traced from it.'

'Did she call anyone else while you were there?'

'No. The agency called her but I heard the conversation. She didn't tell them she had a problem.'

Hitchcock looked across at his colleague to check that he was making notes. 'The thing is, if she didn't call them before you left, how were they able to get to you so quickly?'

'That's a good question,' said Solomon.

'Do you have any enemies?'

'Not in London.'

The inspector's eyes narrowed. 'That's an interesting way of answering the question,' he said.

'I had a bust-up with a pimp in Sarajevo.' Solomon hadn't thought about Petrovic since he'd flown out of Bosnia. But if the Serb had friends in London, he might have been exacting his revenge.

'Connected with this girl?'

Solomon nodded. 'She worked for him.'

'Do you think the pimp might have set you up in London?'

'It's possible.'

'Possible or probable?'

Solomon frowned. Would Petrovic have known that Solomon had gone to London? A phone call to the Sarajevo office was all it would have taken to find out where he had gone. And another phone call to Nicole's new pimp in London. Two phone calls and his life was on the line. 'Probable,' said Solomon eventually. 'If it wasn't him, I don't see who else it could have been.'

'I'm going to need the website details,' said Hitchcock. 'And everything you can tell me about the girl and her flat.'

Solomon talked and Owen scribbled in his notebook.

'You didn't think that turning up at the girl's flat was going to cause problems?' asked Owen.

'You mean, did I know they were going to try to kill me? What do you think? There was no reason to think I was causing anyone any grief. All I wanted to do was talk to her.'

'Did she seem nervous when she was with you?' asked Hitchcock.

'Dead right,' said Solomon. 'She threatened to kill herself.'

The inspector's eyebrows shot skyward. 'What?'

'I don't think she was serious, but she said she'd cut her wrist if I didn't leave.'

'Were you aggressive towards her?' said Hitchcock.

'No, I bloody well wasn't,' said Solomon. 'In case you hadn't noticed I'm the victim here.'

'Is it possible she knew you were being set up?'

Solomon frowned again. He remembered how upset she had been when he'd told her who he was and why he was there. 'No.'

'So they must have had the flat staked out,' said Hitchcock.

'Which makes me bloody stupid, right?'

The inspector shrugged. 'Like you said, you had no reason to think that anyone would object to you talking to her.' He leaned back in his chair and scratched his chin. 'Okay, you don't have to be in Mensa to realise that Russians plus guns with silencers equals Russian Mafia. That means we're not going to get someone on the street giving them up. A woman who lives in one of the flats in Inverness Terrace saw one of them shoot you, but she couldn't give us much of a description. Your descriptions are better and we'll get you to look at mugshots, but there's precious little chance that they have previous because if they did they wouldn't still be in the country.' He cleared his throat. 'We've checked the bullets they took out of you and we don't have a match with anything on file but, again, that's to be expected. Professionals are going to destroy any gun they fire, and the Russian Mafia are as professional as they come. We've got blood spots on the floor and we've had them typed, but I've spoken to my boss and he's not prepared to fund a DNA analysis until we've got a suspect. I think it's the right call. It's only going to help if we've had them in before and, as I said, that's unlikely.'

'Which leaves us where?' asked Solomon.

'We'll check out the flat, but you don't have to be bloody psychic to know that she'll be long gone.'

'But you can bust the agency, can't you?'

'Put them out of business, you mean?' Hitchcock pulled a face. 'That's Vice and Clubs, your old stamping ground.'

'But whoever runs the agency has to be a suspect, right?'

Hitchcock grimaced again. 'The guys who run the agencies go to a lot of trouble to stay hidden, but we'll do what we can. Problem is, all we'll get then is the owner of the agency. Even if we get a face to face, he's not going to roll over on the killers, not if he sent them.'

'You're not inspiring me with confidence.'

Hitchcock smiled thinly. 'You were in the job, you know what the odds are. Most murders are domestic, and we solve them within minutes. Sex murders we get eventually, because they keep on doing it until they get caught. But the professional jobs, the only way we get them is if they fuck up or they're grassed. The Russian Mafia don't fuck up and they only deal with people they know, so they don't get grassed.'

'They're going to get away with it, then?'

'I'm just letting you know the way the land lies. We'll do what we can, but I don't want to raise your expectations.'

Solomon sighed.

Owen picked up the card with the teddy bear on it and opened it. 'Inga?' he said.

Solomon forced himself to smile. He had been surprised to see the card from Inga. Surprised that she'd

267

known he was in hospital and surprised she'd bothered to send him a card. 'A friend in Sarajevo,' he lied.

'It got here quickly,' said Owen.

'She couriered it.'

Owen put the card back on the bedside table. The two policemen stood up. 'We'll send over any mugshots, and if we turn up anything you'll be the first to know.'

'Cheers. And thanks.'

The policemen walked away. Solomon lay looking at the card. Why had Inga sent it? And how had she known where he was?

When Solomon was moved out of the intensive care ward, Danny McLaren was his first visitor. He walked on to the ward along with a dozen others, most of whom were clutching bouquets of flowers and bags of fruit. McLaren held a copy of his paper, which he dropped on Solomon's bed with a paper bag of grapes.

'Seeing as how you were hovering between life and death, you probably didn't get to see the story,' he said, flopping down on a plastic chair and helping himself to a handful of the grapes.

The paper was a week old, from two days after Solomon had been shot. The story was on page seven, half a dozen paragraphs and a head-and-shoulders photograph that had been taken when he was with the Met. The story carried the by-line of the paper's crime correspondent.

'You'd have got a better show if I'd been in town,' said McLaren. 'How are you doing?'

'They keep telling me I was lucky,' said Solomon. 'I was lucky that my leg broke below the knee so it doesn't have to go in traction. I was lucky the bullet in my shoulder didn't go through any nerves so I'll still be able to play the piano.' He flashed McLaren a grin to show that he was joking. 'And I was lucky the bullet in my side didn't go through the gut because then I might have ended up with blood poisoning. Mind you, if I had any sort of luck at all I wouldn't have got shot in the first place.'

'Not bitter, then.' McLaren laughed. 'Who's the card from?'

'One of the girls I met.'

'A hooker sent you a get-well card?'

'She must have read the piece in the paper.'

'Yeah, but even so, you must have made an impression.'

'How's the flat?' asked Solomon, keen to change the subject.

'Window's fixed, and I had the locks changed. I'm not sure what to do about the bullet-holes in the bedroom. They sort of give the place character. I might leave them there.'

'Is it a mess?'

'It's looked better.'

'I'm sorry.'

'It could have been a lot worse, mate. Let's just be grateful for small mercies.'

'Them being what, exactly?'

'At least they didn't steal the family silver,' said McLaren. 'Do you need anything?'

'I'd love a carton of Marlboro, but until I can get about they won't let me smoke. And the only clothes I've got are my jeans – and I haven't even got them, really, because they cut them off me.'

'How bad is it?'

'I should be mobile in a week or two.'

'I gather the cops have been?'

'Have you spoken to them?'

'Yeah. Talked to a DI called Hitchcock. Didn't sound too hopeful.'

'They gave me mugshots to look at but I didn't recognise anyone.'

'They'd have been on the first plane back to Russia, if they had any sense. Lie low until it blows over.'

'They're still looking, though?'

'There's an investigation, but it wasn't murder and you're not high-profile.'

'Worse than that, I'm a cop who left under a cloud and I'd just been in a prostitute's flat.'

McLaren looked sympathetic. 'They're on the case, though. Just don't hold your breath. Did the girl say anything?'

'She clammed right up.'

'What's that about?'

'I don't know. All she had to do was tell me what happened. I could have taken it from there. If she didn't want to give evidence, that would have been okay. But she wouldn't say anything.'

'Do you want me to sniff around?'

'Did Hitchcock say he'd spoken to the girl?'

McLaren shook his head. 'The flat's empty, and she's disappeared from the website. They're trying to talk to the guy who runs the agency, but no joy so far.'

'I got the feeling they weren't going to try too hard on that front.'

'It's a question of resources, it always is these days. The agency uses pay-as-you-go mobiles, so it'd mean a major operation just to find out where their office is. All expenditure has to be justified these days, and, like I said, it's not a murder case.'

'My luck just keeps getting better, doesn't it?'

'I'll make some enquiries,' said McLaren. He took out his notebook. Solomon told him as much as he could remember about Nicole and her apartment, then McLaren left, promising to return with a stack of reading material.

Solomon was exhausted. He had just shut his eyes when a girl's voice said, 'Hello.'

He raised his head long enough to see Inga, but fell back.

'Let me help you,' she said. She propped him up with his pillows.

'What are you doing here?' asked Solomon.

'Visiting,' she said brightly. She was wearing a short black-leather skirt and matching high-heeled boots, with a white-leather jacket that glistened like ice under the overhead fluorescent lights. She was wearing her dyed red hair loose and her eyes were hidden behind wraparound sunglasses. She picked up the card. 'I'm glad this got to you. I wasn't sure which name to use. The paper said your name was Jack.'

Solomon smiled. 'No one uses their right names, you know that. I bet you're not even Inga.'

Inga shrugged. 'Names don't matter, but I like Jack better than David.'

'Yeah, me too.' He nodded at the chair. 'Sit down, please. You're only my second visitor, if you don't count the police.'

Inga sat down and put the card back on the bedside table.

'How did you know I was here?' asked Solomon.

The newspaper was still on the bed and she pointed at it. 'You're famous.'

'Famous for being shot,' he said.

'Do you know who did it?'

'I don't think it was Sasha, if that's what you're worried about.'

She frowned. 'Of course it wasn't Sasha. Why would you think it was him?'

'Forgive me, Inga, but why else would you be here?'

Her frown deepened. 'I was worried about you.'

'We met twice. And the second time I was bundled into the back of a van and given the third degree by your boss.'

'Third degree?'

'Interrogated. Sasha wanted to know why I wanted to talk to Nicole.'

'But that was before he knew who you were and what you wanted.'

'Did Sasha tell you to come here?' asked Solomon.

She looked offended. 'No. Of course not.'

Solomon looked at her closely, but his policeman's instincts failed him and he couldn't tell if she was being truthful or not.

'You think I'm here to spy on you?' asked Inga.

'I don't know.' He smiled. 'I'm doped up on painkillers and my leg's joined together with bits of metal so I'm not thinking too clearly.'

'What was it like being shot?'

'Like being punched, very hard. It was numb for a second or two, then it felt like I'd been burned. I passed out.'

'You will have scars?'

Solomon laughed. 'Oh, yes, I'll have two amazing scars.'

'Scars can be sexy on a man,' said Inga.

'We'll see.'

'On women it's different. I have a friend who works, and she has a knife scar on her stomach. Men hate it.'

'You're still working in the same flat?'

Inga nodded. 'Sure. It's good business.'

'Sasha didn't give you any problems?'

Inga pouted and shook her head.

'I'm sorry if I sound suspicious,' he said. 'It's just that you were the last person I expected to take an interest in me.'

'I like you,' she said quietly.

'You don't have to say that.'

'Why not? It's true. I can see that you're a kind man, a man who cares about people, and most of the men I meet aren't like that. I read the story in the paper and saw your photograph.'

'I'm glad you did.'

Inga flicked through the newspaper. 'The story didn't say who shot you.'

'It was Russians, I think.'

'In your flat?'

'In my friend's flat. I was staying with him.'

'Do you know why they shot you?'

'I suppose they wanted to kill me.'

It was meant as a joke, but Inga took it seriously. 'Why would Russians want to kill you, Jack? Was it about that girl you were looking for?'

Solomon looked at her suspiciously. 'Why do you think that?'

'Because of the way Sasha reacted when he knew you were asking questions. I thought maybe you'd asked somebody else.'

Solomon nodded slowly. 'Yeah, you're right. At least,

I think you are. I found her. She's working for an escort agency. I went to see her and a few hours later they broke into my flat and did this to me.'

She smiled and helped herself to some grapes. 'So how long will you be in hospital?'

'A month, maybe less. They want to make sure that the leg is healing properly before they let me out.'

Inga reached into her coat pocket and took out a piece of paper. 'I've written my phone number here,' she said. She put it on the bedside table. 'Call me when you go home,' she said. 'I'd like to see you.'

'As a customer?' He regretted saying it as soon as the words left his mouth, but she didn't take offence.

'As a friend,' she said. 'We can go for coffee again.'

She stood up, blew him a kiss and walked away. Patients in several beds turned to watch her go, then looked at Solomon, clearly wondering what he was doing with such a pretty visitor. It was a question that Solomon himself was trying to answer. He doubted that Inga had suddenly been overcome with a desire to seek his friendship. There had to be another reason for her visit, and it was almost certainly Sasha.

Inga walked out of the hospital and down the street, raising the collar of her leather jacket. She walked past a telephone box festooned with prostitutes' cards, all promising the ultimate in sexual experience. Inga knew that the photograph on the card never matched the girl in the flat. Most of them were printed by one of three firms, and they had made tens of millions of pounds from the vice trade. Inga's flat alone put out five hundred cards every day. She had laughed when she'd first seen her card. The words were accurate enough, 'Stunning Redhead,

All Services', but underneath was a photograph of a girl with short red hair who looked nothing like her. No one had ever complained, and the punters who spoke to her said that she was much prettier than the girl on the card.

Sasha was parked in a side road from where he could see the entrance to the hospital. He'd driven her from Soho in his Audi convertible. It was the first time she'd been in the sports car: whenever she'd gone anywhere with him before it had always been in the back of his Mercedes with Karic and Rikki. Sasha rarely went anywhere alone. It wasn't that he was afraid, Inga doubted that he was scared of anything or anyone, but he was careful.

Inga climbed into the Audi.

'Well?' said Sasha impatiently, before she'd even closed the door.

'He's been shot twice and his leg is broken,' she said.

'I know that,' snapped Sasha. 'Who did it?'

'He said Russians. He found the girl he was looking for.'

'I knew it,' said Sasha, and he slapped the steering-wheel. 'So she was working for Russians, this girl?'

'For an escort agency, he said.'

'Which one?'

'He didn't say.'

'Did you ask him?'

'Sasha, he was suspicious of me anyway. He wanted to know why I'd gone to see him. If I'd asked too many questions, he'd never have trusted me.'

'Bastard Russians. If he carries on like this, they'll kill him.' Sasha exhaled through clenched teeth. 'Did he talk to the girl?'

'Yes, but he didn't say what they talked about.' She

could see Sasha was about to get angry again and she patted his arm. 'Sasha, he kept asking why I'd gone to see him. I gave him my number and asked him to call me when he gets out.'

'I want to know where she is *now*!' hissed Sasha. 'And get your hand off my arm. When I want you to touch me, I'll tell you.'

Inga flinched. She sat with her hands in her lap as Sasha drove her back to Soho. Back to work.

Solomon spent a week on the general ward before he was released. There was no ambulance available so he asked a porter to call him a black cab. Diane and Sean Milne had told him he could stay with them as long as he liked, and McLaren had offered his spare room but with his leg still in plaster Solomon doubted that he could manage the stairs to the flat.

He called Diane from his mobile on the way to Clapham, and she was waiting at the door when the black cab pulled up. He sighed with annoyance when he saw Sean push a wheelchair out of the house.

'Sean, I can walk,' he said, as he took his change from the taxi driver.

'I'm a nurse, I know what I'm doing,' said Milne.

'I've got crutches.'

'Sit,' said Milne. 'I know how to deal with unruly patients.'

'I bet you do. And I bet it involves an ice-cold bed bath.'

Diane kissed Solomon on both cheeks. 'Thanks for this, Diane,' he said.

'Stay as long as you want,' said Diane, picking up his crutches. 'Until the baby arrives at any rate. Then you're out of here.'

'A week or so at most, I promise,' said Solomon.

Sean pushed the wheelchair to the front door of the house, then expertly manoeuvred it over the threshold. 'We've made up a bed in the front room, save you trying to handle the stairs. And Danny dropped off your gear yesterday.'

Sean wheeled Solomon into the kitchen and Diane made coffee. Solomon was glad to be back among friends in a home that smelt of coffee and freshly cut flowers, rather than vomit and disinfectant.

'How's the investigation going?' asked Sean.

'It's pretty much run out of steam,' said Solomon. 'There's no trace of Nicole on the agency's website. The cops spoke to the girl who runs the agency and she says there's no record of anyone called Amy answering to Nicole's description working for them. There is an Amy and the cops have seen her page, but she doesn't look anything like Nicole, apparently. She said that maybe I was confused and got them mixed up with another agency. They asked her if she knew anything about the shooting and of course she had no idea what they were talking about.'

'Well, she would say that, wouldn't she?' said Diane.

'You know what it's like these days,' said Solomon. 'The cops have to follow PACE, they can't put on the pressure like they used to.' Solomon grinned at Sean. 'Police and Criminal Evidence Act,' he explained.

'I know,' said Sean. 'I watch *The Bill*.'

'But you were attacked after you left the girl's flat,' said Diane, putting mugs of coffee on the table. 'You don't have to be Sherlock Holmes to put two and two together. Even if the woman says it wasn't her agency, you know it was, right?'

'I told the cops that, but they say their hands are tied. And they don't have the resources to mount a major investigation against the agency. They don't even know where its offices are, or who really runs it. Apparently they'd have put more manpower on the case if I'd been killed.' He sipped his coffee. It was rich and aromatic, a far cry from the insipid instant brew they'd given him in hospital.

'What are you planning to do?' asked Diane.

'I'm going to see if I can find out what happened to the girl.'

Sean and Diane exchanged looks of astonishment. 'You are joking,' said Diane.

'I'm not giving up,' said Solomon. 'If I give up, they'll have won.'

'They almost killed you. Next time you might not be so lucky.'

'I wish people would stop telling me how lucky I am,' said Solomon. 'Anyway, I don't mean the men who shot me. The police reckon they'll be long gone. I'm talking about the killers in Kosovo. If I walk away they'll have killed twenty-six people with no consequences.'

'Why are you so set on this case?' asked Sean. 'You must have come across dozens like it.'

'I don't know.'

'That's no answer,' said Diane. 'You didn't take any case so personally when you were a cop.'

'You had to have been there,' said Solomon. 'A whole extended family, murdered together. Someone has to do something, not to make it right but to get justice for them.'

'But why you?' asked Sean.

'I don't think the War Crimes Tribunal will take on the case so it's up to me.'

278

'He's like the bloody Terminator,' said Sean.

'He's going to get himself killed,' Diane said. 'You realise that the girl herself might have had you shot?'

'She's just a kid,' said Solomon. 'She's being used, I'm sure of that. For all we know, they might have killed her too.'

'Jack, please,' said Diane, 'can't you let sleeping dogs lie?'

'No, I can't.'

Diane had a powerful desktop computer in her study and she showed Solomon how to log on to her Internet server before leaving for work. 'There's food in the fridge, so help yourself,' she said, and headed out of the front door.

Solomon used one of his crutches to get himself into the kitchen where he made himself some coffee. His leg didn't hurt, but the cast was heavy and awkward so he needed at least one crutch to steady himself. The biggest problem was the itching inside the cast. A nurse had given him a knitting-needle to get at it but even that only provided temporary relief.

He limped back to the study and put the mug down next to the computer. He lowered himself on to the chair and dialled up the Internet connection. He launched the browser and clicked through to www.legal-escorts.com, then to the page with the pictures of the girls. Nicole had gone. There was a girl called Amy, but she was a statuesque blonde. The agency had a contacts page and he clicked through to it. There was no address, just a mobile phone number and an email address, bookings@legal-escorts.com.

Solomon sat back and sipped his coffee. He was back looking for a needle in a haystack.

His fingers played across the keyboard and he logged on to the Punternet database. He searched for a report on Amy of Legal Escorts, but there was nothing. He went through to the website's message board and posted a message using the alias 'Legman', asking if anyone knew the whereabouts of Amy of Legal Escorts.

He spent the best part of two hours trawling through the various escort-agency sites but couldn't find her. That didn't necessarily mean that she'd left London: she might be working in a Soho walk-up or a massage parlour or a lapdancing club. The only way to find out was to talk to the agency, but if they hadn't told the police anything it was doubtful that they'd open up to him.

Solomon's Bosnian mobile phone rang and he picked it up. There was no incoming number but neither did it show 'Number Withheld'. Solomon pressed the button to accept the call.

'Jack? Is that you?'

It was a woman's voice. Foreign. 'Nicole?'

'Hello, Jack. Can you hear me? It's Arnela.'

Chuck Miller's secretary. It was a bad connection, her voice faded in and out, and there was a satellite delay of almost a second each time she spoke.

'Arnela, yes, I can hear you.'

There was a series of rapid clicks and the line was clearer. 'Do you have an address in London?' she asked. 'I've a letter for you and I need to know where to send it.'

'I'm staying with friends for a few days. Who's the letter from?'

'Mr Miller. Can you give me the address?'

'Just tell me what it says,' said Solomon.

'Mr Miller said I should send it to you right away,' she said.

Solomon could feel that she was uncomfortable, but he pressed her none the less. 'Just read it to me, Arnela.'

'I can't, I'm sorry.'

'Is he there?'

There was a long pause. Solomon felt bad at putting her on the spot, but he knew the letter contained bad news and that Miller was hiding behind her. 'He's here, but he's in a meeting,' said Arnela.

'Come on, Arnela, what's going on?'

'Don't make this difficult for me, Jack. Please.'

'He's sacking me, isn't he?'

'Jack . . .'

'God knows how long a letter's going to take to reach me. Just tell me what Chuck's saying.'

'I'm really sorry.'

'It's not you, I know that.'

Arnela read the letter quickly. It was a typical Chuck Miller communication, carefully worded and impersonal. He used phrases like 'organisational restructuring', 'expenditure forecasts' and 'performance indicators', but the meaning was clear: there was no longer a job for Solomon in the International War-dead Commission. He'd been sacked.

'I want to talk to him, Arnela,' he said, when she'd finished speaking.

'He won't talk to you,' she said.

'He's not in a meeting, is he?'

'Please, Jack.'

'He isn't, is he?'

'No. He's here, but he won't speak to you. I can't put you through.'

'What sparked this off?' asked Solomon.

'I've got to go, I'm sorry.'

'He knows what happened to me here, doesn't he?'

'He knows you were in hospital, yes.'

'How? Who told him?'

'This isn't fair,' whispered the secretary. 'I need this job. If I lose it how will I feed my children?'

Solomon felt guilty for pushing her so hard. She and her family depended on her job in a way that he could never appreciate. The only Bosnians – except criminals – with anything approaching a decent standard of living were those who worked for the internationals. He had no right to jeopardise what little she had. He apologised and cut the connection. There was no point in talking to Miller anyway. He wasn't a man to make snap judgements, or to be swayed by emotive arguments. He would not change his mind.

He sat back in his chair and stared up at the ceiling. He had enough money in his bank account for at least six months, so he wasn't worried about being unemployed. And he knew that he'd have no problem getting work with an aid agency once it became known that he was available.

He lit a Marlboro. Where had Nicole gone? The fact that she had been removed from the agency's website so quickly was a clear sign that she had been involved in some way with the attack in McLaren's flat. He had to find her. Whatever the risk.

Solomon paid the cab driver and eased himself on to the pavement. He was only using one crutch and before long he hoped to manage with just a walking-stick. He'd cut a slit down a pair of his jeans to hide as much of the plaster cast as possible and pulled a pair of hiking socks over the end of the cast to cover his toes.

He pushed open the door and went into the pub. It was

full of lunchtime drinkers, men in suits with soft drinks and worried frowns, builders in dusty overalls with pints of lager, and teenagers drinking alcopops and playing the fruit machine. Colin Duggan was sitting at a corner table reading the *Evening Standard*, a glass of whisky and ice in front of him. He didn't get up as Solomon eased himself down on to a wooden chair, his plaster cast to the side of the table.

'You don't look too bad for a man who's been shot twice,' said Duggan.

'I was lucky.'

'When does the cast come off?'

'Week or two. Do you want another?'

Duggan nodded. Solomon ordered a double Bell's and a pint of lager.

'Did you talk to Hitchcock?'

'Why don't you ask him yourself?'

'Because you're in the job, and I'm not. Did you?'

'Yes but it's the last time I do you any favours.' Duggan leaned across the table. 'They don't know who runs the agency, but they spoke to a woman who claims to be in charge – Anna Gregson, she's from Estonia but married a British teacher a while back.' He slid an envelope across the table. Solomon opened it and took out a single sheet of paper: Anna Gregson's name and address. 'Hitchcock is sure she's fronting for someone.'

'What about the agency? Where's it based?'

'They don't know.'

'Didn't they ask her?'

'She said she runs it from home.'

'Did they search her house?'

'First, why would they want to? Second, what judge would give them a warrant?'

'Because a few hours after I'd seen one of her escorts, two Russians were using me as target practice. She's Estonian, right? That's practically Russian.'

'I'm Welsh, and that doesn't make me English.'

The barman brought their drinks and put them on the table. Solomon paid him and waited until he'd walked away. 'Are they going to try and find out?'

'They've spoken to her. She said she had nothing to do with the shooting.'

'She's running an escort agency. Why don't they do her for living off immoral earnings?'

'They're not Vice cops. And women can't be done for living off immoral earnings. It's controlling prostitution for gain. Have you forgotten the drill already?'

'Why don't they get Vice on to it? Bust the agency, then get her to roll over on the real boss.'

Duggan took a long pull on his whisky. 'They keep a watching brief on the agency, same as they do on all of them. See who's working there. But as long as no punters get hurt they're not going to do anything. Have you any idea how much it would cost to mount an investigation? And for what?'

'Last time I looked it was seven years for controlling prostitution.'

'These days you'd be lucky to find a judge willing to send them down for a year. Out in six months with good behaviour. What's the point?'

'Sequestration of assets?'

'The money's washed faster than a sprinter's jockstrap. They spin it through cash companies then move it to offshore. Even if they went after the money, they'd be lucky to see ten per cent of it. So like I said, what's the point?'

'It's illegal, Colin. It's a fucking crime. Leaving aside

the fact that they shot me.'

'It's a crime nobody cares about. London has a grand total of forty-eight Vice cops. They have more racism advisers than that, which shows you where the priorities lie.'

Solomon stubbed out his cigarette. 'So they're leaving it?'

'Hitchcock says they're still on it. But they're trying to trace the shooters rather than ride roughshod over the agency. The case stays open. If they hit anyone else, they'll be right on to it.'

'I need to find the girl,' said Solomon.

'Last time you spoke to her you spent a month in hospital.'

'And that's a good enough reason to talk to her again. I want to know why she's running.'

'You know damn well why she's running. You said she saw her family massacred in Kosovo. She's got to be terrified that the killers are going to track her down. And then you turn up banging on her door.'

'If she was hiding, she wouldn't have allowed her photograph to go up on the Internet.'

'Let it go,' said Duggan. 'Go back to where you came from and get on with your life.'

'I can't go back, ' said Solomon. 'I've been sacked.'

'Why doesn't that surprise me?' said Duggan dourly.

Solomon held up the piece of paper. 'Who could I get to check out Gregson?'

'What's to check?' asked the policeman. 'She spoke to Hitchcock.'

'She lied to Hitchcock.'

'You don't know that. She might not have known anything about the Russians.'

'I'd bet money that if she doesn't she works for the guy who does.'

'Yeah, well, we'll never know, will we?'

Solomon put down the sheet of paper and sipped his lager. 'What if I go private?'

'You've got to be kidding.'

'I want to know where she works and who she works for. If Hitchcock and Vice aren't interested. I'll pay to have it done.' He slapped his plaster cast. 'It's not as if I can go running after her, is it?'

He drained his glass.

'If you do find out where the agency is, what then? Do you think they're going to break down and confess just because you wave your crutch at them?' Duggan grinned at the accidental pun. 'You know what I mean,' he said.

'Who's good these days?'

'You're serious?'

'Do I look like I'm joking?'

Duggan took out a pen and scribbled a name and phone number on the sheet of paper. 'Don't tell him who sent you,' he said. 'If this goes tits up, I don't want to be involved.'

Solomon hobbled past an upmarket hair salon where all the stylists were model-pretty and dressed from head to foot in black. The customers were all middle-aged, over-weight and dressed in designer clothes with faces stretched tight from plastic surgery. The contrast was stark: the old and ugly being tended by the young and beautiful. One of the stylists was barely out of her teens with straight blonde hair down to her tiny waist. She wore a tight black top that did nothing to conceal the shape of her perfect breasts, and her face could have graced the front cover of any of the top fashion magazines. Solomon wondered how much she earned cutting hair. Five hundred pounds a week, maybe a bit more. Solomon had seen girls on the Internet who were nowhere near as pretty and charged as much for one hour of their time.

He stopped and looked through the window. The girl's scissors flashed around the head of a woman in her late forties who sat flicking through a glossy magazine. He wondered how she had made her money: she didn't look like a high-powered businesswoman so she'd probably married a man with money. Did that make her any different from Nicole and the other agency girls? They sold themselves to lots of men; the woman in the chair had sold herself to one man. The principle was the same.

The woman looked up from her magazine and met Solomon's gaze. Her eyes were cold and flat, like glass. She stared at him with a look of open contempt, then went back to her magazine.

Solomon carried on along the road. To the side of the hairdresser's was a black door. There was a small brass plaque on the wall, labelled 'Alex Knight Security', a button and a speaker grille. Solomon pressed the button and a woman's voice said, 'Hello.'

Solomon gave his name, and the door buzzed. Solomon pushed it open and manoeuvred himself up a narrow flight of stairs. There was a second door at the top and he pushed it open with his shoulder.

A striking brunette looked up at him from a computer terminal. She apologised when she saw the crutch and plaster cast. 'If I'd have known I'd have come down for you,' she said.

'I can walk, it's just a bit awkward,' he said.

'Skiing accident?'

'I fell out of a third-floor window,' said Solomon.

Before she could respond, a door opened and a gangly man in his late twenties strode out, pushing a pair of square-framed spectacles higher up his nose. He was wearing a blue denim shirt with the sleeves rolled up, and khaki pants with pockets above the knees. 'Alex Knight,' said the man. 'Jack?'

They shook hands.

'Come on through,' said Knight. He led the way and held open the door as Solomon limped through. The office was about twenty feet square and lined with metal shelving, which was piled high with technical equipment. Knight sat down behind a large metal desk on which there were three computer terminals.

Solomon passed over the sheet of paper Duggan had given him. He explained who Anna Gregson was and why he wanted her followed.

'Assuming I find where she works, what then?' asked Knight.

'I want to know who runs the agency.'

'Because?'

'Why do you need to know?'

Knight picked up a paperknife in the shape of a miniature sword and toyed with it. 'You're not on some revenge kick, are you?'

'What makes you say that?'

'You've obviously been in the wars. I wouldn't want to lead you to someone for you to beat him to a pulp or worse. Reflects badly on me.'

'This isn't about revenge.'

'So, what is it about?'

Solomon considered. There was no simple answer: it was just something he knew he had to do. But Knight was expecting more than that. He wanted an explanation. Solomon leaned back in his chair and pulled a knitting needle out of his cast. He jiggled it in and out, trying to reach an itch just behind his knee. As he scratched himself he told Knight the whole story.

'So you're hoping that the owner of the agency will tell you where this Nicole has gone?'

'Hopefully,' said Solomon. 'The Gregson woman has spoken to the police and denied all knowledge of Nicole. I might get a different story from her boss. But first I have to know who he is.'

'Okay,' said Knight. 'I can do that. Is there any reason for her to think she'll be under surveillance?'

Solomon shook his head.

'I'll put a car and a bike on it, just to be on the safe side.'

'How much will it cost?' asked Solomon.

'If we get lucky on the first day, five hundred should cover it. It depends. She might go straight to the office, in which case Robert's your mother's brother. If we find the office we can run a check on the landlord and find out who he's leased it to. If it looks more complicated than that, I'll let you know. The thing is, what do you do then? If you want him looked at, that's going to cost more.'

'I can probably get a CRO check done.'

'I'm sure you can. But what if he doesn't have a criminal record? Do you want a home address? Do you want to know what bank accounts he has? Where he spends his money? It all costs.'

Solomon finished scratching and left the knitting needle inside the cast.

'Let's get an ID first. Then take it from there.'

Knight put down the paperknife. 'I'll need a cheque for five hundred.'

Solomon wrote one, and gave Knight the number of his mobile phone.

Two days later Knight phoned. 'Your man's name is Sergei Goncharov,' he said. 'He's Russian, but he's here on a one-year business visa issued by the British embassy in St Petersburg. Date of birth the fifteenth of August 1949. The agency's office is in Earl's Court. Have you got a pen?'

Solomon was in Diane's study and she had a dozen pens in a Snoopy mug. He wrote down the address. An office building in Warwick Road. 'Have you got a photograph of him?' Solomon asked.

'I could get one, but that's going to be another day.'

'Another five hundred?'

'Assuming we get him first go.'

'Do you have a home address for him?'

'I could get one, but again . . .'

'Another five hundred?'

'It depends. He might be listed in the phone book. Or I might have to put a team on him. It's pretty much open-ended, as I explained in the office. The more you're prepared to pay, the more I can find out.'

Solomon scratched his nose. He couldn't see any other way of getting the information he needed. 'Okay, Alex. Get me a photograph and his home address. Then I'll see where I want to go from there.'

He cut the connection. That was the big question, he realised. Once he knew what Goncharov looked like and where he lived, what then? The man was a Russian pimp who'd sent two assassins to kill him. He'd hardly be likely to start talking simply because Solomon turned up on his doorstep. If he was going to stand a chance of getting Goncharov to talk, he'd need help. Serious help.

Solomon carried his coffee mug to a table by the window. He eased himself down into the armchair and watched the traffic cruising down Wardour Street. He opened a copy of the *Daily Telegraph* but he'd barely scanned the front page when he saw Sasha walking down the road.

The man was wearing a knee-length black-leather coat and a black polo-neck sweater; his eyes were hidden behind metal-framed sunglasses even though the sky was overcast. Two big men walked two paces behind him. Sasha pushed his way into Starbucks and looked around – the two heavies stayed on the pavement outside. He saw Solomon and walked across to his table. 'It wasn't my men, if that's why you wanted to see me,' he said.

'Is that what Inga told you, that I thought you'd put me in hospital?'

Sasha pulled a face. 'She said you wanted to meet me, that's all. If I'd wanted to do you any harm. I would have done it in my house, in the basement.'

'I know that.'

'So what do you want?'

'You said you lost family members in Kosovo?'

'So?'

'Didn't you want justice? Or revenge?'

'I got both.'

'How?'

'I went back eighteen months ago. Serbs had moved into the houses where my brother and his family used to live. I killed them and burned down the houses.'

That wasn't the answer Solomon had expected.

'You look disappointed,' said Sasha. He took out a packet of small cigars and lit one with a gold lighter.

'I don't think you can smoke here,' said Solomon.

'If they want me to put it out, they can ask,' said Sasha. Two young brunettes at the next table turned to glare at him. One coughed pointedly. Sasha continued to stare at them until they looked away. He raised his sunglasses so that they rested on top of his head, and looked at Solomon coldly. 'What do you want from me?' he asked.

'Your help,' said Solomon.

'Why should I help you?'

'I was going to offer you the chance of getting revenge on the Serbs, but I guess I'm too late for that.' He leaned across the table. He tapped his plaster cast with his right forefinger. 'The guy who did this is a Russian who runs an Internet escort agency. I know who he is and where he lives.'

Sasha shook his head. 'You want me to fight your battles for you?'

'Just hear me out. Remember the girl I was looking for? Nicole?'

Sasha nodded.

'She worked for him. His name's Sergei Goncharov and his office is in Earl's Court. He has an agency called Legal Escorts with girls all over London. I saw Nicole on his website and went to see her. A few hours later two guys were in my flat trying to kill me. Now Nicole's vanished from the website and some woman representing the agency says they've never heard of her. The cops aren't going to take it any further.'

'But you are?'

'The girl was on the website. This guy Goncharov has either had her killed or sent her somewhere else. I want to find out which. If he's killed her, I want to put the cops on to him. If she's working somewhere else, I want to talk to her.'

'After what happened? Are you stubborn or stupid?'

'I'm not giving up, Sasha. I'm not going to let him win.'

'You think it's a game, with a winner and a loser?'

'No, but I can't let them scare me off. Twenty-six people were murdered in Kosovo, men, women and children. There was nothing Nicole could do to save them and there's nothing I can do that'll bring them back, but I *can* find the men responsible and bring them to justice.'

'And then what? A few years in prison?'

'The War Crimes Tribunal has been handing down major sentences for atrocities in the Balkans. This was mass murder. If we can put together a case, they'll get life.'

Sasha dropped his cigar on to the wooden floor and ground it out with his shoe. He stood up and Solomon thought that he was going to leave, but he said, 'Do you want another coffee?'

Solomon asked for a cappuccino. He watched Sasha walk over to the counter – he had a confident walk, almost a swagger, and Solomon noticed several women, including the two brunettes who'd objected to his smoking, turn to look at him as he picked up the coffee and walked back. He put down the mugs and pulled his seat to the side so that he could see the entrance while he talked to Solomon. 'What are you proposing?'

'You're in the walk-up business,' said Solomon, keeping his voice low so that he couldn't be overheard. 'Goncharov is in the Internet escort-agency business. He's the future and, with respect, you're in the past. That's why the Maltese are so happy for you to take over

293

their flats. They've already moved their girls on-line.'

Sasha scowled. 'We're doing fine.'

'Maybe you are. But how much better could you be doing if you took over Goncharov's business?'

'Why would I want to do that?'

'Because you'd jump straight into the big league. I know where his office is. We can get hold of his records, his computers. We can find out where all his girls are, where he puts his money. You can put him out of business and get his girls working for you.'

Sasha chuckled. 'How naïve are you, Solomon?'

It wasn't the reaction Solomon had expected.

'Girls are easy to get. I could bring in another fifty tomorrow, if I wanted. And why do you think that the Russian's girls would work for me? I don't have any hold on them. If we put him out of business, there's a hundred other agencies they could work for. And do you think the Russian would just let me take his business away from him? What do you think I'd do if someone tried to move in on me?' Sasha leaned across the table. 'There'd be a gang war. And the Russian would react in the same way. I don't need that. There's enough business to go round.'

Solomon stared at his coffee.

When Sasha spoke next, his voice was a husky whisper. 'This girl, who killed her family?'

'We don't know. She's the only one who saw what happened.'

'Who do you think killed them?'

'I think it was well planned and well executed, so I'd guess the military. There was a tidiness about it. If it had been local, I'd have expected more of them to have been shot. Also, no one took over the farm. When locals were behind the atrocities they usually took over the homes and the land.'

'When did it happen?'

'The summer of 1999. There were a lot of troops in the area then, massacring civilians as they headed back to Serbia. Regular troops and special forces. If they were soldiers and Nicole saw their insignia, we'd have a good chance of identifying them.'

'But they'll be back in Serbia now.'

'The Serbs are handing people over to the War Crimes Tribunal. They're scared of sanctions. And they'll be looking for EC membership eventually, so they know they have to co-operate.'

Sasha stirred his coffee but made no move to drink it. 'Why don't the Tribunal launch their own investigation?'

'No witnesses, just the girl. If she'd gone to them in the first place, I'm sure they'd have been on the case.'

Sasha continued to stir his coffee. 'Why didn't the girl talk to you when you confronted her?'

'Maybe she was scared.'

'Maybe she had another reason for not wanting to talk to you.'

'Like what?'

'Who knows? But you might be wasting your time. What is it you English say? A wild-goose chase?'

'I think she was just scared. And it looks like with good reason, because she's disappeared.'

'Because of you, you think?'

'It's a hell of a coincidence if she left the agency for any other reason. I'm sure Goncharov got rid of her.'

'If that's the case, she might be dead.'

'I know.'

Sasha tapped his spoon on the top of his mug. He looked out of the window but his mind was obviously elsewhere. Solomon sat in silence.

'Okay,' said Sasha, eventually. 'I'll help you find the girl. But no one is to know. If this Russian finds out I'm involved, there'll be a gang war. You might be happy getting shot on this quest of yours, but I'm not.'

'Okay,' said Solomon.

'Give me his address and any other details you have. Then leave it to me.'

'Okay. And thanks.'

Sasha fixed Solomon with his pale grey eyes. 'You don't have to thank me. I'm not doing this for you. I'm doing this because I don't want the bastard Serbs to get away with it.'

'Understood,' said Solomon. He handed Sasha a piece of paper on which he'd written down the information Alex Knight had given him. 'I should have a photograph and a home address for Goncharov tomorrow.'

Sasha put the piece of paper in his jacket pocket, then stood up. 'When you've got the photograph, call Inga. I don't want to be seen with you in case he decides he wants to finish what he started – I wouldn't want to get caught in the crossfire.' He walked out of the coffee shop and along Wardour Street, the two heavies in tow.

Solomon pulled out the knitting needle and scratched his leg thoughtfully. Sasha hadn't said how he'd persuade Goncharov to tell him where Nicole had gone, and Solomon hadn't wanted to ask. It was probably best that he didn't know.

Solomon was hunting through Diane's deep freeze for something to eat when his mobile rang. It was Alex

Knight. 'Bingo,' said Knight cheerfully. 'I've got a photograph and a home address.'

'That's great, Alex.'

'Give me your address and I'll bike the information round.'

Solomon gave Knight Diane's address and said he'd give the courier a cheque.

'Do you need anything else?' asked Knight.

Solomon said he'd call if he did, then cut the connection and took out a microwave pizza.

He was eating the last piece when the doorbell rang. A motorcycle courier in black leather gave him an A4 envelope. He signed for it and handed over an envelope containing a cheque.

Inside the A4 envelope was a card with an address in Hampstead and three colour photographs of a man with a massive beer gut and squarish head, receding hair cut close to his skull. He had a small pig-like nose and thin bloodless lips. His eyes were hidden behind wire-framed sunglasses with circular lenses. In one of the photographs he was climbing into the back of what appeared to be a Bentley. It seemed to Solomon as if everyone involved in the London vice trade was making money hand over fist.

Another photograph had been taken in the street and Goncharov had his sunglasses in his hand. He was squinting across at a beautiful blonde woman, a good six inches taller than he was. She was wearing a yellow suit, whose skirt covered little of her long, shapely legs. Solomon looked at the back of the photograph. Two names and an address were scrawled on it: Sergei Goncharov and Anna Gregson, Warwick Road, Earl's Court. It must have been taken outside the Legal Escorts office.

Solomon phoned Inga. She said she was working but

that she'd arrange for another girl to cover for her at the flat, she'd see him in an Italian restaurant close to the coffee bar in Wardour Street at nine o'clock that evening.

Solomon shaved and showered, taking care not to get his cast wet. He grinned at himself in the mirror as he towelled himself. He was behaving as if he was about to go on a date when in fact he was meeting his conduit to a violent pimp.

When Solomon arrived at the restaurant Inga was already sitting at a table studying a menu. She was wearing a black armless polo-neck sweater over which she'd hung a small gold crucifix on a gold chain, and a short black skirt. Her hair was tied back in a ponytail.

She smiled at him as he limped over to her table. He had abandoned the crutches and was using instead a wooden walking-stick that Diane had found in the attic.

'Do you have time to eat?' she asked.

'Of course,' said Solomon, lowering himself into the chair opposite her. The restaurant was called Luigi's and there were photographs of the owner and his celebrity friends on the walls. The tables were covered in starched white cloths and the waiters seemed to be the genuine article, chatting to each other in Italian when they weren't attending to customers.

Inga had a bottle of water in front of her and Solomon ordered a lager. He asked Inga if she wanted wine but she shook her head and said that she had to work later. She looked down as if embarrassed by the reminder of how she earned her living.

Solomon slipped the envelope across the table. 'This is the stuff for Sasha,' he said.

She put it into her bag.

'Thanks for coming to see me in hospital,' he said.

'That's okay.'

'And for the card. It was the only one I got.'

Inga brushed a lock of red hair away from her eyes. 'Don't you have family?'

Solomon wrinkled his nose. 'Not really. I've a brother but he's in America. I only see him every couple of years, if that.'

'What about your parents?'

'My father died when I was a teenager. He was a lorry driver and he drove off the road. He'd been working for almost twenty-four hours. The police said he'd probably fallen asleep.'

'I'm sorry.'

'It was a long time ago.'

'What about your mother?'

'Cancer. About five years after my dad's accident.'

'I am an orphan, too,' Inga said.

'What happened to your parents?'

'I don't know. I was taken to an orphanage when I was just a few months old.'

'No one told you what happened to them?'

'No one at the orphanage knew.'

'So you don't have anyone?'

Inga grimaced. 'I can take care of myself.'

Solomon knew that wasn't true. She was taking care of her pimp, not herself. A waiter brought over his lager and they ordered their food, spaghetti marinara for Inga, and lamb chops with rosemary for Solomon.

'Why don't you have a wife?' asked Inga.

Solomon broke a roll and popped a piece into his mouth. Inga waited until he'd finished chewing, then asked him again.

'I was married,' said Solomon. 'A long time ago.'

'What happened?'

Solomon reached for another piece of bread.

'You don't want to talk about it? said Inga.

'It's not something I'm proud of.'

'Because the marriage didn't work?'

'Sort of.'

He sipped his lager. Inga sat looking at him, waiting for him to speak. Solomon put down his glass. 'It's a long story.'

'We've got time.' Her chocolate brown eyes were still fixed on him.

He realised it was only the second time that he'd seen her without her protective sunglasses. The first time had been in the Soho flat and she'd been wearing the red bra, red stockings and red suspenders with little black bows on them. 'I got married when I was twenty-one,' he said ruefully, 'to my childhood sweetheart. We met at primary school.' It had been years since he'd thought about his schooldays, he reflected. 'She became a teacher, pretty much supported us while I decided what I wanted to do. Then I joined the police. She put up with the shift work, the short haircut, the drinking binges when the stress got too much.'

'What was her name?'

'Jennifer.'

'She sounds like she was a good wife.'

'She was.'

'So what happened?'

The horror of what had happened washed over Solomon. Charlie's death wasn't something he'd talked about for a long, long time. And he wasn't sure that an Italian restaurant in Soho was the place to discuss it now. Or that Inga was the person to discuss it with. 'We had a daughter,' he said quietly. 'Her name was Charlotte. We called her Charlie.'

Inga reached across the table and took his hand. She stroked the palm with her thumb.

'She was a pretty child. Took after her mum.' Solomon felt tears prick his eyes and massaged the bridge of his nose. 'I'm sorry,' he said.

'What's wrong?' she asked. 'What happened?'

'I don't want to talk about it,' he said.

Inga continued to stroke his hand, and he closed his eyes. Images of Charlie flashed through his mind: Charlie running towards him, her arms outstretched, begging to be picked up; Charlie sitting next to him as he read to her; Charlie baking cakes with Jennifer, flour on her cheeks; Charlie in his arms, covered with blood, her eyes closing.

'She died?' asked Inga.

Solomon opened his eyes. A tear trickled down his left cheek and he wiped it off with his shoulder. 'It was my fault,' he said.

'What happened?'

'I was taking her to school. We took it in turns depending on what shift I was working. I was in a hurry and everyone was double-parked near the school so I dropped her about a hundred yards away. I told her to be careful crossing the road.'

He closed his eyes again. More images. Charlie crossing the road, her little blue backpack bouncing between her shoulders. Turning to wave at him, laughing. Her hair blowing in the wind. The little teddy bear swinging from the backpack. The delivery van. The driver lighting a cigarette. Charlie laughing and waving. Then the sickening impact. Solomon running from his car, cradling Charlie in his arms. The van driving away.

'She was hit by a van,' said Solomon quietly. 'I don't think she knew what had happened. One minute she was in the middle of the road, the next she was on the pavement.'

'Oh, my God,' said Inga.

'The driver didn't stop. They never caught him. He'd stolen the van. It was full of mobile phones.'

'Jack, I'm so sorry.'

Solomon barely heard her. 'She was still alive, just about. I picked her up and she opened her eyes. She wanted to hold her teddy. There was a little one clipped to her backpack, she took it everywhere. I got her back into the car and one of the mothers drove us to the hospital. There was so much blood. All over her, all over me. The woman was banging on the horn and screaming at the cars to get out of the way. I kept telling Charlie that it was going to be okay, that I'd take care of her, but I knew that even if we'd got her to the hospital right away . . .' Solomon couldn't say any more.

'It wasn't your fault,' said Inga.

'It was. If I'd parked closer to the school, if I'd walked her across the road, if I hadn't been waving to her . . .'

'You mustn't think that,' said Inga. 'She was your daughter and you loved her.'

'When she needed me most, I let her down.'

'Is that what your wife said?'

'She was right.'

Solomon felt another tear run down his cheek. He pulled his hand away from Inga's and brushed it away.

The food arrived and Solomon kept his head down so that the waiter couldn't see his face. Inga didn't say anything until the man had moved away. She leaned across the table and took his hand again. Solomon tried to pull it away but she held it tightly until he relaxed. 'I'm sorry, Inga,' he said. 'I don't know why I told you that.'

She let go of his hand. 'I don't think you've told anyone before, have you?'

'Not for a long time.' He picked up his knife and fork, then realised he had no appetite.

'Is that why your wife left you?'

'She blamed me. And she was right.'

'No, she wasn't. She might have been the one dropping your daughter off. She might have been the one waving.'

'No,' said Solomon sharply. 'That's the whole point. If Jennifer had been there, she'd have walked Charlie to the gate. If she'd been there, Charlie would still be alive.'

Inga didn't contradict him.

Solomon apologised again, and changed the subject. 'Come on, try your pasta,' he said.

They ate in silence. The waiters kept their distance as if they sensed the strained atmosphere. Solomon could barely taste his lamb. He put down his knife and fork. 'I didn't mean to snap at you.'

'I know,' she said. 'It was my fault for asking about your wife.'

'I guess we could start again,' he said.

'I'm glad you told me. It helps me understand you.'

'Why do you want to?'

'I told you at the hospital. I like you.'

Solomon tutted. 'You hardly know me.'

'Why would I say it if I didn't mean it?'

Solomon wanted to say that she was a prostitute, that it was her job to make men happy, to find out what they wanted and give it to them, but he forced the words back and smiled. He knew it was a poor effort.

'I don't want anything from you, if that's what you're worried about.'

'It's not that,' he said.

'What is it, then?'

Solomon opened his mouth to reply, but put a piece of lamb into it instead and chewed slowly.

Inga twirled spaghetti around her plate. 'What's in the envelope?' she asked. 'Is it okay to ask that?'

'Sasha didn't tell you?'

Inga shook her head. Red hair spilled across her face and she hooked it behind her ear. 'He just said I was to collect something from you. And that if you liked, I could have dinner with you.' She saw from the look on his face that that wasn't what he'd wanted to hear. 'He knew I hadn't eaten, that's all. He said there wouldn't be a problem if I was late back, that the girl who was at the flat would stay there until I arrived.'

'How does he treat you, generally?'

'He's fine.'

'Does he hurt you?'

She frowned at him. 'Why do you ask that?'

'I used to be a policeman, a long time ago. And I used to work Vice. I arrested pimps for beating up their girls. That's how they control them. If the girls aren't scared of their pimps, they wouldn't give them their money, would they?'

'I don't know,' she said quietly. She kept her head down as she toyed with her pasta.

'I guess I shouldn't be asking you about Sasha,' said Solomon.

'He doesn't like anyone talking about him,' she said. She looked up. 'It's hard to find things to talk about, isn't it? You don't like talking about what happened to you, I don't want to talk about what I'm doing now.' She put down her fork. 'Maybe I should go.'

'Please don't,' said Solomon quickly.

She bit her lower lip, then sipped her water.

'What do you want to do eventually?' asked Solomon.

'I'm not sure.'

'But you must have a dream. Something you really want to do.'

'I used to want to own a clothes shop. Maybe design my own clothes. I did drawings when I was younger, but they said I was wasting my time.'

'Who said that?'

'The people at the orphanage. They said I was wasting paper. They said I'd never be a designer, that I'd work on a farm or in a factory. But they were wrong. Now I'm in London and they're still working in the orphanage. They'll never have any money, they'll never travel. They'll never do *anything* with their lives.'

There was excitement in her eyes and her cheeks were flushed. Solomon wondered if she was right: maybe her life as a London prostitute was better than anything she could expect in eastern Europe. Why else would so many thousands of girls be willing to leave their homes to fill the west's brothels and saunas?

'But you're not saving money, are you? You said Sasha took it all.'

'Because he bought my contract. Once I've paid it off, I'll be able to save.'

'When will you have paid it off?'

Inga shrugged. 'That's up to Sasha. But we said we wouldn't talk about him, remember?'

After the meal, Inga and Solomon waited for a black cab on the pavement. They were few and far between and it was a good ten minutes before they saw one with its amber light on.

'We should share,' she said.

'I've got to go to Clapham,' he said. 'What about you?'

She slipped her arm through his. 'I'll come with you,' she said.

They climbed into the black cab. It was a twenty-minute drive to Diane and Sean's house, and they didn't speak again until Solomon had paid the driver and they were standing alone on the pavement.

'Inga, this isn't my house,' he said. 'I'm staying with friends.'

'Are they in?' she asked.

The house was in darkness: Diane had said that she and Sean would be out for most of the evening at a pub quiz. 'I don't think so,' he said.

She looked at him expectantly. At some point during the evening she'd loosened her hair and it rippled in the light breeze as she waited for him to reach a decision. Solomon wanted to ask her if it was her idea or Sasha's, but instead he smiled and put his arm around her. She nestled against him and kissed his neck, then tilted her head until her lips found his. They stood on the doorstep kissing, then Solomon broke away. 'God knows what the neighbours are going to think.' He laughed.

'They'll think we are kissing, that's all,' said Inga.

She ran her hands down between his shoulder-blades as he unlocked the door. As soon as they were inside she kissed him again, softly at first and then with more passion. He dropped his walking-stick and she bent down to retrieve it for him. 'The plaster cast's going to make things awkward,' he said.

'Don't worry,' she said. 'I wasn't planning any gymnastics.'

Solomon fumbled for the door to the front room and they stumbled over to the bed. She helped him undress, then stripped off her clothes and crawled on to the bed next to him.

'I'm a bit limited,' said Solomon. 'Position wise'.

'This is fine,' she whispered, and slipped on top of him.

Later, Solomon heard Diane and Sean come in, stumble up the stairs and collapse into bed.

He chuckled. 'I hope we didn't make so much noise,' he said.

Inga snuggled against him. 'I'd better go,' she said.

Solomon stroked her hair. 'I suppose so,' he said. He doubted that either Diane or Sean would object to him bringing someone back to the house, but he didn't want to explain who Inga was or how he'd met her. 'I can see you again, right?' he said.

'Of course,' she said.

'Sasha won't mind?'

'I won't tell him,' she said, sitting up and running her hands through her hair, 'but I have to work every day, you know that.'

He rolled over and watched her as she dressed. She turned her back on him, and he laughed.

She looked over her shoulder at him as she pulled on her skirt. 'What are you laughing at?' she asked.

'You,' he said. 'After everything we've just done, you're still shy.'

'I'm not,' she said, but she kept her back to him as she continued to dress.

'When are you working again?' he asked.

'I don't want to think about that. It'll spoil what we just had.'

Solomon knew what she meant. The evening had been magical, but it had been an interlude, nothing else. Inga was a prostitute beholden to an Albanian pimp, and Solomon knew he'd be a fool to imagine that the relationship could go anywhere. But that didn't stop him caring about her. Or wanting to see her again. The problem was, next time he saw her would he have to pay her? And if he offered to see her outside work, would she think he was trying to get her on the cheap? It was a minefield. He decided to let things take their course. It would be up to her to make the next move.

'I'll show you out,' he said.

'If you go clumping around in your cast they're bound to hear you,' she laughed. 'Let's try to salvage some of your reputation.'

Solomon lay back on the bed, and she bent over him. She kissed him long and hard on the mouth, ruffled his hair, slipped out of the room and let herself out of the front door.

The Mercedes was waiting for her down the street. The rear door opened as she got closer and she climbed in.

'How was it?' asked Sasha.

Inga took the envelope out of her bag and handed it to him. He opened it, took out the photographs and the card.

'You didn't answer my question,' he said, as he studied the contents of the envelope.

'He's a nice man.'

Sasha slid the photographs and the card back into the envelope. 'Don't get too attached,' he said.

'I won't,' said Inga, and a single tear rolled down her cheek. She turned her head so that Sasha wouldn't see her cry.

Sasha climbed out of the back of the Mercedes. Karic and Rikki followed him down the rutted track to the metal-sided barn. The sun was about to dip below the horizon but the moon was already up. An owl hooted in the distance. Sasha had been brought up on a farm in Kosovo but he hated the countryside, hated the animals, the dirt, the wind. He preferred cities, but some things were better done in the countryside, away from nosy neighbours. He turned up the collar of his leather jacket and put on a pair of black goatskin gloves.

One of his men held open the door. Sasha nodded curtly and went inside.

Goncharov was in the middle of the barn, his hands chained to a metal girder high above his head. He was naked, his clothes and shoes in an untidy pile some distance away. Two more of Sasha's men stood behind the Russian. One was holding a pitchfork.

The Russian's arms were stretched tight and he was up on his toes. Every few seconds he shuffled around to regain his balance. Sweat was pouring off him, even though there was a chill in the air. There were no bruises or cuts on his body: there had been no need for violence.

Goncharov glared at Sasha. 'Who the fuck are you?' he snarled.

Karic and Rikki came up behind Sasha and stood there with their arms folded. 'I need one thing from you, and then we can all go home,' said Sasha. 'The Kosovar girl who worked for you. She used the name Amy. You moved her off the website after your men went to kill the Englishman. Where is she?'

'What is it with this bloody girl? The whole world's after her.'

'All you've got to worry about is me,' said Sasha.

The man with the pitchfork used it to prod the Russian in the back. He tottered forward, then regained his balance. 'She's gone,' said Goncharov. 'She's fucking gone.'

'Where?'

'Sarajevo.'

'Why?'

Goncharov closed his eyes. His beer gut was hanging down over his legs, a mass of flesh that wobbled every time he moved. He was surprisingly hairless and his skin was as white and smooth as boiled chicken.

A mobile phone rang. Sasha looked around at Karic and Rikki, but they shook their heads. Sasha realised that the sound was coming from the Russian's clothes. He grinned at Goncharov. 'That'll be your men, wondering where you are.' He spoke to the man with the pitchfork: 'Any problems?'

The man shook his head. 'Two men in a car outside his house. We left them in the boot.'

'No family?'

'Two hookers in an upstairs bedroom. There was all sorts of bondage gear so we left them strung up.'

The phone stopped ringing.

'You sent your men to kill the Englishman,' Sasha said to Goncharov. 'Why?'

'I was doing a favour for a friend.'

'Who?'

Goncharov sneered at Sasha. 'Who the fuck are you?' he snarled.

Sasha took two quick steps forward and slapped the Russian across the face. His bottom lip split and blood sprayed across his chin. 'I'm not here to answer your questions, you piece of shit. Now, who wanted the Englishman shot?'

'The man who sold me the girl. Ivan Petrovic. He's in Sarajevo.'

'He wanted the Englishman killed?'

'And the girl sent back.'

'Do you know what he planned to do with her?'

Goncharov shook his head. Blood dripped down his chin and plopped on to his heaving chest. The mobile phone started to ring again.

'Who is this Petrovic?'

'A Bosnian Serb. He runs bars and brothels in Bosnia. Some drugs. He sells girls.'

'For your agency?'

Goncharov nodded.

'You didn't kill the Englishman. Were you going to try again?'

Goncharov spat bloody phlegm to the floor. 'Petrovic said we'd done enough.'

The insistent ringing began to annoy Sasha. He walked over to the pile of clothes, pulled out the mobile phone and stamped on it. Then went back to the Russian and folded his arms across his chest. 'The Englishman is a friend of mine,' he said quietly.

'It wasn't personal,' said Goncharov. 'I was paid.'

Sasha gazed at him. Goncharov stared back. There was no fear in the Russian's eyes, Sasha saw. Not even anger. He weighed up his options. He could have the man killed, there and then, just by giving the word. The farm they were on had been sold a few weeks earlier and was deserted. An agricultural conglomerate had bought it from a bankrupt sheep farmer. They were buying up a number of farms in the area and wouldn't move in until they had enough acreage to make it worth while. By then any trace of the Russian's grave would be long gone. Nor did Sasha have any qualms about killing. He'd done it before and he would do it again. But, as Goncharov had said, it had been business, and Sasha understood about business. He also understood about revenge, and he had no way of knowing who might want to avenge the death of the man hanging from the girder. But what if he spared the Russian? Would Goncharov take that as a sign of weakness and wreak his own revenge?

'Your friend is under no threat from me,' said Goncharov, as if he had read Sasha's thoughts. 'But I realise that you have options.'

'And you know what those options are?'

Goncharov nodded.

'If I release you, what will you do?'

The Russian's eyes fixed on Sasha's. There was still no fear. 'I have a business to run,' said Goncharov.

'You would not come looking for me?'

The Russian snorted. 'If I did, you seem well protected. And I've come to realise that my men are not all that they might be.' Sasha's face remained impassive. 'No,' said Goncharov. 'I would not come looking for you.'

'And you would not tell Petrovic of our conversation?'

'My relationship with him is purely business. And it was doing him a favour that has put me in this position. I owe him nothing.'

Sasha looked deep into the Russian's eyes. He could see no guile, no sign that the man was lying. They were both professionals and London was a big city. Business was business: there was no need to go to war over a single hooker. 'I apologise for hitting you,' Sasha said.

'No offence taken,' said the Russian.

Sasha nodded and walked away. Karic and Rikki fell into step behind him. 'Untie him and take him home,' Sasha said, to the man by the door.

Solomon's mobile rang and he leaned out of bed to pick it up.

It was Sasha, and it was two o'clock in the morning. 'The girl is back in Bosnia,' he said.

'Damn,' said Solomon.

'She was on a plane back to Sarajevo right after they shot you.'

'So she must have been in on it?'

'Either that or they wanted her out of the way.'

'You spoke to Goncharov?'

'We had a conversation, yes, but he didn't know much.'

'He sent the men to kill me?' asked Solomon.

'Yes, but he was doing it for a pimp in Sarajevo. Ivan Petrovic. You know him?'

'He's the guy who employed Nicole in Sarajevo.' Solomon didn't want to tell Sasha what he had done to Petrovic.

'Goncharov says they won't be coming after you again.'

'And what about Nicole?'

'He sent her back to Petrovic.'

Solomon cursed.

'What do you want to do?' asked Sasha.

'What do you mean? She's gone.'

'She's in Sarajevo. She wouldn't be hard to find.'

Solomon had only been asleep for an hour and he felt

bone-weary. 'Petrovic traffics in girls. He could have sent her anywhere in Europe.'

'I didn't think you would give up so easily. I thought you were serious about wanting to find this girl.'

Solomon frowned, wondering why Sasha was suddenly so interested in Nicole.

'Jack, are you there?' asked Sasha.

'I'm serious, Sasha. I'm in bed with my leg in a cast and two nearly healed bullet wounds. I think that shows how serious I am.'

'So, what do you want to do?'

Solomon wiped his forehead with the back of his arm. He wanted to sit down and talk with Nicole. He wanted her to tell him who had murdered her family. He wanted her to go with him to the War Crimes Tribunal and tell investigators everything she knew. 'I want to find her,' he said. 'I've a friend in Sarajevo. I'll call him and get him to make some enquiries.'

'And then?'

'If he can find out where she's gone, I'll go back.'

There was a long pause. 'If you do go, you'll need help,' said Sasha.

'I know my way around Bosnia,' said Solomon defensively.

'You can't even take care of yourself in London,' said Sasha, harshly. 'But you do what you have to do.' He cut the connection.

Solomon put the phone back on the bedside table and lay down. At least now he knew where Nicole had gone. And who had tried to kill him.

The man stank of engine oil and beer, and he grunted with every thrust. Nicole turned her head to the side. She felt ill, but she knew that if she vomited the man would beat her again. He was a lorry driver, her fourteenth customer of the day.

The man pushed himself up and told her to roll over on to her front. She did as she was told. The chain that ran from her left wrist to the metal bedstead rattled as she moved. She had been manacled to the bed since she'd arrived at the brothel in Arizona, like all the other girls on the top floor. The chain was just long enough for her to reach a small wash-basin in the corner of the room: she could drink from the tap and wash herself with a grubby cloth. There was a pot underneath the bed in which she could relieve herself.

The man began to pound into her, faster and faster. He grabbed her hips and pulled her up on to her knees. Nicole made no sound. She had blanked her mind as she always did when customers had sex with her. It had been different in London: there they had behaved as if she was a girlfriend. They had talked and laughed, maybe had a drink, and then she'd led them to the bedroom and undressed them, and had sex on a bed with clean sheets and towels in the bathroom. It hadn't been like making love, she was still only doing it for the money, but at least there had been a pretence of affection. Some of her regular clients even brought her little presents – chocolates or perfume. But the men who visited the brothel in Arizona were different: they didn't want affection or tenderness, they only wanted to relieve themselves, to use her as a receptacle.

Nicole had no idea how much they paid to have sex with her, but she knew it entitled them to do whatever they wanted with her. She wasn't allowed to refuse anything; that much had been made clear to her when she'd first been chained to the bed. On the floor below there were rooms where the dancers took their customers. Nicole could hear them sometimes. The girls would laugh and the men would laugh, and then the bedsprings would creak and the women would moan with pleasure. Nicole knew they uttered the same counterfeit sighs and groans as she'd used with her clients in London – it was part of the act: the better the act the bigger the tip, and the more likely it was that the man would return. That was how the girls made money. But on the floor where Nicole was held, the rules were different: the men paid for half an hour with her, and during that time no one would disturb them. No matter how much she cried, no matter how much she screamed, the door stayed closed until the half-hour was up. Not that Nicole screamed any more. The first time she'd screamed two pimps had come upstairs and beaten her black and blue while her customer stood at the end of the bed and grinned. Then, after the pimps had gone, the man had beaten her to the edge of unconsciousness and raped her.

Some of the men beat her before sex, some hit her while they were raping her, others waited until afterwards. Nicole had learned not to try to fight back, physically or verbally. The more submissive she was, the quicker it was over. Until the next man came into the room.

Sasha finished his coffee and took a last drag on his cigar. He looked at his watch. It was just before midday and he'd only been up for half an hour. He'd spent the evening in a bar in Chelsea with Katrina, the Moldavian girl he'd bought in Belgrade, and two Slovakian girls who'd worked with him for the past three months. All three were stunningly pretty and among his top earners. Katrina alone was bringing in more than nine thousand pounds a week. She had a particular talent for oral and, according to the maid at her flat, she had a dozen regulars who returned at least once a week.

He still had a hangover from the six bottles of Dom Pérignon they'd drunk at the bar. He'd brought the three girls back to his mansion and spent the best part of two hours putting them through their paces with the help of a 100-milligram Viagra tablet and half a dozen lines of high-grade cocaine. He'd kicked the Slovakian girls out of bed in the early hours but had allowed Katrina to sleep with him.

He went through to the hall and shouted at her to hurry up. When there was no reply he went up the staircase and along to the master bedroom. She was sitting at the dressing-table, applying mascara. She was wearing the black dress he'd bought for her, cut low at the top to show off her impressive cleavage, and so short she had to keep her thighs clamped together when she sat down. He'd bought similar dresses for the Slovakians, and had taken great delight in the number of heads that had turned when he walked into the bar with them.

'You'll be late,' said Sasha. She stood up, hurried across the room and flung her arms around him. Her tongue moved between his lips, urging, and her hand slid down the front of his trousers. Sasha felt himself grow hard, but he pushed her away. 'You don't have time,' he said.

'You're the boss, they'll wait.' She was trying to undo his zip.

'You're already late for work,' he told her. 'You were supposed to be in the flat at noon.'

Katrina pouted. 'Do I have to go?' she whined.

Sasha grabbed her wrist. 'You're here to work,' he said coldly. 'Never forget that. I might screw you for fun every now and then, but that doesn't mean you miss your shift. Understand?'

'I'm sorry.'

Sasha kept a tight grip on her wrist, but with his right hand he reached up to stroke her hair. He slipped his hand around the back of her neck and pulled her towards him. He kissed her lips, then twisted her hair savagely. She wailed, but his mouth smothered her cries. He kissed her harder, then pulled her head away from his face. Her lower lip was trembling but there were no tears in her eyes.

Sasha smiled. 'Downstairs,' he said. 'Now.'

Katrina grabbed her bag, slipped on her shoes and tottered out of the bedroom.

Sasha followed her, watching as she stumbled downstairs, grabbing at the banister for balance. Rikki came out of the sitting room and opened the front door. Katrina hurried out and went over to the waiting Mercedes. Karic already had the rear door open and she climbed in.

Rikki closed the front door and got into the Mercedes next to the driver. Sasha slid into the back next to Katrina, Karic got in next to him and slammed the door.

'Soho,' Sasha said to the driver, and settled back. Katrina slipped her hand on to his leg and massaged his thigh.

The driver pressed the remote control to open the security gates and slipped the gear selector into drive. Katrina's hand became more insistent. Sasha pushed it away and flashed her an angry look. The girl had yet to learn that business was business and pleasure was pleasure, and that the two were only mixed when Sasha wanted it that way. Katrina sat with her hands in her lap and stared out of the window as the Mercedes drove through the gates and on to the road.

Sasha took out his mobile phone, flicked to his address book, then called the number of one of his Soho flats. The maid answered, and he told her he was running late, that she should have the money ready for him at one o'clock. The maid told him that the girl had earned a little under two thousand pounds during her night shift. 'Why so much?' asked Sasha.

'We had three football supporters in and they wanted to be with her at the same time,' said the maid. 'I agreed a higher price and told Julia to get on with it.' Julia had been with Sasha for almost six months. She was from Latvia, and while she wasn't one of his prettiest girls she made up for it with her enthusiasm and her willingness to do anything for money.

'Did you hear that, Katrina?' said Sasha, as he cut the connection. 'Two thousand pounds in one shift.'

The Mercedes braked suddenly, and Sasha put his hand on the seat in front to steady himself. A white van had stopped unexpectedly and Sasha's driver pounded on the horn.

'I've done more than that,' said Katrina, sulkily.

'I don't think so,' said Sasha, and gripped her chin between finger and thumb. 'I think the best you've done is one thousand six hundred.'

'I can do two thousand, no problem,' she said.

'We'll see,' he said.

Her face exploded in a shower of blood and bone, and cubes of broken glass ripped through the Mercedes. Sasha's ears were ringing from the deafening bangs of high-powered guns fired at close range. What was left of Katrina's head slumped forward on to his shoulder and her blood streamed down his shirt. Sasha screamed at the driver to get out of there but they were too close to the white van to drive round it. Bullets hammered into the side of the car and the driver's window burst inwards. The back of the driver's head blew apart. There were two louder bangs and the right side of the car lurched down. They'd shot out the tyres, Sasha realised.

Karic pushed Sasha down so that his face was pressed against the bloody seat and pulled a gun from under it. He fired off three quick shots through the smashed window and screamed at Rikki to get the car moving.

Rikki was hunched forward, grabbing for a gun in the glove compartment. He found it, released the safety and fired twice through the driver's window. There were more ear-splitting cracks and bullets thwacked into the seat rests, sending leather and foam-rubber fragments fluttering around the car interior. Sasha tried to lift his head but Karic held it down and fired again, two shots in rapid succession. 'Move us!' he screamed at Rikki. 'Come on, or we're all dead.' He threw himself forward, covering Sasha with his body as he fired another two shots. Sasha's eyes were stinging from the cordite and his ears were ringing.

Rikki pushed aside the driver and thrust his leg into the footwell, then slammed the gear selector into reverse and stamped on the accelerator. The Mercedes leaped backwards. The wheel rims on the driver's side shrieked and sparked along the Tarmac. There were more rapid bangs and the windscreen shattered into a thousand glass cubes. Karic carried on firing out of the side window until his clip was empty, then dropped down over Sasha again.

Rikki had his left hand on the steering-wheel, trying to

keep the car heading straight back while he continued to fire through the driver's window, but with the driver's-side tyres blown away the rear end swung wildly to the right, into the middle of the road, then the car spun round. A motorcyclist smashed into the rear wing, hurtled through the air and slammed into a lamp-post.

Karic lifted his head, leaned across and slammed the gear selector into drive. The Mercedes roared and accelerated away, the steering-wheel juddering in Rikki's hand.

More bullets thwacked into the back, and the rear window disintegrated. Sasha shook glass cubes from his hair. He could hear a far-off siren. The driver's shattered head was hanging out of the window and banging against the door with each juddering movement of the car.

Karic was shouting at Rikki to keep his foot down on the accelerator. They were on the wrong side of the road now and cars were pulling frantically into the side to avoid colliding with the Mercedes. Showers of sparks sprayed out from the tortured wheel rims.

Sasha tried to look out of the rear window but Karic screamed at him to get down, and pushed him on to Katrina's body.

The siren was getting louder. A police car.

Ahead a van driver banged on his horn and tried to swing his vehicle out of the way but the Mercedes was moving too quickly and slammed into it. The airbags erupted but Sasha's driver hadn't been wearing his seat-belt and the body flew over the airbag and across the bonnet, smearing blood and brain matter over the crumpled metal before it rolled into the side of the van.

Rikki pushed aside his airbag and looked back down the street. There was no sign of the four gunmen. The white van that had forced the Mercedes to stop was disappearing into the distance, black smoke belching from its exhaust.

Sasha sat up. Katrina's blood was dripping down his face and he wiped it away with his sleeve.

'They've gone,' said Rikki.

Sasha pulled Karic's gun from his hand and thrust it at Rikki. 'Go,' he said. 'If the cops find us with those, we're dead.'

Rikki grabbed the weapon, opened the passenger door, pushed away the airbag.

'And, Rikki. . .'

Rikki turned.

'Well done,' Sasha said.

Rikki nodded, then leaped out of the car and ran down the street. Sasha slumped in the seat. 'That fucking Russian. I should have killed him when I had the chance.' He clapped Karic on the shoulder. 'That's twice you've saved my life,' he said.

But Karic was deathly pale and there was a look of shocked surprise on his face. Sasha punched the air. 'The bastards, huh? We'll show them.' Karic didn't say anything. He was panting. Sasha frowned. 'Are you okay?' he asked. Karic coughed and a dribble of blood ran down his chin. Sasha opened the man's coat. There was a small black hole in the middle of his chest. Blood was pumping from it in regular spurts.

'Oh, God,' gasped Sasha. He snatched a large linen handkerchief out of his pocket and pressed it against the bubbling wound. 'Don't you die on me,' he shouted. 'Don't you fucking die on me!'

Solomon waited until early afternoon in Sarajevo before he phoned Dragan Jovanovic at the Sarajevo Canton

Police Headquarters. He wasn't at his desk and one of his colleagues had to fetch him. 'Jack?' asked the detective. 'How the hell are you?'

'I've been better,' said Solomon, but he didn't go into details. He told Dragan that Nicole had returned to Sarajevo. 'Do you think you can find her?'

'I'm not going to trawl around the brothels for you again,' said the policeman.

'I don't expect you to,' said Solomon. 'She arrived three or four weeks ago. Couldn't you check with Immigration?'

'Are you sure she travelled under her own name? Most hookers fly on false papers, remember?'

He was right, of course. And if she had used another name, there would be little or no chance of tracing her through official channels. 'What about Petrovic?' he asked.

'I don't think you should come back at the moment, if that's what you mean.'

'I meant, maybe she's gone back to work for him.'

'So you want me to have a quiet word with Sarajevo's most wanted, do you, on the basis of your long-standing friendship?'

'You could get someone to swing by the bar. See if she's there.'

'And what if she is? Are you going to fly over and walk into Petrovic's bar for another head-to-head? Because if so, you'd better hope there's another SFOR patrol passing by.'

'Are you okay?' Solomon asked. 'You sound a bit stressed.'

'No more than usual,' said the policeman. 'But you worry me. This girl has become an obsession.'

'Bollocks!' said Solomon. 'I just asked you to do me a favour, that's all. If you can't do it, fine.'

'Don't sulk,' said Dragan. 'I'll ask around. But if I were you, I'd forget about her. Move on with your life.'

'As of a few days ago, my life is on hold,' said Solomon. 'I've been sacked.'

'Why?'

'My boss says it's a budgetary problem but he's talking through his arse.'

'It might be for the best. The last thing you want right now is to be back here.'

'We'll see,' said Solomon. 'First things first. See if you can find out what's happened to Nicole.'

Dragan promised to do what he could, then cut the connection.

Solomon pulled the knitting needle out of his cast and dealt with an itch six inches below his knee. The doctor had said that it would be at least another three weeks before the cast could come off, then several months of physiotherapy. There was no point in Solomon looking for a new job until he was a hundred per cent fit. Aid work was demanding, and out of the question for a man who needed a walking-stick. Maybe Dragan had been right: if Petrovic was still on the warpath, Bosnia was the last place he should be thinking of going to.

Anna Gregson ran the last stack of twenty-pound notes through the electronic counter. Two thousand six hundred and eighty pounds. She used a calculator to add up the numbers she'd written down on a yellow legal pad. Thirteen thousand, seven hundred and twenty pounds in total, the receipts from two days. They hadn't been especially busy days, either.

To the left of the desk was a large safe and she put the money on top of the pile that was already in it, a little under a hundred thousand pounds altogether. Goncharov's accountant was due in later that evening: he would take the money away with him and ensure that it was paid into several different bank accounts. Anything over ten thousand pounds had to be reported to the authorities.

She closed the safe door and spun the dial, then went out to the main office. Six girls were sitting at desks, each wearing a headset connected to a mobile phone with a computer terminal in front of them. Each was taking bookings for an individual agency. The procedure was always the same. A call came in and the receptionist asked which girl the client wanted to see. If the caller was concealing his phone number, the receptionist would ask for a contact number so that they could confirm the booking. It was entered into a database and cross-referenced against the phone numbers of men who had used the agency before. That allowed the receptionist to recognise regulars, and punters who had caused problems in the past. Assuming there was no problem with the number, the receptionist would take the booking, then phone the girl to confirm it. Then she called back the client and told him the address. Most of the business was incall because many clients were married. Goncharov preferred it that way. It was easier to control the girls if he knew where they were.

A seventh girl, a Spanish brunette called Chloë, was making coffee in the kitchenette at the far end of the office. Anna called her over. Chloë had worked as an escort for six months but had been taken to hospital with a burst ovary and was still unable to work. Anna had offered her the chance to work in the office and she was doing such a good job that she probably wouldn't return to escorting. A good receptionist could earn a hundred thousand pounds a year. They had to have a good phone manner and a confident sales technique so that if the girl a client wanted was busy they could sell him another. They had to be able to handle the girls, too. Sometimes a client would call in with a special request – for a sexual activity that many would regard as perverse: a good receptionist could often persuade a hesitant escort to expand her limits. It no longer surprised Anna how quickly they adapted to the work. The girls Goncharov brought into the country had no say in the services they had to provide, but there were several dozen English girls on the books who started work declaring that they wouldn't do anal, oral without a condom, or allow clients to urinate over them. Within months they had usually agreed to virtually anything, providing that the price was right. A good receptionist knew exactly what each girl was prepared to do, which meant clients were never disappointed. And happy clients meant regular clients.

Anna told Chloë to go to three post-office-box locations around the city – one in Chelsea, one in Kensington and one in Battersea. Most of the girls who worked for Goncharov's agencies had no idea where the main office was. And few got to meet him in person. Contact was usually through Anna or two other senior girls, who helped handle problems with Immigration, landlords or difficult customers.

The escorts paid their money to the agency twice a week. Each girl was issued with a notebook in which she had to record the name of each client, the day, times at which he arrived and left, the amount he paid, and the one-third share that was due to the agency, unless the girl was indebted to Goncharov in which case the agency received all the money. They were instructed to put the cash due to the agency in an envelope along with all the written details of their bookings and deliver it by hand to the post-office-box nearest them. The boxes were opened every day and the money checked against the agency's computer records.

Chloë picked up her jacket and opened the door. She screamed as a heavy-set man in a leather jacket pushed her in the chest and sent her sprawling on her back. He was holding a handgun, which he pointed menacingly at the receptionists as he told them to step away from the terminals. Two more men piled into the office, also waving handguns. One of the girls was sobbing hysterically. The man in the leather jacket pistol-whipped her across the face, knocking her to the floor.

'No!' Anna shouted. 'Leave her alone!'

A fourth man walked into the office. He was in his thirties with a square face and short, dark brown hair. He was wearing sunglasses and a black-leather knee-length coat. A small cigar was stuck between his lips. 'Where is Goncharov?' he asked. He didn't have a gun but there was something in his hand, something that glinted under the overhead lights.

'He's not here,' said Anna. 'If it's money you want, it's in the safe.' There was never more than a few days' money in the office and Anna would rather hand it over than have any of her girls hurt.

'Show me,' said the man.

One of the others bolted the door as Anna took him into Goncharov's office. 'If you know Sergei, you know what he'll do to you when he finds you,' she said.

The man gestured at the safe. 'Open it,' he said. He stubbed out the cigar in a crystal ashtray on the desk.

Anna twisted the dial and pulled open the door. The man looked over her shoulder and nodded. He tossed her a Harrods carrier-bag and told her to fill it.

She did so, and he took it, then showed her what he was holding in his right hand. It was a Stanley knife with two blades that had been separated with a matchstick. 'You see this?' said the man.

Anna nodded.

'I slash your face with this, there's not a plastic surgeon in the world who can fix the scar. Now, where is Goncharov?'

Anna stared at the double-bladed knife. 'Sarajevo,' she said.

'When did he go?'

'This morning.'

'When's he coming back?'

'He didn't say.'

'He left you in charge?'

'Yes.'

The man indicated that she should move away from the safe. He bent down, checked that there was no money left in it and rooted through the papers that were there. He found a manila envelope and emptied the contents on to the desk. There were more than two dozen passports – Russian, Latvian, Bosnian, Ukrainian, Thai, all belonging to girls working for the agencies. He scooped the passports into the Harrods bag. 'Sergei Goncharov is out of business, as of today,' said the man. 'Do you understand?'

Anna nodded.

'If you want to set up on your own, that's fine. I don't

have a problem with you. But I will be running these agencies, and I will be taking over the girls.'

'You can't do that—' began Anna.

The man stepped forward and pushed the knife against her throat. 'I can do whatever I want,' he hissed. 'Understand?'

'Yes,' said Anna, her voice quivering.

The man pushed her back to the main office. The receptionists were all lying face down on the carpet. One of the men was switching off the mobile phones and putting them into a blue nylon holdall. Another was unplugging the computers and disconnecting the VDUs.

'Lie down,' the man told Anna.

The man with the sunglasses spoke to his colleagues in a language Anna didn't recognise. She didn't know who the men were, but she knew one thing for sure – that when Sergei Goncharov discovered what they'd done, they would be dead. And that before they died, they would suffer.

Solomon eased himself down on to the wooden bench and stuck out his cast in front of him. He took out a bag of peanuts. Two grey squirrels scampered down a tree and sat watching him, rubbing their paws together. Solomon tossed them each a nut, which they grabbed then ran away.

It was a sunny day. He was wearing a red polo shirt and yet another pair of jeans with the left leg slashed up to the thigh to accommodate the cast. When it came off, he was going to have to buy a whole new wardrobe of trousers.

The squirrels returned, wary but eager for more peanuts. Solomon tossed a couple in their direction. As the squirrels headed back to the tree with their booty,

Solomon heard footsteps behind him. He turned. Two men were walking towards him. They were big men in dark coats and his stomach lurched. He looked around frantically, but no one else was within earshot. He looked back at the men, now only a dozen yards away. One was familiar. He had a square jaw, a crew-cut and thin, blood-less lips. His hands were in his coat pockets and he was saying something to his colleague.

Solomon reached for his stick, but he knew there was no point in trying to escape or to fight them off. His heart pounded and his breath caught in his throat.

The two men moved apart as they approached the bench, the square-jawed man came to stand in front of him, his colleague stayed behind the bench. Solomon glanced around. The nearest person was a young woman striding purposefully along a path, a briefcase in one hand, a mobile phone clamped to her ear with the other. His mobile phone was in the back pocket of his jeans and he grabbed for it, but even as he started to tap out nine-nine-nine he knew he'd never make it. He was going to die on Clapham Common, shot on a park bench by men who killed for a living.

The square-jawed man pulled his right hand out of his coat pocket. Solomon flinched, then saw there was no gun. 'Sasha wants to talk to you,' the man said, his accent almost impenetrable.

Solomon remembered where he'd seen him before: he had been in the front seat of the Mercedes that had taken him from Sasha's flat to Bayswater. He cancelled the nine-nine-nine call. 'He can talk to me here,' he said.

The man pointed to a BMW parked at the far side of the common. 'He wants you to come to him.'

'Some sort of power game?' asked Solomon. He was

angry with the men for frightening him, and even angrier with himself for being scared. 'I'm through playing games. If he wants to see me, he can come here.'

The man behind Solomon bent down. 'We were attacked yesterday,' he said. 'Sasha was almost killed. We would prefer him to stay in the car.'

For the first time Solomon noticed the small cuts on the square-jawed man's face and a bruise above his left cheekbone. 'Who was it?' he asked.

The man didn't reply. The pair waited in silence. Solomon pushed himself up with his stick and walked towards the car.

As Solomon reached the BMW the rear door opened. He climbed in. Sasha was sitting in the back. He pushed his sunglasses on top of his head before he spoke. 'That fucking Russian tried to kill me yesterday,' he said. 'If I'd been sitting in my regular seat, I'd be dead now. He killed one of my girls, and one of my friends.'

'Not Inga?' said Solomon, quickly. Too quickly.

Sasha looked at him scornfully. 'No, it wasn't Inga. But she was a good girl and she didn't deserve it. Neither did Karic.'

'I'm sorry,' said Solomon. He was relieved it wasn't Inga, but Sasha was right. It didn't matter who had been killed: what mattered was that the Russian who'd tried to kill Solomon was on the warpath again and it was Solomon's fault. 'Jesus, I'm sorry, Sasha. This is all because of me, isn't it?'

Sasha pulled a face. 'It was my own fault for not killing the bastard when I had the chance. I won't make the same mistake again.'

Solomon nodded slowly, not sure what to say.

'Now the bastard Russian has run off to Sarajevo.

Probably thinks I can't get him there. He's got another think coming,' Sasha went on.

'You're going after him?'

'What do you think? How long would I last in this business if I let him get away with it?' He looked at his wristwatch, a white-gold Breitling. 'I'm on a flight to Sarajevo in three hours. Do you want to come?'

Solomon's jaw dropped.

'Goncharov's taken four of his men with him, probably the guys who shot at me. And two are probably the ones who were in your flat. You saw them, I didn't.'

'I can identify them.'

'Might be a help. And if that girl you're looking for is still there, we could kill two birds with one stone.'

'That's what we're going to do? Kill birds?'

'I'm offering you the chance to find the girl, and to take revenge on the men who shot you.' Sasha looked at his watch again. 'Of course, if you don't want to come . . .'

'I'm there,' said Solomon, hurriedly. 'Just let me get my passport.'

Sasha reached into his jacket pocket and pulled out an airline ticket. He handed it to Solomon. It was a British Airways flight to Sarajevo via Zagreb. In Solomon's name. Solomon looked up and Sasha was grinning. 'I knew you'd want to be in at the kill,' he said.

Nicole woke up, gasping for breath, her mouth full of cold water. She spat it out and coughed. A hand grabbed her hair and pulled her into a sitting position, then shook her.

'Wake up, bitch!' hissed the man. He was one of the owners of the brothel, a tall, lanky man with shrapnel scars across his cheek and neck. His right eye was a milky white and half of his right ear was missing.

Nicole struggled to keep her eyes open. She was dog-tired. The brothel was open for business twenty-four hours a day and the upstairs windows had been boarded up so she had no way of knowing what time it was. Nor did she know how long she'd been in the room. Time had lost all meaning. The men came, they abused her, and they left. That was her life.

'You're not here to sleep, bitch!' the man hissed. 'You're here to screw.' He slapped her, twice. Nicole didn't try to defend herself. A lot of the men who came to the room slapped her, or punched her, or bit her. They seemed to enjoy inflicting pain as much as having sex with her.

There was another man behind the owner, a man in his fifties with a beer gut straining at a dirty white T-shirt. He was naked below the waist but he still had on his socks. He had one hand on a semi-erect penis and he was wiping his mouth with the other.

Nicole's eyes fluttered closed. The man swore at her again and twisted her hair savagely. When she didn't react he pushed her back on to the bed. Nicole rolled over into the foetal position, her knees drawn up to her chest. Suddenly cold water splashed over her face and chest and she gasped and spluttered. The owner grabbed her by the hair again and pulled her upright. Nicole opened her eyes. The man's hand was inches from her face holding a white tablet. She clamped her teeth shut but the owner yanked her hair and when she yelped he pushed the tablet between her lips.

'Swallow it, bitch, or I'll kick you around the room,' he hissed.

Nicole tried to swallow but she gagged and began to

choke. The owner thrust a glass of water to her lips. Nicole drank and swallowed. The owner picked up another tablet and held it to her mouth. It was smaller than the first. This time she swallowed without choking and the owner pushed her back on the bed.

'The ecstasy will get her in the mood, the speed will keep her going,' he said to the customer. 'Give it a couple of minutes for the stuff to kick in. Sorry about the inconvenience.'

The owner left the room. Nicole lay on her back with one arm across her face, her legs wide apart. The customer stood staring down at her, breathing heavily. Then he grunted and knelt down on the bed. He rolled Nicole on to her front and entered her roughly from behind, swearing at her and calling her a cheap whore. Nicole barely heard him. She tried to blot him out, to blot it all out. She tried to imagine that she was somewhere else, somewhere safe and warm, somewhere where she could sleep in peace.

The British Airways jet touched down at Sarajevo airport shortly after nine p.m. There were long queues at Immigration, and it was after ten o'clock by the time Solomon, Sasha and Rikki walked out of the terminal building. Four other men had joined the flight in Zagreb. They had sat together at the back of the plane but Solomon had seen them nod to Sasha when they boarded and they had joined him at the luggage carousel. They were big men, not as big as Rikki but broad-shouldered and thick-waisted with army haircuts and designer stubble. They all wore bomber jackets, cargo pants and matching diving watches. They followed Sasha and Solomon as they headed for two black stretch limousines. Each car had a driver, and a man in a waxed cotton jacket was sitting in the second.

The four men in bomber jackets got into the front car while Sasha, Solomon and Rikki climbed into the other. The man in the waxed jacket nodded at Sasha, who took a brown envelope from his inside pocket and gave it to him. He slit it open with his thumbnail and Solomon glimpsed a wad of banknotes before the envelope vanished inside the man's jacket.

Rikki pulled open a concealed lid to reveal a large drinks cabinet. He lifted a bottle of Cognac and Sasha nodded. Rikki filled three crystal tumblers and handed one each to Sasha and Solomon.

Sasha clinked his glass against Solomon's, then drank deeply.

Solomon took a sip from his glass, then put it on a shelf behind the driver's glass partition. His leg had begun to itch and he pulled the knitting-needle out of the cast and scratched away.

Sasha frowned at the knitting-needle. 'How were you able to take that on the plane? Didn't it set off the metal detector?'

Solomon shrugged as he scratched. 'It went off but I told them my leg had been pinned. Anyway, I'm not even sure it's metal. Might be some composite material. Some sort of plastic.' He stuck it back down the cast and worked away at the itch. 'What's your plan, Sasha?' he asked. 'Where do we go from here?'

The man in the waxed jacket handed Sasha a black-leather holdall. Sasha opened it and took out something bulky wrapped in an oily cloth. It was a black machine pistol, just over a foot long with an oblong magazine sticking out of the bottom. He passed it to Rikki and took out a second weapon for himself. 'I'm going to kill that bastard Russian and anyone who's helping him,' he said flatly.

'And what about me?' said Solomon. 'Don't I get a gun?'

'Have you ever fired one of these?'

'No.'

'Any sort of gun?'

'No. Vice cops don't need guns, not in the UK.'

'Even with a silencer these are loud, and they jump around a lot,' said Sasha. 'You don't want to fire one unless you've had a lot of practice. A bullet from this will tear off a limb.'

Solomon settled back in the seat. 'So I'm just along for the ride?'

'You're here to identify the two guys who shot at you. And this Petrovic, do you know what he looks like?'

'I met him once, yeah.'

'You never told me the full story about that, did you?'

Solomon tried to play innocent, but he knew he was wasting his time.

'Petrovic didn't go to all this trouble just because of the girl, did he?' Sasha said. 'All he had to do was yank her back to Bosnia. There was no need to have you killed.'

'I put him in hospital,' said Solomon.

Rikki chuckled, and took a swig of Cognac.

'How did you manage that?' asked Sasha. 'I've been told he's one tough son of a bitch.'

'I burst his spleen. Lucky kick, maybe. I don't know. It all happened so fast.'

Sasha slapped Solomon's plaster cast. 'I'm going to have to watch you,' he said. 'Maybe you're not as soft as you look.'

The car in front pulled away from the terminal. 'Who are those guys?' asked Solomon.

'Croats. Good men. I've used them before.'

Solomon knew without asking that Sasha was referring to the revenge he'd taken on the Serbs who'd killed his brother. The limousine edged forward, then accelerated quickly after the first vehicle. 'Where are we going?' asked Solomon.

'To see Petrovic,' said Sasha. 'You can ask him about his spleen.'

'Now?'

'Later tonight.'

'How do you know where he is?'

'I have friends in Belgrade, where he gets some of his girls.'

'Won't they tip him off?'

'Give me some credit. He's back in his clubs. Usually he hangs out in one called the Butterfly.'

'I know it.'

'You've been there?'

'It's where I had my altercation with him.'

'The busted spleen?'

Solomon nodded. 'What about Goncharov?'

'My friends don't know him. But we can ask Petrovic, can't we?' Sasha broke the machine pistol expertly into its individual components and reassembled it. He slotted in the magazine. Clicked on the safety, then screwed a bulbous silencer into the barrel. For the first time Solomon realised the enormity of what they were soon to do. The adrenaline had kicked in the moment Sasha had told him they were going to Sarajevo, but he hadn't considered what they would do when they arrived. The guns were a tangible symbol of what lay ahead.

As they reached the centre of the city, the first limousine peeled off and drove south towards the hills. Sasha saw Solomon frown and explained that the Croats were going to stake out the Butterfly.

They drove to the Holiday Inn, and Solomon waited in the limousine while Sasha and Rikki checked in. Sasha had offered to get him a room, but Solomon still had his apartment. Sasha and Rikki left their guns on the back seat. The tinted windows of the limousine were opaque from the outside but Solomon still flinched every time someone walked past. He wondered what the penalty was for having a loaded machine pistol, then remembered that possession of a weapon was the least of the crimes they'd be committing that night. He leaned over and picked up one of the pistols. He was surprised by how heavy it was. He doubted that he'd be able to fire it with one hand. He put it down and tried not to look at it again.

A short time later, Sasha and Rikki returned, and the limousine headed out of the city. As they got closer to the Butterfly, they checked their guns again. They parked a short walk away from the bar. Sasha and Rikki opened their jackets: they were wearing nylon shoulder holsters and slotted in their weapons.

Rikki spoke to the driver, who opened the glove compartment, then handed him two ski masks and a Polaroid camera. Rikki gave one of the masks to Sasha, then got out of the car. Sasha turned to Solomon. 'You wait here. No matter what happens, you wait for us.' He grinned suddenly. 'Don't worry, it'll be okay.'

A figure walked towards the limousine and Solomon tensed, but then he recognised one of the Croats. Rikki went over to talk to him.

Sasha slapped Solomon's shoulder and climbed out of

the car. He joined Rikki and the Croat, and the three men headed down the road towards the Butterfly.

Solomon sat staring at the back of the driver's head and listening to the soft clicks of the limousine engine as it cooled. He was breathing heavily and forced himself to relax. Whatever was happening to Petrovic, he deserved it. He was a violent criminal who corrupted the police, who trafficked in women, who thought he was above the law – and probably was. Solomon knew that there was no way he could ever have persuaded Petrovic to tell him where Nicole had been sent, so Sasha was the only option. Petrovic had brought it upon himself. The limousine engine stopped clicking.

He jumped as he saw two men jogging towards the limousine and it was a second or two before he realised that it was Sasha with one of the Croats. Sasha climbed into the back of the limousine, and thrust a dozen Polaroid photographs at Solomon. 'Which one's Petrovic?' he asked.

Solomon flicked through them. They were all men – some defiant, some confused, some scared. Solomon tapped the one of Petrovic, who was glaring at the camera – he could feel the hate burning out of the photograph.

'Recognise anyone else?' asked Sasha.

None of the pictures were of Goncharov and Solomon couldn't see either of the men who'd been in McLaren's flat. He pointed out the men who'd been in the bar when he'd had his run-in with Petrovic but said he didn't know their names.

'Right, you can leave the rest to us,' said Sasha.

'What are you planning?'

Sasha put the photographs into his pocket. 'I'm going to have a quiet word with him. The driver will take you back to your apartment and I'll phone you when I have something. Try to get some sleep.'

Solomon took several deep breaths to calm himself. He doubted that he would be getting any sleep that night.

Sasha kept the gun jammed hard against Petrovic's neck as they drove along the twisting hillside road. The man was lying face down on the floor of the limousine, a black hood over his head.

'Do you have any idea who the fuck I am?' Petrovic snarled.

Sasha put his mouth close to the hood. 'Of course I know who you are,' he hissed.

Rikki was in the front, sitting next to the driver. The four Croats were in the back with Sasha. They had their feet on Petrovic, keeping him pinned to the floor. The Bosnian's hands were tied behind his back and his feet had been taped together.

Half-way up the hill there was a ruined house, its roof long gone, the walls peppered with shrapnel scars. There was no glass in the windows and all the doors had been stripped out. Its nearest neighbour was half a mile away. One of the Croats had told Sasha about the house, and its basement – he had used the basement before, he had said, but he hadn't explained why.

They pulled up behind the house and the driver switched off the lights. There was a near full moon and the sky was cloudless. Rikki opened the door, and he and Sasha got out of the car. The Croats bundled Petrovic out and dragged him across the grass into the house. Two of the Croats had torches and switched them on as they went inside.

Sasha and Rikki stood at the rear of the limousine.

'Have you got them?' asked Sasha. Rikki pulled a pair of bolt-cutters out of his coat pocket. Sasha nodded his approval.

'Fingers or toes?' asked Rikki.

'Your call,' said Sasha.

'If it was you, which would you rather lose?'

Sasha scowled at him.

'Just asking.'

They walked into the house and stood looking down the stairs that led to the basement. Petrovic was screaming but the noise barely reached the kitchen.

An hour later, Sasha went back to the limousine. There was blood on his right hand and he stopped to wipe it on the grass. He took out his mobile and called Jack Solomon. 'She's in Arizona,' said Sasha. 'So is Goncharov.'

'Petrovic told you that?'

'Petrovic told me everything. I'm driving up tomorrow. Do you want to come?'

'Of course.'

'We'll pick you up at your flat at midday or thereabouts.'

'Is everything okay?' asked Solomon.

'Why do you ask?'

'You sound tense.'

'It's been a tense evening,' said Sasha. There was blood on the toe of his right shoe and he wiped it on the grass. 'Just be ready to go tomorrow.'

Solomon rolled over on to his side but the cast made sleep impossible in that position – he could only sleep on his back or his front with any comfort. He tried to clear his mind but the events of the past few days kept buzzing through it. It was as if he no longer had any control over what was happening: it was Sasha's show, and Solomon was just along for the ride.

He sniffed. He could smell smoke – but he'd smoked his last Marlboro on the balcony as he drank a bottle of Heineken before he'd turned in. He'd not smoked in bed since he was a uniformed police officer and had been called to a house where an old woman had burned to death after falling asleep with a cigarette in her hand. Now he didn't even have an ashtray in the bedroom. He sniffed again. It *was* cigarette smoke, but it wasn't a Marlboro: it was a sweet-smelling local brand.

Solomon sat up. Dragan Jovanovic was lounging in an armchair by the window, his legs crossed, his right hand draped over the back of the chair.

'For God's sake, Dragan, don't you ever knock?' said Solomon.

'I'm a policeman, I don't have to knock. And you should lock your door, Jack. There are many dangerous men in Sarajevo.' He ran his left hand through his close-cropped greying hair. 'What are you doing back in town?'

'First, I'm pretty sure I locked my door. And second, how did you know I was back?'

'I just said, I'm a policeman. It's my job to know what's happening in this city.'

'And what is happening?'

Dragan took a long drag on his cigarette and blew smoke across Solomon's bed. 'We could do this down at the station,' he said.

'Are you playing good-cop-bad-cop all on your own?'

Dragan didn't say anything, just stared at Solomon.

'And now the silent treatment?'

'We've known each other a long time, haven't we?' asked Dragan.

'Sure.'

'So why are you treating me like shit? Why won't you answer a few simple questions?'

'Because it's God knows what time and you've just broken into my flat, that's why. What's going on, Dragan?'

'Ivan Petrovic, that's what's going on. My boss is going to have to find someone else to play pool with. They've just fished his body out of the Miljacka. And he was missing a few fingers. So, I think, Jack, old friend, that *I* should be asking *you* what's going on, don't you?'

Solomon sighed. 'Let's go outside, yeah? I don't feel like having this conversation in my bedroom.'

Dragan went out as Solomon swung his cast off the bed. The policeman went into the kitchen, reappeared with two bottles of Heineken and opened the sliding window that led to the balcony. They sat in plastic chairs. Dragan used his slab-like teeth to prise the caps off the bottles, then handed one to Solomon. They drank their beer looking out over the darkened graveyard opposite the apartment block. Solomon handed his friend a Marlboro, lit it, then one for himself.

'You have a nice flat here. I've always said that.'

'I know.'

'Are you going to stay now that your job's gone?'

Solomon shrugged. He was wearing baggy pyjama bottoms and nothing else, but it was a warm night. Dragan had on a dark grey suit and he'd loosened his collar and tie. He looked exhausted.

'I'm not sure,' said Solomon. 'Depends if I can land another job here.'

'But that's not why you've come back, is it? You're not here to hand out your CV.'

'A few fingers?'

'A bolt-cutter, it looked like. Somebody wanted him to talk. And he must have done, otherwise they would have carried on cutting. I wonder what they wanted to know. What do you think?'

Solomon took a long pull on his Heineken but didn't reply. Two white UN four-wheel-drives rattled by on the road below.

'It's about that bloody girl, isn't it?'

Solomon squinted across at the policeman. 'That's a hell of a leap,' he said.

'You're not denying it, then?'

Solomon drained his bottle and put it down next to his chair. 'I didn't kill him,' he said quietly.

'I never said you did. With that cast, you're hardly likely to have thrown him in the river. But you know who did, don't you?'

Solomon didn't reply.

'Do you have any idea what a difficult position this puts me in?' asked Dragan. 'You called me from London and asked me to talk to Petrovic. A few days later he's butchered and murdered.'

'I didn't ask you to talk to him. I asked you to check out the bar to see if Nicole was there, that's all.'

'You put me in the firing line, Jack, and I think I have the right to know what the hell's going on. Don't you?'

Solomon rubbed the back of his neck. The muscles had tensed and he had the beginnings of a headache. 'What do you know?' he asked.

'I know that six guys went into the Butterfly club late last night wearing ski masks. They had silenced machine pistols – Hungarian KGP-9s, we think. They shot three of Petrovic's men. One is dead, two are in intensive care. That's when it all got a bit weird.'

'Weird?'

'They wanted to know which one was Petrovic. No one said anything, so one of the men produced a Polaroid camera and started snapping at all the men in the place. Then he took the Polaroids outside. He was gone for a couple of minutes. When he came back he went straight up to Petrovic and slammed him with the gun. They dragged him out and that was that.'

Solomon's hand shook as he lit another Marlboro.

'At first I couldn't work out why they needed the camera,' said Dragan.

'To identify him, right?'

The policeman wagged a finger at Solomon. 'Once a cop, always a cop, hey? But if they needed someone to identify him, that means they aren't local because Petrovic is a celebrity in these parts. But whoever was there to identify Petrovic could have worn a ski mask, too, and gone in with them.' Dragan leaned over and slapped Solomon's plaster cast. 'Unless something else might give him away. Something a ski mask couldn't hide.'

Solomon sat back in his chair. 'Why are you here, Dragan?' he asked. 'Looks to me like you already know all there is to know.'

'You were there, weren't you?'

There was no point in denying it.

'And the men in ski masks?'

'One is a friend from London. He brought one of the heavies with him and the other four were Croatians. Ex-army, I think.'

'That's some friend you have there.'

'He's Albanian. Kosovar Albanian.'

'Name?'

'Sasha's the name he uses. Are you going to arrest me?'

345

Dragan drained his bottle and pushed himself out of the chair. He ambled off to the kitchen and returned with two fresh Heinekens. He opened them and handed one to Solomon before dropping back into his chair.

'Well?' said Solomon. 'Are you going to take me in?'

'For what?'

'You know.'

Dragan shrugged his massive shoulders. 'No one in the Butterfly mentioned a guy with his leg in plaster,' he said. 'I don't see that I'd have a case. And I don't think you'd want to confess, would you?' He took a long pull at his bottle, then wiped his mouth with the back of his hand. 'You really should get some decent beer in,' he said.

'I'll do that,' said Solomon. 'I might as well get you a key cut, too.'

Dragan flashed Solomon a tight smile. 'Where is the girl?'

'Arizona. Petrovic has sent her to a brothel there.'

'You're going after her?'

'They're picking me up this afternoon.'

'Arizona's a dangerous place,' said Dragan.

'I know.'

'No, a *really* dangerous place. There's no law up there. Wild West.'

'Sasha can take care of himself. He knows what he's doing.'

'Yes – but do you?'

Solomon leaned forward in his chair. 'Petrovic had me shot.' He tapped his cast. 'And this wasn't a warning, Dragan. They dug two bullets out of me and if the cops hadn't turned up they'd have finished me off. They tried to kill Sasha, too. Shot one of his bodyguards and killed a girl who worked for him.'

'It wasn't Petrovic. He hasn't left Sarajevo.'

'He got an associate to do the dirty work. Name of Goncharov. A Russian. He's in Arizona, too.'

'So, your new best friend is heading up there for another shoot-out, is he?'

'We're going to rescue the girl. The eyewitness.'

'Hasn't it occurred to you that maybe she doesn't want to be rescued?'

'I don't believe that. Her family were murdered, she's got to want justice.'

'This doesn't sound like justice,' said Dragan. 'It sounds like revenge.'

'It's a thin line,' said Solomon. 'But I'm happy to see her family's killer answer to the War Crimes Tribunal.'

'But this Sasha isn't doing it out of the goodness of his heart, is he? He wants Goncharov.'

'I'm not going to shed any tears for the Russian. Not after what he did to me. And *he* sent the girl back to Bosnia.'

Dragan held out his hand for a cigarette. Solomon tossed him one. He caught it deftly and put it to his lips, then lit a match with his thumbnail. 'You're sure about this?' asked Dragan. 'You're sure you want to go through with it?'

'I can't explain why I feel the way I do, Dragan. I wish I could. It's like I'm trapped on some sort of roller-coaster and I can't get off.'

'No matter what?'

'No matter what.'

Dragan put his beer bottle on the floor. 'You don't leave me with any choice, then,' he said. 'I'll have to come with you.'

'What?' exclaimed Solomon.

'You heard me,' said the policeman. 'You need taking care of.'

'Sasha will do that.'

'How well do you know this guy?' asked Dragan. 'What if he's got another agenda? If he decided to do something to you in Arizona, there'd be nothing to stop him.'

Solomon toyed with his bottle of Heineken. He knew that Dragan was right. Sasha had already tortured and killed Petrovic. And he was heading up to Arizona to kill Goncharov and his thugs. He might well decide that he was better off with no witnesses around.

'How do I explain you to Sasha?' he asked. 'No way he's going to want a cop around.'

Dragan grinned. 'I'll dress casual,' he said. 'Don't forget I worked undercover with the federal police. You just tell him I'm a friend from the Commission. I know enough about your work to get by.'

'And why are you going to Arizona? He'll want to know.'

'You can say I've been there a few times. Which is true. And that I'm worried about your safety. Which is also true.'

'You're sure about this, Dragan?'

'If I don't take care of you, who else will?'

Solomon was sitting on his balcony eating a fried-egg sandwich and drinking a mug of coffee when he saw a black Range Rover and a blue Toyota four-wheel-drive park below his building. He peered down and saw Sasha climb out of the Toyota. A few seconds later his intercom buzzed. He limped over and picked up the handset. He asked Sasha if he wanted a coffee but was told that they should head off straight away.

Solomon picked up his holdall, which contained a change of clothes and his washbag, and took the lift to ground level. Sasha was waiting for him outside the main doors.

'What happened to the limos?' asked Solomon.

'These are less conspicuous,' said Sasha. He took the holdall and walked towards the Toyota.

'I want a friend to come with us,' said Solomon.

Sasha stopped dead in his tracks. 'You what?'

'A friend of mine from the Commission.'

'This isn't a road trip,' said Sasha. 'Arizona's a no man's land.'

'He knows Arizona. He's been there before.'

'It's practically a war zone,' said Sasha.

'So the more manpower, the better.'

'Who is he?'

'His name's Dragan. He used to be in the army, but now he's one of our exhumation officers. He'll be useful.' He had agreed the cover story with Dragan before the policeman had left.

'What do you mean "useful"? This isn't a game of cricket. We're going to war. Last night was a walkover compared with what's waiting for us up in Arizona.'

'Look, Sasha, you need me to identify the two men who shot me because they're probably the ones who killed your man and the girl. And I want Dragan here.'

Sasha pointed a finger at him. 'I have Goncharov's photograph, remember? And I won't have any problem getting him to tell me where his men are, believe me. The only reason you're still part of this is because you want to get that girl from Kosovo.'

Solomon put a hand on his shoulder. 'Okay, you're right. I need you more than you need me. There's no way

I could have done what you did last night, no way I could have taken Petrovic and got him to tell me where Nicole is. And I know how dangerous Arizona can be. I don't have the manpower or the firepower to go up there on my own and get her. So I'm asking you. Please. Let Dragan come with us. If nothing else, he can watch my back.'

Sasha was suspicious. 'You don't trust me?'

Solomon took his hand off Sasha's shoulder. 'I wouldn't be here in Bosnia if I didn't. I just mean that if Dragan's there to keep an eye on me, you have an extra man.' He gesticulated at his plaster cast. 'I'm not going to be any good in a firefight, am I? And I see you don't have drivers this time. Dragan can drive one of the cars.'

Sasha took out a packet of small cigars from the inside pocket of his leather bomber jacket and lit one. He blew out a cloud of bluish smoke, which dissipated slowly as he stared at Solomon with his pale grey eyes. Then he smiled slowly. 'You're scared, aren't you?' he asked.

'What do you think, Sasha? Even when I was a cop, I didn't see guns like the ones you used last night. And I've seen heavy guys before, but those Croats would put the fear of God into anyone.'

'You could stay here, in Sarajevo.'

'No,' Solomon said. 'I want to be around when you get Nicole out. She's not going to know who you are or why you're there.'

Sasha blew another cloud of smoke. 'If he comes, you're responsible for him.'

'Sure.'

Sasha fixed him with a cold stare. 'You understand what that means?' he said, his voice devoid of emotion. 'If he fucks up, I'll hold you responsible.'

'He won't.'

★

Dragan paced around his apartment like a big cat confined in a cage. He lit a cigarette, then flicked the spent match out of the open window. It was the fifteenth he'd smoked since he'd returned to his apartment. He'd seen the stars fade as the sky brightened, and the first rays of the sun creep over the edge of the hills that surrounded the city. In the early hours his wife had asked him what was wrong, but he'd sent her back to bed and told her not to worry. It was work, he'd said, nothing he couldn't handle. He just needed to think. He told her he'd have to go away for a day or two. She didn't protest: she'd been a policeman's wife for long enough to know that there was no point. The job was his life. She'd muttered something, and left him to it. Dragan had paced, smoked and cursed Jack Solomon for being one stubborn son-of-a-bitch.

Anyone else would have given up long ago, and Solomon was lucky not to have been killed on his first visit to the Butterfly. Even luckier not to have died in London. The men who'd tried to kill him were gangsters and assassins, yet he hadn't given up. Arizona was one of the most lawless places in the world, ruled by the gun: life wasn't just cheap there, it was disposable. Solomon knew that, yet he was still prepared to go in to rescue a prostitute who might not even want to be rescued.

'Damn you, Solomon,' said Dragan aloud. 'Damn you to hell and back.'

If Solomon had let things lie, the girl would have disappeared, Petrovic would have gone back to running his criminal organisation, Solomon could have started afresh in London, and Dragan could have carried on doing what he did best. Now the girl was back in Bosnia, Petrovic was lying in the city morgue, Solomon was in the firing line again, and Dragan would have to risk everything to clear up the mess.

He went over to his big-screen TV and pulled open the bottom drawer beneath it. Among the pirated video-cassettes of blockbuster movies there was a plastic case. Dragan opened it. Inside was a Yugoslavian M70 pocket pistol, a cleaning kit, a box of ammunition and several spare clips, a souvenir of his days with the Odjeljenje Za Organizovani Kriminalitec I Droge. When he had been in uniform he'd carried it as a back-up weapon, strapped to his right ankle. When he was undercover, it had been the only gun he carried.

He took the case over to the coffee table and methodically field-stripped, cleaned and reassembled the weapon. He slotted eight cartridges into the clip and rammed it home. In a perfect world he'd have carried spare clips with him, but there was no point in having a concealed gun if ammunition was rattling around in his pockets.

His nylon ankle-holster with its Velcro straps was in a cupboard in the hall and he strapped the gun to his ankle, rolled down his trouser-leg and examined his reflection in the bedroom mirror. Perfect.

Solomon called Dragan on his mobile and the policeman was waiting for him on the pavement when the Range Rover and the Toyota pulled up.

'That's him?' asked Sasha. Dragan was wearing a blue fur-trimmed parka, baggy brown trousers and Timberland boots. Over one shoulder he carried a green nylon holdall.

Solomon nodded.

'Stay here.' Sasha got out of the car and walked over to Dragan. The two men shook hands, then Sasha pointed to the Range Rover, which contained the four Croats. Dragan looked across at Solomon, winked, then climbed into it. Sasha walked back to Solomon, rubbing his hands, and got in. 'Right, let's go,' he said. Rikki was driving.

'What was that about?' asked Solomon.

'What?' asked Sasha, lighting a fresh cigar.

'You know what. He could have ridden with us.'

'It means we can talk without worrying about what's said.'

'You can trust Dragan,' said Solomon.

'I don't trust anyone,' said Sasha. He clapped Rikki on the shoulder. 'Except Rikki.'

Rikki pulled away from the kerb and the Range Rover followed as they left Sarajevo. It took almost four hours to drive to Tuzla. Rikki was a careful driver, bordering on obsessive. He checked his rear-view mirror every few seconds, and looked back over his shoulder before every manoeuvre.

Several times, Sasha turned the conversation to Dragan. His questions were innocuous and casually asked, but Solomon knew he was being tested. Sasha wanted to know how they'd met, how long they'd worked together, jobs they'd done, places they'd been. It was phrased as idle chit-chat but he was sure that Sasha intended to ask the same questions of Dragan. Any discrepancies would have to be explained. Their cover story was based on the truth, the only lies about Dragan's supposed job with the Commission.

The four Croatians were a taciturn bunch, except the one called Otto, who was sitting on Dragan's right in the back of the Range Rover. They had introduced themselves by first name only. The driver was the biggest of the four

with a wicked scar across his left cheek. He grunted that
his name was Mirko, then didn't say another word. The
man in the front passenger seat was Tafik. He hadn't
turned round when Dragan had climbed into the car so
he didn't know what the man looked like.

On his left was Tomislav, the only one of the quartet
who had offered to shake hands.

Otto's breath reeked of garlic, and Dragan took out a
packet of cigarettes and offered them round – if nothing
else the smoke might mask the smell. Tomislav and Otto
produced gun-metal Zippos and lit the cigarettes. The
Zippos bore the same crest, and Dragan asked what it
represented. Otto told him it was the crest of their
Croatian Army unit, but didn't go into details. That they
were army was without question: they were all well
muscled with short haircuts and faces sprinkled with
ruptured capillaries from too many nights spent outside
in rough country. Their hard, soulless eyes suggested that
they'd seen too much killing to be bothered any longer by
death. Dragan tried not to think about the fact that he was
surrounded by four trained killers, who had already
tortured and murdered one of the country's most ruth-
less gangsters.

Otto kept grinning at him with grey teeth and asking
him about his work with the International War-dead
Commission. Dragan talked at length about identifying
the victims of the ethnic-cleansing atrocities but kept the
details vague. From time to time Otto would ask a question that required a specific answer – the location of an
office, the name of an official – and Dragan knew he was
being tested. He continued to smoke and act as if he
was at ease, but inside his mind was racing, cross-
checking everything he said with the cover story. He had

been involved in enough interrogations to know what the signs of lying were and how to conceal them, but that didn't make the process any less stressful.

Otto also asked him about Arizona, and there he was on firmer ground. He'd visited the area several times when he'd been with the federal police, once undercover while investigating a drugs ring operated by former senior officers of the Kosovo Liberation Army. The name had stuck after the Americans had renamed the roads. When they had moved into the former Yugoslavia to keep apart the warring factions, they had found the road names unpronounceable: the main road from Bosnia to Croatia became Arizona.

With the huge volume of troops and commerce passing along the road, it hadn't taken long for the entrepreneurs to move in, initially offering food, drinks and cigarettes, then prostitutes and drugs. What started as a few roadside shacks swiftly grew to a shanty-town that wasn't shown on any maps. The Chinese moved in, funnelling counterfeit designer clothes and CDs from Far Eastern sweatshops. The Russians sold weapons and ammunition raided from the fracturing Soviet military. The Bosnian and Albanian pimps moved in their girls. Side-roads sprang up, with brothels and illegal bars, and shops with heroin from Afghanistan. Amphetamines from China were sold under the watchful eye of armed gangsters. Because the shanty-town was so close to the Bosnian–Croatian border, it remained unpoliced. People disappeared regularly and no one went looking for them. Stolen cars were stamped with new identity plates, driven across the border and on to Italy and Germany, no questions asked. False passports and papers for virtually every country in the world were available: all you needed to know was who to ask and how much to pay.

Traders and shopkeepers drove up from all over Bosnia to load up with cheap cigarettes and counterfeit goods, and get laid in the area's brothels. Arizona became one of the major prostitute-auction centres, with hundreds of girls arriving from around the Balkans and the former Soviet Union to be traded like cattle then shipped off to the West. The same smuggling routes were used to transport drugs, weapons and counterfeit goods. Arizona generated millions of dollars of profits every month, and with that sort of money at stake, law-enforcement officers were either bought off or killed. Dragan's undercover operation had been blown by a senior officer taking bribes from the KLA gang. He had been lucky to escape with his life, and it wasn't long after that that he had left the federal police. He hadn't been back to Arizona since.

Otto asked more and more questions about Arizona, and it became clear that he was no longer testing Dragan: he was interested. He wanted details about transport, roads, population levels, communications, and as his questions became increasingly specific, Dragan realised he was briefing a soldier who was planning a military attack.

It was almost four o'clock in the afternoon when the two vehicles reached the massive coal-fired power station and chemical factories on the edge of Tuzla. The Croat driver beeped his horn and Rikki pulled over to let him pass, then followed him some ten car-lengths behind, his foot alternating between the accelerator and brake.

The Croat drove to a roadside restaurant and pulled up behind it. Rikki parked. Sasha opened the door. 'We'll eat here,' he said.

He handed Solomon his walking-stick as he eased himself out of the vehicle. They walked together into the restaurant, a whitewashed single-storey building with a sloping, red-tiled roof. There was a large conservatory to one side filled with tables. The Croats were already inside, helping the owner to push two together. Dragan walked over to Solomon, who lit cigarettes for them both.

'How's the leg holding up?' he asked.

'Fine,' he said. He nodded at the Croats. 'How are the guys?'

'Not very talkative,' said Dragan. 'Wouldn't want to meet them on a dark night.'

'They're on our side,' said Solomon.

The owner, a bald, portly man with a bushy moustache, produced a large white tablecloth, which he threw over the two tables with a flourish. Then a young waitress in a black and white uniform appeared with knives, forks and spoons.

Dragan and Solomon sat at one end of the table, the Croats at the other. Otto patted the waitress on the backside and ordered nine bottles of the local Pilsner beer. Sasha nodded at Otto and the two men went outside to stand by the Range Rover. Dragan and Solomon could see them talking and tried to look unconcerned, joking with the Croats about whether or not the waitress was a virgin. Both men knew that Sasha was cross-checking Dragan's story with Otto.

Their beers arrived with a tray of glasses, and they poured and toasted each other, clinking glasses and shouting, '*Zivjeli*'. Then platters of smoked fish, smoked meats and cream cheese appeared, with baskets of sweet-smelling bread. The Croats ate hungrily, but Dragan and Solomon sipped their beer, waiting for Sasha to return.

'Come on, eat up!' urged Rikki, and nudged Dragan.

Dragan grinned and stabbed at a chunk of fish with his knife. Solomon sipped his beer and watched Sasha and Otto: they were standing so close together that their heads were almost touching, and Sasha had his arm around the Croat's shoulders. Solomon forced himself to look away. He didn't want to appear nervous, because Rikki kept looking in his direction.

He wanted to ask Dragan what he'd said while he was in the Range Rover, but he knew that Rikki at least spoke some English and the Croats might know some too. He could only hope for the best. He wondered what Sasha would do if he decided that their stories didn't match up.

'Come on, Jack,' said Dragan. He nodded at the Croats, who were devouring the food as if they hadn't eaten for days. 'If you don't get started, they'll have had it all.' He pushed a platter towards Solomon and winked.

Solomon helped himself to slices of smoked meat and a dollop of cream cheese. He took one of the rolls and broke it in half, then smeared it with cheese. He tried to chew but his mouth was dry so he took a gulp of beer to wash it down. Eating was the last thing he felt like doing, but as Sasha would pick up on any sign of nerves he fought the urge to retch and took another bite.

Rikki had already finished his Pilsner and was ordering another round when Sasha and Otto came back. Otto sat with the three other Croats and Sasha took the chair between Solomon and Rikki.

'How's the food?' asked Sasha.

'Good,' said Solomon. 'Everything okay?'

Sasha held his eyes for several seconds. Then he said, 'Everything's fine.'

Solomon's stomach stopped churning and he reached

over to help himself to more meat. 'What's the plan?' he asked.

'We'll drive up to Arizona after this and take a look at the place from the outside by daylight. Then Otto and his guys will go in. He knows a place where we can lie low until it gets dark.'

'What about Nicole?'

Sasha picked up a platter and used his fork to scrape a pile of meat, fish and cheese on to his plate. 'If she's there, we get her out.'

'And Goncharov? What are you going to do with him?'

Sasha looked suddenly like a shark preparing to strike. 'What do you think?'

'I think I'm glad I'm not in his shoes,' said Solomon.

Sasha laughed and slapped him on the back. He told the Croats what Solomon had said and all four laughed and nodded. Tomislav made a cut-throat gesture with his knife, which made them laugh all the more.

The Range Rover led the way to Arizona with Rikki following a hundred yards behind. Sasha had told Dragan that he could ride in the Toyota now, so he'd obviously passed the test with Otto.

He sat in the back with Solomon whilst Sasha rode up front with Rikki. Dragan flashed him a reassuring grin, but didn't say anything.

They drove in silence for two hours along a single-carriageway road until Rikki announced that they had arrived. Solomon peered around his shoulder. In the distance he could see that wooden shacks lined both sides of the road, with cars and trucks parked nearby.

The Range Rover slowed and Rikki eased back on the accelerator to keep pace. They reached the outskirts of the shanty-town. The first shacks they passed were filled with cases of brand-name whisky – Johnnie Walker, Famous Grouse, Suntory.

'Is it the real thing?' asked Solomon.

'Difficult to tell,' said Dragan. 'If it's cheap, it's probably been smuggled in duty-free. If it's really cheap it's counterfeit.'

Some of the shacks they drove past were packed with boxes of cigarettes, American and local brands. One had dozens of fridges stacked outside it, another had televisions and microwave ovens, while yet another offered more than a hundred pedestal fans in different colours. Chinese women in sheepskin fleeces were selling plastic flowers and artificial trees, old Muslim women were surrounded by boxes of soap powder, and children stood guard over piles of car parts while their parents polished complete engines.

'They'll have been stripped from stolen cars,' said Dragan. 'You can get parts for practically any make here. Or you can order a car. Tell them what make, model and colour you want, and come back a week later to pick it up, complete with false documentation. The further back from the road you go, the more illegal the stuff gets. Counterfeit currency, drugs, guns. There's supposed to be a group of Russians here who can order Soviet weaponry to be delivered to any country of your choosing. Grenades, bazookas, mines. They have auctions of girls here, too. They bring them from all over and sell them on.'

'Not so much now,' said Sasha. 'A lot of the auctions have moved to Belgrade. There were too many fights out here.'

They passed a parking lot filled with four-wheel drives,

all used vehicles but with no registration plates. They had handwritten prices on pieces of cardboard tucked under their windscreen wipers and all were at least half the price they would fetch in Sarajevo. An Arab was walking around with two Bosnian heavies, kicking tyres and shaking his head. 'A lot of cars end up in the Middle East,' said Dragan. 'They put them in containers and drive them overland. A few bribes to Customs are their only overheads.'

Otto stopped beside a shack selling cigarettes, and Rikki pulled up next to the Range Rover. By the time Solomon had climbed out, Sasha was beckoning him into the cigarette shack.

Otto was giving a big bearded man a bear-hug and kissing his cheek. Then the man hugged the other three Croats, and shook hands with Sasha. He nodded at Solomon and Dragan. He took them between stacks of cigarette cartons and through a wooden door to a large room that contained a rattling refrigerator, a Formica-covered table and a dozen rusting, metal-framed chairs with canvas seats and backs.

Sasha took the seat at the head of the table, the bearded man sat on his left and Rikki on his right. Rikki was carrying a large manila envelope. The four Croats took the seats in the middle, leaving Solomon and Dragan at the end facing Sasha. Sasha gestured at the bearded man with his thumb, 'This is Bruno,' he said to Solomon. 'He knows the place we're going to. It doesn't have a name because they don't cater for the internationals and all the locals know where it is. The bad news is that it's one of Petrovic's places, but the good news, of course, is that Petrovic isn't around any more.'

Solomon remembered to fake surprise – Sasha hadn't

told him what he'd done with the Serbian gang-leader. 'What's happened to him?' he asked.

'Who's Petrovic?' asked Dragan.

'You don't have to worry who Petrovic is,' said Sasha, jabbing a finger at Dragan. 'He's been taken care of.' He held out his hand to Rikki, who gave him the envelope. He opened the flap and slid out the contents. Solomon recognised the photographs of Goncharov that Alex Knight had given him in London. Sasha passed the pictures around the table. 'This is the man we're looking for. Sergei Goncharov, a Russian.' He tapped the picture of the blonde woman talking at Goncharov's side. 'Ignore her, she's in London,' he said. 'He'll have protection. Two men at least, probably more. No pictures, but Jack here has had a close look at them so he can tell us what they look like.'

Solomon described the two men who had broken into McLaren's flat as best he could. It seemed like a lifetime ago.

When he'd finished, Sasha passed around the photograph of Nicole, the blown-up shot taken from the wedding picture. 'This girl's in the building somewhere. We're going to get her out.' Tomislav looked at the picture and said something to Mirko, who grinned, showing two metal front teeth in his upper jaw.

'English,' said Sasha. 'Here we speak English so that we can all understand each other.'

Tomislav apologised. 'I was just saying she was pretty,' he said.

'Pretty or pig ugly, we're getting her out,' said Sasha. 'That was taken three years ago. She's dyed her hair black or brown.'

Solomon reached into his jacket pocket and pulled out

the printout of Nicole's agency page that he'd taken from the Internet café. He passed it across the table to Sasha. 'That's what she looks like now.'

Sasha looked at it and frowned. 'This is off Goncharov's website?'

Solomon nodded. 'They took the page down after I went to see her.'

Sasha passed it round.

'Right, this is how we play this,' said Sasha. 'Goncharov knows me and Rikki and he's seen Solomon. Same goes for his heavies. We stay outside until the last moment. Otto, you and your guys go in this afternoon for a look round. Check out the girls, see if you can locate Goncharov and find out where Nicole is. Two groups of two would make sense.'

Otto nodded at Tomislav. 'You and me,' he said.

'I'm not sharing a girl with you again,' said Tomislav, and grinned.

'What about me?' asked Dragan. 'Goncharov doesn't know me.'

'It's a dangerous place if you don't know what you're doing,' said Sasha. 'Your friend was shot twice in London for asking the wrong questions. If he did that here, he'd be dead.'

'I've been to brothels before,' said Dragan.

Sasha gave him a long, hard look, then nodded slowly. 'Okay, you go in, but you go in alone. Any trouble and you take care of yourself.' He turned to look at Otto. 'You don't stick your neck out for him, okay?'

'Understood.'

'No guns the first time,' said Sasha. 'You're just there to look around. If anyone asks, you're construction workers on the way to Sarajevo. You can tell them there's an agent down there who's promised you work in London. Don't ask questions, don't stick out.'

'What if the Russian isn't there?' asked Tomislav.

'Then we keep going back until he is,' said Sasha. 'What we can't do is ask if anyone has seen him.'

'Why is he here?' asked Dragan.

'He told Petrovic he was here to buy girls,' said Sasha. 'The truth is he got out of London because he knows I'm after him.'

'And why are you after him?' asked Dragan.

Sasha stood up and pushed back his chair. He pulled out a revolver, cocked it and pointed it at Dragan's face.

'Sasha!' shouted Solomon, and tried to get to his feet, but Tomislav forced him back into his seat.

Dragan stared back at Sasha, unfazed.

'You ask too many questions, you know that?' Sasha snapped.

'I just want to know what we're getting into, that's all.'

'It's none of your business,' said Sasha. 'If you don't like it, go back to Sarajevo.' He pointed at Solomon. 'You're here because he wants you here.'

Dragan reached into his jacket, and Sasha's finger tightened on the trigger of his gun. Dragan smiled sarcastically as he brought out a packet of cigarettes and a box of matches. He lit a cigarette, then tossed the packet to Solomon. His hands were rock steady. 'I'm not interfering,' said Dragan, 'but if I don't know what the situation is, I'm going to be a liability. If this Russian is scared of you he's going to be jumpy, and if he's jumpy he might be sitting in that brothel with a loaded gun.'

'If you're scared, stay here.'

'Not much scares me, Sasha. Least of all a gun with its safety on,' Dragan responded. Sasha twisted his gun to the side. The safety was off. When he looked up, Dragan was grinning from ear to ear. 'Made you look,' he said.

'Sasha, put the gun down,' said Solomon. 'It's my fault. I hardly told him anything about what's going on.'

Sasha continued to stare at Dragan. Then he put the gun on the table and sat down. 'The Russian tried to kill me. He killed one of my friends and one of my girls.'

'So you're here to kill him? Is that it?'

'Dragan, leave it,' said Solomon.

Dragan turned to him. 'If he goes in there shooting, where does that leave us?' he asked.

'Goncharov's a gangster. He tried to kill me,' said Solomon. 'Besides, even if we weren't here, it'd still happen.' He looked at Sasha. 'Right?'

'Right,' agreed Sasha.

'That's all right, then,' Dragan said easily. 'Sorry about the interruption.'

Tomislav and Otto took the Range Rover, and Dragan sat in the back of the Toyota with Mirko and Tafik in the front. It was just after six o'clock in the evening and the sky was darkening. They drove back on to the main road and headed north for a couple of minutes, then turned left. They slowed to a little over walking pace as the road was heavily pot-holed. They passed a metal-fenced enclave of building equipment and a yard filled with fibre glass septic tanks. Soon they reached a three-storey house with a blue-tiled roof. In front a large car park held a dozen or so vehicles. It was surrounded by a six-foot-high chain-link fence, and a small concrete guardhouse stood at the entrance. Two security guards waited by it, in dark blue bomber jackets and peaked caps.

Mirko brought the Toyota to a halt and twisted in

his seat. 'That's the place,' he said, in Serbo-Croatian.

'Have you been before?' asked Dragan.

Mirko shook his head. 'Seen one, seen them all,' he said. They watched as Tomislav spoke to the security guards, then drove into the car park. He and Otto climbed out of the Range Rover, knocked on the front door of the building and went in.

'You can walk in now,' said Mirko. 'We'll be in after about fifteen minutes. Don't look at us, don't talk to us. There are two sorts of girls in there. There's the dancers, they take customers up to the second floor. Half an hour or an hour. Then there are girls on the top floor. They don't come down.'

'What do you mean?' asked Dragan.

'They're just hookers. They don't dance, they don't drink with customers, they just screw. You tell one of the waiters what you want, pay and go up. If the girl isn't dancing, she could be upstairs.'

'Are they cheaper?'

'Depends,' said Mirko.

'On what?'

'On what you want to do with them. Look, find out for yourself, I don't have time to hold your hand.'

Dragan climbed out and headed towards the building. The windows on the ground floor were of darkened glass so he couldn't see in. On the first floor there were blinds, and on the second curtains were drawn. He nodded at the two security guards but they barely acknowledged his presence. Most of the vehicles had been parked near the entrance, including the Range Rover. There were two top-of-the-range Mercedes and several new four-wheel-drives but most were commercial vehicles, trucks and vans. Dragan rapped on the door, which opened almost immediately. A well-muscled man in a grey T-shirt and tight black trousers stepped aside to let him in. He had a thick gold chain around his neck and another round his right wrist.

Music was playing, a rock song Dragan recognised only vaguely. There were three podiums, each with four girls dancing around silver poles. They were all young, barely out of their teens. More girls were sitting on sofas scattered around the smoky room, and others on a line of wooden booths by the windows. In all there must have been thirty girls in the room. Those who weren't dancing were smoking, as were most of the customers.

Dragan walked slowly to an empty sofa and sat down. A teenage waiter in a black polo-neck sweater and black jeans walked over to him and he ordered a beer. He lit a cigarette and glanced around the room. Tomislav and Otto were in one of the booths with two dyed-blonde girls.

Three men in oil-stained overalls were sitting on stools by a bar, laughing and knocking back tumblers of slivovitz. Another half-dozen rough-looking men in baggy pullovers were sitting at one of the podiums, gazing at the dancing girls.

There was a door to the left of the bar and as his beer arrived a dancer and her customer came through it. The girl went to sit in one of the booths and cadged a cigarette from one of her friends while the man walked outside, adjusting the crotch of his stained work jeans.

'Do you want a girl?' asked the waiter.

'That's why I'm here,' said Dragan.

The waiter went over to a group of dancers. Seconds later four were lined up opposite him, pouting sexily and thrusting out their breasts. They all wore sheer robes in pastel colours over bikinis. Niçole wasn't among them. Nor was she dancing.

Dragan pointed lazily at two. 'Bring them drinks,' he told the waiter. The girls he'd selected giggled and slid on to the sofa at either side of him.

Dragan chatted to his girls. They were Latvian and had been in Bosnia for three months – a month in Sarajevo and two months in Arizona. They spoke reasonable English and said they wanted to work in London. Or Rome. Or Zurich. His eyes scanned the room as he talked. Three men were sitting at a table near the bar drinking Cokes and looked as if they might be security. They had expensive leather jackets and whenever they leaned forward he could see the telltale bulge of a concealed weapon.

The girls said they were drinking vodka and ice but the speed at which they knocked them back suggested it was only water. He lit a cigarette and offered the packet to them. They were amazed at his ability to light a match with his thumbnail, and asked him to repeat the trick several times. They tried themselves but failed and accused him of trickery. He held out his hands and let them inspect his fingernails. It was all technique, he said, and years of practice.

Like pole-dancing, one of the girls put it, and they all laughed.

Dragan finished his beer and ordered another. Two men walked in from the hallway, one telling a dirty joke in guttural Serbo-Croatian: Mirko and Tafik. They went over to sit by one of the podiums.

'Do you want to go upstairs?' asked one of Dragan's girls. She'd said her name was Angelica and that she used to work in a shoe factory. He sipped his beer. During the fifteen minutes he'd been sitting in the bar, half a dozen dancers had come through the door with customers and four had gone upstairs. There was still no sign of Nicole. She must be upstairs on the second floor, but if he asked for her, he'd draw attention to himself. Angelica was rubbing his thigh and nibbling his ear, and Dragan knew that the only way through the door by the bar was with a girl. But if he went upstairs with one girl, he'd have to do something with her.

Otto and Tomislav walked by his sofa. Tomislav had his hand on one girl's backside while Otto's arm was round another's shoulder. They stopped at the bar, handed money to the barman, went through the door and up the stairs.

'I can do everything,' whispered Angelica. 'Anything you want.'

Jovanovic patted her knee. 'Okay, let's go,' he said.

'One hour?' she said hopefully.

'Half,' said Dragan.

'What about me?' asked the other girl. He couldn't even remember her name.

'One is enough for me,' he said. She flounced away to sit down at a booth with two of her colleagues.

Dragan and Angelica went over to the bar, where he gave the barman fifty konvertible marks. The barman gave Angelica a key attached to a block of wood on which was written a number. She took Dragan by the hand and led him through the door and upstairs.

The landing was covered with a threadbare carpet that had worn through in places. Bundles of dried flowers and grass had been tied to hooks on the wall, and cobwebbed glass lampshades hung from the ceiling.

Angelica unlocked a door and ushered Dragan into a small room with a single bed. She switched on the light, a bare, low-wattage bulb. The sheet on the bed had once been white but was now grey and stained. There was a small washbasin in a corner with a single dripping tap, and a carrier-bag hanging on the bedhead. Each wall had a travel poster tacked to it: Turkey, Greece, Holland, Switzerland.

Angelica slipped off her robe. She reached for Dragan's jacket, but he stopped her and told her to take off her bikini. She did as he asked.

Then he told her to sit on the bed and stood in front of her. 'Aren't you going to take off your clothes?' she asked.

He shook his head. She smiled up at him and unzipped his trousers.

'Condom?' asked Dragan.

'You want one? For a blow-job?'

'Sure.' He knew that even oral sex carried with it the risk of disease, especially from a girl who worked in a place like Arizona. God alone knew how many men she serviced in a day and what she did for them.

She reached over to the carrier-bag, pulled out a condom and ripped open the packet with her teeth. She slipped the condom on to him and went to work with her mouth.

Dragan stared at the poster of Switzerland. Snow-covered mountains. A skiing chalet. A happy couple in brightly coloured jackets toasting each other with huge glasses of wine. He wondered if Angelica would ever get there, or if she'd spend the rest of her working life servicing men in an Arizonan brothel until she had nothing left to offer and was sent back to the shoe factory in Latvia.

Her head bobbed back and forth, her eyes closed. She

stroked his thighs with her hands. He closed his eyes and concentrated. It was over in seconds. He grunted and pulled back.

Angelica took off the condom. He zipped up his pants and headed for the door.

'Do you want to make love?' asked the girl.

'I have to go,' Dragan replied, slipped out of the room and closed the door quietly behind him. He moved to the stairs, checked that no one was around and hurried to the second floor. He stopped on the landing and looked around. He was still alone.

He moved along a corridor, the floor bare concrete. There were doors on either side. Heavy wooden doors with rugged metal bolts, top and bottom. The bolts on the first door to the left were undone and when he pressed his ear against it he heard grunts and cursing from inside. The opposite door was bolted, which he assumed meant that the girl wasn't working. He shot the two bolts and pushed open the door.

The room was dark, the only illumination coming from a small nightlight. He stepped into the room and shut the door. The room stank of bleach and stale perspiration.

A girl was sitting on the bed, her head down, her hands in her lap. She had short, frizzy black hair and she was dumpy, almost fat. Definitely not Nicole. Without looking at him she swung her legs on to the bed and lay back. She was wearing a short, grubby nightdress and she pulled it up over her thighs. She opened her legs and draped an arm over her eyes.

Dragan looked around the room. A door on the right led to a cramped shower room. On the floor there was a battered metal plate with some sort of stew on it and a hunk of bread. A cockroach scuttled off it and ran under the bed. Planks were nailed across the window, and behind them were curtains.

Dragan went out. The next door wasn't bolted, and grunts floated out from inside. The door opposite was bolted. Dragan slid back the bolts and opened it. A girl was curled up on her bed, crying softly and whispering, 'Mama, Mama.' She was wearing a red T-shirt with a Nike tick across the back. Dragan couldn't see her face, but she was a big girl with a mane of red hair. Not Nicole. He closed the door.

The next two doors on either side were unbolted, the girls occupied with customers. Inside one room the girl was being slapped, hard, but she made no sound. Part of Dragan wanted to kick open the door and beat the hell out of the bully, but he knew it was impossible. He could do nothing but move silently along the landing to the next door, trying to blot out the sounds of the slapping.

The next two doors he came to were bolted. He slid back the bolts of the door to his left and peered into the room. A girl was lying on her back, staring up at the ceiling, her arms folded across her abdomen. She was breathing heavily as if she was asleep, but her eyes were wide open. There was a lamp on the floor by the bed with a single red bulb, and a chain ran from her left hand to the headboard. He pushed the door and the girl turned to look at him. Her face was blank, her eyes without expression, but Dragan knew she was Nicole.

'What are you doing?' asked a harsh Bosnian voice.

He pulled the door closed and turned to face a tall man with scarred cheeks and neck. His right eye was a milky white and half of his right ear was missing. He was wearing a leather jacket, and Dragan recognised him as one of the three who had been sitting by the bar.

Dragan didn't smile, but he didn't show any hostility either. He stared at the man impassively. 'Checking the merchandise,' he said.

'You do that downstairs,' said the man.

'I was told that the girls up here were a bit special,' he said.

The man's eyes narrowed. 'What do you mean?'

'That it was okay to be rough with them. That they wouldn't complain.'

'Is that what you want? To be rough?' The man grinned cruelly. 'That one will let you do anything to her, she's doped up to the eyeballs.'

'What's her name?'

The man snorted contemptuously, 'They don't have names up here,' he said. 'Just the numbers on the door.'

Dragan looked at the door he was still holding open. Thirty-eight.

'If you want to play with the merchandise, you have to pay downstairs.'

Dragan shut the door. 'I can do anything with her?'

'They complain for the first day or two, then they realise it's better not to say anything. Don't worry, you'll enjoy yourself. And the amount of ecstasy we give her, she'll probably enjoy it, too.'

Dragan walked away. When he got back to the bar, Angelica was talking to one of the barmen. 'Where were you?' she asked.

'I needed the bathroom.'

'How was she?' the barman asked in Bosnian, nodding at Angelica.

'Excellent,' replied Dragan, with a wink. 'Best blow-job I've had in years.'

As he turned, he almost bumped into a man with a huge beer gut. He grunted an apology, but the man pushed him aside and walked past him. He had a small, flattened nose with large nostrils and bloodless lips. Goncharov. Walking close behind him were two other men, as big as Goncharov but well muscled rather than fat. One glared at Dragan who raised his hands and smiled amiably. All three went through the door and upstairs.

Mirko and Tafik were still sitting at the podium, eyeing up two blonde girls who were dancing topless. Mirko was drinking beer from a bottle. He wiped his mouth as Dragan sat down next to him.

'Did you see him?' whispered Dragan, out of the side of his mouth.

Mirko nodded and turned his back to talk to Tafik. Dragan ordered a beer and swivelled on his bar stool.

'I've found the girl,' he murmured to Mirko's back, and smiled as the Croat stiffened.

The sky had darkened and Bruno had brought two oil lamps into the back room along with a plate of thickly cut cheese sandwiches and half a dozen large bottles of Heineken. While Rikki, Solomon and Sasha helped themselves to food and beer, he nailed a whiteboard to one of the walls. There was a tray at the bottom of the board with three marker-pens, blue, black and red.

Solomon was on his second sandwich when he heard a car pull up outside. Rikki and Sasha pulled out handguns and hurried to the door, but returned a few seconds later followed by Dragan, Mirko and Tafik.

'They're in there now,' said Mirko, reaching for a bottle of Heineken. 'Goncharov and two heavies.'

'They look like the guys you described,' said Dragan to Solomon. 'Hard bastards.'

Sasha and Rikki put their guns down on the table. Tafik helped himself to a beer and a sandwich and sat down heavily.

'The girl's there, too,' said Dragan.

'You're sure?' asked Solomon.

Dragan flashed him a withering look. 'Second floor, chained to a bed.'

'Chained?'

'They do that, sometimes,' said Sasha, 'if the girl's being difficult.'

'She's drugged, too.'

Sasha sat down and took out a packet of cigars. As he bit off the end and spat it away, Dragan leaned over and struck a match with his thumbnail. Sasha took a light and nodded his thanks. 'Where are Otto and Tomislav?' Sasha asked.

'They went upstairs with girls,' said Dragan. 'I think they're getting their money's worth.'

'They won't be long,' said Tafik.

'Let's get started,' said Sasha. He stood up, picked up the black marker-pen and handed it to Mirko.

Mirko sketched a ground-plan of the brothel on the left-hand side of the whiteboard, marking in all the doors, windows and internal walls. He drew in the podiums, the booths and the sofas. It was a professional job, drawn to scale from memory. Next to it he sketched out the first floor, showing the location of the stairs and the doors to the bedrooms.

Then Sasha motioned at Dragan, who went to the whiteboard, took a pen and drew a plan of the second floor. He put in the doors leading to the bedroom, and wrote '38' next to one. 'This is where the girl is,' he said. 'The windows to all these bedrooms have been boarded up, and I only saw one staircase.'

He put down the pen and sat down.

They all heard the Toyota drive up. Sasha nodded at Rikki, who picked up his gun and went out. He returned with Otto and Tomislav.

Otto went straight to the whiteboard and studied it intently. 'That's good enough,' he said. 'What's the plan?'

Sasha picked up the red marker-pen and went to the whiteboard. Solomon looked anxiously at Dragan, who winked at him. He wished he felt half as confident as his friend seemed. The hardest part was yet to come.

Solomon gunned the engine and Sasha grinned across at him. 'See? You can handle it just fine,' he said, and lit a small cigar. He gestured with it. 'Do you want one?'

'I'll stick with Marlboro,' Solomon replied. He gunned the engine again. When Sasha had suggested he drive one of the cars, Solomon had pointed out that his cast ruled out any Formula One antics. But Sasha had said that the Range Rover was an automatic and that there was plenty of room in the footwell for the cast. He'd been right: with the front seat right back Solomon had no trouble handling the vehicle.

Sasha had wanted Dragan to drive the Toyota, which had led to a short but fiery argument: Dragan had said he wanted to go inside with the Croats but Sasha had insisted that he was an unknown quantity and that he'd be a liability. He had eventually been forced to accept Sasha's argument and was sitting at the wheel of the Toyota, still fuming. Rikki was sitting in the front passenger seat with

Otto and Tomislav in the back. Mirko and Tafik were sitting behind Sasha and Solomon in the Range Rover, giving their handguns a last check.

'Right, let's go,' said Sasha. He waved at Dragan, who switched on the Toyota's headlights and drove towards the main road.

Solomon waited a full minute, then drove after him. Rikki said something in Albanian to Sasha, who laughed.

'What?' asked Solomon, sensing that it was about him.

'He says you drive like a woman,' said Sasha. 'An old woman.'

'You said they had to get there first,' said Solomon. 'I'm giving them plenty of room. And Rikki drives like a grandmother.'

Sasha laughed again and told Solomon he was over-sensitive. Maybe he was right, thought Solomon, but he reckoned that sitting in a car with an Albanian pimp, his bodyguard and two heavily armed Croatian thugs on the way to a shoot-out in a Bosnian brothel would make anyone nervous.

The Croats had field-stripped four machine pistols and loaded a dozen magazines as Solomon and Dragan had watched. Three of the guns were now in a black holdall at Sasha's feet. Rikki had taken the fourth with him in the Range Rover.

The Croats were wearing nylon shoulder holsters under their jackets, as was Sasha, and all were carrying large handguns. The Croats had automatics while Sasha had a revolver. Dragan had asked why he wasn't given a weapon: Sasha had told him that they were for profes-sionals and that he was just along for the ride.

Solomon turned down the track that led to the brothel, the beams of the Range Rover carving two tunnels of light in the night sky. Most of the shacks had closed for the day although a few had stayed open, illuminated with oil lamps. As he drove by he saw shopkeepers sitting inside them, wrapped up in thick jackets and wool hats, talking animatedly and drinking whisky from the bottle.

Ahead, he spotted the Toyota parking outside the brothel. There were more than two dozen cars in the car park now, a mix of battered commercial vehicles and expensive luxury cars. Otto and Tomislav climbed out and headed for the main entrance while Rikki and Dragan remained in the vehicle, smoking cigarettes.

Solomon stopped at the guardhouse. The evening guards were young and fit, but they were more interested in watching a football match on a small portable television than in checking the occupants of the Range Rover. Solomon decided they were there primarily to watch over the vehicles in the car park rather than to inspect visitors.

One raised the red and white painted pole that acted as a barrier, and waved the Range Rover through. As he drove in, Solomon noticed two shotguns leaning against the portable television.

'It's going to be okay, Jack,' said Sasha.

'I'm fine,' said Solomon.

'You're breathing like a train.'

'Didn't you see the shotguns?'

Sasha smiled. 'They won't hear a thing out here,' he said. He patted the holdall at his feet. 'And even if they did, one look at these and they'll head for the hills. Shotguns are for show, beyond fifty feet or so they're useless.'

Solomon parked well away from the Toyota, on the other side of the entrance to the building. He wasn't sure whether Sasha was being honest about the shotguns. He'd seen clay-pigeon shooting on television, and the participants hadn't had any problem blowing small discs out of the sky at distances of well over fifty feet.

Mirko and Tafik got out of the Range Rover, adjusted their jackets, and walked to the front door. Mirko knocked and a few seconds later they disappeared inside.

Sasha put his mobile phone on the dashboard, took a long drag on his cigar and settled back in his seat. He looked so calm, thought Solomon. Serene, almost.

Otto reached for his beer, and drank half. Tomislav was looking up at a big-breasted Belarussian who was licking her upper lip suggestively and making wide eyes at him. Otto slapped him on the back and slid off his stool. 'See you later,' he said.

Tomislav nodded. 'Enjoy yourself,' he said. He took out his mobile phone and put it next to his beer.

Otto went over to the bar and gestured at one of the barmen, a man in his forties with grey hair and a jet black moustache, who leaned over to hear him above the music blaring from the speakers. 'Friend of mine says there's a girl upstairs that I can, you know, be a bit rough with,' said Otto.

Goncharov was sitting at a table, talking to a thin man with a bad eye and a mutilated ear. The Russian's two bodyguards were sitting at another table drinking Black Label whisky with two of the brothel's security men. Otto turned his back on them.

The barman leered suggestively at him. 'Pay enough, you can get as rough as you want with any of them,' he said. 'Just don't kill them.' He grinned. 'You kill her, you pay more, right?'

'He said she was in thirty-eight. Is she still here?'

'She ain't going anywhere,' said the grey-haired

barman. 'She's popular. Just turned nineteen. You can give it to her any way you want.'

'My friend said a hundred for the hour.' Otto handed the barman the money.

The barman nodded at the door. 'Enjoy yourself,' he said. 'Try not to mark her. And the boss doesn't like blood. She bleeds, you pay more.'

Otto went through the door, the barman's guffaws echoing behind him. He went up the stairs quickly and found room thirty-eight. He unbolted the door and went inside. The girl was lying on her side, her hair across her face. Otto went to the bed and brushed away her hair so that he could get a good look at her features. It was Nicole.

Hey eyes fluttered open. 'Don't hurt me,' she croaked.

'Don't worry, little sister,' said Otto, and stroked her brow. 'We're not here to hurt you.'

Nicole closed her eyes. She was wearing a short pale blue nightgown with lace ties and dark blue flowers along the hem. She undid the ties and the nightgown fell open, revealing her breasts.

Otto bent down and pulled it around her. 'There's no need for that, little sister,' he said. He reached into his jacket and brought out a pair of metal cutters. He cut the chain, close to her wrist.

Tomislav swivelled on his barstool and drank some beer. Goncharov was still deep in conversation at one of the tables, his two men knocking back tumblers of whisky and laughing. Tomislav saw Mirko and Tafik walk in, their faces hard. They looked round the room and Tomislav saw Mirko nod in the Russian's direction. Tafik was scanning the room for possible threats.

The two men went to sit on one of the sofas. Tomislav's

mobile phone beeped. It was a text message from Otto. 'I have the girl,' it said.

Tomislav stood up and nodded at Mirko, who got to his feet and walked back to the hallway, taking a ski mask from his pocket. He pulled it on, grabbed his gun from his shoulder holster, and raised it high in the air.

Tomislav put on his own ski mask as he headed towards Goncharov's table. He pulled out his gun and aimed it at the Russian's head. His men started to get up but Tomislav yelled at them to stay where they were. They dropped back on to their chairs.

'Everyone down on the ground!' shouted Mirko, in Serbo-Croatian, then repeated it in English.

Tafik pulled on his ski mask before he stood up. He held his gun in both hands, and swept it around the room.

'Hands on the table!' Tomislav yelled at the body-guards. 'Hands on the table or I blow his head off.' They complied. One said something in Russian. 'One more word and I pull the trigger!' screamed Tomislav.

Customers and girls were dropping to the ground. Several of the girls were crying.

'No one is going to get hurt,' shouted Mirko. 'Just do as you're told and we'll be on our way.'

Tomislav took out his mobile phone with his left hand.

Sasha's phone rang twice and then went silent. 'Right, that's it,' he said. 'Whatever happens, you stay here until we come out. If you leave for any reason I will hunt you down and kill you.'

'Bloody hell, Sasha, I heard what you said,' said Solomon.

'I mean it,' said Sasha, pointing a warning finger at him. 'This is serious.'

'You think I don't know that?'

Sasha threw open the door and stepped out, taking the holdall with him. Across the car park, Rikki climbed out of the Toyota. Rikki had put on his ski mask, but it was rolled up like a hat. He jogged towards the entrance and got there at the same time as Sasha. He opened his jacket, to reveal a machine pistol, and pulled his mask over his face. Sasha put on his own mask, then knelt down and put the holdall on the ground. He unzipped it and took out another machine pistol, switched off the safety and nodded at Rikki.

Rikki banged on the door and Mirko opened it. Rikki moved inside quickly, cradling his weapon. Sasha followed him and Mirko closed the door.

Rikki ran into the bar, waving his machine pistol and yelling for everyone to stay down.

Sasha handed Mirko his gun, then went into the bar with the holdall.

He walked quickly towards Goncharov's table, handing another machine pistol from the holdall to Tafik on the way. Tafik tucked his own gun into the waistband of his jeans and clicked the safety off the machine pistol. A customer in overalls was whispering to one of the girls: Tafik went over to him and stamped on him between the shoulder-blades. 'Shut the fuck up!' he yelled.

Rikki was moving around the bar, kicking men and threatening anyone who moved.

Sasha went over to Goncharov's table and handed the holdall to Tomislav as he pulled out his revolver and pointed it at Goncharov. 'Stand up,' he said.

Goncharov pushed back his chair and got to his feet with his hands up.

Tomislav took a machine pistol out of the holdall and

aimed it at the Russian's guards. Sasha told them to stand up, too.

When all three men were on their feet, Sasha gestured for them to stand by the door that led upstairs. They grouped together. The thugs looked at Goncharov, waiting for instructions, but the Russian said nothing.

Tomislav frisked all three and took their guns from them. He ejected the clips then tossed them behind the bar.

'Upstairs,' said Sasha, nodding at the door.

Tomislav opened the door and gestured with his machine pistol. 'This isn't my place,' said Goncharov. 'This is nothing to do with me.'

Rikki came over and shoved the barrel of his machine pistol into the Russian's stomach and pushed him through the door, then took him up the stairs with the gun pressing into the base of his spine.

Sasha told the bodyguards to follow Goncharov and covered them with his gun as they went up the stairs, with Tomislav in the rear. He stayed on the first-floor landing as Sasha and Rikki took the three captives up to the second floor. Sasha lined them up against the wall as Rikki knocked three times on the door to room thirty-eight. Otto was standing by the bed, masked, his gun levelled at the door; the girl was curled up in a tight ball, her eyes closed.

'Is she okay?' asked Sasha.

'Asleep,' said Otto. 'Out for the count.'

'Take her downstairs,' said Sasha.

Otto swung the girl effortlessly over his shoulder and left the room.

Sasha ordered the three men into the room. They walked in, their hands on their heads. Sasha covered them with his revolver as they lined up by the bed. Rikki closed the door and went to stand next to Sasha.

Sasha gestured at Goncharov. 'Kneel down,' he said.

'Fuck you.'

Sasha took a silencer from his pocket and screwed it into the barrel of his revolver.

'I already told you, this isn't my place. I'm a Russian. I'm just visiting.'

'I know who you are,' said Sasha. He pulled up his ski mask so that the Russian could see his face.

'You!' hissed Goncharov. 'You trashed my office, didn't you?'

'The bitch called you, did she? I've done more than trash your business, you piece of shit. I've taken it over. It's mine. Now get down on your knees.'

'Fuck you.'

'Suit yourself.' Sasha pointed the gun at the Russian's chest and pulled the trigger. He fired again. And again. The silencer reduced the sound of the gun to a muffled pop, like a balloon bursting underwater. The Russian fell backwards on to the bed and the springs groaned under his weight. He bounced up and down several times, then lay like a beached whale as blood seeped through his shirt. A loud rasping noise escaped his throat, a spasm ran the length of his body, then he lay still.

Rikki kicked the legs out from under one of the heavies and he hit the floor hard. Sasha told the other man to get to his knees. He did, grunting as he went down. The two men knelt together, heads bowed, as if they were about to receive communion.

'Is he your father?' asked Sasha.

The men shook their heads without looking up.

'Your brother? Your cousin?'

More headshaking.

'So he's not your family. Just an employer?'

Both men nodded. The bigger of the two crossed himself and muttered something in Russian.

'So you don't owe this man anything,' said Sasha. 'He's dead, you find someone else to work for.'

The men looked up at him, confused.

'If I give you your lives, I want you to take away his body and bury it where it'll never be found.'

The big man crossed himself again. The other was staring at Sasha, unable to believe what he'd heard.

'Do you understand? I want the body hidden.'

Both men nodded, unable to believe their luck.

Sasha lowered his gun, pulled down his mask and turned to go. Rikki put a hand on his shoulder. Sasha looked at him. He could see the concern in Rikki's eyes. He had made a mistake with Goncharov: sparing his life had led to the deaths of Karic and Katrina. Was he about to make the same mistake again?

Sasha cursed under his breath. In one smooth movement he turned to face the kneeling men again, levelled the gun at the big man's forehead and pulled the trigger. Blood and brain matter splattered across the wall behind him and he slumped backwards. The other man's mouth dropped open but before he could say anything Sasha shot him just above the nose. He fell backwards, his mouth still open in surprise.

Rikki nodded approval and opened the door.

Solomon sat tapping on the steering-wheel. He looked at his watch. Sasha had been inside for a little over five minutes. He looked across at the Toyota. Dragan was staring fixedly at the door to the brothel. Solomon was grateful that he was close by, but he couldn't help wondering why the policeman was prepared to risk so much to help him. If his bosses discovered that he had been involved in the raid on the Bosnian brothel, his job would be on the line. But the raid was only part of it: there was no doubt that Sasha intended to kill Goncharov, and while Solomon would shed no tears for the Russian, murder was still murder, and if it was ever discovered that Dragan had been involved, they'd throw away the key.

Solomon's train of thought was interrupted by the opening of the brothel's front door. It was one of the Croatians, wearing a mask and holding his machine pistol high in the air. He scanned the car park, then held the door wide. Another man in a mask ran out, a bundle over his shoulder. White arms swung from side to side as he ran across the car park. It was Otto, carrying Nicole. He ran towards the Range Rover at full pelt. Another man ran out and headed for the Toyota, a machine pistol in one hand, the black holdall in the other. It was Tomislav. Dragan already had the doors open for him and he climbed into the front seat.

Solomon gunned the engine, then took a quick look over at the guardhouse. There was no sign of the guards: they must be inside, watching television.

Sasha ducked through the door, slipping his handgun into his shoulder holster as he jogged towards the Range Rover, followed by Rikki, who cradled his machine pistol as he ran.

The man who'd opened the door stood in the doorway, his back to the outside, covering the bar with his machine pistol. Solomon figured it was Mirko. Another figure appeared next to him. Tafik. They kept their machine pistols aimed inside the brothel. Mirko looked over his shoulder, checking that the car park was still clear.

Otto reached the Range Rover, pulled open the rear door and tossed the girl on to the back seat, then climbed in next to her.

'Is she okay?' asked Solomon.

Otto pulled off his mask and used it to wipe perspiration from his face. 'She's drugged, and exhausted,' he said, 'but she'll be fine.'

Nicole was on her side, her eyes closed, a line of frothy dribble down her chin. Otto took off his leather jacket and draped it over her, then slipped off his shoulder holster and placed it on the seat next to him.

Sasha got into the front passenger seat and ripped off his mask. 'Perfect,' he said. Solomon stared at his right hand. There were flecks of blood on it.

Rikki appeared at Sasha's window and gave a thumbs-up. 'Right, let's go!' said Sasha.

Solomon put the gear selector in drive and headed for the car-park exit. Rikki's hand reached for his gun. He waved at Dragan and pointed to the main entrance of the brothel. Dragan drove over to Mirko and Tafik, who climbed into the four-wheel-drive.

Solomon blipped the horn as he approached the guard-house. Sasha's right hand disappeared inside his jacket, but the guard didn't give them a second look as he raised the barrier. They drove out of the car park and on to the pot-holed track. The guard lowered the barrier and went back into the guardhouse.

Solomon sighed. He'd been holding his breath without realising it. He looked into the rear-view mirror. Rikki was climbing into the front passenger seat of the Toyota.

'Eyes on the road, Jack,' hissed Sasha, and twisted in his seat. Men were running out of the brothel, yelling and pointing at the Toyota. Dragan accelerated towards the barrier. One of the guards stepped out brandishing a shotgun, but jumped back as the Toyota leaped forward.

The wooden barrier shattered as the four-wheel-drive smashed through it. The guard got off a shot but it went high. By the time he'd pumped in a second cartridge the Toyota was driving along the track towards the main road.

'They're clear,' said Sasha. He settled back in his seat and lit a cigar.

His hands were rock steady, Solomon noticed. Not a trace of nerves. 'They'll come after us,' he said, looking into the rear-view mirror.

'No, they won't,' said Sasha. 'They've seen our weaponry. And they know what happened to Goncharov. They won't be keen to have the same.'

'What did happen to Goncharov?' asked Solomon.

'I got my revenge,' Sasha said. He looked over his shoulder at the girl, who was still fast asleep. 'I hope she's grateful,' he said.

'You didn't do it for her,' said Solomon.

'No, but you did,' said Sasha. 'Now, put your foot down, we've a long way to go.'

Solomon parked the Range Rover outside his apartment block and glanced over his shoulder. Nicole was lying across the back seat, her head in Otto's lap. She was snoring softly.

He climbed awkwardly out of the car and Sasha handed him his walking-stick. 'I'll come up with you,' said Sasha.

Otto looked at his chunky diving watch. 'As soon as the

others get here, we should be going,' he said. It was just after eight o'clock in the morning; they had seen dawn break on twisting mountain roads between Tuzla and Sarajevo.

'Rikki can drive you to the airport,' said Sasha.

Solomon offered Otto coffee and the Croat nodded. He eased Nicole into his arms and lifted her gently out of the car.

Solomon opened the door to his building and held it open as Otto came in, followed by Sasha. He looked up and down the street but there was still no sign of the Toyota. The last time he'd seen Dragan had been on the road to Tuzla. They'd stopped and checked that nobody was hurt, and agreed to drive back to Sarajevo separately. Sasha had probably been right: there was little chance of anyone coming after them, they were more easily spotted if they were in convoy.

Solomon pressed for the lift and rode up in it with Otto. It barely held two people so Sasha took the stairs. He was standing by the door to Solomon's flat when the lift doors opened. Solomon let them in and showed Otto to the bedroom.

He went into the kitchen and made a pot of coffee. The intercom buzzed while he was pouring it into mugs. He shouted at Sasha to get the door. It was Dragan. Sasha buzzed him in and a few minutes later he was in the flat with Rikki and the rest of the Croats, raiding Solomon's fridge and handing out bottles of Heineken, apologising for Solomon's taste in beer. Tomislav had the black holdall, which he handed to Sasha. Sasha put it behind an armchair.

Dragan collapsed on to one of the sofas and raised his bottle in salute. There was a chorus of '*Zivjeli!*'

Solomon went through to the bedroom with a mug of coffee for Nicole. She was lying on his bed, her tousled hair across the pillow. She was wearing a short blue nightgown that had ridden up her thighs. There were old bruises all over her skin in various shades of green and blue, and livid red scratch marks across her legs and arms.

Solomon sat on the edge of the bed and put the mug on the bedside table. Nicole's eyes flickered open. She looked at Solomon, a slight frown on her face, then gazed around the room. 'Where am I?' she asked, in Serbo-Croatian.

'Sarajevo,' he said. 'You're safe now.'

Her frown deepened. 'Who are you?' she asked, in English this time. 'What am I doing here?'

From the next room came the sound of raucous laughter. Nicole glanced at the bedroom door. 'It's okay,' said Solomon. 'They're friends . . . Do you remember me?' he asked.

Nicole tried to sit up but the effort was too much for her and she flopped back, exhausted. The nightdress had ridden even further up but she didn't seem aware of her nakedness. Solomon pushed himself up off the bed, limped over to his wardrobe and took out a denim shirt and a pair of boxer shorts.

'What happened to your leg?' she asked.

'It's a long story,' he said. He handed her the shirt and shorts. 'Put these on,' he said. 'You can have a shower when you're ready.' He turned his back.

'It's been a long time since a man did that,' she said.

'Did what?'

'Tried to avoid seeing me naked.'

Solomon turned round. She was sitting on the bed, clasping her knees to her chest. 'That's over now,' he said.

'Have you bought me?' she asked. 'Is that it? Do I work for you now?'

Solomon sat down again. 'Nobody owns you, Nicole. Not any more.'

She stiffened at the mention of her name. 'Who are you?' she asked.

'My name is Jack,' he said. 'I saw you in London, remember?'

'London?' she repeated. She frowned as if it was the first time she'd heard the word.

'It doesn't matter,' he said. 'We can talk later. Are you hungry?'

She shook her head.

Solomon gave her the coffee. 'Try to drink some of this,' he said.

She took it from him and sipped. There was more laughter from outside and she flinched. Solomon reassured her again that they were friends and there was nothing to worry about. 'You came to St John's Wood, didn't you?' she asked.

'That's right.'

'And after that they sent me back to Bosnia.' She shuddered. 'To that place.' Her hands trembled and coffee slopped on to the duvet.

Solomon took the mug from her and put it on the bedside table. 'I'm sorry,' he said.

'I was happy in London,' she said quietly. 'I had a nice place to live. The men were kind to me.' He saw tears in her eyes. 'They brought me presents.' She sniffed. 'Do you know what they did to me in that place?' She showed him her arms. They were covered in welts and bruises, some fresh, some old.

'Nicole, I'm sorry.'

She wiped her eyes. 'You ruined my life.'

'I didn't,' said Solomon.

'You ruined the life I had,' said Nicole. 'I had a job, decent customers. I could have stayed in London and made a lot of money. Now I've lost everything. Everything.'

She began to cry and Solomon put his arm round her. 'I didn't know this would happen,' he said. 'I just wanted to know who killed your family. That's all.'

Her body was racked with sobs and she pushed him away.

'Nicole, I'm sorry,' said Solomon.

'You don't get it, do you?' she sobbed. 'You don't understand.'

'What do you mean?'

She looked up at him, her cheeks wet. 'It was me,' she sobbed. 'I killed them.' She threw herself down and buried her face in the pillow.

There was a knock on the bedroom door. It was Sasha. 'Rikki's going to run the guys to the airport. You should say goodbye.'

Solomon nodded. He gave Nicole's shoulder a squeeze and followed Sasha out of the room.

Dragan was hugging Otto and patting him on the back. Solomon shook hands with the four men, and thanked each one, although he could barely concentrate on what he was saying. All he could think of was Nicole, and what she'd said. How could she have killed her family? It didn't make sense.

Dragan tossed Rikki the Toyota keys. 'Try to get it out of second gear or the plane'll have gone by the time you get there,' he joked.

Rikki and the Croats left. Dragan grabbed another

Heineken and lay on the sofa, his feet crossed at the ankles. 'How's the girl?' he asked.

'Shaken up,' said Solomon.

'What are you going to do with her now?' asked Sasha.

'Get her to talk to investigators at the War Crimes Tribunal,' said Solomon, 'and tell them what she saw.'

'What did she see?' asked Dragan.

'I don't know yet,' said Solomon.

He went back to the bedroom and closed the door. Nicole was lying in the same position as he'd left her. Solomon limped over to sit beside her. 'Nicole?'

'Go away.'

'We have to talk,' he said.

'I don't want to talk.'

'You said you killed your family. That can't be true. You can't blame yourself for what happened. It wasn't your fault.'

'It was my fault.'

'You're just saying that because you were spared, that's all. It's called survivor's guilt. You're blaming yourself. I know all about it, Nicole.'

'You don't know what you're talking about.' She pushed herself up into a sitting position, her back against the headboard.

'I know you mustn't blame yourself.'

'I told them where the drugs were.' She put up her hands to cover her face. 'And when they came for them they took away my family.'

'What are you talking about?' Nicole didn't reply. 'Nicole, what drugs?'

'My father, he let some people store boxes on our farm. In one of the barns. Boxes wrapped in black plastic. He thought I didn't know but I saw them being brought in

393

one night. They were hidden under the floor. There was a trapdoor under sacks of potatoes.'

'And it was drugs?'

'Heroin. I didn't know that, not then. I didn't know what it was, other than that it was a secret.'

'And who did you tell?'

Nicole wiped her face. 'I had a boyfriend.'

'Emir?'

Nicole laughed harshly. 'Emir wasn't my boyfriend. He's just a boy. A lovesick boy.' She sighed. 'His name was Mirsad, and he worked on one of the farms near ours. He was older than me, he'd been to Priština loads of times. He said we could run away there and start a new life. But we needed money.'

'So you told him about the drugs?'

'I showed him the secret place. It was Mirsad who said it was heroin. He said we could sell some, just a bit, and we'd have enough money to buy a restaurant. I was going to cook and he'd be the manager. I thought if we took just a little no one would know.'

She sniffed and wiped away tears.

'Three days later, the men came. I'd been to see Mirsad. He kept telling me not to go home but it was getting late. When I got back they were making everyone get into the truck.'

'Who were they?'

Nicole shrugged. 'I don't know. They were wearing masks. And they had guns like the soldiers carry. Big guns.'

'Were they soldiers?'

'I don't know. They weren't wearing uniforms.'

'Mirsad must have told them – is that what you think?'

'No one else knew where the drugs were hidden. He

betrayed me. He used me. And because of that my family died. So it was my fault.'

Solomon didn't know what to say. She rolled over and buried her face in the pillow again.

Solomon looked down at her helplessly. He patted her, lost for words, then stood up and went back to the sitting room. Sasha and Dragan looked up as he closed the bedroom door behind him. Dragan swung his feet off the sofa and sat looking expectantly at Solomon. 'Well?' he said.

'She didn't see the men who took her family away.'

'After all this?' said Sasha. 'After all this she didn't see them?'

'She saw them. But they were wearing masks. She didn't see their faces.'

Dragan shook his head. 'Why the hell didn't she say that in the first place? She could have gone to the police after her family were taken.'

Solomon went over to the sofa and sat down next to him. 'It's a long story,' he said, reaching for a beer.

'We've got time,' said Sasha.

'It's about drugs,' said Solomon. He repeated what Nicole had told him.

'So it was nothing to do with ethnic cleansing?' said Sasha. 'Nothing to do with them being Muslims?'

'She told her boyfriend where the drugs were stored. Three days later the family were put into the back of the truck and driven away. She saw men in masks take away the drugs. Now she blames herself.'

'With good reason,' said Sasha.

'She didn't know what would happen,' said Solomon. 'She had some romantic idea that she could run away with her boyfriend on the proceeds of a couple of kilos of heroin.'

Sasha took out his cigars. Dragan reached for his matches.

The bedroom door opened. Nicole came into the sitting room, her face still wet from crying.

Solomon introduced Sasha and Dragan. 'They helped get you out of Arizona,' he said.

'Thank you. I want to go,' she said. 'I can't stay here. I want to go.'

'Go where?' asked Solomon.

'Anywhere. London, maybe. I want to go and work for the agency again.'

Dragan lit a match with his thumbnail and offered the light to Sasha, who held it to his cigar.

Nicole froze. 'You!' she said.

Sasha and Dragan looked at her, bewildered.

'It was you!' she hissed. 'You killed my family!'

Sasha groped for his gun, but Dragan moved quickly, bending down and pulling his semi-automatic out of its ankle holster. He had it in his hand before Sasha had pulled out his revolver. He swung it towards Sasha and fired. The bullet caught him in the chest and he staggered back. He looked at Dragan with a puzzled frown, then slumped to the floor, blood blossoming across his shirt-front. Dragan got to his feet and stood looking down at Sasha. He kicked him in the side. Sasha's leg twitched once, then went still.

Solomon stared at the policeman in horror. 'It was Sasha, all the time?' he said. 'He killed them?'

Dragan said nothing. He prodded Sasha, looking for any sign of life.

Nicole was standing by the bedroom door, her hands to her face. 'It's okay,' said Solomon. 'He can't hurt you now.'

'Not him,' she said, and pointed an accusing finger at Dragan. 'Him.'

'What?' said Solomon.

'Him. I saw him. At the farm.'

Dragan turned to look at Nicole. 'She's hysterical,' he said.

'You were there,' she said. 'You were in charge.'

'You said they wore masks,' said Dragan.

'The man in charge lit matches like you did. With his nail.'

'It's an easy trick,' said Dragan.

'No, it isn't,' said Solomon quietly. 'You know it isn't.'

'Jack, come on. You saw Sasha going for his gun.'

'Because he knew it wasn't him who had killed her family. So if it wasn't him, she was accusing you.'

Nicole slid down the wall and sat with her arms clasped around her legs.

Dragan's eyes hardened. He turned slowly and levelled the gun at Solomon.

'Why?' asked Solomon.

'Why?' repeated Dragan. 'Why do you think?'

'Money.'

'Not just money, a lot of money. More money than I can earn in ten years as a policeman. In a hundred years.'

'You killed twenty-six people!' shouted Solomon. 'Men, women and children.'

'No,' hissed Dragan. 'I didn't kill anyone.'

'You herded them into the back of a truck.' He pointed at Nicole, who was huddled by the bedroom door. 'She saw you.'

'That's all I did,' said Dragan. 'We just wanted them out of the way while we got the drugs. I didn't say they were to be killed.'

'They were Serbs? The guys you were working with?'

'Her boyfriend had a friend who was a Serb. He told one of his friends who had a friend who was one of my informers. I put together the crew, men I knew from my days in the federal police.'

'Other cops?'

Dragan shrugged. 'Some were cops. A couple of soldiers. Guys I knew who could be trusted. Some were Serbs, but this wasn't about race. It was about money. They weren't supposed to kill them.'

'What did you think they were going to do? Take them out for pizza and beer?'

'I keep telling you, I didn't tell them to drive the truck into the fucking lake!' shouted Dragan. 'All I was interested in was the heroin. It wasn't about killing people. It was about drugs. It was good-quality Afghan heroin. Her father was looking after it for a drug-smuggling gang who were shipping it from Turkey into the EC. Hundreds of kilos a month were moving through that farm. Millions of dollars' worth.'

'And how much did you get?'

'Why does that matter?'

'Because I want to know what value you put on those lives, Dragan. A hundred thousand dollars a head? A million? How much for the little girl?'

Dragan crossed the room and held his gun to Solomon's head. 'Fuck you!'

'No!' shouted Nicole. 'Don't!'

Dragan looked across at her, but kept the gun pointing at Solomon's head. 'What choice do I have?' he asked. 'You know what happened. He knows what happened. I can't let you tell anyone.'

Nicole stood up, her back to the bedroom door. 'I

won't say anything. I didn't before, why would I now?'

'But he will,' said Dragan, jerking his head at Solomon, 'and he'll get the Tribunal to make you talk. I'll spend the rest of my life in a cage.'

'I don't want to die!' sobbed Nicole.

'I don't have any choice in this,' said Dragan. 'You haven't left me any choice.' He glared at Solomon. 'You should have walked away when you had the chance.'

'I couldn't,' said Solomon.

'I know you couldn't!' shouted Dragan. 'You think I don't know that, you stupid bastard?'

'No!' screamed Nicole. She ran at Dragan, her fingers hooked into claws, her lips curled back in an animal snarl.

He took a step away from Solomon and backhanded Nicole with the gun, smashing it against her chin. She fell to the side, arms flailing, and crashed on to the coffee table. It shattered under her weight and she hit the floor. She rolled on to her back. 'You stupid bitch! This is all your own fault!' screamed Dragan.

Nicole tried to get to her feet, but Dragan put his foot on her chest and pinned her to the floor. He swung his gun at her face.

Solomon looked around for something to use as a weapon. The holdall containing the machine pistols was behind an armchair, half a dozen steps away, but with his leg in plaster there was no way he could reach it.

Dragan's finger tightened on the trigger. 'Dragan, don't!' shouted Solomon, but he knew that he was wasting his breath. Dragan didn't have a choice. He couldn't afford to leave any witnesses. He was going to shoot Nicole and then, as sure as night follows day, he would shoot Solomon.

Solomon pushed himself up off the sofa, cursing his

broken leg. Then he remembered the knitting-needle, snug in its place beneath the plaster cast. He pulled it out and lunged forward, thrusting it between the policeman's ribs.

Dragan stiffened and gasped. Solomon kept pushing the knitting-needle in and up, driving it towards Dragan's heart.

The gun fell from his hand and clattered to the floor. Solomon pushed with all his might, and he and Dragan toppled over. Nicole scrambled out of the way as they crashed into the remains of the coffee table. Solomon kept the knitting-needle in his hand, pushing hard. Dragan's mouth was moving soundlessly, his eyes wide and staring. Frothy blood trickled from between his lips.

Nicole crawled to the wall and sat there, her hands covering her mouth.

Solomon was on top of the policeman, staring down into his face, his hand still clamped around the knitting-needle.

A bubble of blood popped in Dragan's mouth. He frowned, then his whole body tensed, his back arched, and he lay still.

Solomon rolled away from the body and crawled over to Nicole. He sat beside her and put his arm round her shoulders. 'Is he dead?' she whispered.

'Yes.'

'It's over?'

Solomon nodded. 'Yeah. It's over.'

'Can I go back to London, now?'

'I don't know.'

'I want to go back to London. I was happy there.' She rested her head on his shoulder and closed her eyes.

Solomon looked across at Sasha. And at Dragan. He

thought about the bodies in Arizona, and in London. A lot of people had died, and all because Solomon had wanted justice for a family he'd never met. Maybe Dragan had been right. Maybe it would have been better if he'd walked away in the first place.

Then Sasha's arm moved, just an inch or so. 'Sasha?' whispered Solomon, unable to believe what he'd seen. The arm moved again and the fingers clenched into a fist, then slowly relaxed. 'Sasha!'

The man groaned. Solomon crawled across the floor, dragging his cast. He flopped down next to Sasha as he opened his eyes. His shirt was soaked in blood. 'Don't try to say anything, just lie still,' Solomon said. 'Nicole, get me towels from the bathroom.' Nicole didn't move. She was staring into the middle distance, her eyes dead. 'Nicole!' he yelled. Nicole jerked and looked at him, as if she was seeing him for the first time. Solomon pointed at the bathroom door. 'Towels, now! Come on!'

Nicole scrambled to her feet and rushed into the bathroom. Solomon put his fingers on the side of Sasha's neck and found a pulse. It was faint but regular. 'It's going to be all right, Sasha,' he whispered.

'Bullshit,' croaked Sasha.

'I know what I'm talking about,' said Solomon. 'I've been shot myself, remember?'

Sasha forced a smile, then his body was racked by a coughing fit. Spittle flecked his lips but Solomon was relieved to see that there was no blood.

Nicole hurried back into the sitting room with two hand-towels. Solomon grabbed them and pressed one to Sasha's a chest. 'Phone for an ambulance,' he told Nicole, nodding at the telephone.

Nicole picked up the receiver and dialled. Solomon

kept the towel pressed hard against Sasha's chest. He had no way of knowing if there was an exit wound but he didn't want to risk turning Sasha over to find out. Sasha's face was deathly white but his mouth was open and Solomon could hear him breathing and feel the rise and fall of his chest. It had been years since Solomon had been on a first-aid course, but he could remember the basics. Sasha was breathing, he had a pulse, and Solomon was doing what he could to stem the bleeding. Other than that, all he could do was wait for the emergency services to arrive.

'Where are we?' Nicole asked, her hand over the receiver.

Solomon told her the address of the apartment and she repeated it into the phone. 'They're on their way,' she said. 'They want to know if he's still breathing.'

Solomon looked down at Sasha. The blood was seeping through the towel and on to his hands. 'Yes,' said Solomon. 'Just about.'

Solomon stirred his cappuccino. He reached for his packet of Marlboro and as he took out a cigarette an overweight woman wearing too much makeup glared at him pointedly. Solomon glared back at her and lit the cigarette. He kept staring at her until she looked away. After what he'd been through, Solomon figured he'd earned the right to a cigarette with his coffee.

He sat looking out of the window at the Wardour Street traffic. His leg itched but he had nothing to scratch inside his cast: Rikki had taken away the knitting-needle when he'd removed Dragan's body and Solomon couldn't bring himself to replace it. He blew smoke at the window, then grinned as he saw Inga walking along the pavement from Oxford Street. Her red hair was swinging loose and, as usual, her eyes were hidden behind her sunglasses. She was wearing a long black coat and black boots and he could hear the tap-tap-tap of the heels over the sound of the traffic. She waved when she saw him, then pushed through the door and rushed over to his table. He was already on his feet and hugged her. She buried her face in his neck and kissed him. 'I'm so glad you're all right,' she said.

'You and me both.'

She released him and stood back, holding his hands. 'I thought I'd never see you again,' she said.

'Bad penny,' said Solomon, but he could see from the blank look that she didn't get the joke. 'It doesn't matter,' he said. 'I'm just glad to be back.' They sat down and Inga took off her sunglasses. Solomon stubbed out his cigarette. He'd told Inga the bare bones of what had happened in Bosnia when he phoned and asked to meet her. The only questions she'd asked were if he was okay and when and where they could meet. There was a long silence as if neither was sure what to say.

'Sasha phoned me last night,' said Inga, eventually.

'From hospital?' said Solomon, surprised. The last time Solomon had seen him it was through the window of the intensive-care unit at Sarajevo's main hospital, hooked up to machines and connected to a drip. Nicole had been there, and so had Rikki. That was before Rikki had gone back to Solomon's flat and taken away the body. He'd even cleaned up the two patches of blood, Dragan's and Sasha's. When Solomon had gone home it was as if nothing had happened. A bad dream.

An elderly doctor with an eye-patch and old shrapnel scars on his forehead had said that the bullet had missed

Sasha's aorta by less than an inch but that he was going to be okay. The accident and emergency doctors in Sarajevo were among the most experienced in the world when it came to dealing with gunshot wounds.

'He had a mobile,' said Inga. 'He said he was going to be fine.'

'Yeah, the doctors said he was lucky.' Solomon grinned ruefully. 'Funny how they always say that when someone gets shot. You're either dead or you're lucky.'

'He said he'll be back in London in a week or so.'

Solomon nodded. 'Back to business,' he said sourly.

'He said it would be okay if I saw you,' she said, hesitantly.

'Saw me?'

She nodded. 'Outside work.' She looked down, avoiding his eyes. 'If you wanted to.'

Solomon wasn't sure what to say. He felt as if Sasha was somehow giving his blessing to the relationship, and he resented that the other man still had power over her. His blessing was a painful reminder of what she was. A hooker.

Inga looked up at him and brushed a stray lock of hair behind her ear. 'Do you want to?'

'Of course I do,' said Solomon, but he could hear the hesitation in his voice.

'Really?'

Solomon nodded. More sure this time. 'Really.'

'Good,' she said, and her smile brightened.

There was another long silence. Again Inga spoke first. 'Did you find her?'

'Who?'

'The girl you were looking for. Nicole.'

Solomon nodded and stirred his coffee. 'Oh, yes, we found her.'

'And she spoke to you?'

'She told us what happened, yes. The man who killed her family was the man who shot Sasha. He's dead now.'

'And what's going to happen to her?'

Solomon was glad that she didn't ask him how Dragan had died. The image of Dragan impaled on the knitting-needle kept flashing through his mind. The feel of it squeezing through flesh, popping through the heart muscle, the look of fear in Dragan's eyes as his lifeblood drained away. Solomon shuddered. 'She's coming back to London,' he said.

'To work?'

Solomon nodded. 'The man who killed her family's dead, she has no one in Bosnia apart from one old lady. There's no reason for her to stay there, so she's coming back to work for Sasha.' Solomon had been with Nicole when she'd spoken to Rikki, who had said he was sure that Sasha could use her in London. If that was what she wanted. Nicole had said yes, that was exactly what she wanted.

'I'll take care of her,' said Inga. She reached across the table and held Solomon's hand. 'She'll be okay.'

Solomon shrugged but didn't say anything. He doubted that Nicole would ever be okay. The guilt she felt for the death of her family would be with her for ever, and working as a prostitute would do nothing for her self-esteem. He felt a sudden wave of helplessness. There was nothing he could do to help her, nothing he could offer as an alternative to prostitution.

'It's just a job, Jack,' said Inga, as if reading his mind.

'It isn't,' said Solomon. 'And you know it isn't. She's selling herself. She's letting men use her. Abuse her.'

'Are you talking about her, or me?' said Inga quietly.

'I'm sorry,' said Solomon. 'I'm not being judgemental, about her or you. I know what your lives were, and I know how much money you can earn here. If our positions were reversed, maybe I'd be selling myself.'

Inga grinned mischievously. 'I hope it never comes to that,' she said. 'I don't think you'd make much money selling your body.'

Solomon laughed. 'You know what I mean,' he said. 'What can I say to her? Go back to Kosovo and work in a factory? There are hardly any factories there. Get an office job? There aren't any. The only people making money in Kosovo are criminals and the internationals. At least in London she can have a decent place to live, maybe save some money. Start a new life. But I've seen the damage prostitution can do, physically and mentally. And I'm not sure she'll cope. She's just a kid.'

'I'll help her,' said Inga.

'And who'll help you?' asked Solomon bitterly.

'My life isn't so bad,' said Inga, 'not compared with what it was like in Bulgaria. I don't do drugs and I'm careful, so I won't get sick. I'll have worked off my contract eventually. Then I'll be able to save money. Enough to start a small business, maybe.'

'You think Sasha will ever let you go?'

'Maybe,' said Inga. 'Eventually.' She squeezed his hand. 'Jack, it's all right. I chose this life, I wasn't forced into it.'

'That's not true,' said Solomon. 'If you had money, you wouldn't have to do what you do.'

'And if you were rich, would you do your job? Would

406

you spend your time telling people that their loved ones are dead?'

'It's not the same,' said Solomon.

'To me it is,' said Inga. 'We do what we must to survive. Neither of us takes pleasure in what we do, but we do it, and we make the best of it.'

They sat in silence for a while, watching the traffic go by outside the window.

'What if I were to buy out your contract?' asked Solomon.

'No,' she said firmly.

'I've got some money. I could talk to Sasha.'

'No,' she repeated. 'You'd be buying me, Jack, and I wouldn't want that. I don't want to be owned by anyone. I'll work off my debt.'

Solomon nodded. He knew how she felt and she was right. If he paid Sasha he'd be buying Inga, and he didn't want that. She had to come to him of her own free will, because she wanted to, not because he'd paid for her.

'Are you okay with this?' she asked.

Solomon smiled and took her hand in his. She bit down on her lower lip as she waited for his answer. He nodded slowly. 'Yeah, I'm okay with it,' he said. And realised, to his surprise, that he meant it.

STEPHEN LEATHER

Tango One

'In the top rank of thriller writers' Jack Higgins

In different parts of London, three recruits prepare for their first day at the Metropolitan Police's training centre at Hendon. All three have secrets in their past they are keen to put behind them.

But the Met has other plans for Jamie, Bunny and Tina. They are to join a team of undercover detectives, a secret unit involved in the long-term penetration of criminal gangs.

Their target? One of the world's biggest drug dealers: Ben Donovan – alias 'Tango One'. A man so rich and powerful he's virtually untouchable, despite being number one on HM Customs and Excise list of most wanted criminals.

But as the three recruits close in on their quarry, they are unaware that someone is pursuing an alternative agenda. Someone who has deliberately put their lives on the line . . .

CORONET BOOKS
Hodder & Stoughton